Vampire Vic² Morbius Reborn

Vampire Vic Trilogy, Book 2

Harris Gray

*Here's to drinking what we need,
and not one ounce more.*

ALSO BY HARRIS GRAY

Vampire Vic (Book 1 in the Vampire Vic Trilogy)
Java Man

8 May 1586

A most unfortunate thing happened to me last night. I hesitate to write about it; as if I could otherwise go on with my former life, pretending it did not happen. I struggle to write about it; because I cannot come to grips with what I've become.

I was warned by everyone who knew. Everyone who saw what had become my love affair with M. And no external alarm was necessary. The voice of reason spoke plainly to me throughout, as these pages bear witness. Over the past months I documented every argument for abandoning what has now become the tragedy of my life. I heard, I wrote, I did not listen.

'Unfortunate,' indeed. How that word fails to convey the enormity of my situation. Last night I was bitten by M. Today I have become cursed. My life is ruined. My life has ended.

Leading up to last night, and at that fateful moment, I believed this would instead be the beginning. The beginning of a new chapter, a new life. An exciting change of direction, away from my dull heading. How naïve.

This morning, my sister confirmed my ruin. O my precious, beloved Celestina! To see your face, the horror when you beheld me. Your expression at that instant transformed our relationship. Ended it, I am certain, forevermore.

Never had I been more certain than I was last night. Know that there was no wine to blind me to apprehension, to blur my reservations; we drank not a drop, and I lay down with M. harboring neither apprehension nor reservation. I was intoxicated by our love. I had waited months for that moment.

I knew I would be bitten. As we crossed sacred barriers I have dreamed night after night of breaching, I knew my blood would cross a barrier, too. M.'s mouth at my throat! How can I describe the ecstasy, the agony, and finally the transcendent gift no other lover could bestow?

In the Arabian Desert with my father long ago, I saw a mirage radiating the warmest colors and promising the coolest reception. So with transcendence. Father, if only you were still here, you would have cautioned me, again, against the reckless pursuit of mirages.

Holy Father, I trust that in Heaven's sanctuary from suffering, You did not allow my father to see M. carry me to my bed, or afterward flee with me screaming and drenched in blood. Blood enough to fill the bottomless cup from which Death can never quite quench its thirst.

I would take my own life if I were braver. Although it is hardly necessary. There are any number of slayers ready to do that taking. Even now, my sister is undoubtedly leading one or more this way. Every day there are new accounts of M.'s kind—now my kind!— here in the city, in the Carpathians to the north and Constantinople to the south. From the Black Sea to the Adriatic, the number grows.

As does the slayers' difficulty in killing them. They will not find such a difficult monster here.

My sadness knows no bounds, and I curse M.

In the next breath, and if it be my final, I am content. I will not be the first to have chosen the fullness of love over empty living.

N.

[translated from Romanian]

29 August 1586

'Unfortunate.' I see that word in my prior entry. A peculiar word! Unfortunate that not four months ago I knew my new life to be a death sentence. Self-condemned, eager to kneel at the executioner's block and stretch my neck for the axe, to bare my breast for the point of the slayer's stake.

And now today, tonight, and every night hereafter, I live a Heavenly eternity in every second.

M., I owe you all that I am! Wherever you are, I pray that my hasty curses went unheeded by Him and have done you no harm. And that someday we will meet again.

A vampire, I am a vampire! The feeling is beyond anything I had contemplated. To hold Life in my hands, and to bring Death, if, when and as I choose. At those precarious moments, and every moment in between, the sensation is incomparable.

M., you promised much and still inadequately prepared me. Maybe because I can honestly say that I am so much more than you. More than any other vampire. I harbor so much passion; and yes, so much hatred. I shudder to tell you the visions I have, and the acts they allow me to commit.

What a dull excuse for Life I was, before M. gave me this gift. How I shuffled through the world. Conflict rages within me and I love it. The strife breeds energy that reanimates long-buried ideas. Finally I have the respect and, yes, the fear, to allow me to accomplish everything I've ever dreamed.

But of course, they will never allow it. I am feared like no other, and I am hunted like no other. They hate me and anyone close to me. And so I have left my home, my beloved Bucharest, and moved north. To Tirgu Mures. I have shed my former life like a drab winter's coat, and with it—to protect those I love, even as they too forevermore loathe me—I have shed my name.

Soft, dull N. is no more. My flesh is turned to armor, my teeth to daggers. I turn away your spears, and I spill your blood, more than I could ever drink. Tremble as you should before the vampire who is now called Morbius.

[translated from Romanian]

From the "Ask the Slayer" fan page on the *Sage Slayer* website

"I've learned there are three types in this world: slayers, people who need slayers, and those about to be slain. No matter which group you're in, I'm here to help." – Eugene the Vampire Slayer

From: Slayer Sven
Posted: Sat Jan 4, 7:02 a.m.
Subject: Urgent!!

SOS!! Calling all Vampire Slayers!!! Urgent!!!!
^STOP^

I am collecting a multitude of V. Slayers.
^STOP^

To eradicate the outbreak of Vamps in France.
^STOP^

There have been an unusual number of Gypsies "disappearing" from the Provence region in the South of France.
^STOP^

In the city of Cassis, it has been especially severe. After the city's yearly festival honoring the patron Saint of the Gypsies (Saint Sarah) there has been an extraordinary amount of vampire activity. So many homes abandoned or vacant. No one seems to care because they are Gypsies. That's not right; we need to help out people in need.
^STOP^

I can't do this alone. I need your help. I am trying to amass at least 100 V. Slayers by the end of the month.

^STOP^

Your humble servant,
^STOP^

Slayer Sven

p.s. I'm stateside kicking it with a few Up With People homies, maybe I could pop in?

p.s.s. Not really humble or your servant. I will be in charge.

—

Sven,
Happy to see your e mail. I love the south of France!! Gypsies of course don't own homes—otherwise we'd call them "Romanians"—but nonetheless, if the vacancy is what you say it is in Cassis, I bet the price of real estate is rock bottom. I was in Marseille a few years ago and prices are outrageous there. I would love to own a bit of real estate on the Mediterranean. Thanks for the tip. Please don't tell too many people about this. Is this some pyramid scheme? If so, that is fine. I am already a diamond member of Amway & I have the pink Escalade from Mary Kay. All I ask is that I am up the pyramid as much as possible.

I'm actually on the Continent for some Slaying training & could use some down time. Offing French vamps definitely qualifies. The trick is killing them before they surrender. I will be in Cassis by mid-week. Eugene > The Vampire Slayer <

p.s. Don't ask me to STOP, that's weird.

From: Gus
Posted: Sat Jan 4, 5:12 p.m.
Subject: Vampire nests

Mr. Slayer,
You have quite the reputation. I really think I have a job/problem right up your alley. As you know, the outskirts of Detroit are overrun with the undead. Vampires seem to be everywhere. They are unchecked and killing with reckless abandon. With all the foreclosures & abandoned homes, they have free reign. I have lost countless friends & several family members. Can you help? I need a Slayer out here immediately. Please help.

Your fervent fan,
Gus

—

Gus,
I feel your pain. With all the foreclosures & abandoned homes our country is a mess. It takes a monstrous effort from all of us to make it better. Good thing is that with the interest rates so low & Fannie Mae once again willing to work with you, buying & flipping those homes is a great option. I happen to co-own a consulting firm that can help walk you through the process, slayer-investments.com. It really is easy & super practical. With the market the way it is, this country is ripe for these kinds of solutions. It's up to us to get the country back on its financial feet.

Good luck,
Eugene > The Vampire Slayer <

From: Edna Campbell
Posted: Sat Jan 4, 9:32 p.m.
Subject: Eating Meat(eaters)

Dearest Eugene,
I want to do an apprenticeship with you. I think the work you do killing meat-eaters is amazing. Recently, I have been let go from PETA and I must disassociate myself with that compliant, apathetic & submissive tree hugging association. I believe all meat-eaters should die!! This includes vampires. They are no better than the meat-eaters on this planet. Essentially they eat meat, blood, whatever, I am in. The only redeeming value they have is that sometimes they prey upon meat eating people of this despicable world we live on. I would love to work under your tutelage. My only question is, are you a vegan? This is very important to me. I could not work with someone who eats animals. I love them so much. I do practice pescetarianism. I love me some fresh Atlantic salmon over a bed of greens. Can't wait to work with you and do some killing.

Eternally Yours,
Edna Campbell

—

Edna,
What kind of wacko are you??? I can't believe this email, totally disgusting. Atlantic salmon is an abomination. Do you realize that those salmon are "farm raised"? Fed & over-fed until they almost burst. They taste horrible. Flat, soggy and tasteless. They add chemically-enhanced color to the salmon just to make them look edible. Their nutrition is less than

nutritious, having less than 1/3 of the health benefits of a Pacific Northwest or Alaskan salmon. Alaskan salmon has 120% of your daily Omega-3s. That alone should keep you away from Atlantic salmon. I would rather eat juicy, pen-fed young veal than any farmed fish. Meat of any kind is good, & good for you. I could never work with or be around such a buffoon. I would rather hunt you, ala *The Hunger Games* or *Logan's Run*. Only for sport, don't worry, I would not eat you.

Yours truly,
Eugene > The Vampire Slayer <

p.s. Don't get me started on Tilapia, the poop fish.

Slayer Sven comments:
Edna, I like where your tête is. When apathy reigns, the guillotine must awaken! You sound beautiful. I could use your organizational and perhaps some of your fundraising skills. How old are you? Let us meet.

S.S.

Eugene replies:
This isn't eHarmony. Both your privileges have been revoked.

XTREME REVAMP

Florence looked good.

Black, glossy hair spilled over smooth bare shoulders and rested atop uplifted breasts. Florence's shimmering dress of golden mermaid scales hugged her sleek body, from thin shoulder straps to a high, tattered hemline. Her long legs were lightly muscled, her ankles tapering sweetly above Aphrodite sandals. Her toes were straight.

And she smiled, baring white uniform teeth. Florence laughed, her mouth the perfect complement to her incandescent indigo and lavender eyes.

For Victor Thetherson, feasting his eyes upon this heavenly body was just another day at the office. He had never seen Florence otherwise, from the first time he gazed upon her in college to his final visit to the Bizco accounting floor. Victor saw one's immutable essence, be it real or imagined.

Still unnoticed just inside the backstage entrance to the Gulf Waters television studio, Victor and his ex-wife Barbara took in the scene. This was a special, live "Xtreme ReVamp" episode of the previously dormant *Extreme Makeover* television program. The director's carefully crafted evening was just beginning to unfold, an over-the-top spectacle with minor and a few major celebrities in attendance. Staff and guests alike milled about, trying to predict the story arc of the evening, everyone with their own ideas and hopes for how the show would be a night to remember.

Florence held court ten minutes before air time. Arrayed before her were the show's corporate sponsors—executives from EnerGreen, the oil industry joint venture that was committed to "revamping" the nation's energy supply—and their guests: Don Chleber, Mel Parish and Jay Hansen from Bizco Diversified, which was a rubberstamp away from being officially tapped to build the JV's manufacturing facility in suburban Houston.

"I've known Flo since she started working for Vic Thetherson, our resident vampire," Parish the barrel-chested Bizco construction chief was telling the EnerGreen execs in his bullhorn voice. "One of the great things about being in construction, I can tell a woman what I think. Flo, you are drop-dead gorgeous."

Barbara cinched her arm tighter through Victor's. "So, Gale is back." She hadn't let go since hugging him in the parking lot, a reunion after many weeks apart. She also hadn't stopped looking at his mouth. "That's how I remember her, driving all the boys crazy on campus."

With hand and lips, Victor masked his teeth. "Gale," he recalled Florence's nickname, short for Nightingale, back before she dropped out of nursing school and ran off with a New Zealand sheep rancher.

"She's gorgeous, isn't she?"

"Sure, Florence is great." Victor said the right thing in the right way.

Not that Barbara owned an official right of possessiveness; they were no longer married. And neither was Barbara the jealous type. She was confident in her appeal, and looking good in her own right. In the three months Victor had been sequestered at the Longevity Labs as a live-in lab rat and rehab patient of sorts, Barbara had completed "the PX-90," as she used to call it. She got the name right now, and had the exercises figured out, too, judging from the body filling out her Jackie O. dress.

"Let's say hello," she said.

Basking in the spotlight, Florence finally saw Victor, and began to tremble. Sam Saboura had hosted enough "revealings" of his made-over subjects to sense that Florence's primary audience had arrived; yet he was curious whether her reaction was excitement or fear. Taking Saboura's cue, the show's staffers, sponsors and guests moved aside, opening a lane to Victor.

Don Chleber, Victor's corpulent boss, spread his arms and mouthed *What the hell?*, wondering why his employee had time to make the social scene but not the Bizco workplace. This was more a greeting than a challenge, finished with a wink.

Florence took a deep breath and a step forward, arms raised to put herself on full display. "Well?" It was obvious from this first word that she had been coached away from her sharp Texas twang, and cigarettes, and perhaps had her vocal chords tightened and polished to boot. "What do you think?"

Having religiously watched *Extreme Makeover* before it was canceled years ago, when the Thetherson routine was to settle nightly in front of the television with a different pint of Ben & Jerry's for each day of the week, Victor knew he was ruining what was supposed to be the televised surprise. "I'm early."

Florence pirouetted with a feminine flourish, glowing. Anyone in the Bizco accounting department simply would not have recognized her. "You didn't answer the question."

"You are beautiful, as always. We were just commenting on it."

Barbara embraced her college buddy. This wasn't their first meeting in the intervening 30 years, but it was their first hug. "You look stunning, honey. I called you Gale when I saw you."

Saboura looked on, nodding. "Sounds like a story in there."

The tenor of his voice prompted Victor to belatedly look and find a camera, and then another and another, capturing this informal unveiling.

Saboura's studio smile stayed in place as he continued to stare at Barbara, prompting her with his slowly elevating eyebrows.

"We knew each other in college," said Barbara.

"Ah," said Saboura.

"Florence was always so beautiful."

"Uh-huh," said Saboura. "And now look at her, right?" After waiting out another stretch of silence, he turned to a small woman with e-pad, earpiece and headset who was positioned off Saboura's right hip, strategically out of the cameras' eyes. He took her a couple steps aside. "I knew getting The Shot from the vampire was going to be tough." He betrayed his tension over the show's ratings. "I should have figured everyone would be reserved around him."

Jay Hansen, Bizco's chief financial officer, snickered and spoke quietly for his business companions. "Re*pulsed* is more like it." He winked at Chleber and turned his back on Victor and the scene to check his BlackBerry.

No one paid him attention, all eyes on Victor. This was not lost on Chleber. From the satisfied tug at the corner of his lips, Bizco's head of Strategic Development was happy to see that Victor still had it.

Having a vampire on staff had done wonders for business. Victor was closing deals even while on medical leave; he may have been locked away at the Longevity Labs, but the vampire's presence was always in the room. Victor was a big reason why Bizco would win the EnerGreen contract. Chleber jangled the keys in his pocket, ignored Hansen, and settled on his heels, content to watch the show.

One foot placed in front of the other as if following the director's tape marks, perhaps executing a scene she had been mentally rehearsing, Florence approached Victor, stopping inches away.

Before checking into the Longevity Labs, Victor's physique had been coming along nicely, vampirism brokering a swap of fat for muscle. At Dr. Speer's insistence he had been on a sedative targeted to his blood cravings, with the side effect of snuffing desires of every sort. Victor hadn't thought of women, work or working out. As the treatment progressed, Speer had allowed the staff to gradually back off the sedative. For this outing, Tripp had shut it off.

Victor had only really "come-to" this morning, and had been alarmed to see the state of his body. In fact he hadn't gained much weight—the Labs fed him 2,000 calories a day, heavy on blood-substitute in the first couple weeks, the ratio trending to favor "human" nutrients over the last month. His muscle tone was still decent. But right now all he knew was that Florence was brushing up against his spare tire.

She didn't seem to notice, or care. A microphone dangling from its runner above them struggled to pick up her surgically-softened voice. "You know this is for you, right?"

Victor met her hungry gaze, and shook his head.

"Of course you do. This," Florence indicated her physical appearance. "We both know it's temporary. Your transformation, that's permanent. I want that, Victor."

Ignoring the *Makeover* staff's signals to keep a respectful distance, Barbara gravitated toward their conversation, straining to hear.

Florence twiddled a button on Victor's shirt. Her finger slipped between buttons, inside. "We both have something the other one wants, don't we?" she purred, closer yet, warm breath, midnight garden scent. "Let's make a deal."

His lifelong infatuation tickled Victor above the eyes and deep in his gut. His voice came out low, the words muted by his hand. "It's not possible."

Barbara walked into the frame. "Excuse me."

Florence moved Victor's hand away from his face, and touched his lips. With a distressed glance at the camera, and then at Barbara, Victor bared his teeth.

Everyone was watching, and the gasp was pronounced.

"It actually worked," Jay Hansen marveled.

Florence stepped back, shaking her head, gaze unfocusing and mind retreating as her eyes recorded Victor's straight white teeth ... in particular his short, rounded canines.

"There goes the show," said a beefy staffer against the wall, remotely controlling the room's microphones.

"Two minutes to air time," said Saboura's assistant.

Sam Saboura brought his hands together in a single clap. "That, ladies and germs, is why we have a backup plan."

Reserved front-row seats for Victor and Barbara. They sat in silence waiting for the show to begin, neither really noticing the staff hustling to ready the host and the gothic set, or the glitterati sitting behind them. A vampire-themed show would have been draw enough, but rumor had it something big was going to happen.

Saboura, spreader of rumors, stood conferring with his assistant under an iron-and-candles chandelier, in a chamber of faux stone walls dressed up with crisscrossed pikes, more candles and a painting of baleful Vlad the Impaler. A wooden coffin stood in the corner, the lid ajar but reconnected with cobwebs. On the corner of a nearby table set for two, a staffer positioned a stuffed red-eyed rat to sniff at the main course, waiting on a large platter under sterling silver cover.

"I heard Snipes is the special guest," said Robert Downey, Jr., two rows behind Victor and Barbara. "I'm going to be severely disappointed if it turns out his work in *Blade* was just a cameo."

"I hope Wesley drinks your blood first," said Chelsea Handler from two chairs down. "I know I can fend off a stoned vampire."

"First of all, that's dated." Downey, Jr. gave Handler closer inspection. "Second, vampires don't bite each other, so you have nothing to worry about. You're like a turnip."

Amidst the banter, Barbara squeezed Victor's hand, arrhythmic in time with her distressed heart. She attempted a supportive smile. "Quite the event, isn't it?" After seeing the evidence of his in-process cure, Barbara had struggled to find words, her excited energy replaced by uncertainty.

What had she expected? Victor thundered inside. After what had happened to Amberly, bitten by a vampire, in their *home* for God's sake, what choice did he have? None, and Barbara knew it. This was exactly what he had feared when he checked into the Longevity Labs, finally agreeing to Tripp's pleadings to allow the Labs' scientists a final chance to study vampirism's impact on his aging while they cured him.

Before embracing vampirism, Victor had been timid and inconsequential. Barbara had not been impressed. He couldn't blame her if she was worried about Old Victor's return. He was, too. But during his near-incarceration at the Labs, her phone messages and handwritten letters had expressed support for what he was doing, and a longing to simply have him back.

They had been lies. Lies, like finding herself "in the picture she dreamed of painting" during her aggressive pursuit in their final college days. Like her wedding vows, and her feeling of "overwhelming completeness" when she held Amberly for the first time in their home. When would he learn?

Victor could feel disappointment pulsating through her tepid fingers. He didn't have to look to see her expression; she had worn it for years before his transformation as a vampire.

"You okay?"

She asked innocently, as if his pain were a mystery to her.

"You were counting on it not working, weren't you?"

Barbara appeared stung and confused—an affectation, in Victor's eyes. "What?"

"Don't."

Staring straight ahead, Barbara took a long moment. "Can't I have a little time to adjust?" Her voice was a mixture of anger and pain, cutting Victor all the deeper.

He wrested his hand from hers. "Take all the time you want."

Before Victor could rise, a scrawny straggly-haired woman with luminescent eyes and snaggle teeth threw herself into his lap. "Master!" His ex-admin, his former Renfield, Nikki, twice-bitten and hungering for the third in a tied-off t-shirt doing poor work as a bra, exposing ribcage and—for the teenage boy in the next row briefly distracted from ogling Jennifer Lawrence— a little bit of breast.

Victor felt the sudden attention from his immediate neighbors, checking their ears and the "master's" face: Was there a vampire in their midst? He pulled down Nikki's t-shirt.

"I heard a terrible rumor." Arms around his neck, Nikki now reached for his mouth. Victor caught that hand but not the other. Nikki's fingers weren't content to simply raise his lip; they forced their way in, searching for fangs and instead finding chompers better suited to biting an apple. "No! Master! It's over, already?" She gripped his cheeks like the crazy auntie about to plant a kiss on her favorite nephew. "Why didn't you tell me?"

The nurses and orderlies at the Longevity Labs had finally started to enjoy intercepting Nikki's attempts to reach Victor. The mad dashes through the front door, the smoke bomb diversions in the parking lot, the deliveries "for VV's eyes only." Just last week Nikki had disguised herself as a mustachioed man in an oversized suit who suffered from "Benjamin Button disease," volunteering to be admitted, poked, prodded and dissected—whatever sacrifice Science demanded of her.

She fantasized the third bite would flip a switch and make a vampire out of her. This despite Tripp running periodic blood tests to confirm that Victor's bloodletting had put no vampire spoor in her.

The disappointment in Nikki's face was too much for Victor to bear. He shoved her off his lap, looking for the nearest exit as the house lights winked off and two "On Air" signs popped on, bookends for descending neon-lit letters, "Xtreme ReVamp," billboard-sized in Gothic font, the "V" elongated to a sharp, red, fanged tip. Victor remained seated.

Where all those workers scurried a moment ago, Sam Saboura stood alone, welcoming the local and television audiences. "After a long hiatus, we're back, and we couldn't be more excited. In the coming months we will bring you unique stories of new beginnings. Emotional tales of rebirth that reflect our rapidly changing and sometimes unfamiliar new world. Tonight ... well tonight it's about the vampire."

The other neon letters turned off and the blood-red V pulsated over Saboura's shoulder.

"Just as you've come to expect from our show, tonight's guest, Florence Blankenship, is seeking a fresh start. But her goal might surprise you."

A large video screen rose beside Saboura, frozen in close-up of Florence's old pre-*Makeover* face. Terribly, there were murmurs of pity in the audience, only intensifying when Florence's face came to life.

"I'm a local girl," old Florence said. "From Spring, Texas. Went to the University of Houston. Got swept off my feet and moved to New Zealand. Things didn't go like I'd hoped. What was it Joe Walsh said? 'I can't complain, but sometimes I still do.'"

As she spoke, her college picture flashed momentarily onscreen. Even Victor was forced to acknowledge the contrast.

"Joe Walsh needs to quit his bellyaching," said Bill O'Reilly in a low rumble to Larry King, right behind Victor and Barbara. "But this lady has a legitimate beef."

"I had given up hoping for a change," Florence said onscreen. "As the years go by, it finally sinks in: This is my life." She straightened the Lone Star clasp of her bolo tie, her stringy neck flesh shimmying like a bead curtain. "And then my manager at work became a vampire."

Victor stiffened, expecting his picture to appear. Florence remained on the monitor. "Let's just say he had always had his own problems. But becoming a vampire changed that."

Saboura stepped in front of the screen, which faded to gray and recessed below the stage. "Without further ado, let's meet Florence Blankenship ... ReVamped!"

Florence emerged from the dungeon door stage left and the audience came to its feet, cheering ever louder as they registered the extent of the makeover. Now Victor received unwanted attention, in chain reaction from Florence to Saboura to the audience, and finally from the nearest camera. He laid a finger across his closed lips and sank lower in his chair.

"Welcome, Florence," said Saboura. "You look beautiful."

"Thank you." Florence's hand went to her chest, perhaps reflexively to cinch a bolo tie, fingering instead a delicate gold chain and pendant, a miniature red and black gaming dart.

"Have you received any feedback from your family and friends?"

"They're impressed, of course." She cleared her

throat and triggered a cough, harsh and bubbly, a disturbance of the layers coating her lungs. Cosmetic repair only went so deep. "They're ecstatic for me. Which makes it all the harder ..."

"Why is that?" Saboura probed.

She cleared her throat, softer this time. "Because I know it really doesn't matter what I look like. It's what's on the inside that counts."

"So true, isn't it?" Saboura let everyone ponder that for a second. "Our first time around, there was a legitimate criticism that our makeovers were presented as the happy ending. With our new show, the makeover you've experienced is just the beginning. This time around, we're going to go deeper."

He put his arm around Florence, turning her to fully face the audience. "This brings us to the surprise I alluded to in my introduction. You have a unique goal, don't you Florence? I'd like you to share that goal here tonight."

Florence's eyes flitted defensively to the studio audience. She flicked her hands down and up her body. "I don't care about this. Back when I was younger, I used to attack the world. No one told me what I could or couldn't do. *I* decided. There are people like that, you know."

Saboura nodded encouragement, and prodded her toward the punchline. "What do you want, Florence?"

"I want to change on the *inside*. I want what I used to be." She turned and stared at Victor. "I saw the changes. Deep, life-altering changes."

Nothing changed! Victor wanted to scream at her. *I was the same inside. Vampirism just stripped away all the* shit *that Barbara and Jay and everyone else piled on me.*

The audience stretched to get a look at him, with those within striking distance more circumspect. Except for Bill O'Reilly. "Excuse me, son." He clapped a hand on Victor's shoulder. "Are you a vampire?"

Victor ignored him, enjoying the pain in Barbara's face from Florence's public lust.

"I saw the way people looked at you ... the way they *saw* you." Florence's voice went hoarse, stumbling over old smoking wounds. "It had nothing to do with your appearance." She turned to the audience and paused for effect. "I want what Victor had. I want to be a vampire."

The audience gasped. Scattered catcalls pro and con weighed her desire, the scales tipping in support, applause building as converts were made, voyeurism outweighing horror.

Had, Florence said. *What I* had. Victor raged at the past tense—then in the next instant he foundered, suddenly unable to picture exactly who he was, the most vivid image in his mind a sudden recall of last night's nightmare, of Barbara at her canvas and painting his face, fat jowls showing behind a gruesome vampire mask.

For Saboura, Victor had had his moment, backstage. He wouldn't allow the cameras to find Victor—the show's ratings demanded something more dramatic than a defanged, former vampire. He took Florence's hands, turning her back on her vamp crush. "Did you think changing your look like this would improve your chances of becoming a vampire?"

"You saw what my throat used to look like," said Florence. "A vampire would take one look at that throat and think, 'Dry hole.'"

"Oh, Florence," Saboura chided her.

"Top to bottom," said Florence. "Dry hole."

"And now he—the vampire—he would look at you and think ..." Saboura drew it out, theatrically reluctant to say it. " ... juicy?"

Florence smiled.

Saboura raised his eyebrows. "Do you want to find out?" He included his audience in this question. "Should we see?"

The studio audience was now effectively unanimous in support of a vampire experience for Florence. Those around Victor assumed he was about to be called forth. While they hadn't seen any flash of fang, Nikki's visit and Florence's longing looks suggested there was a vampire in their midst.

Victor sensed a spark of hopefulness from Barbara, too. That there might be something of VV left in him, the cure imperfect, his humanity still laced with the vampire's power.

This only compounded Victor's frustration. What was Victor and what was the product of vampirism, Vampire Vic? The question was meaningless! Vampirism had only freed his true self, stripping away the insecurity that had coated his mind, the filter that had recast all inputs in a negative light and quality-checked every single output for potential embarrassment, until thoughts and words and emotion were bottled up, mixed up, shaking him up, while his real self screamed noiselessly for recognition.

If anyone should have seen this, should have loved him unconditionally either way, should have always seen the immutable essence that was Victor Thetherson, it was Barbara. She claimed to have seen it, needed it, loved it. And she had lied. Inviting her here was a mistake.

Women were screaming even before the vampire appeared. The coffin lid blew off with a muffled explosion and a wave of smoke from a low-key pyrotechnic and the stogie clenched in the jutting jaw of the Manhattan hot dog vendor and socialite vampire.

"Florence." Saboura stood back and swept his arm in presentation. "Your vampire. We're pleased he could take a break from his number one rated Cinemax reality series, *Nocturnal Elations*. Everyone, join me in giving it up, for Sennett McGumphrey!"

During the applause McGumphrey snuffed the cigar

in his palm, tucked it in the pocket of his way-off-white linen shirt, and advanced on Florence. The Bizco accountant swooned. McGumphrey covered the last yards at smooth speed, his arm around the small of Florence's back before her knees buckled. She was head back and throat exposed.

McGumphrey was mesmerized by tan smooth skin above the dress's golden scales, adorned by a curled lock of lustrous black hair. He drew Florence closer, bending to her—and then turned to the audience and bared his magnificent triangular fangs.

"Do it!" was the general roared consensus.

"Wait!" said Saboura, brave and mad to thrust his hand between a vampire's mouth and meal. "Sennett, you know the point of this show. You know why Florence is here." He was rushing a bit, because McGumphrey had his wrist and was applying pressure. "Will this bite do it, Sennett? Will one bite transform Florence into a vampire?"

"No," McGumphrey said. "But it's a nice start." He opened his mouth extra wide and dropped it on Florence's throat.

"Whoa, big boy." Saboura was quick and crazy, free hand on McGumphrey's forehead, forcing him away from Florence's flesh. "Not on my show."

"Then let's agree to call it *my* show." McGumphrey came off like a cross between Colin Farrell and Jesse "the Body" Ventura. He grabbed Saboura's fine silk shirt, lowered into a squat and then powered up, lifting the *Makeover* host and shotputting him into the dinner table. The stuffed rat went flying, bouncing on its head and into the coffin. Saboura's head clanked against the sterling silver platter cover, unveiling a wooden stake labeled "rare," likely a staffer's joke never intended for prime-time viewing. Saboura checked for obvious injuries, shot his off-camera team a look, and picked up the stake.

In the front row Victor Thetherson stood. Three

things occupied his mind:

Protect Florence. Former employee and forever fantasy. She hung limp in McGumphrey's arms.

I hate that McGumphrey. Victor had glanced at this glamour vampire on TV and paged right past him in Barbara's magazines with no reaction. But now, in person, he hated McGumphrey, wanted him dead and gone with an intensity he had never experienced.

Bloodlust.

Victor wasn't the only audience member standing, although most had remained in their seats, reflexively pressed deeper into the theater-style padding. He was the only one to charge the stage.

"Go get him, VV!" Nikki pumped her fist and exposed some chest, her cheerleading lost on the anxious audience, except for the teenage boy in the next row.

McGumphrey took a poll. "Who would love to see me give our contestant a taste of the good life?"

There were actually a few cheers of encouragement, amidst the buzzing undercurrent of uncertainty. Staffers scrambled on the periphery, chattering into headsets, looking at each other for direction.

McGumphrey laid eyes on Victor, striding toward him. "I've heard about you. I was hoping you'd show up. You've become quite infamous in our little circle—"

Victor kick-stomped McGumphrey in the chest, knocking him to the floor. Florence tumbled free, semi-conscious enough to break her fall. She reached for Victor, but he was lunging for the strapping, sexy, hot dog vendor vampire. Victor landed on McGumphrey and bit his exposed throat.

"What do you know," said Robert Downey, Jr. to Chelsea Handler. "I stand corrected."

The Irish-American vampire barked with fear. Victor raised his head, confused why McGumphrey's blood wasn't flowing. Where puncture marks should have been was an oval of imprints that would make a dentist proud.

McGumphrey punched Victor in the side of the head. Blooms of light came between his eyes and mind as he tumbled to the floor. He felt but couldn't see McGumphrey raise a foot and stomp his solar plexus, leaving him mute as well as blind, writhing like a fish in the bottom of McGumphrey's boat. He could still hear—there was Nikki, screaming for her master, and possibly Barbara as well, another constricted fearful voice in the babble.

The glamour vamp retrieved Florence, clamped a veiny hand on the junction of shoulder and neck and dragged her to Victor as she feebly tried to pry away his fingers. Nikki flew at him—"Not in VV's house!"— and was cuffed to the floor. No one crumpled like scrawny, flexible Nikki.

McGumphrey admired his handiwork, assigning a spot in his mental queue for Nikki. He hauled Florence to her feet, hand around her throat, on display. "This time, Victor doesn't get the spoils."

The audience was hesitantly, haltingly closing in. McGumphrey gave them a snarl before yanking Florence to him.

The show's host gripped the stake double-fisted over his head, exorcised demons with a tortured wail, "Up yours, AMC!" and slammed the polished cedar spike into McGumphrey's back.

McGumphrey reared and roared. Saboura fairly vibrated, absorbing all the energy he had put into his strike. Rugged features distorted in rage and pain, the hotdog vampire wheeled on Saboura and gave the audience full view of his unmolested back, his linen shirt ruined but not punctured. Saboura tried again, but he was dumbfounded by his first failure, in his heart aware that he was not to be cast as Van Helsing today. McGumphrey caught the stake, snapped it, head-butted Saboura, and spun back on the emboldened crowd.

Bill O'Reilly and Chelsea Handler were at the forefront of the audience's charge, really more like an amoeba's probing pseudopod. McGumphrey was big to begin with, and muscular enough to fill out his shirt (to be fair, probably a size too small). Now his vamp blood was up, and his bulging veined neck gave a hint to the power lurking below. His eyes were crazy and his smile wicked. McGumphrey looked famished. O'Reilly and Handler exchanged a glance, slapped away the prodding of Robert Downey, Jr., and stepped back.

McGumphrey laughed. He pulled Florence's face to his. "Wait for me, toots. I'll make it worth your while." He gave her a shove, and brought Victor to his feet. "So you took the cure. What a schmuck."

Movement stage left caught McGumphrey's eye—a cameraman, getting a better angle. The vampire beckoned him closer. "Let's see if we can boost our ratings. Florence, you were so right. Appearances mean nothing." He slugged Victor on the same side of the head, to the same effect. "This country appears strong. But it has grown soft." Seemingly unable to help himself, again he hit Victor, who was now on his feet only because McGumphrey insisted. "All the while our enemies grow bolder. It sickens me." He took his patriotic frustrations out on Victor, headbutting him, opening up a gash below his eyebrow. "A change is coming," he announced. "This country is about to get aggressive."

If the audience was cowed before, at the word "aggressive" they submitted to the vampire's will.

McGumphrey read the vibe and understood he now had free reign. As a hot dog cart vendor, he had been a showman, making more on tips than sales, more than the street musicians entertaining the Times Square throngs. He was sexy and salacious, able to belt out an '80s hair metal ballad and willing to show enough skin to please the women and stay in health code compliance.

Now he returned to Florence and planted a kiss on her lips. The audience sighed, maybe relieved he hadn't bitten her. And then McGumphrey began to theatrically beat Victor, broad sweeping punches and wind-up tosses into the gothic set walls that knocked loose the Styrofoam pikes and flickered the electric candles. He was action hero and professional wrestler, giving the crowd what they loved.

It didn't hurt that Victor was bigger than him, soft in the belly, and not all that attractive. Never mind that Victor had tried to prevent a bloodletting. He was now recast as the villain.

McGumphrey had the audience figured out, but he hadn't a clue about Victor's state of mind. For so very long he had been locked away in the Longevity Labs, drugged and sedentary. After some weeks in that condition, Victor had equated mental dullness with the cure and the return to his former, human drudgery. But as the last of the sedative left his brain while he caromed off the walls, which weren't as flimsy as one might assume, he couldn't have felt more alive.

And because of the tapering of the blood substitute, he was increasingly famished. Hunger is a powerful motivator.

The repeated head shots left him too dazed to see. Victor wanted to find Barbara, to make eye contact right before unleashing the fury that grew with every bombastic blow from McGumphrey. But his vision swam and swirled, preventing him from getting his feet under him. There was only one thing he could see, and it appeared to Victor as if through a tunnel in the concussion fog: McGumphrey's armpit. That was a good start. Victor swung for all he was worth.

Showboating, McGumphrey had his hand to his ear, a pro wrestler or Roman gladiator, wondering whether the crowd was ready for the *coup de grâce*. Victor's blow seemed to break a rib, instantly rendering

McGumphrey debilitated, bent, weakened. The vampire tried but was unable to turn to look at his assailant.

Victor's head was now clear, his vision sharp. He was eager for battle.

"Oh no," said McGumphrey. Dirty white dots appeared on his arm and hand, spreading in number and size, sweeping up his face and blossoming on his other hand. The milky blotches grew until they merged, turning McGumphrey's skin the color of his shirt. Now his skin oozed liquid, some of that 60-to-80 percent of vampires and humans alike that is water, fouled by McGumphrey's dissolute lifestyle. The vampire sucked a last labored breath and hit the floor with a great wet thud.

With half the crowd holding its breath and the rest demanding to know what just happened, Saboura's petite assistant crept forward and bent close to McGumphrey, unwilling to touch him, repelled by his gooey skin. "I think he's dead," she reported, making a note in her e-pad.

"Fucking really?" said Chelsea Handler.

Victor wasn't sure what had happened. He felt cheated by McGumphrey's easy dispatch. His soul screamed for a release. As the crowd closed in on him, he removed the falsies Tripp had given him and bared his skinny fangs.

After a collective gasp, the assembled clapped and stomped and raised their voices.

"That's our VV!" Parish bellowed. The moniker swept the crowd, becoming a chant: "V-V, V-V, V-V!"

Over the heads of his adoring fans, Victor found Barbara and gave her a grim nod, bringing tears of pride to her eyes.

"Master!" Nikki leaped into his arms and wrapped her arms around his neck. "I knew you could do it!" She stretched out her throat. "Are you thirsty after that workout?"

Parched was more like it. Victor raised his former admin, lifted her high as if carrying her to safety above rising floodwaters, and sank his fangs into her flesh, tapping her carotid artery, giving Nikki her long-sought third bite.

And how the crowd loved it. Their adoration grew to wild cheers. For the television audience it might as well have been a college basketball game, the decibel level challenging their TV speakers, the thrill of competition married with a girl-gets-her-man happy ending. Sam Saboura drank it in as he regained consciousness, imagining them trending on Twitter. An 8.5 share was not unthinkable. He mapped out a series of vampire-related shows.

All the while, Victor drank. He had been so good, taking the cure. But a human Victor clearly wasn't meant to be. And why was that "good"? Would this crowd ever cheer Human Victor? They would never even notice him; if he ever competed for their attention, he would come off the stumbling, stuttering fool.

Were Parish and the other execs in attendance eager to have Human Victor back, and to continue paying him a fat multiple of what he had earned as an accountant? For Bizco, the vampire was a wise investment with meaty returns.

Barbara's opinion went without asking. Victor's thoughts returned to their first meeting in college, their first days together, back to that brief moment in time when his mind was clicking on all cylinders. She had loved him, she had craved him—and loving her back had felt *good*. Barbara wanted nothing less than the best that he could be, heroic and aggressive and successful—an alpha male. There was nothing wrong with that. Victor would give his woman what she wanted, and he would be fulfilled.

These thoughts took some time to play out. Time enough for Victor to fully slake his thirst. He lifted his fangs from Nikki's throat and laid her gently to the floor.

The applause died down. Cameras and the closest of the studio audience studied Nikki's inert, bloodless body. Perhaps some expected her eyes to spring open and her transformed body to sit up, newly undead. Others began to cry for help. Sirens joined the increasingly frantic chirping as the soundstage doors opened and the police hustled in.

JAILED AND SLAPPED AROUND

Round in the face and body, an optimized endomorph, approachable and mischievous, fluid and graceful, Dr. Winnie Linciome laid an encouraging hand on Victor's shoulder at the tinted door to the Longevity Labs on the Rice University campus. "Are you ready?"

"No," said Victor. He pulled the door open and stepped inside.

This was his first stop after two nights in the Houston lock-up. The cops had stored him in what they called the vamp pit, a holding cell crowded with 60 or so fanged men and women who had crossed the line (a blurry, inconsistent line, according to the ACLU's recent national survey of policing practices) and languished while the system decided what to do with them. Victor was given a disproportionate amount of space by the other vamps, big and small, male and female, vicious and metaphorically toothless. They wanted nothing to do with him.

The feeling was mutual. Just as he had instantly despised Sennett McGumphrey, Victor was repelled by this crowd. He bristled when one would stumble close. The very sight of these vamps constricted his chest and bludgeoned his brain so violently that Victor could think only of exterminating them.

Exterminate them. Like vermin. What did that say about himself? He physically stood apart from these bloodsuckers, but could not claim to be any different.

Not after what had happened on the *Xtreme ReVamp* set. Over the course of 40 hours' sleepless crouching and pacing in the pit, Victor's loathing hadn't been restricted to the vampires around him.

And yet, intertwined with the anguish over Nikki's death—there would be no rising from the grave sporting the fangs she had coveted—he was at peace. The cure had not worked. During his de facto incarceration at the Labs, even as his fangs remained sharp, Victor had convinced himself the cure was in process. He had assumed the change was so slow as to be imperceptible, the tipping point at hand and so tenuous that a misstep would jeopardize all the hard work from Dr. Speer, Dr. Linciome and Tripp.

Every day Victor had felt guilty for not wanting the cure as badly as Tripp did. But every day he had done his duty and stayed in his room, hooked to his IV, turned away from temptation, on course for an uncertain, unwanted future.

But in a flash the truth had been revealed to the world and to Victor. The struggle, the anguish, was over. Tripp and company had done what they could, but there would be no turning back for Victor. He was a vampire. He looked forward to figuring out what came next.

Certainly his future didn't include Tripp and the Labs. Tripp hadn't visited him in jail. Victor had hoped and then been disappointed when it was a nurse and not Tripp making the daily rounds from the Labs, which had a deal with the Houston police department to procure blood samples from each of the incarcerated vamps. Tripp hated him, Victor was certain. He had protested on the drive from the jailhouse but Dr. Linciome had insisted, and the scientist was right. A final visit was in order.

Tripp Nicklus, doctoral candidate and the Labs' assistant genetic researcher, stood in the waiting area in his typically elaborate cowboy garb. He was obviously prepared to tear into Victor, sorting through all the accusations jockeying to be first. Behind him, where the receptionist might have been, sat the lab's glowering director, Dr. Regnald Speer.

"I'm sorry," said Victor.

That broke the logjam. "Not a chance," said Tripp. "You're just mouthing what humans say when they're remorseful."

"I am truly sorry—"

"You killed her!" Tripp put the brim of his cowboy hat on Victor's forehead. "You killed Nikki!"

Victor took the verbal beating, prepared to likewise absorb it physically if Tripp needed the release. "I cared for her," he said, throat thickening and stomach roiling all over again as he was confronted by what he had done to his longtime assistant. "I've bitten so many people—how could I know?"

"We both knew it was possible every time, Victor." Tripp seethed. "Every time. And don't tell me—"

"Come now," said Dr. Linciome. "How many times was Nikki here, looking for exactly what Victor finally gave her?"

Tripp spread his orangutan arms, brushing the wall with one hand and swatting the double-helix wind chime hanging over the reception desk with the other, making the colorful spiraling metal rungs twist and tinkle. He gaped at his boss. "Why did you bring him here, Winnie? You bailed him out!"

Dr. Linciome rested a warm, calm hand on Victor's shoulder. "You're right. I could have waited another day or two for the charges to be dropped."

"Says who?" said Tripp.

"It was an act of self-defense against Sennett McGumphrey. And a lame one at that. Did you see the video? Victor punched him in the armpit."

Dr. Speer frowned. "Then how did McGumphrey die?"

"Ah," said Dr. Linciome. "That is very interesting.

The skin on this vampire's torso was chitinous, thick and leathery, nearly impenetrable. He had basically grown a bulletproof vest. A punch, a stake, maybe even a bullet would have done no damage."

Dr. Speer was unconvinced. "Why haven't we come across anything like that before?"

"I believe HPD has only provided us what they're calling 'lesser vampires.' There are a certain few who have evolved various defense mechanisms. So I've read." Dr. Linciome raised an arm and fingered his armpit like a monkey. "Here, McGumphrey was unprotected. The chink in his armor. According to the coroner, Victor's punch exploded the lymph node, triggering system-wide cell death."

Tripp was impatient throughout. "Who gives a damn about McGumphrey? Nikki was murdered."

"We all know the law surrounding vampire bites is very unsettled." Dr. Linciome talked to Tripp, but he was making his case to Dr. Speer.

Tripp stabbed a finger at Victor. "This one might settle it."

Dr. Linciome clucked softly. "We need to avoid overreacting. I have it on good authority that Nikki's family is not going to press charges."

"Good authority?" said Tripp. "Whose?"

"Nikki's family."

Tripp was incredulous. "You talked to them?"

"I felt terrible for them. And somewhat responsible. After all ..." Dr. Linciome arched an eyebrow at Dr. Speer. "Nikki received her second bite right here in one of our exam rooms."

Victor was embarrassed, Tripp mortified.

"The only thing that doesn't last long at the Longer Labs are secrets." Dr. Linciome used their pet name for the place. Normally that would prompt Tripp to hold his hands about ten inches apart, suggesting the science of enhancement more than longevity. Not now. "Don't beat yourself up. I was as eager to read the results of Nikki's before-and-after bloodwork as you were."

From his expression, Dr. Speer was the only one previously unaware that Victor had bitten Nikki in his laboratory. He rose.

"It could also be argued," Dr. Linciome said, slowing Dr. Speer's momentum, "that we erred by backing off the blood substitute. We have to shoulder a large portion of the blame, Reggie. We unleashed a starving vampire on that set."

"Which is exactly what I feared from the start." Dr. Speer rounded the desk. "Your time here is over, Mr. Thetherson. Your belongings have been shipped to your house. I've asked campus security to join us to make it official."

"What's done is done," Dr. Linciome appealed, leaving Victor's side and talking fast. "This is not the end of the world. We've learned so much from Victor— his data has accelerated our longevity research by a decade. And enormous strides remain."

Tripp turned on Dr. Linciome. "I can't believe you're arguing to keep him here."

"You have no idea what this vampire can do for humanity."

Tripp went boggle-eyed. "That's completely unethical." He pointed at Victor, unable or unwilling to look at him. "He doesn't want to be here. He doesn't want to be cured."

"I did everything you asked," said Victor. His false teeth were like a slight inebriation, messing with his lips and tongue, maddening as he tried to spark a glimpse of the affection Tripp always had for him. "I didn't want this."

"*Do* you want to be cured?"

Victor sputtered through aborted attempts to explain the conflict that raged within him.

"Are we even capable of curing Victor?" Dr. Linciome rescued him. "Isn't that the question? Isn't it we who failed in our promise to Victor?"

"We made no such promise," said Dr. Speer. "It's irrelevant now."

Dr. Linciome shifted smoothly, never letting the lab's bulldozer of a director meet firm resistance. "Yes, exactly. This is not a treatment center. Our full attention must be on discovering the secret of Victor's longevity."

Tripp's anguish was laid bare. "What happened is my fault. First having him bite Nikki again, and now with the botched treatment. I should have seen this coming. I knew the cure wasn't progressing as quickly as we thought—but the inhibitors were in his bloodstream! They were in his cells. I *saw* them, Reggie. They *had* to be blocking the manufacture of the vampire protein. It should have been just a matter of time."

Dr. Speer pointed at Vic's falsies. "Did you provide Victor with this disguise?"

"That was a mistake," said Tripp. "I wanted Vic to feel human when he went out." The scientist in him came back to the fore. "Reggie, the cure will work! Our data proves it. There's no reason to give up." He turned on Victor. "What about your daughter? Aren't you willing to do whatever it takes to perfect the cure—for Amberly?"

"Of course," Victor snapped.

Tripp had managed to obtain samples from a few of the women Victor had bitten, verifying in each case that no vampire markers were present in their blood. This had lulled them all into complacency when Amberly didn't exhibit any symptoms after being bitten by Bob the appraiser vampire.

On one of her visits to see her father during his extended stay, as an afterthought Tripp had coaxed her to give him a sample. It had come back positive.

"We can't guarantee what's inside her is going to remain dormant," said Tripp.

"I said *yes*. I will do whatever I can."

"Perhaps we should be testing a cure on a different vampire," said Dr. Linciome. "In my professional opinion, Victor likely isn't representative of the species."

"Curing vampires is not our business," said Dr. Speer.

Dr. Linciome appeared to have just brokered a grand compromise. "Couldn't agree more."

"Hello?" Barbara poked her head in the door. "I'm sorry to interrupt. I just knew Tripp would get to you before I could. How can a woman compete with a man-crush?"

Tripp winced. "Barbie, we're here to officially part ways with Victor."

She was holding the door open for Larry Cocachello to make a reluctant entrance. "Look who I ran into in the parking lot."

When Victor checked in for extended treatment, Chleber had looked to hire him an assistant. Victor had insisted on Larry. Victor didn't really like him, but aiding his fellow former citizen of tiny Milford had always made Victor feel good. The position was a plum—a 50 percent pay bump over his job as construction accountant, and ten times the fun. Larry owed Victor for his former position, and he owed him now.

And hated him for it.

"Chleber told me to go see you at the police station." Larry's eyes threw Bowie knives at Victor and the Labs' scientists. "They told me you were bailed out."

Barbara went to Victor, brought his hand to her chest. "You're not staying? You're coming home?"

"They're not forcing you to take the cure?" Disgust deepened Larry's hangdog lines as he took a couple bowlegged strides forward. "After what you did to Nikki?"

Victor answered for Barbara's benefit as well. "I

don't think it works for me."

"Bullshit." Larry stuck his finger in Victor's face. "That's pure b.s. You don't want it. Because then you'd never get a second look from *any*body." Larry's twitching eye delivered a Morse code message: *You had no right to change.* "You can't succeed without intimidating people. You're just a thug."

"Larry!" said Barbara. "What's gotten into you?"

He continued to point at Victor as he backed toward the door. "I better not see you at Nikki's funeral."

He ran into a vial held like a pistol in the hand of a young man dressed like a mime with a gas mask clipped to his hip and what resembled a giant angled razor blade mounted on an axe handle, hoisted high aloft.

Larry squawked and threw an elbow. The vial went flying.

Frenchie's little old lady companion dove in a crackling volley of popping synovial fluid and flaking cartilage-free joints, laying out and catching the vial a hands-breadth from the floor. "I'd like to see a 60-year-old meat-eater do that," she said. "Much less one 80 years old."

Frenchie plucked the vial from her wrinkled claw and thrust the blade above his chapeau'd head. "*Vive la resistancers!*"

His wizened associate got to her hands and knees, clutched at his vacuum-sealed capris pantleg, slipped down, set down her gas mask and grabbed Frenchie's leg again, now with both hands, letting go briefly to wave off Barbara's offer of help, grunting and cackling as she regained her feet. "Edna Campbell," she introduced herself while gingerly bending to retrieve her gas mask. "Pescetarian. Former member of that all-talk-and-no-action bunch of radical poseurs, PETA. And U.S. leader of the anti-vampire resistance!" She had a pronounced humpback.

"For *moi?*" said Frenchie. "Slayer Sven." It was

difficult to determine whether he was speaking English with a French accent or vice versa.

Larry hiked up his pantleg, unclasped and unholstered his Bowie knife. "I hope you're here for Vic."

"Vic*tor*?" said Slayer Sven, eyes boggling. "Victor Tetterson? I have zee happy moment of meeting Victor Tetterson?"

Edna cocked her head and moved for a closer look. "You're the talk of the town out on the World Wide Web."

"On zee slayer sites," said Sven. "It is all, 'Victor, he is zee Chosen One des vampires.' 'Victor, he is zee second coming of Morbius!' 'Victor, he must die!'"

Barbara glowed with pride. Larry wiped sweat off his upper lip with the back of his knife hand.

Sven bowed his head, humble. "Zees weel be a great honor to slay you."

Tripp looked at Victor. "See what you have to look forward to?"

"No-no," said Sven. "You have nothing to look forward to."

"Prepare to die, Vampire!" Edna crowed. "Along with any meat-eaters who'd like to join you!"

"This is a private facility," said Dr. Speer. "Please leave."

"Hey guys." Dr. Linciome approached, conversational, hands in his pockets behind woolen double pleats. "Protestors are always getting us mixed up with the ag genetics lab on the other side of campus. All kinds of nefarious GMO experimentation going on over there. We'll get you an escort."

"We're in the right place," Edna cackled. "The genetically modified *people* laboratory!"

Sven pointed at Victor, and then took finger shots at everyone in the room. "Zee vampire factory."

Tripp turned to Dr. Speer. "When did you say security was coming?"

Sven laughed with a French accent. "Just like Americans, trying to solve every problem with a gun. You can fix Iraq and Syria and Russia with guns, yes-yes? And vampires. You weel just shoot all the vampires, *oui*?"

"Shoot them like a Hydra." Edna stomped her little feet while holding her rear end to keep everything together. "And then turn your back while ten more vamps rise from the grave!" She broke into song. "Ain't it the way, having a nice day, along comes a vamp to get in your way. Hack off a hand, grows it right back, stake in the heart, lays down for a nap!"

Dr. Speer returned to the desk and picked up the phone. "I'll see how close they are."

"*Voila,* zee anti-Hydra!" Sven held the vial high in his tanned fist. "Shoot it with your American bullets, and watch zee virus spread!"

"What do you have there?" said Dr. Linciome.

Sven stared affectionately at what looked like an empty vial. "Zee end of your wicked laboratory, and all your vampire patients. And your poor, miserable animal subjects."

"Sorry, we just turned loose the latest horde of animal vamps," said Dr. Linciome. "A fresh crop of monkeys aren't due in until tomorrow."

"No more monsters will be created in zees laboratory." Sven brandished the vial. "Zees microbe, there is no cleaning it up. Zee entire building weel need to be burned to zee ground. And unfortunately you weel all most likely die. Except you." He pointed the long-handled razor at Victor. "You weel already be dead."

"You're currently undead," said Edna. "Pretty soon you'll just be dead."

"Victor is very much alive," said Barbara, moving to Victor's side. "You two fruitcakes should think twice before trying your luck."

Victor swelled with pride and slid a protective arm

around his ex.

"As my esteemed countryman once said," said Sven, "luck favors zee prepared mind." He tapped the flat of the blade to his forehead. "I am feeling très lucky." After having no luck squeezing the vial into the pocket of his capris, he held it in his mouth, lips cradling the precious cargo in an "O." With a two-handed grip he admired the blade and then removed the vial to speak. "You may remember zee life of zee party from *la Revolution Française*, yes-yes? We call it zee National Razor!"

"Good news for the axe," said Tripp. "I guess it can retire now that we have the guillotine on a stick."

Sven adopted a John Wayne accent on top of his questionable French. "If you're looking for a close shave, you came to za right party, cow-poker." He put the vial back in his mouth.

Edna dancing a jig at the anticipated slaying. "This shave is for you, Eugene!"

Victor grimaced. "Of course you know Eugene Foreman."

"Our leader, Eugene V.S.E.," Edna crowed. "Vampire Slayer Extraordinaire!"

Sven took out the vial again. "I am affiliated but do not directly report to Eugene." He replaced the vial and charged.

Victor had been lulled to complacency by the ease in repelling Eugene's attacks. He was still guiding Barbara safely behind him when Sven swung his portable guillotine in a whistling arc at Victor's neck.

Dr. Linciome's cry joined Barbara's scream. Victor was too slow to defend himself. But the wooden handle shattered on impact, the blade twisting ineffectually, taking a small bite from his neck before thudding to the floor.

Barbara's knees momentarily buckled when she saw Victor's head attached to his body. Larry bawled like a branded steer and dropped his Bowie knife, a splinter from Sven's busted weapon buried in his nostril.

Tripp charged Sven. He took a swing but came up short, with Sven's heel in his gut, right on the big longhorn belt buckle. Tripp staggered back, clutching his stomach. "Frenchie," he gasped, "you're as nuts as Eugene."

"I weel take zat as a *merci*," said Sven.

"Almost forgot," said Edna. In the melee she had retrieved a bucket of red paint. She swung the bucket back and then stumbled sideways, dumping the paint on Larry.

He stopped bawling. "Gol*dammit!*" The profanity whistled through his pierced nose. "What in the hell was that for?"

"Old time's sake," said Edna. "Sorry, though. I was aiming for the other meat-eater."

"I have never agreed with ruining clothing." Sven watched Larry daintily wipe his eyes with a small dry patch of his plaid chamois shirt without disturbing the mini stake. "But your apparel will not be missed."

"They're vandalizing my office," Dr. Speer reported into the phone. "Please be prompt."

Sven secured the vial under his armpit and donned his gas mask while Edna did likewise. "You are inviting zem to zer funeral, I have fear." His voice was muffled through the mask. He started to remove the vial's cork.

Edna snatched the vial from her compatriot. "Allow me." She worked at the cork while tilting her head just so to see through the mask's scratched plasti-glass face shield.

Blood oozing from his wound, Victor strode toward her. Edna dodged left and right. "How thick is your finger, vamp?" Edna grunted through her cork-popping exertions. "Good luck plugging this dike!"

Victor karate-chopped the little old lady on the back of her neck.

Edna hit the floor with a soft plunk. She was out

cold. The possibly microbe-filled vial hit the tile floor. Plastic, still corked, the tube bounced and skittered under an end table covered with outdated *GolfWorld* magazines. Sven dashed for it and slipped on a patch of paint, landing hard on his hip, head bouncing off the tile.

Larry holstered his knife and jumped on Sven just as two campus security officers burst in the door with guns drawn.

The officers took in the various injuries, trying to sort good guys from bad. "Everyone freeze," one of them commanded.

"It's over now, officers." Hands half-raised, Dr. Linciome looked for their buy-in as he shuffled over to the end table to retrieve the vial.

"Victor took them out," said Barbara.

"I got this one," Larry called out with a whistle and a honk as if he was talking through a kazoo. He jammed woozy Sven's head into the floor.

"Nicely done," the officer congratulated Victor.

Tripp scowled at Victor and pointed at Edna's inert form. "That didn't take a vampire."

The drive into their neighborhood stirred warm feelings for Victor. He was worried about coming back to what had been a place of tension and unhappiness for so long. Barbara's hand in his helped—not just squeezing him, but feeling him, her fingertips becoming very acquainted with the back of his hand, his fingers, his palm. Barbara turned this into a homecoming, remodeled their home as a soul-soothing refuge.

Even so, the house suddenly looked small and exposed. Impulsively Victor said, "There are neighborhoods close to the new EnerGreen plant going up in Spring. Bigger houses, bigger trees. Let's move there."

Barbara's eyes flashed with excitement, but she

muted her response. "So you're going back to work? And you're done at the Labs? That would be wonderful—but only if that's what you want. If you need to continue to be treated, of course that's fine, I understand, with Nikki ... . I'm just looking forward to, if you want, to being together again."

"I do want that." Victor liked seeing that Barbara had kept half the two-car garage devoted to P90X training, chin-up bar affixed to the rafters, spongy mats on the floor, the stall bordered with dumbbells, medicine balls and Tony Horton's poster on the wall. "I'm not going back to the Labs. Speer is done with me." He put the midnight blue Charger in park, giving the engine a final purring rev before hitting the off button. "Tripp, too."

Barbara turned in her seat to give him her full, physical attention. "You tried. Maybe a cure just isn't meant to be."

"He doesn't see it that way. He won't forgive me for Nikki."

"Just give him some time." Barbara leaned over and put a soothing, lingering kiss on her ex-husband's cheek. "They should all be thankful you were there today. And that you are who you are."

"I knocked out a little old lady."

"You acted. That's what mattered. Just like at the television show. You're the one who acts."

"Tripp was wrong. It probably does take a vampire to hit an old lady."

"That one deserved it." Barbara kissed him at the corner of his lips. "Weren't you worried about the vial?"

"I assumed it was fake."

"Because you think you're invincible." They exited the car. Barbara took his hand and led him to the house.

As she opened the entry door, Victor had the intoxicating sensation that Barbara was deciding to open herself to him. She seemed vulnerable like never before. This was the first time he had ever felt like she was inviting him in. Maybe only a vampire could appreciate the symbolism.

Her comment about his perceived invincibility had moved him. She wasn't chastising him for that mindset. It seemed to excite her. He now realized how different Barbara looked when she was simply going through the motions. Barbara was truly excited. She was excited by *him*. And so Victor was moved physically, too.

They hurried through the kitchen. "There's something I need to tell— Oh, Barb."

Three paintings adorned the living room walls. Barbara's work, it was obvious, even though he hadn't seen anything new from her in years. She painted in the colors and patterns of a children's book, fanciful and warm, extending beyond the canvas boundaries and pulling Victor into a fantasy realm where he could draw the sky into his lungs and taste its textures. He felt the vibrations humming from the paintings' striking figures, fated and eager to join this world.

"You like?"

On the easel in the middle of the room, a steam locomotive plowed through a lush valley, no tracks in sight, sending in its wake waves of grain, earth and warning signs: STOP, CAUTION, YIELD, AUTHORIZED PERSONNEL ONLY. Victor wanted to touch it. He sighed with delight. "You're painting again."

Barbara's breathing was shallow, watching him see her work. "I've been inspired. It's like I'm 20 years old."

He was reaching for her as he lost himself in her art, gripping her arms and then inappropriate places, squeezing and caressing and now plunged deep into her hair, pulled back into a ponytail and woven through his fingers, fingers gripping her skull, his mouth on hers.

Barbara moaned. "I've missed you." She clawed at his mouth, removing the false teeth and mashing her mouth against his, cutting them both on his fangs.

The familiar warning bells clanged in Victor's brain. "I can't. I can't do this." He kissed her again and again. "I'm so sorry," said Victor, now pulling away. "There's something I need to tell you. I have a ... problem."

"Tripp told me." Barbara gave him the most serious smile; and then ripped the bandage off his neck.

"Ouch! Barb, what the hell?"

Barbara squeezed his balls so hard he forgot about his neck, nearly passed out. "Silly boy. You don't have to orgasm for us to make love."

She kissed him a while, standing surrounded by her paintings, giving Victor alternating images of her sweet bone structure and her art. Barbara had let go of his balls to hold his hands in hers, refusing to let go, sensing his need to reacquaint himself with her body, no doubt remembering how excited he would get so long ago, when he would run his hands along the pinch point of her hourglass, ribs to waist to hips and back up again, occasionally coming around the front to palm her stellar abdominals. Victor's knuckles cracked from his pull and Barbara's restraint.

Still his excitement rose. Barbara broke away. "Let's move this party, shall we?"

They made snail's pace progress to the bedroom. Barbara paused to straighten a lampshade and check the moisture of the soil supporting her little lemon tree. Victor wanted to throw her over his shoulder. They finally sat together on the bed.

"So ... you haven't had sex since you became a vampire? All those times you were out all night?"

"I only bit them."

"And not with what's-her-name?"

"Darla?" Victor shook his head emphatically. "Never."

Barbara kissed him. They made out, until Victor's

physical state again shifted from simple enjoyment to serious involvement. Barbara let him feel her up and down; when he unclasped her bra, she pinched the inside of his thigh.

Victor yelped. "That really hurt, Barb."

Barbara stood up. "Yes, I know. We both know the consequences if you, if *we* go too far. It will kill you."

Victor stood before her. Barbara leaned in for a kiss, slowly explored his mouth with her tongue, being careful not to touch his fangs. She bit his lip. Just a bit of a bite.

"Oh, Barbara."

She ran her fingers along his widow's peak and to the back of his head, tousling out his Brylcreemed pompadour, making fists in his thick, collar-length hair, making him moan. Then abruptly and violently Barbara slammed his face down onto the top of her forehead.

"Fuck!!" Victor screamed.

Barbara smiled sweetly as blood trickled from Victor's nose. "I love you," she whispered as her hands made quick work of his pants. She began to work on his cock.

Victor's mind was spinning, a carousel of pain and pleasure. He growled a warning that his lips refused to translate, unintelligible, as Barbara kissed his chin, her hand working feverishly.

He was angry, and he was close, the warning bells now merged into one long cathedral-sized peal, reverberating and deafening in his skull.

Another few moments and he would make her stop.

Barbara's one hand and then the other caressed their way up his body, stroking his stomach and tickling his ribs. Victor was passionately returning the favor as she gripped his shoulders for leverage, and kneed him in the groin with all her might.

"Bitch," Victor gasped. He doubled over, hands on his knees. Tried to raise his head. Resisted the urge to punch her in the thigh.

Barbara pushed him back onto the bed. She sat astride his stomach, removing her shirt and now her bra.

"You made your point," Victor wheezed. "I promise I'll slow down."

For his bargaining Victor received a hard slap between the legs, and Barbara's nipple in his mouth. Starbursts filled his viewing screen and queasiness swirled in his gut while he enjoyed that nipple. He heard the snap of an elastic band giving way and then was enveloped in the glossy deep-brown curtain of Barbara's hair.

He cupped and nuzzled her breast while breathing in the dizzying scents of her hair and skin. He slid his hand down her back and beneath pants and panties to squeeze her butt cheek and force her hips harder to his.

"I was afraid of that," he was vaguely aware of Barbara saying, amidst all sorts of alarms and cravings demanding his attention.

She planted a hand on his chest to lever up and plop her butt onto his solar plexus, forcing wind from his lungs. "I can't have you that excited." Barbara reached to the nightstand and came back gripping a pair of long-bladed silver scissors. "I'm sorry, Victor."

"Holy shit, Barb!"

The scissors flashed. A foot of her hair was gone. She set it carefully on the nightstand, and then cut another swath, and another, stacked like a bumper crop of burnt amber silk. "I'll run that over to my hairdresser as soon as we're done. She can donate it." A couple more quick clips and Barbara now wore shoulder-length hair, chopped but remarkably even.

Victor sighed and finger combed her new 'do. "I'm warning you, I still like your hair."

Barbara kissed him, melted into him, unbuttoning her pants, working them past her hips. "That's okay."

She guided his hand between her legs and then rolled to the side, eyes closed and a slight frown on her face. "I've got something to take your mind off my hair."

"Yes, you do." Victor went to work. Barbara felt for him, found him too far along again, and clamped down on his balls.

He was enthralled with the response he was receiving from his manipulations while the pain brought tears to his eyes, made it hard to draw a good breath. Barbara escalated in stages over the next few minutes. When she was there, and when she could take no more, Victor was bathed in sweat, fully spent himself, balls bruised and blue, and never happier.

EUGENE FOREMAN

The old Civil War Soldier didn't believe in anything other than live-fire training. Because modern-day vamps had evolved to thrive in broad daylight and insinuated themselves into the daily lives of their human prey, Eugene Foreman, Vampire Slayer, only hoped to minimize the collateral damage.

He also hoped to close on a nice three-bedroom row house in Cassis before it hit the south of France real estate listings.

His filthy vamp target ran the Chenonceaux Castle visitor center in north central France. The CWS briefed Eugene as they ate crepes on the TGV bullet train southwest out of Paris, CWS's assistant Hilda three seats back and as always on high alert.

The CWS fought side by side with Charles Valery in the Belgian cleansing three years ago. Only recently had he learned that Valery had been turned at some point during a battle in Brussels. Not involuntarily.

"It breaks my heart to have to kill him," the CWS drawled, drinking hard apple cider—a cold beverage, but the old slayer slurped it like a cup of piping hot tea. "Charlie was a fine young man. He has a wonderful family." He smacked on a shrimp-filled crepe. "But for as long as I've lived, yesiree, I've had my heart broken more than once. I always get over it."

Just how long the CWS had lived was hinted at but never quantified, left open to Eugene's speculation thanks to Hilda and her extremely tight lips.

"Has he been terrorizing the countryside?" Eugene pictured the French landscape as the foothills of the Swiss Alps, dotted with thatch-roof chalets manned by striped-shirted mimes who provided wholly inadequate protection to rosy-cheeked, goat-milking women in Dutch hats, all in the shadow of a vampire's castle. This despite the broad, gentle Loire valley outside their window, field after field of row crops, gleaming steel corporate farming complexes, and wind turbines strung along the valley's rim.

"Not so much. I could use a Perrier." The CWS doffed his floppy white hat, wiped his high forehead with a once-white hanky, and pulled the bellman cord, which was in fact the "next stop" signal. "I've told you how the vampires are organizing."

"Like a union with unfair bargaining position, I believe is how you described it." Eugene was distracted by his BlackBerry, the businessman's communication weapon. He had received an email from a young Gypsy boy he paid peanuts to be his finger on the local Cassis pulse. "Dammit," he muttered, now perturbed for the umpteenth time with the device, which was taking forever to load the picture from young Milo the Gypsy. He cast a covetous glance at a man in short pants across the aisle, watching a funny cat video on his Galaxy.

"Focus, Gene," the CWS said calmly, ominously. He looked into his hat.

"It's *Eu*gene." He couldn't help himself; he craned for a look. He had no idea what was in that hat, only that what the CWS saw always portended poorly for him.

Take the slaying in the Sonora Desert in December. The flies had been unbearable. The CWS had received a tip on a smugglers' route, illegal vampire immigrants. Sure enough, the little cabin they commandeered was stocked with water, GMO-free dry goods proven to be easy on vampire tummies, dry socks, and Spanish-to-English flashcards.

After a three-hour stakeout they watched a motorized rickshaw rise out of the smelly baking sand as if extruded from the mouth of Hades, the trapdoor to the tunnel well disguised. The rickshaw pulled an ice cream cart. Hilda stopped the driver, a Renfield of a creature, thick twisted torso porting a distorted blockhead with google eyes and a friar fringe. Before she was long into torturing the Renfield, the cart tipped over and a clown car's worth of Guatemalan vampires spilled out the top hatch.

They were small and emaciated and gray with oxygen-depletion, weak from hunger and sucking greedily at what Eugene considered putrid desert air, dilated pupils starved for light and now getting too much of a good thing, guiding their owners blindly into cacti, yucca, each other, and slayers.

If like Eugene you were one who thought the world had gone insane welcoming vampires into our midst, who saw vampires as a plague to be eradicated, a human-form virus manifested by the dark side of evolution, it was no different and just as easy as slaying newborn baby mice. The CWS had described these vamps as "interrupted" in their evolution and all of a piece, dispatched via the traditional stake through the heart. Each of them had a role. Hilda would hamstring them with her sword—in truth she probably only managed a classic hamstringing on half the unfortunate creatures, but was 100 percent on incapacitation—and Eugene would stake their vampire hearts.

The CWS was there to aggravate their last seconds on earth. He sat in his lawn chair under a beach parasol, braying, "You should have stayed below the border where you belong!" and "This is my land, comprende?" and "Si se puede." Each statement was followed by a toast and a toot of tequila sunrise from his canteen.

Finally even Eugene had been taken aback by the old slayer's venom. With three still to slay, feeling like a psycho border patrolman and overwhelmed by nausea from the hot, fly-studded stench, Eugene had unbuckled his bandolier of stakes and made for the shelter of the cabin. Hilda's high-heeled jackboot had streaked across the bug-infested sand and stabbed him bluntly in the spleen. Eugene had cursed her with a sailor's gusto and limped into the clapboard hut.

Later the CWS had stood outside, looking into that hat while carrying on about preparation for the coming war, about sacrifice. Ten minutes later and for the next ten hours Eugene was running for the dry creek bed beyond the big disfigured saguaro cactus to empty his bowels. He learned quickly to take his sword with him. Hilda and the broadside of her sword had no shame or pity, deciding that "young boys always with their pants down must be looking for a spanking." Also, it could have been her armadillo gumbo.

Eugene set what he now thought of as his CrapBerry on the seat and put down his crepe. "I am listening."

"You are all ears." The CWS took a last look into his hat before reluctantly putting it back on his head. "This vampire, Charlie Valery, he's not formidable to look at. Very French."

"So I need to make sure I kill him before he surrenders." Eugene waited for the belly laugh.

Hilda leaned over the seat, studying him. The CWS leaned back, the wide brim of his hat in Hilda's face. She stared one-eyed at Eugene. "You wonder why the other slayers dislike you?" said the CWS.

"They hate me, actually." Eugene had just come from a Bucharest convention, his first chance to meet the other guardians of humanity previously known only by their code names on the slayer sites. "They hated me before they met me. The local slayers in particular."

"Yep." Into the CWS's mouth went a cracker dripping with ripe, runny Camembert. "Your name is legendary for slayers. *Maistru*, in Romanian." Through cheese and cracker the CWS pronounced the name like he had grown up in Bucharest. "Foreman was an Ellis Island translation. One of the better, actually."

He was a smacker, one of the banes of Eugene's misophonia. Despite all the other surrounding sounds—the hum of the train, the omnipresent Euro club music on the sound system, the singing parrot video on the Galaxy across the aisle—all he could hear was that smacking.

"'Infamous' is what they said."

"Trust me when I tell you," said the CWS, slurping cider. "Your great, great, dot-dot-dot great-grandfather Trubadur Maistru was the best slayer I've ever seen. He went up against the evilest vamp of them all. Morbius. The vampire who will bring the other vamps together to enslave humanity. Your gran-pappy killed Morbius."

Eugene swelled with pride. The slayer chat boards always lit up when the name Morbius was mentioned. Slayers at the convention barely dared speak the vampire's name, while in the same breath having no problem besmirching the Foreman name. Eugene's research on Ancestry.com revealed references to the vampire but with frustratingly little context. "Are you saying you knew my great-great-whatever grandfather?"

"Slayed Morbius," the CWS repeated. "Saved humanity. Only the most talented and *committed* slayer could have pulled it off." He stared intently at Eugene. To reinforce the moment, and even though Eugene was staring back, Hilda snapped her fingers beside her boss's head, like a photographer drawing her subject's attention to the camera lens. "Morbius has a unique soft spot."

That was the CWS's term for the unique Achilles'

heel possessed by the evolved strains of vamps. For most, like the Guatemalans in the ice cream cart, a stake to the heart did the trick. But some bloodsuckers had evolved to the point where a good staking was nearly impossible to achieve, thanks to adaptations like leathery skin, ribcages like armored breastplates, and vital organs that had shrunk like prunes or become "slippery."

Fortunately, every one of these evolved vamps was handicapped with an alternate termination site. To Eugene's reckoning, while God's code of honor prohibited Him from interfering after setting the natural laws in motion, vamps were just too much of an insult and so He had insisted on a backdoor kill switch. The knowledge of each strain's soft spot—kept close to the vest by the CWS, perhaps kept in that hat—was a big reason why Eugene continued to associate with the aggravating, demanding old coot.

"Morbius is dead. What's it matter?"

"Because Morbius's heir is not."

"Are you talking about Victor Thetherson? *Again*? He's a putz. I doubt he's evolved, and if he wasn't already cured, I could slay him in a second."

The CWS cleared his throat, kept at it until Eugene couldn't take it.

"Coughing! Coughing works better!"

"Coughing's hard on my bladder."

Eugene casually slid the crackers out of the CWS's reach. "Sounds like I need to get my hands on Morbius's diary."

The CWS wrapped up another staccato measure of throat clearing. "What?"

"The local slayers were obsessed with it at the convention. Everybody's looking for it. Everyone kept diaries back then, you know."

"No, I know. Why do they care?"

"Supposedly the diary identifies Morbius's soft spot."

"They are wasting valuable time worrying about that diary." Without Eugene noticing the CWS had repossessed the crackers. "It's one thing to know *how*. It's another to be willing to *do* it." He waited for Hilda to Camembert his cracker. "Besides, I'm sure your ancestor, Trubadur Maistru, took it."

"Why would he care about a vamp's journal?" Eugene scoffed.

"You know how Indians count coup? Back in the day you took your victim's diary."

"Cool."

Smack *smack*, the CWS enjoyed his cracker. "Maybe your mother has it? One of your relatives?"

When forced to be near someone's maddening noises, mimicry was Eugene's only defense. He started smacking. "My family refuses to acknowledge our glorious history. I can't even get them to sign up for my blog feed." *Smack-smack.* "Listen," said Eugene, clenching his jaw. "The other slayers talked about a highly-evolved vampire named Claudius, terrorizing Europe, killing slayers. They say he's impossible to slay. Offing him will truly be a service to humanity. The other slayers will love me."

"Claudius isn't your destiny." *Smack, smack-smack.* "I'm concerned, Eugene." *Smack, smack, smack, smack-smack.*

"About?!?"

"Your dedication." The CWS stared.

"Ironclad."

"We don't slay for the fame."

Eugene snorted.

"And we don't slay for the fortune."

Eugene knew the CWS referenced the real estate plays, the various multi-level marketing endeavors, the Slaying Made Satisfying book series. "Sidelights," said Eugene.

"Slaying requires *sacrifice*."

"I know, I know."

The CWS nodded, for some time. "We'll be at Chenonceaux soon. Let's us focus on today's task at hand. Charlie Valery, your target."

Smackety-smack went Eugene, gritting his teeth. "Fine. Just tell me his soft spot."

"Well," *smack*, "he was turned by a vamp who could only be killed by gluten."

Smack-smack. "So I'll shove a loaf of au bon pain in his mouth."

The CWS brandished a cracker. "You can't be sure anymore." He ate it, crunching with his mouth open. "Could be made of nuts and rice flour."

Smack-smack-smack! "Crepes then! I'll use crepes!"

"I was kidding about the gluten." Somehow the CWS now had a handful of grapes. He tossed one into his mouth and started sucking on it.

"Aaagh!" Eugene gripped his head in both hands and threw himself back in the seat.

"You have to slit his wrist." The CWS peeled a grape with lips, tongue and teeth. "Soft wrists. No ability to coagulate. He'll bleed out in 90 seconds."

"Okay, I got it."

"Charlie's not physically intimidating," the CWS continued, while Eugene stared out the window with a finger in the near ear. "But he's crafty. Like I said, this vampire uprising is like a union movement. And Charlie is an organizer. Their leaders know there are more evolved vampires out there than anyone understands. And that they possess a quality that makes them very well suited to positions of power."

"Right. Fangs."

The CWS stared at Eugene for some time, evaluating whether he had his complete attention, whether or not he needed to take off his hat. "Balls."

"Like your friend, Victor Thetherson," said Hilda. She pronounced Victor's last name better than most.

"He's not my friend." Victor was a trigger for Eugene. The CWS and his mean, swashbuckling henchwoman Hilda rode him mercilessly after discovering he had a thing for Amberly Thetherson and then erroneously deducing that he must then have a "soft spot" for her father. "And he's been neutered."

The train pulled into the Chenonceaux station. "Where's my Perrier?" said the CWS. Hilda took a break from glaring at Eugene to glare at her seatmate, who merely turned his knees so that Hilda had to squeeze past to gain the aisle.

She seized the man by the forehead and peeled back his upper lip. No fangs. "You are lucky." Fists clenched and jaw muscles dancing, she stalked off in search of a Perrier.

The CWS took off his hat, not to look into but to allow him to put his face very close to Eugene's. "Did you see *Extreme Makeover* the other night?"

"No." Eugene sat as far back as the seat and headrest would allow. "Did you TiVo it?"

The CWS shook his head slowly and closed the gap. "Victor Thetherson is not cured." Pungent, putrid fumes poured from his mouth. Eugene used to love French cheese. "He will never be cured. Some say he's the second coming of Morbius." The CWS finally sat back in his seat. "And they would be correct. If you want to go down in history like your ancestor, you will need to slay him. And you are nowhere near ready."

As Eugene rounded up the spiraling staircase that seemed to go forever, he could not clear his mind. "Focus," he muttered to himself, as he texted Amberly.

France rocks, remind me to take u next time.

He was chasing a Class III vamp. Needed to block everything else out, take care of this bloodsucker and get back to the task at hand. He had been scampering in and around castle Chenonceaux for hours. Trying to close in on Charles, the vamp who knew this castle and the surrounding acres of gardens like he had lived here a thousand years. Trying to close a terrific land deal at the same time.

Right now he was waiting for a call from his international real estate broker, aka Milo the Gypsy. His new ultralight 2.5-pound graphite crossbow in one hand, CrapBerry in the other. A classic Honshu samurai sword strapped to his back and a Bluetooth ear bud in each ear. Chugging up the stairs, he looked at the CB. His text hadn't left the building. "No bars? Ahhg!" Just then a phone call came through his left ear bud. "Yes? Yes? *Yes?*"

It was the CWS. "What on God's green earth are you doing?"

"I am climbing up this spiraling staircase to kill your vamp."

"Gene, I handed you Charles on a silver platter, this is too—"

"It's *Eu*gene."

"*Yoo*-gene, kill that vamp then hop the next train to Tours to finish your training."

"Can't stay. As soon as I finish Chuckles, I'm off to Detroit."

"This is exactly what I was referring to," said the CWS with regret and his Southern brand of portent-rich intensity.

As Eugene closed in on the top of the spire, he slowed his pace to read Amberly's text.

France isn't the only place with french.

"Oh, hold on, I have a call on my other Bluetooth."

The CWS was confused. "A call? On your other line?"

"No, on my other Bluetooth, I have one in each ear. Please hold."

Eugene rounded the bend of the staircase and Charles the organizer vampire grabbed hold of his arm and made to twist it from Eugene's shoulder socket. "Ow," said Eugene. He hit Charles with his crossbow to set his arm free. "Jeepers, you startled me."

Charles ripped the crossbow from Eugene's hands

and chucked it down the staircase. He moved in extra close to Eugene's face. "Why are you hunting me? I don't know who you are. I have done nothing to you."

"Yes, yes, I know. No, no, you can't do that," Eugene pleaded.

"What?" Charles was confused.

Eugene held his finger up, whispered as he covered his ear piece. "Not you." He uncovered his ear piece. "I know I am not a legal citizen. I get it. But where there's a will ..." Eugene turned his back on Charles.

Charles shook his head in disbelief. The vamp leaned in toward Eugene's neck.

"NO!!! NO, NO!! That will not do." Eugene paced down and back up the broad stone stairs.

Charles turned around and headed up the staircase. After a moment Eugene realized the vampire was not there.

"Hold on, my reception sucks, damn castles." Eugene started for the top of the spire. His other Bluetooth beeped. "What?!?" said Eugene.

"Eugene, kill that vampire."

"Fine, fine. I'll call you back."

Long pause, Eugene listening to insistent chatter on his Blueteeth while thinking of something witty to say to Amberly. "Both of you, yes, I will. Get off my back ... not you, yes you ... fine ... bye, I will call you back. Yes, yes, both of you." Eugene quickened his pace up the spiral staircase. As he turned the last corner into the uppermost chamber, he had it.

You have to be here to really get the tongue.

Charles surprised him with a punch to the chest. Even through Eugene's chest protector there was the audible *crack* of ribs. He flew against the wall, dazed.

"I want to know why!" the French vampire roared. "Why are you hunting me?"

Slumped against the wall, Eugene coughed and regained his breath. "Because you're a vamp. There needs to be no other reason. You are the vermin of the earth." A Bluetooth beeped at him. "Yes? Hello? Damn, no reception."

Charles was on him, grabbing him by the collar. "You have messed with the wrong man," he hissed and tossed Eugene halfway up the other wall. Eugene hit the floor upside-down. "I am a peaceful, loving man. A man for the ages, a collector of the arts and benefactor to all of Europe. Also, I am a very private person."

"Vampire," Eugene muttered as he spit up blood. "You are not a person."

"I am more of a person, more human than most." Charles was pacing in the cramped chamber. "I have made this world a better place, despite monsters like you."

Eugene was fading in and out. *Where did the CWS say his soft spot was?* "Better place, that's a good one." He feebly rolled onto his stomach, reached behind him, realized that his Honshu samurai sword was nowhere to be found. Worse, he saw his Blueteeth in the middle of the room, possibly damaged. "Damn, I don't have those insured."

Charles walked over to and on-to the ear pieces. Then he kicked Eugene in the head like he was booting a 60-yard field goal. The organizer vamp effortlessly lifted the semi-conscious Eugene over his head and marched toward the lone window. He had an epiphany. "Did Cornelius send you?"

Eugene pictured the "CWS" monogram on his Seersucker jacket. "Is that his name?"

This was confirmation enough for Charles. "How dare you? How dare you judge me, hunt me, try to kill me!" Eugene dripped blood and other essential fluids on Charles. As the vampire threw him through the window, Eugene's last-ditch effort earned him a handful of matted hair. Charles bleated and followed Eugene out the window. Both tumbled end-over-end to the River Cher some 80 feet below.

HIGH POINT

Bizco had found its swagger. The new downtown headquarters stabbed the Houston sky, that partially-dissolved cloud that puts a moist lid on the city. The Bizco spire punctured that lid, tapping fresh blue air that flowed down the tapered glass tower to enrich the people below. Here were former Texahoma and Westchase construction rivals, a couple thousand centralized Texans from the metro outskirts, uprooted Chicagoans from the old Texahoma corporate office, and a band of Germans relocated from Bizco's parent company in Dresden. All were ridiculously proud to be in this building.

The entire tower was theirs. Right now, some 3,000 newly-settled employees occupied the 53 floors. Everyone downtown knew that anyone entering that bayonet of a building was Bizco. Bizco had energized Houston. It was EnerGreen, the oil and gas joint venture that promised to subjugate the new energy industry to King Houston, just as Houston had ruled the fossil-based world. But until EnerGreen took physical form on its new campus, Bizco was the emblem of New Energy's talent, drive and power. And so its employees fairly strutted to work.

Like the rising taper of the slender prism tower, credit for success inside the company focused on an increasingly narrow band of individuals: The team of architects whose Atlantis-inspired design for the suburban Houston campus wowed EnerGreen. The handful of construction supervisors, superstars in the industry with the proven power to meet budget on projects in some of the globe's more inhospitable sites. The few executives who lived and breathed dedication to EnerGreen and its much-publicized devotion to a depletable-to-sustainable energy transition (*"Natural gas and fracking, great for now. But we have the answer for-ever."*) And at the sharp tip, the vampire.

The alternative energy approach was real, far beyond a façade, but EnerGreen was run by oilmen. Big Oil-men. Texas oilmen. Plus a couple prim, power-mad Brits. These very different groups shared an innate attraction to displays of strength and muscular brilliance. Before he had retreated to the Longevity Labs, Victor Thetherson's final act for Bizco wowed EnerGreen. At a banquet where Bizco and its only competitor had made their pitches, Victor had rhapsodized about Bizco's historical construction highlights in front of a big-screen Hollywood-polished film. And at the Brits' request, he had elegantly, efficiently bit a pretty blond looker on the catering staff.

"You might as well bite me now, so everyone will get back to work." This from Sally Bornel, Human Resources. They stood where she had intercepted Victor on his way to Don Chleber's desk. The floor configuration was "collaborative," open from wall to wall: no cubes, no offices, no doors. Executives were as exposed as the rank and file. Many employees on this southwest side of the 49th floor were currently "collaborating", discussing the arrival of their vampire. Whether they were waiting for Victor to bite Sally was debatable.

She leaned in, although no one was within earshot. "This crew"—this was the strategic development floor—"would probably have us on a Vine loop in their online marketing brochure: 'At Bizco, we're expanding the concept of human resources.'"

After the *Xtreme Revamp* nightmare, Victor might have sworn he would never bite anyone again. But then he had found out he couldn't be cured, that perhaps the only scientists in the world with a viable treatment had taken their best shot and failed. And Barbara couldn't be happier or more committed to him, in her own special way. The past haunted, but the future beckoned; now he had to figure out what kind of vampire he was going to be.

"My lawyer advised me to lay low while charges are pending. Sucking your blood for all to see on the Bizco sales website would be a problem. Considering what I did to Nikki."

That squelched Sally's devilish grin. She nodded at Chleber, rocking heel to toe, silhouetted by the slanted window bordering his desk. "Go be a good boy and say hello to your boss so he can get some work done." She took hold of the lapels of Victor's golden brown sport jacket and gave it a lift so that it settled afresh over the crimson dress shirt and his broad shoulders. "Don hasn't been able to keep his butt in his chair all morning."

Victor lightly touched Sally's ribs as he left her, enjoying the catch in her breath.

"Welcome back, Victor," he was greeted by the first Bizco employee he passed, a young man he didn't know. He shook the man's hand, the first of five such greetings as he wended his way toward his boss. A few employees eyed him nervously, and a couple others with near-hostility.

"It's good to be back." This Victor said in greeting Chleber, who hung back, not smiling, but nodding, before stepping forward to hug him.

Chleber pointed at the bandage on his neck. "Is that from McGumphrey?"

The guillotine wound was healing fast, already starting to itch. "Slayer attack."

"Slayer attack." Chleber laughed so that his gut

bounced. "I stubbed the hell out of my toe helping the wife change the sheets. I gave her hell for buying a bed frame with legs that stick out beyond the mattress. Might have broken my pinky toe. But you probably don't feel bad for me." The Bizco exec chuckled affectionately at Victor.

"Sally informed me that my leave-of-absence benefit is about to expire. You'd better put me back to work."

"Can do, Mr. V. EnerGreen is upstairs waiting for me. I'll score some unearned points by showing up with you." Chleber steered him to the elevator, the hub of the circular floor, with Star Trekkie whisper doors fronting the clear plasti-glass tube, in keeping with the building's transparent floor plan. Waiting for their car, the business development exec spoke loudly enough for most to hear. "I'm sorry about what happened with your secretary."

Victor dipped his head in acknowledgment.

"I know you didn't mean for that to happen."

"I promise you it will not happen again." Victor could hear Tripp mocking his ability to make good on that vow.

A smattering of applause followed them into the elevator car. Victor gave a small wave. Chleber selected the 52nd floor. And then as the doors swished closed, someone jeered, "Get staked, Morbius."

At high speed, Chleber unbuckled and lowered his pants to re-tuck his shirt, counting on rising past the intervening floors too quickly for anyone to get much of a glimpse. When Victor didn't volunteer, Chleber asked. "What's that about?"

"Couldn't say." Someone had obviously been doing some Internet research. "Why are we meeting with EnerGreen today?"

"They had another round of questions as they vet our project plan. It's a formality at this point." Chleber winked while buttoning his trousers. "Especially now." They crested the 52nd floor. The admin and the occupants of the glass-walled conference room behind her were an audience for the buckling of his belt. Chleber gave Victor a wry grimace as they exited the car. "At least the bathroom walls are opaque."

The admin greeted Victor with a sly, extended glance. "Welcome back, sir."

"Thank you …"

"Miss Moneypenny?" Chleber offered, before Victor could recall Vanessa's name. Chleber wagged his finger. "Come on, Bond. Your next assignment awaits."

"Ladies and gentlemen," big gruff Mel Parish announced their entrance, bringing his meaty palms together with a shockwave-generating *whomp*. "We are full strength again. Vic, it's about goddamned time."

Victor bowed his head in greeting, keeping his fangs for the most part masked. "I'm glad to be back." He extended his hand to the nearest EnerGreen exec, tall and fresh-skinned, older than his boyish face and hairstyle suggested. "Victor Thetherson."

"Tim Waters. We met at the TV show. I saw you, anyway."

"You put on quite an exhibition, I think everyone might agree?" said Gerry Whitehouse, one of the Brits Victor had met at an earlier meeting. "I was unable to attend live or catch the original programming. Thank goodness for Hulu. Very sorry to hear about your young employee. Dreadful result."

Victor shook his head. "I'm not doing that anymore."

No one present seemed worried. The nine men and two women had left the back half of the conference room nearly unoccupied, magnetized by the big vampire.

"Terribly uncouth of me to ask," said Whitehouse, "but if you no longer intend to bite the ladies, how will you expect to find sustenance?"

The lone man at the far end of the table looked up from his BlackBerry. "Back to soaking your fries in blood bank donations?" said Jay Hansen. "For God's sake, Mel, let your people build Vic a real cube with real walls. No one wants to see him slurping up his dinner." Before anyone could respond, Jay continued. "Just kidding of course." He slid the BlackBerry toward the center of the polished marble table, but still within reach. "John, Daniel," he addressed the CEOs of EnerGreen and Bizco. "We should get started, hmm?"

"Fascinating topic," Whitehouse squeezed in as Bizco CEO Daniel Fasset smiled and invited everyone to take their seats.

Chleber left Victor's side, sitting as far away from his charge as the table permitted. This was their norm. Chleber led Bizco's presentations and had a knack for creating openings for Victor, from their kitty-corner placement able to simultaneously survey the group and gauge Victor's readiness, feeding him the perfect question at the right moment. Except this time.

"We really appreciate the EnerGreen team making the trip here today. I reviewed the questions you provided with the agenda, so I know we have a lot of ground to cover. But I'd like to open by telling you that Victor is back with us full time. Victor, why don't you give everyone your vision for this partnership."

He was caught off guard. Since "enrolling" in the Longevity Labs' full-time research and treatment endeavor, he hadn't spent a moment thinking about the campus that Bizco hoped to build for this new-energy joint venture.

He looked around the table. "I wasn't, uh ..." Victor blushed in anticipation of the terribly familiar constriction of his throat and vision, brain soon to be gridlocked, in a tunnel, claustrophobic, all the things he could have said jammed and jumbled and coming out in stammered nonsense.

"I'm glad you led off with that topic," said Waters, the clean-scrubbed EnerGreen exec. "As you know, we're impressed with what Bizco has to offer.

Including the contributions from Mr. Thetherson. But we're concerned about the negative publicity from *Xtreme Makeover.*"

John Anderson the bearded EnerGreen CEO pushed back from the table to rest a cowboy boot on his knee. "Our board of directors needs to sign off on the final decision. That meeting is not quite three weeks from today. It would be good if Mr. Thetherson was invisible in the meantime."

Turned out, Victor hadn't entered the tunnel. Rather, he was seeing the conference room with an open floor plan far beyond what the architects had imagined—open to the sky, in crystal clear air coursing with electric blue freshness, high above the rest of Bizco, above the city, the floor a transparent platform perched upon a slate-and-steel spire that disappeared into the muggy mists below, with no communication lines, no lifelines, those present cut off from the world, at Victor's mercy.

Each person around that table was soft and vulnerable. Speaking was like drinking their blood. Victor held up his hand, preempting his boss's reply. "Visibility. Yes. That is the question. What do we see? What do we want the world to see? The essential question. We are going to build this campus like it belongs to us. Like it belongs to everyone. Every step of the way, we will tell the world just how revolutionary this joint venture is. How important it is to them, their children, and the generations to come."

He felt as though he was hovering over the attendees, thirteen leashes of energy crackling from his chest to theirs, holding them in place and in thrall. In fact he had risen to his feet, gliding around the table, brushing fingers across the back of each leather swivel chair.

"The campus is going to be built for New Energy, using New Energy. It is going to seem as if it sprang from the ground, as if it had been germinating all along, waiting for spring to arrive, to break through the crust and emerge in full bloom. The people you see before you, around this table, they are simply the vanguard of a fanatical army, obsessed with only one goal: to create your world."

Hansen chuckled and tapped his BlackBerry to keep it awake. "While you were institutionalized, Vic, we moved past platitudes. Our client is looking for specifics."

"Nope," said Anderson the EnerGreen CEO. "It's called vision. And it's exactly what we were looking for." He clapped three times. "Bravo."

Hansen nodded as if Anderson had agreed with him. "It makes great sense, as you said, for Vic to lay low. While he waits for the murder charges."

Victor stood behind him. He swiveled Jay gently back and forth, making eye contact with each person on the EnerGreen team. "I am going to be everywhere. You will see me regularly at the site, and everyone at Bizco will see me here. I will be the driving force behind this project. During construction, I will be the face of EnerGreen." CEO Anderson was his final target. "EnerGreen willing, of course."

Anderson nodded. "Yes we are."

Whitehouse leaned his head out over the table. "The power of the vampire compels us, after all."

The remainder of the meeting was devoted to answering EnerGreen's outstanding questions on timelines and costs. Victor was largely quiet, which gave him time to ponder why Jay was involved in a four-way text conversation labeled "Project Well Done" with three past or current Bizco employees: David Copperfield, Teddy the foreman, and Larry Cocachello.

A picture of his renewed relationship with Barbara needed to include fireworks and flaming arrows from Cupid and an army of besieging crusaders, love and war, a raucous celebration in a warm home where a

naked sweaty couple writhes together with reckless
abandon while their future selves look on approvingly
from their rocking chairs. Thrills and commitment.
Victor's perfect marital picture.

He had no business visiting Darla. It was
completely appropriate that he stop by the Accounting
floor to say hello after his long absence. But not at 5:30
when Darla would certainly be alone, her clock-
punching staff long gone. And not with what was
occupying his mind—and what would be occupying
Darla's after he left.

Floor fourteen. Same collaborative style as on the
upper levels. But rather than teak desks, soft lights,
sound-absorbing carpeting and stylish art on
pedestals, the accountants got pine and fluorescence,
nonskid concrete and filing cabinets. Their digs were
no worse than accountants ever got, and in fact Victor
felt the peacefulness of familiarity, of being home.

Good to visit home, occasionally and briefly. Victor
had grown out of Accounting, couldn't imagine going
back.

"Heeeyyy." Kirby Backer, one of Darla's team
leaders, came eagerly around his desk. "It's VV. How
are you? Back, are you back? Nooo, you're missing
everyone! I'm afraid it's just me."

Victor received Kirby's double-handed shake and the
fluff-headed accountant's perpetual fixation on his
mouth. "It's good to see you, Kirby."

"Gosh." Kirby stared. "I was so sad to hear about
Nikki. To see it, actually, I was home with my wife and
our kids, everyone settled in around the television, we
had had a long argument about whether it was a wise
move to watch the first half of *CSI: Wichita* and the
last half of *CSI: Little Rock*—did you know that
Xtreme Makeover show started at 7:30? Do you know
why they didn't start it at 7 or 8? That really put us in
a bind. It got heated, if you want to know the truth."

"Kirby, it was good to see you." Victor was looking at

Darla, who stood at her desk with a weary smile, leaning toward him with everything except her body. "Please let everyone know how disappointed I was to have missed them."

"Oh, I will. I don't think Florence is in tomorrow. She hasn't been feeling well since that program—I don't know if you noticed whether she looked a little peaked that night? Were her hands clammy? That's a sure sign for me. I'll go to rub the edema out of my wife's calves and she'll say, 'Mr. Clammy, you have a bug!' There's a bug going around I've heard. Mostly the southeastern metro if Channel Four News is right and, I have to say, they are pretty darn reliable. I've been worried about Larry too, he lives near Florence, you know. Have you seen him lately?"

Victor was now 20 feet away in Darla's cube. "Larry seems to be doing fine."

I haven't bought any Amway product yet. Is that going to be a problem?

That was from Larry to the "Project Well Done" text group, the only message Victor was able to read on Jay's BlackBerry. He had no clue what it meant, but it did serve to rub out most of his curiosity.

"And Darla?" Darla with her sensible blue suit and pretty, tired eyes. "How is Darla?"

"Oh, you know." When forced to verbalize her status, the weariness couldn't be contained. "Busy. On top of everything else, Jay is having us create all the reporting templates we'll use for the EnerGreen project. Everybody is swamped and stressed." She gave her head a tiny shake, to dislodge the gear that had momentarily shifted her back into business mode. "I'm sorry about Nikki."

"I'm the one who's sorry."

"I called her sister. I told her we were all grieving here. She asked about you."

Victor frowned. "Wondering where I hide my coffin so they can sneak in and put a stake in my heart."

"I'm sure they're going through a lot of emotions But she seemed mostly curious. I didn't think you'd be out so soon. I was going to visit you in jail—"

"The vampire pit. That's where they put me. I'm glad you didn't."

"And where do things stand now?"

"Now I'm glad."

Darla blushed. "I meant legally."

"That might depend on Nikki's family."

"If they're anything like Nikki, they probably march to different drummers. So ... first day back, and I heard through the grapevine you already had a big meeting. Everything go well?"

"Despite Jay's best efforts? I almost feel bad for him. I really am his worst nightmare."

"Now that you don't work for him, I was hoping you would be able to move past your issues."

"Not with this." Victor tapped a fang. "Did you know I met Jay in college? When I was interviewing with the big accounting firms. His recruiting team included a vampire. Jay's boss."

"That doesn't sound like a good fit."

"I think it left a mark. This guy was something else. An ugly little toad, but he radiated power. He had Jay completely cowed."

"I didn't know you two went that far back."

"Neither did we, until ..." Victor was about to say "Germany," before recalling how badly that trip had ended for Darla. "It all came back to me at the perfect moment. Just when Jay thought he had the upper hand." This was all it took to trigger an emotional recall of all the times Jay had abused him, ridiculed him, tried to ruin him. "Jay will never bully me again."

"You know, he's been great to us. He really has. After everything blew up with Raj and his attempted coup, I was surprised Jay stayed on. And then I was worried how he'd treat us. But he's been very supportive."

"Because he likes you. Because you fit his expectation of what an accountant should be." Victor couldn't help himself; he reached across the desk. Was the power of the vampire compelling him? A self-compulsion? He willed Darla to place her hand in his. "Because you're wonderful."

Darla blushed and leaned in before remembering Kirby, standing at his cube watching and following the conversation, nodding and murmuring *Oh my gosh* and *Uh-huh* and *You don't say* at all the appropriate junctures.

"You can knock off now. We're in good shape for tonight."

"Right," said Kirby. "Good."

"So go ahead and wrap it up."

"Thank you. Will do. Well, VV, it was so wonderful to see you again, everyone is going to be so jealous tomorrow when I tell them I saw you, and listened to your conversation with Darla, and hey, maybe you could stop by tomorrow—"

Victor cut him off, to restore blood flow cut off by Darla's ratcheting grip. "Good night, Kirby."

"Good night. Both of you." Kirby marveled at the two of them while donning his ear muffs, then shouldered the dual straps of his duffel bag and made for the elevator.

Darla waited for him to clear the floor. "There's something I want you to see." She invited Victor behind her desk, sat him in her chair and then leaned over him, firm against his arm, causing the silk lining of his sport coat to slide up and down against his shirt sleeve while she worked her mouse to call up a file: a picture drawn in slightly smeared charcoal of Victor, Darla and their daughters, Amberly and Kimberly, side by side on a Six Flags rollercoaster, arms up and hair blown back by the acceleration of their descent, screaming with delirious fright.

Victor studied the drawing. They had their heads

tilted affectionately toward each other. He touched the
screen, tapped his flat charcoal teeth. "The cure didn't
work, you know." He took Darla's hand off his
shoulder, folded her fingers into a fist save one, and
pressed the exposed pad into the point of his fang.

Darla tensed but did not pull away. A drop of blood
bubbled on her fingertip. It elongated and ran toward
her chewed fingernail. Victor kissed it, sealed it with
his lips, and drank a little of Darla's blood.

"Oh. I really wish you wouldn't." She plucked a
tissue from the dispenser on her desk and wrapped the
tiny puncture. "I feel like, like you shouldn't let that
define you." She opened another file. "Kimberly's first
draft was a little different."

Stewing a little over Darla's reaction, Victor only
noticed the slightest ripple in the image.

With her tissue-wrapped finger Darla pointed at his
teeth. First Draft Victor had fangs, thin ones, Eddie
Munster–style, accurate. Victor was self-conscious
about his slender fangs.

"I made her change it." Darla clicked to close both
pictures. She sat on the edge of her desk, noticing his
bother. "I don't picture you with fangs and I don't want
Kimberly to, either."

Victor kept his hands on the arms of Darla's chair,
his eyes on hers. "If not for vampirism, I wouldn't be
here."

"I don't agree. It's like when I tell Monique not to let
her looks define her."

Victor grinned at the mention of the gorgeous,
silent, vacant staff accountant. "When has Monique
ever used her looks?"

Darla smiled bigger. "Actually I've never told her
that. She can use all the help she can get."

"I *use* these." Victor pointed to his fangs. "Believe
me, *everything* good for me has happened because I do.
You wouldn't know, but I am not the same person."

"You forget." Darla slid closer and rested her hand

on his, her pricked, tissue-wrapped finger levitating above his wrist. "I did know you before, for a bit. I liked you when you presented at that conference. It's your face. Your face makes me feel good. And your smell."

"Really?"

Darla brought the back of his hand to her nose. "You probably don't want to hear this, but you smell like a McRib."

"That's awful."

Darla refused to let Victor pull his hand away from her face. "I love the way you smell. Smoky, a little meaty. And a deeper spice I can't place."

Victor let his knuckles brush against her lips. "You are odd."

She gave him the sweetest smile. "Yep."

He returned his hand to the chair arm. "I wanted to tell you. I'm moving north, to be closer to the EnerGreen campus."

"I think that's a great idea."

Victor knew that Darla lived on that end of the metro. He held her eyes, as if he could influence how she received his next words. "With Barbara."

The smile remained on Darla's lips, but her eyes couldn't hold it, or Victor's gaze. "Good. That's good. I'm glad. For your work. For you."

Victor squeezed his lips as tightly as his fangs allowed. Again he regretted coming to her, and started convincing himself to make this the last time, as Darla patted his arm and stood. She was so plain, and so warm, ready to be wrapped in his arms, crushed against him, melting into him. Darla would give herself to him completely. That was the last thing he needed. "I will let you get back to work."

"I'm done for the day. Do you mind walking me out?"

"I would like that." Victor waited for her to log off her computer, exchange pumps for sneakers, and shoulder her carryall bag. As they crossed the floor the elevator flew past. Too fast to identify the occupants, and yet Victor had glimpsed Jay Hansen.

Casually he asked Darla, "Is David Copperfield working for you?"

"No, remember he had that accident before we went to Germany."

"I do recall."

"He hasn't been back since. I got the green light from HR to hire Larry and haven't thought about David since. Why? What made you think of him?"

"No good reason. Just reminiscing, I guess."

BANISHED

Nikki's funeral should have been gloomier. It was put off for two rainy weeks—rumor had it the body had disappeared, fueled by sightings of a scarecrow-like figure dancing along misty Buffalo Bayou. Turned out to be a heroin-addicted vegetarian vampire catching bats along the waterway, dressed as a clown. That revelation didn't soothe any nerves, but it did put a damper on the Nikki rumors. The delay was likely due to all the authorities and laboratories wanting dibs on the few remaining ounces of Nikki's blood.

Thursday was a beautiful Houston winter day, 65 and sunny, light pouring into the chapel of the church in which Nikki's parents considered her a member, despite the pastor's discreet, contrary claim.

Nikki's family and friends could have been sadder. Yes, periodically they mourned in startling group-bursts of wailing and pew-pounding. In between they chattered and sometimes broke out laughing, whispering nonstop during the ceremony. Always with an eye toward the vampire. Victor knew his presence would be a distraction.

A distraction at the very least; probably wildly inappropriate, considering he had killed her. A dialogue had played in his mind as he contemplated whether to attend the funeral:

I was her boss for seven years.

- Which makes sucking her blood ten times as abhorrent. Why remind everyone?

I want them to know how much I owe to Nikki. If it weren't for her I would still be a fat, balding, timid accounting manager.

- If it weren't for you, Nikki would still be alive.

In the end he had come because Darla had asked him to. And because Larry told him not to.

As Victor debated visiting her closed casket, the voices were back at it.

It looks callous for me to just sit here in the back of the church while everyone else pays their respects.

- You're a vampire; you're allowed.

I never got a chance to say goodbye. I'd like one final opportunity to tell her how much I miss her.

- It would look like you're trying to raise her from the dead.

Of course that was Tripp in his head, his big Jiminy Cricket. Tripp would be pleased to know he had become Victor's conscience.

His former staff wasn't helping to set the funereal mood. As the pastor read scripture on lambs and their shepherds, Bizco's accountants carried on.

"See, I told you he was back," said Quinten.

"Gee, Quinten," said Tessa, "if you hadn't told me, I wouldn't believe my eyes."

In fact, Tessa had seen him in the lobby. Victor had started toward her, cut short by her glare. She had turned away shaking her head and hurrying into the chapel.

"I couldn't believe my eyes when Kirby told me," said Casey.

Sitting in front of them, Kirby turned around and craned his pencil neck over the pew. "I should have taken a picture, shouldn't've I?"

"You should have stayed home, that's what," Florence whispered loudly enough to echo off the ribbed ceiling. She still looked good revamped, but cracks were showing in her eyes and mouth and posture, allowing glimpses of the marks that men and choices had put on her body and mind. Her midnight blue dress hung on her frame, only filled out by the hint of her former hump.

When Quinten opened his mouth to respond, Florence leaned over Larry and seized his throat until the junior accountant sealed his own lips.

"We all failed that girl." Larry rubbed the dent in his sternum from Florence's pointed elbow. "None of us deserve to be here." He had a hanky to dab at the weeping piercing of his nostril.

When Larry had caught sight of Victor walking up the church sidewalk, the violence of his reaction—face contorted into a bloodhound fright mask—had opened his wound inside and out, sending a trickle of blood out his nose. The pastor happened to see this, naturally assuming he was witnessing the vampire's unholy power. He crossed himself as he retreated into the chapel.

Now Darla grew exasperated. She left Victor's side and hurried the five pews forward, whispering apologies as she squeezed down the row, forcing Quinten and Larry to create space. She took a seat between them and soon everyone's eyes were respectfully pointed forward.

"Nikki, I am told," said the pastor, casting a quick glance at her mother, "wanted. She wanted for love and adventure. She wanted for all the excitement this world offers, and tempts us with. Wanting can be such a terrible burden for us. Especially now when the Devil's temptations are more cleverly disguised than ever.

"And so I am overjoyed to comfort you all with good news. From this day forward, Nikki shall not want."

The pastor's final "amen" reverberated over the chapel sound system as Victor strode through the lobby. Jiminy Tripp could celebrate a victory; he would not attend the basement potluck. Certainly Nikki's family had suffered enough from his presence. And

Victor didn't want to see them—he mourned for Nikki, he trusted himself to say the right things, but not to look right as he said them.

Victor didn't want anyone to see the struggle inside. He deserved condemnation for killing Nikki. Yet the judgment hanging over the funeral, in the pastor's sermon and the mourners faces, seemed to be for his vampirism. He could take the guilt for killing Nikki. Not for being a vampire.

A woman caught him before he reached the door. She was 40ish, a fuller version of stringy Nikki, her eyes a little smaller, teeth about the same. "Thanks for coming. You're Nikki's boss, right?"

"I was." Victor gladly followed her outside. "I am very sorry for ... what happened."

"Thank you." She took his arm as they strolled the sidewalk, skirting the parking lot. "Nikki loved you, you know."

Hearing this was wonderful, terrible. "She was very good to me."

They rounded the rear corner of the church and stopped on the matted, dormant grass, a few yards from a thin belt of trees separating them from a sprawling equipment dealership. The church blocked the street noise and mercifully for Victor the sun as well. "Nikki told me about your relationship." She kept a pinch of Victor's suit sleeve between finger and thumb, gathering fabric. "She was very proud but tight-lipped at the same time. She reminded me of a guy I dated who worked for the CIA. A handler for the agents. Nikki told enough to make us jealous, but not so much that it could put you in danger."

"Our relationship was special, I guess."

"I'm Nikki's sister. Cat." She took his hand in both of hers. "Special is perfect. You're a precious commodity, Victor."

He stared into Cat's eyes and enjoyed the moment.

"Even if it's just to bring some excitement into our

lives." Cat moved closer. "Nikki knew she was living dangerously. Not just with you. She hung out with a wild crowd." Her eyes welled up with tears. "We knew this day would come. We just didn't know how."

"I wanted to protect her."

"That's not the agent's job, is it?" Cat laid her fingers at the corner of his mouth. "I can't say I have the same need, to always live on the edge." With her thumb she applied just enough pressure to part Victor's lips. "But there's a thrill, thinking about being on one of your missions."

Cat backed away, until she was half outside the building's shadow. "Our family is having a testimonial for Nikki tonight at the Holiday Inn a mile down the street. It'll be over by midnight. Are you available?"

"It wouldn't be appropriate. Nothing I could say would make your family feel—"

"*After*, Victor." Cat retreated, now in full sunlight. She waved to someone exiting the church. "I want you to find me *after*."

Somehow Barbara had created a new-house smell. For Victor, equipped with the vampire's nose, the scent colored his vision, giving the formerly familiar, burnt umber surroundings a crisp, freshly-unwrapped, aquamarine glow. He looked twice at the carpet, performed a soft-shoe tap dance on it, thicker and spongier and richer than he remembered, and still wasn't sure whether it was new. Most of their furniture was gone, a couple replaced by smaller pieces. The formal dining room was no longer Barbara's workshop, her easel, paints and brushes cleared out, the walls bared but for her tamest works, four rich oils from her Romantic period that had begun shortly after they married and ended before their second anniversary. Stacks of taped-up moving boxes huddled in the middle of the room.

Barbara descended the stairs like a real estate

agent, arms inviting appraisal. "What do you think?" A
sexy real estate agent, how the makers of Halloween
costumes envisioned them, in a black leather skirt, a
white blouse that didn't own buttons above the
diaphragm, high heels, and the red jacket favored by
bull fighters, small so as not to interfere with the tools
of the trade. From her hand dangled a broad leather
strap which in turn dangled, hammock-like, a leather
cup. The contraption was a cross between a
weightlifter's belt and an early prototype for the
jockstrap.

"I think you are eager to move. Maybe we should
start house hunting."

"I'm way ahead of you. After we're done here I'll
take you up to our new house."

"We bought a house?"

Barbara slung her free arm around his neck and
kissed him full. "They'll need your signature. It's
gorgeous. You're going to love it." Another kiss, wetter,
warmer, longer. "Wait 'til you see the workout room. It
has mirrors everywhere." The folded belt smacked him
behind the knee.

Victor's first reaction was a scowl. Then he threw
his head back and laughed—and grabbed the belt as it
came for his butt. He raised the leather cup for
inspection. "What is this?"

"That's where the hot wax goes." Barbara
disengaged and sashayed to the kitchen, beckoning
him to follow. Her butt was flat but her hips gave it
fabulous range of motion. He reached her at the two
rooms' threshold, one hand on her hip and the other
squeezing her backside. She removed the hip hand and
made them point together at the fondue pot on the
table. "That is not cheese."

The wax bubbling in the pot was what Victor had
smelled. His new olfactory system still needed fine-
tuning.

Barbara peeled off his jacket. "I was hoping you

wouldn't head to the office to work on your system after the funeral."

Victor left the University of Houston with an accounting major, a computer programming minor, and a Platonic ideal of "Accounting System." During his time as an auditor, privy to the inner workings of perhaps 40 different companies, and then as an accountant at Bizco's predecessor, he had been severely disappointed by the real-world versions. So he had designed his own.

Tweaking his creation, adding back-end features and experimenting with the user interface had been a hobby like his trains. He never contemplated trying to *use* it. When he left Accounting behind, along with the fogged-over insecurities vampirism had no time for, Victor saw his system in a new light. Bigger, beyond Accounting. And badder, beyond what Plato could have envisioned. In between keeping Chleber happy and drinking blood, Victor had devoted more and more time to retooling his System.

"No programming today. But I do have to go out later tonight."

Barbara unbuttoned his pants. "That's fine, we need to stay on schedule here. We can't have prospective buyers walking in and finding me with your bald balls in my mouth."

Victor backed away, grinning and truly a little scared. "My private parts already fear you."

Barbara pursued him. "We'll start with the inside of your nose."

Victor's eyes widened. "I hate to ask what you have in store for my nose."

"No, it just needs it."

"I'll give you the nose. But you are not hot-waxing my balls."

"I understand it's painless."

"You're lying."

She cackled and caught him in the formal living

room, pushing him into a small formal chair, a new addition to their furnishings that groaned and flexed dangerously under his weight. "That one falls in the white lie category." Off came Victor's shoes and then his pants. "Told for your own good." She purred at the erection under his skivvies.

"Shouldn't we close the curtains?" He yelped as she dragged her long nails down his stomach and past his waistline.

There came a knock at the door.

"Come back in an hour," Barbara called over her shoulder.

"Knock-knock," said Dr. Winnie Linciome as he came on in. He plunged his hands in his well-pleated pants and whistled. "Barb, I really like the heels." He sniffed the air. "Do I smell hot wax?"

"That's to seal the sale of our house." Victor snapped his fingers for his pants. "Our realtor is old-school."

"You're moving?" Dr. Linciome frowned. " Did you clear it with the D.A.?"

"Not yet." Victor zipped up his pants. "It's been easy to forget I'm out on bail."

"That's because ..." Dr. Linciome paused, as sheepish as he ever got. "This sounds awful. You did what vampires do. More importantly, you did what *you* do. And the world is going to be better for it."

"I was just at Nikki's funeral."

"I said 'going to be' better. Going to be."

Victor couldn't stay offended. Everything was falling into place, thanks to his so-called curse. Now he was ready to give back. He was glad Linciome had come— he was the only one who could appeal to Dr. Speer to let Victor again start contributing to their longevity research.

"Speaking of charges, we're urging the D.A. to throw the book at Sven and Edna. Terrorism, attempted murder. Five counts." Dr. Linciome held up each finger in turn, pinkie to thumb. Then he wagged a sixth finger at Victor. "You don't count."

"They tried to cut his *head* off." Barbara laid her hand on his wound, which couldn't elicit much sympathy, already healed to look like an old scar.

"Fair's fair if we don't want McGumphrey's death ruled a murder. But the rest of the charges should be severe enough to act as a deterrent to other slayers." Dr. Linciome winked at Victor. "Not that you can't take care of yourself."

"I was lucky the handle of his French axe was rotten. I thought Eugene was the only lame slayer. In the slayer versus vampire battle, the table is definitely tilted in our favor."

"The wood was just fine. You broke that axe, Victor."

"How?" Barbara demanded, intrigued more than skeptical.

"The same way McGumphrey evolved thick, leathery skin." Dr. Linciome peered at Victor's neck. "Besides possessing an incredible repair rate—the key to your longevity—I'm guessing your muscle tissue has evolved to become incredibly dense." He dug a finger into Victor's chest.

"Those pecs are all mine." Barbara playfully pushed between them and laid possessive hands on Victor's chest.

The scientist winked at them. "These defense mechanisms are only present in certain vampires. You are fortunate to be one of them."

"So I can't be killed?"

"Oh, no-no. Just look at McGumphrey. You undoubtedly have a weak spot."

Victor and Barbara exchanged a look.

Dr. Linciome grinned. "In addition to sex. Which, by the way ... what I walked in on ..."

"Don't worry." Barbara twisted Victor's nipple, eliciting a yelp. "We practice safe sex."

Dr. Linciome enjoyed the moment. He took a few meandering steps, absentmindedly nudging the protojockstrap with his foot. "You were right about one thing, Victor. We don't seem to have any evolved slayers. The playing field is definitely tilted in favor of the vampires." He looked at the moving boxes. "Barbara, I don't suppose you have any munchies laying around? Just plastic fruit now, I suppose."

"I'll get you something." Barbara planted a kiss alongside Victor's widow's peak and headed for the kitchen.

The scientist admired her progress. "Let me tell you something, Victor. You haven't even begun to pay your debt to society."

"Exactly." Victor sat back in the poorly-jointed chair. "I wasn't ready last time. I was tortured—part of me excited, the other part fighting it. But I'm ready to give back, for everything vampirism has done for me. I know what I did to Nikki was wrong ..."

The scientist knelt at his side. "Poor Tripp is haunted thinking he encouraged Nikki's unfortunate pursuit. And then to put a starving vampire in her path. But you and I know that certain things are beyond our control. And others are meant to be."

"I want you to know—I want Dr. *Speer* to know—I am dedicated to controlling my anger. I promise you. I will learn to maintain control."

Dr. Linciome's eyes moved to the painting over Victor's shoulder, a businessman resembling a younger Victor at an 18th-century writing desk, in a modern suit, dipping a quill pen into an inkwell. The room was furnished consistent with the desk, while the cityscape view out the far window set the businessman's study in a skyscraper. A computer monitor served as a paper stand for a curled sheet of parchment.

"She's good, isn't she?"

"Phenomenal. I had no idea. I know the owner of the Corpus d'Art Gallery downtown. I think she'd dig Barbara's style if you'd like me to make the introduction."

"Yes," Barbara called from the kitchen.

"Shooting Mikhaila some shots right now," Dr. Linciome called back, on his smart phone taking and sending pictures of Barbara's paintings. Now he lowered his voice without dampening his enthusiasm. "Barb is phenomenally perceptive the way she sees you. A man of two eras. Victor, you descend from a very special vampire."

Victor waited through the dramatic pause. Dr. Linciome wasn't one who needed prompting.

"Ever since you started making your big contribution to our longevity research I've been a little bloodsucker gaga. Sven and Edna's comments prompted me to try to learn more about you, specifically. Understand that I've been limited to online resources, which are full of holes and often contradictory. But I think they were right about your ancestor."

"Morbius."

"Yes! The legendary vampire who made a brief appearance in the 16th century. What's incredible about—"

"What's incredible is that you'd listen to anything these slayers say. I used to think Eugene was a lone nut-job. After seeing those two in action, I realize he fits right in."

"I'll admit it." The scientist feigned a painful confession. "I have been spending time in the slayer chat rooms." He grinned. "I had to pass an extremely shallow background check: 'Do you or either of your birth parents look really good for their age?' It also seemed necessary to come up with a *nom de guerre*. You can call me Winnie-the-Pooh-fect-Slayer."

"That's really awful."

Dr. Linciome was stung. "Better than ColinCaseThere'sTrouble." He got no reaction. "I guess you have to see it to be annoyed." After a glance to confirm an empty kitchen doorway, he dropped his voice further. "Your name does come up regularly in relation to Morbius."

"Thanks to that idiot Eugene. He has the slayer community vying for the honor of killing me."

"I don't think this Eugene fellow is to blame. He's out there—the only one without a code name. He has his own website and a huge Twitter following. But he seems to be focused on selling real estate and Mary Kay cosmetics."

"Then who is it?"

"Best I can tell, a blogger named Publicola. Latin for 'friend of the people.' He's slaying you, online." Dr. Linciome gave Victor a sympathetic grin. "If it's any consolation, the picture of you is flattering. You're striking a formidable pose."

"He posted my picture?"

"The good news is his assassination campaign doesn't appear to be working. Sven and Edna only stumbled upon you by accident. Slayers aren't falling over themselves to take a crack at you." Dr. Linciome leaned in closer. "Because they don't know your weak spot. Your Achilles' heel. The Heel, in the slaying vernacular."

Victor's Achilles' tendons tightened. "From all the testing you've done ... do you know?"

"No clue." The scientist frowned. "Supposedly there's a diary out there that belonged to Morbius. They say it identifies your Heel. A lot of people are looking for that diary." He tapped a finger into his own chest. "Before that happens I want to help you show the world how *good* you can be."

They heard Barbara coming. Victor didn't want her worried that her man was a target for an army of batty slayers; and he needed to make sure Linciome understood his commitment to furthering the Labs' longevity research. He would be a *good* vampire. "I promise to do anything you need from me."

Barbara brought them wedge-cut Monte Cristo

sandwiches on a paper plate, as Tripp barged through the front door. He pointed at Dr. Linciome, kneeling beside Victor.

"You son of a bitch."

Dr. Linciome was taken aback. "Nice to see you, too."

Tripp threw down his cowboy hat and charged.

Victor knocked Dr. Linciome aside and picked Tripp off, and up, lifted him to his tiptoes.

Tripp stared at him through a couple rapid breaths. "Vic, buddy. You've been swindled."

Hearing Tripp call him 'buddy' again was sweet for an instant, before a sinking premonition set in. Victor released his sheepskin vest.

Dr. Linciome was anchored to the floor, his sweater under Victor's foot. He pulled free, fell on his butt, got to his feet. "No one's swindling anyone here."

Tripp staggered the soft-bodied scientist with a palm strike to his chest.

"Tripp!" Barbara set down the sandwiches and went to Dr. Linciome's aid. "What is wrong with you?"

"You sabotaged Vic's cure," Tripp accused the Labs' senior researcher. "Didn't you?"

"Take a breath, big boy." Dr. Linciome was trying to do the same. "Victor and I were just talking about this."

"We were? I remember hearing my vampirism was meant to be."

"Exactly!" Dr. Linciome steered clear of Tripp, keeping a new and much smaller end table between the two of them as he directed his defense to Victor and Barbara. "I simply cannot tell you what the world loses if you are cured. No one believes it now but it won't be long before it's apparent. Barbara," he appealed to what he had walked in on, what had been written all over her face. "Victor as a vampire—he isn't an evil creature, is he? He's wonderful, isn't he?"

"Of course," said Barbara. "Tell me what you did."

"Allow me." Tripp pulled a sheaf of rolled-up papers from an interior vest pocket. "You don't need to understand what this says—because he does." He attempted to smooth the curled papers for a moment before flinging them at Dr. Linciome. "That's the analysis from the blood we drew from Vic when he was in the slammer. It has your fingerprints all over it, Winnie. You evil son of a bitch. You used your little time-release capsule to counteract the cure."

Dr. Linciome threw caution to the wind and approached Tripp, retrieving his ten-gallon hat, stepping on the papers strewn in his path. "Can I ask you to trust me? You know me—"

"If I knew you this wouldn't have come as a surprise." Tripp snatched away his hat. "If I *knew* you, I never would have worked with you."

Dr. Linciome started to appeal, then closed his mouth in resignation. "I guess I have a lot of explaining and making up to do."

"It's way beyond that." Tripp stood protectively in front of Victor and Barbara. "Dr. Speer cleaned out your office. He alerted the Rice oversight committee and the national bioethics commission. Anyone and everyone. You're done, Winnie. Your career is over."

Dr. Linciome's chin dropped to his chest. His sweater bunched around his pudgy middle and the skin in his face drooped to layer his neck. "I'm sorry."

"Tell it to the judge, hombre." Tripp shook his head, stupefied. "The D.A.'s involved, too. They're considering pressing charges. As an accomplice to Nikki's murder."

Dr. Linciome pulled the door open like it weighed a ton. He stood with his back to them, slumped in the doorway.

With a guttural moan Victor stalked him. "Do you realize what you've done to me?"

The scientist faced Victor. "I'm not apologizing to you. This *is* what you were meant to be. Vampirism is your destiny."

Tripp advanced. "Get the hell out of here."

At the scientist's hesitation, Victor growled, "Go."

Dr. Linciome backed away, eyes only on Victor. "Don't let them cure you."

Tripp slammed the door in Dr. Linciome's face. The emptied house rang with silence, everyone alone for the moment with their thoughts. Victor was seeing the future—and saw Barbara trying to do the same.

"Dr. Linciome blocked Victor's treatment for his longevity research?" Barbara looked for confirmation.

Tripp slapped his hat against his chaps. "He is involuntary-commitment nuts. I've read about scientists without a moral compass, willingly sacrificing their subjects—supposedly for the good of humanity, justified by the ends, by the knowledge gained. I never thought I'd witness it."

Barbara's body was tight with worry as she sat in the cheap chair. Victor couldn't help but admire the strength in her legs, the controlled grace of her movement. He didn't want to hear the question on her lips.

She looked at Tripp, and then Victor. "What does this mean?"

Tripp's intensity became enthusiasm. "We're going to cure your man." He grabbed a sandwich. "I could always see our inhibitor molecules in your cells." He picked up one of the papers he had thrown, brandishing it, the smoking gun. "But it turns out Linciome's implant was releasing enzymes that deactivated those molecules. Basically tied them up. If we take out his implant and re-start the treatment, you'll be human again in no time." Tripp fairly glowed with the good news.

In a small voice Barbara said, "That is wonderful."

Victor's fangs ached to be bared, to be used, to bite to bite to bite. He shook his head violently, warding off the compulsion, working to be level-headed. "I don't know. I'll have to think about it."

"No, no, no." Tripp came between the two of them, literally, symbolically. "You have the chance to be cured, you *take* it. There is no debate."

"Of course there is!" Victor peeled his lip back to give full rein to his fangs. "What this has done for me ..." *I have everything to lose. The respect. My job. My wife.* He couldn't voice his fears in front of Barbara— that was exactly the type of weakness she hated.

But of course he could pretend nothing was going to change, and Barbara would see it for herself soon enough. "I *told* you. I'm working to control myself. I can control it."

"Of course you can't, buddy." Tripp slung his arm around Victor. "It doesn't work that way."

Blood roared in Victor's ears and his vision shaded red, every muscle from jaw to toes yearning to hurl Tripp against the wall. The word *buddy* mocked him, belittled him, reminded him of everything he used to be.

Soothing hands were on his neck, cool on his face. Barbara's sweet scent enveloped him. She pushed Tripp away, saving him. "We'll get through whatever happens. Together."

Victor breathed heavily, wanting to believe. *Whatever happens.* Maybe Barbara believed that the cure could fail again, or somehow leave him otherwise unchanged but for a loss of pointy teeth and a red diet.

He dared to look in her eyes. Her words were just a brave front. Barbara knew as well as he did what was to come. She was moving in close, but already shrinking from him.

"It really isn't a decision." Tripp sounded like a marriage counselor shooting them straight and confident he could guide them through the rough stretch. "The D.A.'s primed to lay all the blame on Linciome. He's in favor of dropping the charges against you. *If* you take the cure."

"But he was already leaning toward dropping the charges," said Victor.

Tripp snorted. "That was before you had a cure available. He didn't think he could get a conviction if being a vampire was out of your control. But if you *choose* to stay a vampire? He'll come after you."

"Then why did you tell him?"

Victor heard how ridiculous he sounded, but Barbara seemed of the same mind. He could imagine her nodding as he overpowered Tripp, perhaps helping to restrain him as Victor bit him, drank him dry, silenced him.

The thought was fleeting, intoxicating, then vanishing, leaving him ill. "You always know what's best. Don't you."

"Just the obvious stuff." Tripp was pleased as punch, gripping his belt buckle and ready to dance a jig. "Going to the D.A., I took my lead from Speer as you can probably imagine. But sure. I would have done it, too."

"I'm not going back to the Labs." The thought was physically distressing. Sweat beaded along his thick widow's peak.

"Then you are of a mind with the big man. Speer would never allow it. Good thing you don't need to." Again Tripp went for the sandwich plate and referenced the lab papers that Barbara gathered from the floor. "Not the way he planned it, but Linciome lent us a hand. I'm going to use his time-release implant to deliver your cure."

The rangy post-doc researcher placed his hand on Victor's shoulder, and then dug his finger under his clavicle. Victor seized his wrist, fangs bared.

Tripp marveled at the aggression in Victor. "That's where your implant is, I'll guarantee it. Right under your collarbone. Linciome would have slipped in through the catheter insertion site we used to administer your treatment. Our inhibitors were compromised right out of the gate."

Victor lost the desire to twist Tripp's wrist and bring him to his knees. He shuffled toward the kitchen ... and realized he was heading to the garage. To his trains. But of course they were long-since packed away and stored in the attic.

"I'm excited to package your treatment in Linciome's delivery system. It won't take me long, brother. Tell your doc to book us a room at his favorite surgery center." He knelt beside Barbara and nodded at the sandwich plate. "The Monte Cristo, huh? You're the whole package." He put a kiss on her cheek. "Don't fret, Barbie. We'll have Vic back to normal before you know it."

The door closed with a soft *click*. Victor longed for it to be the hypnotist's signal, telling the two of them to wake from a trance and find themselves back where they were before Linciome's arrival. Not the position— the giddy feeling, created by a future vibrating with untapped potential, a future of experiences that college graduate Victor had fantasized about, occupying a corner office in a skyscraper, consumed with his job and in passionate love with his wife.

That part, the love affair—without it there was no perfect future. Victor was a romantic; and he had always understood that romance for a woman required a hero. Pudgy as a kid, a big kid yes, but all brain and no body, young Victor had no business fancying himself a hero. The books he had read—like the chronicles of Thomas Covenant, a leper healed and revealed to possess wonderful power—those stories didn't turn young Victor into a romantic; they resonated with one.

No less than the leper Covenant, Victor was afflicted. As he had suspected as a boy and becoming awfully apparent as the years passed, no woman dreaming of romance would ever love him. Only some sort of magic could allow his true self to come forth.

Until Tripp walked in, Victor believed vampirism

had healed him. Now he understood that he had simply been under a spell, cloaked in a magical fanged costume. Underneath, the leper remained.

Victor had his hand on the door to the garage; he was ready to hear the wonderful squeak the hinges would make, a thin echo of the mournful toot of his tiny train engine, welcoming him to his solitary world, a perfect getaway to an island no one cared to find.

Some part of him, the vampire perhaps, remembered the shame that would immediately follow. He prayed for Barbara to stop him.

And there she was at the kitchen threshold. "I love you, Victor."

There would be no better moment, if she ran to him now. When she didn't, he went to her. They hugged, making contact in as many places as Victor could achieve, hips, knees, shoulders, stomach, reluctantly trading one for another when all were simultaneously impossible. He was the aggressor, Barbara submitting. He would take her there, sink his fangs into her throat and drink. In that position no compromise was necessary. Barbara would feel him against her from head to toe.

But that wasn't the way Victor wanted his ex-wife. He wanted Barbara to see him not rising from a coffin but silhouetted against the window in the corner office, taking in a view of the city.

Victor kissed her neck, her jaw, her mouth. He drew blood, welling up on her lower lip and dribbling down her chin, without apology. "I love you, too. You are meant to be with me. I don't care whether I'm a vampire or not."

But even as she kissed him feverishly and recklessly, Victor was afraid that Barbara did care.

BROKEN EUGENE

Eugene woke up with the now familiar pain of getting his ass kicked, to the smell of musk and a mint julep. He could hear ice clanking in the small glass the CWS always seemed to hold and the sound of his heavy but graceful feet on the stone floor. Eugene could not open his eyes. "Where am I?"

The footsteps stopped. Eugene heard the slow sip of a mint julep. "We are in one of the Chateau d'Ussé complementary buildings. Jean-Jean, the current owner of the Chateau, has given us use of this building for the last two weeks. Gene, you have barely survived." The soldier paused and took another sip, top lip working through a floating layer of leaves. "Barely survived yet another encounter with a vampire."

One of Eugene's eyes popped open. "*Eu*gene, not Gene."

"My apologies." The CWS raised his glass in Eugene's direction.

"What happened?"

The soldier walked to Eugene's bed, stood for a moment. "Well, Eu-gene, somehow you did it again. You slayed Charles."

Eugene tried to recollect the castle, the fight, and could remember very little. Gingerly he touched the bandages swaddling his head. "I remember going up the spire, trying to catch the vamp."

"Do you remember the land deal that you were trying to close as Charles was kicking the crap out of your insides?"

Eugene tried to roll to his side and found it impossible. He thought for a moment. "Yes, I needed someone to vouch for my citizenship or take me on as a partner."

The CWS's usual calm demeanor broke for a moment. "Eugene, you have a natural gift and a lineage that gives you the right, honor and obligation to hunt the Vampire Menace. The last thing you need to do is, is ... land deals."

"*Well?* I can't remember what happened. Tell me."

"Somehow you fell out of the top of the castle into the river. Charles fell out with you. With slit wrists, and a crossbow bolt in his back. Not very sporting," the timeless old soldier kidded him with a chuckle.

"No, no, the land deal! What happened to my land deal?"

The soldier sat on the edge of Eugene's bed. "I surely don't know. What I do know is that my assistant fished you out of the river, whisked you down here to my friend Jean-Jean's place, and we have been nursing your ungrateful, broken self for weeks now. You almost died, again. Should have been dead, again."

Eugene hated to kowtow to anyone, but the CWS had taught him many things. About his family history, and his destiny. He taught him how to hone his skills. How to hunt and kill vamps. But his land deals, Amway and other multi-level marketing strategies had suffered.

The CWS had saved his life more than a couple times. Eugene changed his tone. "Yes, yes, thanks, and sorry I have not been as attentive as you would have liked." Eugene said this as sincerely as possible. Which came out even more sarcastic than usual.

"Eugene." The Soldier took a deep breath. "When I brought you to this country for training, you blossomed." The CWS was right. He now performed all the drills with precision. What he lacked in focus he made up for with a calm mind, confidence, and an aloofness that made him deadly. "I let you do your blog thing, and build the pyramids of Amway. And when you wanted to go to the South of France to speculate on land, I let you."

"I have to do those things." Eugene had been blogging and serving as an online Dear Abby, Dr. Phil and Jumping Jim Cramer wrapped into one. He had a huge online following, 160,000 Twitter followers, 14,000 Facebook friends, and 13 newspapers in the U.S and abroad where he doled out advice on real estate, love and vampire slaying, just to name a few of his specialties. "For my followers."

CWS raised an understanding hand. "Gene—oops, sorry. Eugene, you need to give up all outside influences and concentrate on your craft, your calling. Just for the next few months, until you're ready. Then you can resume these *sidelights*. In a week or so you will be well enough to move and we can get back to my place in the mountains for more training."

Eugene shook his head. "I need to get to Detroit. They need me there."

The soldier stood up slowly and dug his fists into the small of his back. "If you don't complete your training—after Charles nearly did you in, trust me, you're not ready to do what needs to be done to slay Victor Thetherson." There came a loud pop from his back, and he sighed. "Morbius can only be slain by the best. By a slayer willing to put in the time and make the sacrifice. Like your ancestor, Trubadur Maistru. Eugene, your preparation now must be just as much mental as physical."

Eugene shook his head emphatically. "I have to meet four men from Detroit. I am their only hope."

The old soldier stared in disbelief. "Really?"

"Yes. They want to pay me some big dough to slay some Vampire. While I'm there I'm planning to capitalize on the housing market before they come out of bankruptcy. It's a win-win."

The CWS polished off the mint julep and walked to the makeshift bar. He pawed around the countertop, turned his head this way and that, bent down as far as his back would allow to peer into the glass doors, couldn't find what he was looking for. Settled for a gin and tonic sans lime. He looked forlornly at his beverage. "Pitiful." Shook his head again and took a big swig. Looked hard at his glass. "Not bad." Turned back to Eugene. "A win-win is you staying here and resting up until we can safely move you back to my place in the mountains."

A soft but firm rap on the door, an incoherent declaration, and Hilda entered abruptly. After a brief pause to press her skirt to her legs, she walked three steps forward, stopped and clicked her heels. "Sir, your bed is ready and your chambermaid is present in your room."

The CWS toasted Hilda. "Thanks, I will be there shortly." His gaze turned back to Eugene. "As I was saying, we'll head to the mountains to complete your training." He slammed the rest of his gin and tonic, smiled at his glass, set it on the bar and left the room.

Eugene was in a fix. He needed to finish his training—he had learned a lot but knew the CWS had more to teach him. At every training session the old vampire slayer showed him a new move, another unusual way to kill a vamp. And every vamp Eugene encountered was tougher to kill than the last, each seemingly with his or her own brand of armor and unique soft spot.

But how did that trend apply to Victor Thetherson? No matter how many times the CWS said it, Eugene couldn't picture the fatty as Morbius reincarnate.

Truth be told, Eugene couldn't picture a future worth living in if he were to kill Victor. It would mean living without Amberly. When they were together, she sometimes joked about him slaying her dad. This level of trust was worth a hundred times more than if she had made him promise not to do it.

He had been falling in love with Amberly from the first time he put her under surveillance at her boarding school, to get to her father. Their connection deepened when he slew Bob the appraiser vampire for biting her. The feeling had grown stronger when they were apart; it consumed him when Amberly was in his arms. In Eugene's mind, Victor existed merely to bring the two of them together. They were meant for each other. That was a destiny Eugene believed in.

And then there were his various ventures. Eugene had been scrolling down the list of unread emails and texts on his CrapBerry for three minutes without reaching bottom. In his latest coma he had left everything hanging, every*one* hanging. Beyond the money to be made, Eugene wanted to help people. He saw how badly they needed him.

The question was how to maximize the number of people he could save in the long run. And yes, to make money doing it.

In his heart he wanted to be in Detroit; he *needed* to be in Detroit. He had made his decision.

JAY HANSEN

Jay heard the bleep from his BlackBerry as he left the Bizco elevator bank. He squinched his eyes to ward off an oncoming headache and checked the incoming text. It was from Teddy Mook, formerly a foreman on Mel Parish's construction team, to the Project Well Done chat group.

You a-holes up for pool tonight at the Ground Round?

Jay slowed his walking, typing an excuse. *Sorry, I can't. I have—*

David Copperfield had replied: *Whuz theyr happy hour like, wont support a joint that wont support the masses. Unless its ladys night.*

—two appointments—

The waitresses r foxes, Teddy responded. *Dont give a shit about happy hour, nothing but oil traders talking bout the killing they made in the market, ruins my karma.*

—busy night—

Their shrimp fettuccine is top notch. This was Larry. *I'm in.*

—and we have an early flight ...

Jay's fingers misplayed one tiny key after another until he gave up with a muttered curse, deleted his draft message, pocketed the device and plowed through the revolving doors.

The wind was up in the downtown skyscraper canyon. The breeze entered at the north end of Milam

Street, funneled, focused and accelerated past the Bizco tower, splitting and lifting Jay's single-vented suit coat, giving him two broad flapping tails, ratcheting up his aggravation level. He swatted at the tails, beat them back down to his butt, only to have them float and flap against his shoulder blades as soon as he let go.

Chicago was obviously no less windy, but Jay had always looked for excuses to walk around. He hated walking downtown Houston. He drove in every morning, parked in the subterranean Bizco ramp, all the way down to level six, took the elevator up to his office and then back down ten hours later, got in his Audi and punched it all the way back up, around and around, one long tight corkscrew turn, a little smile on his face and a measure of stress gone from his chest before leaving downtown as fast as he could.

Tonight he had an appointment with his counterpart at Playco Construction down the street, in their nondescript concrete tower. In the battle with Bizco for the EnerGreen contract, Playco was the last bidder standing. Teetering, really, out on their feet and waiting for EnerGreen to knock them over with the final, formal "sorry."

To be safe, Jay should have taken the elevator down to his Audi and corkscrewed up and out of downtown like every other day, and then driven back in to park below Playco's building, to avoid being spotted. The last thing he needed was a rumor in tomorrow's Business section, "Construction Execs Cozy on EnerGreen Bid?" But he was running late—he had a habit, his worst according to his wife, of always wanting to send one more email.

And there was a third person joining the two CFOs tonight, someone Jay was bringing to the table. Jay didn't want to disappoint him.

Jay had been born in the wrong era. He envied accountants of the previous decades who had been, first and foremost, businessmen. Accounting, public accounting in particular, was where business talent had launched their careers. When he started out of college at the public accounting firm Arthur Andersen & Company, Jay had the pleasure and thrill of observing that last free generation.

They were powerful men and women, many of them former college athletes, intense competitors, attractive, outgoing and well-rounded, prime movers who cut to the chase, who were able to focus on nothing but the bottom line, helping their clients build revenue, satisfy customers and make money. Most of them moved on to join those clients, rising to lead not the Accounting or Finance areas but the companies themselves.

That all perfectly described young Jay Hansen in background, personality and future. That was the man who won the heart of his gorgeous, vivacious wife.

And then seemingly hand in hand the two scourges of the modern era had emerged, and multiplied, and become increasingly powerful. Regulators and vampires. Both had been harmless in the early days, something to joke about, to circumvent and to mock. Now they were too many, and worse, they were esteemed, able to assume power by the adulation of the people.

Regulators were largely faceless, bland men and women coming and going. Dealing with them had been treated as a cost of business, and it had fallen to the Chief Finance Officer's team to minimize that cost. Originally a small fraction of their duties, that proportion had grown under a rising tide of new regulations—and before Jay could escape, Finance had been walled off from the rest of the company, deemed synonymous with "Compliance" and pictured wearing belt and suspenders, both, no-men who avoided risk at all costs. Trapped and by now permanently tainted, Jay really didn't have anyone to hate other than himself.

But vampires, they had a face, and a name: Victor Thetherson, darling of the Bizco executive team, of the entire company. At Victor's core, the essence of the man, was weakness. An intelligent guy who knew his accounting rules, but too timid, too deferential, too unsure of himself to ever win an argument. The art of debate—that was the defining skill in the world of business competition, and Victor didn't have it. Not without his fright mask.

Unlike the nearly imperceptible, incremental advance of the regulators, Vampire Vic's attack had been startlingly, grotesquely abrupt. Jay couldn't kick himself enough for not firing Victor the day he showed up with fangs. Or the day of the announcement of Texahoma's merger with Oklarkana. Victor could have found himself a nice government job. Now Chleber had smugly plucked him out of Finance and put him beyond Jay's reach.

There was one other important difference between regulators and vampires: It wasn't illegal to kill vampires.

This was the "good news" side of a phone call Jay received a few days prior, from the district attorney. Jay had tried to dodge him, but his admin, usually quite good at the brush-off, had ignored her boss and put Stuart Goodnight through.

"I hope I'm not catching you at a bad time."

"Never a great time these days," Jay had said. "We're incredibly busy. But I'm happy to give you a few minutes."

"First I want to say how fortunate the city is that you chose us for your headquarters."

"Truth be told?" Jay didn't appreciate the escort down memory lane, back to the city park where his ill-conceived alliance with Raj Dajiv had come to an end, where he had his first good look at Bizco's new tower. "It felt more like fate than a choice."

"I'm guessing the bid for the EnerGreen campus

might have had something to do with it. Sounds like they've all but awarded it to you."

Now Jay could smile. "Barring some eleventh-hour bombshell."

"Let's get to the reason for my call." The D.A. was regularly on television announcing indictments of prominent Texas businessmen for ventures that had not previously been considered illegal. Goodnight was Houston's version of former New York attorney general Eliot Spitzer, he of the kinky, adulterous tastes. Jay hoped some similar revelation would soon sink the D.A. and his smooth, righteous face. "I understand you're a recent investor in the Longevity Labs."

Jay had been mentally sifting through various Bizco contracts to anticipate the D.A.'s approach, and so was caught off guard. He wondered which one of his fellow investors had divulged the confidential investment.

"Your laboratory was supposed to cure Victor Thetherson," said Goodnight. "It failed. And so there are people here in my office who believe you bear responsibility for the two people murdered on that television program."

"Stuart, that's ridiculous, right? The Labs aren't in business to cure vampires. Longevity research is its end-all be-all. Maybe they gained a research benefit from having vampires in their study. And if they happened on a cure as a byproduct, great. But that's an unplanned bonus. There were no expectations created."

"Bizco gave Mr. Thetherson a paid leave of absence while he was taking the cure at the Labs. You are highly placed at both companies. Don't you think a rational observer would assume you *expected* the cure to work?"

When Jay didn't immediately respond, Goodnight continued.

"Of course they would. And it brings us to your other problem. Bizco employed Mr. Thetherson before his failed cure, knowing full well he was dangerous. And you're employing him now, after he admittedly murdered two people."

Goodnight had hit upon a real concern within Bizco, so much so that Darla's attempt to have Bizco buy a floral arrangement for Nikki's funeral was nixed by their lawyers for fear of creating any perception of guilt.

"I'm sure we've received this same call from corporate ambulance chasers. Shouldn't you be spending your time putting Thetherson away for life?"

"You think there's a case?" said the D.A., as if he was sincerely interested in Jay's legal opinion. "Don't you think he would argue self-defense on McGumphrey? And don't forget, that point of contention is irrelevant. McGumphrey was a vampire. They get slain all the time."

That was the good news. The rest was all bad.

"What about the woman he killed? Nikki."

"We've passed a thousand times on prosecuting vampires for biting people. There's too much precedent to overcome on her death."

"You're dropping the charges? You have to be kidding me."

"Don't worry, Mr. Hansen." Goodnight moved smoothly to threatening. "It's not like I won't have something to work on. We have ample precedent for you to be held liable for the acts of your employees."

"You called the wrong person. You need to be talking to our corporate counsel."

"No, Mr. Hansen. I'm talking personal liability."

There was malevolence in the word *personal*. Jay tried to ignore it. "Bizco's insurance policies still cover executives personally, so our legal staff—"

"Insurance coverage won't protect you. Jay."

Jay had hurriedly searched the web and found the D.A.'s latest press conference. He muted the volume and watched it, while Goodnight breathed on the line.

Rumor had it he was a vampire. Jay peered at the screen but it was impossible to tell. The prosthetics vampires used to mask their fangs were incredible. Those falsie manufacturers should be prosecuted!

"I'm a big fan of community policing," said Goodnight. "Citizens taking responsibility for their neighborhoods. In my mind, in the jury's mind, we've successfully placed Mr. Thetherson in your neighborhood. Established your responsibility. Since there doesn't seem to be a cure for your vampire, I need to know how you propose to clean up your neighborhood."

"What are you asking me to do?"

Jay sweated through the silence on the other end of the line. Houston's district attorney couldn't be a vampire, right? And why would he be targeting another vampire? Turf battle? Surely there was blood enough in the city for all of them.

More likely, the D.A. simply wanted a professional embarrassment to go away.

"Are you saying you won't pursue anything against Bizco or the Longevity Labs, if I ... if I clean up the neighborhood?"

"Law enforcement doesn't need to spend much time in communities that police themselves."

Until that call, Jay considered his investment in the Longevity Labs the best in his portfolio. Not for the potential economic return on any commercial longevity treatments. That was at best a long-shot bonus he would enjoy but could live without. (The running joke with his wife: A successful longevity product was a bonus no one could live without!) The real reason for his buy-in was information, and it had paid off better than expected.

The other investors had been impressed with Jay's desire to go beyond the Labs' published findings and dig into the researchers' notes. Well they should have been impressed, because the reading was mind-numbing. But days into his nighttime pastime, buried in that unpublished documentation, encoded in jargon, Jay had learned something extremely valuable about Victor Thetherson.

The D.A.'s attention was an ugly hidden cost to his investment. It could be worse; at least Goodnight was asking for something Jay also desired. Thanks to the Labs' notes on Vic's origin, and Florence's display at the *Xtreme ReVamp* show, Jay had a plan to satisfy them both.

With virtually no risk. The universe felt a little less unjust knowing that vampires came equipped with an iron-clad defense for their murderers.

The biggest problem was the uncertainty. His plan placed too much reliance on Florence, which was why Jay was still suffering through Project Well Done with the three buffoons. He was meeting Larry "Mellow" Cocachello, "Foreman" Teddy Mook and David "Magic Man" Copperfield the next day in Detroit. Bizco's parent company, Verrstagg, had a subsidiary there. Jay had no authority outside Bizco but liked to keep tabs on developments in the Verrstagg empire. This trip was such an opportunity.

And he didn't want to be seen in Houston with the three buffoons. Project Well Done was an extremely distasteful backup plan.

As was this meeting with the Playco CFO, and the arrangement with their special guest. Distasteful, arduous tasks that appeared to suck valuable time away from the business at hand—such was the nature of contingency planning. Jay excelled at it. Very often it was the edge that determined the winner in a business competition. Victor might not know it, but right now he was competing for his life. Jay would walk away the winner.

In his heart and soul Jay Hansen was still a businessman. Still the man his wife had been thrilled to love. He was long overdue in stepping outside his

Finance box and bringing home a work story worth telling.

Jay walked onto the Playco accounting floor. Mitchell Harms officed there—to hear him describe it, a great place to get work done, as the company's accountants feared him and did all they could to avoid him, steering clear of his office like the plague just in case he was inside.

The floor was quiet, whether empty or harboring accounting mice heads down at their desks, no desire to be noticed by the higher powers. Harms' office was ten steps from the elevator, windowless, door closed.

Jay would term this meeting a hedge. Hedges protected your downside, but they cost money. This meeting was costing Jay—and Bizco—dearly. But in the long run the cost would be well worth the benefit. At least for Jay.

He knocked and entered. Immediately he felt claustrophobic. Suffocated and regretful. Mitchell Harms didn't look any better off. Neither man said a word in greeting. Mitchell merely waved Jay to a chair sitting all too close to their special guest.

DETROIT (AND WARREN)

As Eugene moved from concourse to terminal and approached all of the friends and family awaiting their loved ones, he looked and looked but did not see a scantily clad Detroit Lions cheerleader holding up a big sign, **EUGENE V.S.**, as he requested.

He wandered about the terminal severely disappointed and now fully pissed because he could not find his customers. "Another five minutes of walking around here and I will have four more people to take care of, on the house," he muttered to himself.

Now at the baggage claim he waited for his luggage in livid silence. After waiting another 23 minutes for his suitcases, skis and steamer trunk, and after everyone else had collected their belongings and left arm in arm with the people who cared enough to follow directions, Eugene heard over the intercom, "Will Professor Plum please come to the Air France baggage claim office? Professor Plum, please go to the Air France baggage claim office to meet your party."

His codename. Eugene approached the row of airline complaint offices and the dark Air France room. The door was unlocked. Eugene glanced around the baggage area before entering the room casually. He was met by the comforting aroma of garlic. "Knock, knock."

Three men emerged from under the desk, one from the closet.

Eugene closed the door and flipped on the lights. "Come on, guys, were my orders that hard to follow?"

The closeted gent was dressed for business. He had been on his BlackBerry, wrapping up an email while he approached Eugene ... letter-letter-letter, delete-delete ... letter-letter ... punctuation mark. Send. "You must be our slayer."

"Am I?" said Eugene. "If I were, wouldn't I have a Cuban in my mouth and a Lions cheerleader on my arm?"

"Yo-yo-yo, we knew you were testing us," said a big dude, too loud for the room and loving it, swaggering to take his place beside BlackBerry as co-leader of their foursome, big head and big chest, bigger gut, flashing signs like a slow-motion hand jive. "Didn't make sense, you wanting to make a scene and draw everyone's attention."

Eugene considered this a decent explanation. "Next time don't make me wait so long."

A deformed man piped up. "We wanted to make sure we weren't being followed." Judging by the roll of his speech, the tousled hair and the layered Lucky shirts and pre-worn Lucky jeans, at one time he was quite the looker. But he was beaten, physically and mentally. Eugene could see it in his eyes. He really could: One of Lucky's eyes was slow and discolored. He had a slouch and a bent spine; a young hunchback. He was the one wearing garlic, in ropes like leis around his neck.

"Sorry. You're right," the hunchback decided. "Making you wait wasn't a good idea." He shot a guilty glare at the back of BlackBerry's head.

Eugene surveyed the four men. They were each timid, broken in some way. Even the two leaders. Beneath Big Boy's bluster and BlackBerry's arrogance, there was fear. Both of them had been terrorized by a vampire and were looking for a savior.

BlackBerry looked Eugene up and down. Took in the gleaming silver buckles on his black boots. The Michael Jackson high-ranking admiral jacket. The Trotsky chapeau. The peach fuzz. "How old are you?"

"Old enough to use online banking. I saw the initial payment was wired to my account." Eugene pressed his palms together and dipped his head in thanks. "But ..." He paused, halfway up from half a bow. "I did not see your required first purchase of Mary Kay, Amway or Young Living. Nor did I see your required investment in the EVS crowdfunded real estate investment trust. Should I assume it will all be done by midnight? Or is my business here concluded?"

BlackBerry made it clear he was standing up and speaking for the lesser men. "We have no problem if you want to use the money we sent you to buy some makeup."

A small, wiry and soon to be arthritic man in a dark brown western-cut suit, oldest and most reluctant of the bunch, finally spoke. "Mr. Plum—"

Eugene cut him off. "Good. Code names are essential. We'll call you Li'l Cowpoke." He pointed at the hunchback. "For you—"

"I already have one," said the hunchback. "Magic Man."

Eugene vetoed that, and resisted the obvious. "You're Lucky. This one is BlackBerry. No, just Berry."

"Berry," Big Boy sniggered.

"And you're Chet," Eugene gave him the worst name he could think of.

"I'm partial to 'The Foreman,'" said Chet.

"Not a chance," said Eugene. "For me, Gene is fine."

"Gene," Li'l Cowpoke drawled.

Eugene winced. "No, nope, Professor Plum is better."

Li'l looked puzzled. "Okay. Professor Plum. We're prepared to wire you the other half of your fee when the job is done, as requested. But we don't have additional funds for the other, for your—"

At a grunt from Berry, Li'l Cowpoke started over. "We don't want to buy the Mary Kay stuff."

"Or your crowdfunded REIT," said Berry.

Eugene had heard this many times. People didn't just hand over their money. One had to take it from them. He smiled, arms open wide.

"Gentlemen, this is an investment. Not only is it an investment in great companies like Mary Kay and Amway and the soon-to-be-booming Detroit real estate market—but in yourselves and your future. The money you wired is mine, to do the job you have asked of me. The money to build the pyramids and fund the REIT is for you, you, you and you!" Eugene pointed at each of them in turn. "For your future! For your families' future. For your grandchildren."

Eugene opened the door and stepped into the baggage claim area. He smiled a big toothy grin. "Besides, it's fucking non-negotiable. Now get my goddamn luggage!"

Li'l, Chet and Lucky scrambled to get his bags. A big one and a not-as-big one for each. They struggled to keep up with Eugene. Berry shook his head in disgust and followed at his own speed. He was the key to this sale and he was going to take some more selling.

Eugene's pace quickened like he knew where he was going. He had a good 30 yards on the men, who were not sure when to tell Eugene that he was going the wrong way.

Eugene darted into a bathroom and into a stall, waiting until Berry straggled in. Then he kicked the stall door open. "Okay, you sons of bitches. I will be at the Waldorf Astoria, on your tab of course. Meet me at my room at 8 a.m. sharp." Eugene gazed at the bathroom ceiling and shook his head. "Make that 11 a.m. sharp." He paused again. "Nope, 11:45."

Berry laughed a dry ho-ho. "This is Detroit. Could we interest you in a Holiday Inn?"

Eugene advanced on Berry. He wore an indigo dress coat over suit jacket over open-collared starched white shirt. He had a manicure, had just had his Bostonians polished by the airport bootblack, and didn't see what all the smartphone fuss was about. After replacing his own CrapBerry, Eugene had no patience for such ignorance.

"I won't be sleeping, Berry. I've got properties to inspect and vamps to kill."

"Then let's make it Super 8."

Emboldened, Chet sidled closer and measured himself against the slayer. "No offense, but I thought you'd be bigger."

"More like Blade?" said Eugene.

"Just less like Where's Waldo," Berry retorted.

Eugene made his living being underestimated. That being said, these four had now lost their introductory discount. "Maybe you're looking for a demo?"

"I'd love it." Berry straddled a piss puddle at the urinal, unzipped with one hand and thumbed his CrapBerry with the other. Eugene had to admit, a pretty fair demonstration of coordination and multi-tasking. "No offense on your choice of slayers," he tossed a token apology to Li'l Cowpoke, who must have been the one to contact Eugene via his online application. "But I'm not blown away, right? Feels like we're in a shakedown. So even better," Berry said to Eugene, "you could just kill our vampire."

"I was wondering, Professor Plum," said Li'l. "Do you offer any other packages besides slaying? Crippling, for instance?"

"Sweet Jesus." Chet spread his arms and looked to Heaven. "Answer my prayers and promise me I'll never ever have to work with accountants again."

Lucky the hunchback piled on Li'l. "We all agreed, Larry."

"We're not here to break his leg," said Berry.

"Any slayer will tell you ..." Eugene recorded in his little notepad, *Li'l Cowpoke = Larry*. "You start trying to wing 'em instead of slay them? That's how you get hurt." He snapped his fingers at his steamer trunk. Lucky dragged it to him and Eugene solved the combination lock, popped the clasps, rummaged inside and pulled out his GoPro head-mount camera. "Look for the footage on my website tomorrow."

Berry wrapped up his business one-handed. Like an unsanitary magician, that same hand produced a business card. "We'll pass on your slaying services. But send me pictures of the properties you're looking at. Maybe I'll be interested."

Eugene gave him an appraising nod. "I couldn't help but notice your generalized inflammation and inconsistent skin tone." He ignored Berry's sour reaction, briefly eyeballing each of them in turn as he knelt at the trunk again. "It's obvious you could all use a sample of what I would call a wonder drug. You see this?" Eugene doffed his cap and parted his mop to reveal a scabby hole in his skull. "Took a vamp for a ride off the top of Castle Chenonceaux. Luckily it straddles a river. Unluckily it's shallow. I went headfirst onto a circa 1943 spike-topped Nazi helmet. They pulled me out with it embedded in my skull. I got $400 for that helmet on eBay. Paid for having the swelling in my skull drained." He blanched at the fuzzy memory of the drill bit Hilda used, and the vivid recollection of the bill she presented later. "I was in a coma for a month. Broke three vertebrae in my neck. You should be looking at the Stephen Hawking of slaying."

He let it all sink in, subtly displaying a bottle of essential oils. "I wouldn't be here without this product. I have a free sample for each of you. $6.95 for processing and handling."

"Can we just focus on Victor?" said Larry, while Lucky put down a five and two ones.

Eugene's eyes widened. Now their accents made sense. "You gentlemen aren't locals, are you? Let me guess ... Houston."

"See," said Lucky to Berry. "He's good."

"You want me to slay Victor Thetherson."

Chet guffawed. "You know the douche?"

Eugene's head spun and rolled like a state fair Tilt-a-Whirl. "We've crossed paths."

"Then I'll bet you're willing to do this one for free," said Berry.

"Did an old Civil War soldier put you up to this?"

The men stared blankly.

Eugene knelt and pretended to search through the trunk while he regained his equilibrium. The CWS wouldn't hire four to do a job that took one. He wouldn't quadruple the chance for something to go wrong. He certainly wouldn't hire *these* four.

No, they were here on their own. Four men who each hated and feared Victor enough to want him dead. Eugene's stomach twisted and his heart ached, as the CWS's warning rang true.

"I heard he took the cure," said Eugene.

"Didn't take," said Larry.

Why hadn't Amberly told him? Stupid question. Eugene advanced on Lucky the hunchback, a one-man pack of wolves picking off a diseased elk unable to keep up with the herd. "Vic did this to you."

"Did what?" said Lucky, as if he had been born that way, as if the world didn't have mirrors.

"I've seen it before." He pulled aside Lucky's layers of shirt collars and slapped down the hunchback's attempted defense, looking for fang tracks. "You're his blood bitch."

"No! It was just the once." Lucky looked cornered, even though he was closest to the door.

Chet shook his head. "You little blood bitch."

On bow legs Larry moved protectively in front of Lucky. "We're sorry to take up so much of your time, Mr. Eugene. Plum. I'm probably more sensitive than the next guy, but I'm up to here on the smell in here. Can we move our discussion out into the hall? Or we can reconvene after a nice continental breakfast at the Super 8."

"Better yet," said Berry. "We'll just give you Vic's address and call it a deal."

"I know everything about Victor Thetherson." Eugene saw that Berry considered himself quite the negotiator. "Including his address."

"Then you know how hard he is to kill," said Larry. "I saw a slayer try and lop his head off with a gillo-teen. Gillo-teen mounted on an axe handle."

"Ghee-o-teen," Berry corrected.

Chet waggled his hands in the air. "Whoop-de-doo, Jay knows his foo-foo frigging French. You shoulda asked Jay how to pronounce it before you opened your trap, you douche-ay."

Eugene made note in his little pad, *Berry = Jay.* "And?"

"It broke on Vic's neck." Larry looked troubled by the memory. "This Sven Slayer gentleman had a bead on Vic's gullet, and his aim was true. That blade was edge-on." He relived and reenacted the moment, his hand the blade, his own neck Victor's, staring at himself in the flecked mirror. "It was like trying to chop down mesquite." His blade burst into an array of fluttering fingers, falling to his side. "Vic walked away with razor burn."

"Sven?" Eugene demanded. "The slayer's name was Sven? Capris?"

"Tight and shiny as apple skin. Shirt, too. Dressed like a mime."

Eugene absorbed, processed. As always the CWS was right. "So Vic has evolved."

"I really doubt that," said Jay.

"Two types of vamps." Eugene struggled to hide his angst as he watched a time-lapse video: Medium focus on himself striding grimly forward; widen the shot to witness him coldly and efficiently slaying Victor; then cut to an extreme close-up of Amberly as her loving expression dissolved into hatred. "Two types, Berry. Evolved and not. The evolved vamps, it's like their genes sat through every vampire flick ever made, and then adapted."

He robotically echoed the lesson from the CWS. "There's only one way to kill an evolved vamp. Find their soft spot."

"Beer and barbecue for Vic," said Jay, garnering a big laugh from the rest of the Houston Four.

"Good idea. Lock him overnight in a Bubba's Buffet, he'll be dead by morning." Eugene's boots snickered on the sticky floor as he headed for the lavatory door. "Clearly you don't need me."

The skin under Jay's eyes went to white.

Gotcha.

Jay was living in the shadow of the vampire. It was written all over his pasty face. Still, he mustered corporate bravado. "Vampire slaying isn't our business. You don't start a dairy farm because you're thirsty. You just go buy a carton off the shelf."

Eugene glared at one after the next until they were all squirming, each in his unique way. "Then it's time to figure out just how thirsty you are." Eugene now hated vampires more than ever before, which was saying something. For what he was doing to Amberly, Eugene hated Victor most of all. "Get us a room in Warren."

"The Holiday Inn Express downtown has four different HBOs," said Lucky.

Eugene had four different pains in his ass. "I've never heard anyone so eager to stay in Detroit."

"What's Warren like?" Chet wanted to know.

"Twice as entertaining as HBO," said Eugene. "Chop-chop, get on it. Somebody with a smartphone." He shoved his steamer trunk at Jay. "No smarts here. You must be the muscle." He checked his watch. "We'll give everyone time for a nice little siesta at the motel and then you'll get your demo." He left the bathroom, and returned. "And then you're going to buy some fucking makeup."

They arrived at the Deer-Horn Inn in Warren in two rental cars, Jay in a Mustang and the other four in a Fusion.

"Make that two rooms," Jay told the motel desk clerk, and then to no one in particular, "I have a conference call in ten minutes."

Chet checked his watch. "At 5:23?"

"It starts when I call in," said Jay.

"Just twisting your titties, dude. Halfsies on the room?"

"No," said Jay.

To Jay's displeasure their rooms were side by side. He was in his room with the bolt thrown and the chain slung before Larry successfully keyed the adjoining door.

Living quarters were tight after everyone's luggage was inside. "There's no room for a cot in here." Chet stumbled navigating between the steamer trunk and two double beds. "Shit, did I forget to bring my sleep apnea machine?"

"You and me?" Lucky whispered to Larry, trying to lock down a decent bed partner.

"Congratulations, you're the first Deer-Horn guests interested in a good night's sleep," said Eugene, before informing them he'd be back soon.

He hotwired the Mustang and drove to the nearest cinderblock bar. Under a Hamm's Beer sign Professor Plum made arrangements with a vamp to meet back at the Deer-Horn in two hours, for a blood "donation."

Two hours later, three of the Houston Four peered out a smeary motel window while Eugene worked with pestle and mortar over a Bunsen burner in the bathroom. "Guys, stop, you are going to scare off the vamp."

"You're not making meth, are you, Professor?" Chet chuckled to himself.

Lucky was highly agitated. "I can't believe you got the vamp to come here. Are we going to jump him and stake him all together?"

Eugene didn't have time to even glance up from his work. "If I were you I'd keep as far away from this vamp as possible. She looked a little under-nourished."

"It's a she?" said Larry, mortified.

"Tonight we're going to recreate a classic slaying of an Evolved Vamp. Not that this little biter is evolved, mind you. A stake would do just fine. But I thought you'd appreciate seeing how a pro handles a custom job." He wished Jay was there. "You can't buy this one off the shelf."

Most vamps just wanted blood. No confrontation, no mess, no desire to draw attention to themselves or to hurt anyone. This vamp seemed to fit that bill; otherwise she probably wouldn't have agreed to meet "Professor Plum" (who looked younger than his 22 years) and his voyeur friends at the sleazy Deer-Horn.

Eugene didn't care. Never had and especially not now. These guys needed a highlight reel playing in their heads when he quadrupled the price on Victor tomorrow.

More than that, they and the rest of humanity needed to wake up and realize that vampires needed to be dealt with. Whether the bloodsuckers wanted confrontation or not.

And no matter who they were related to.

A young lady bundled against the elements walked briskly across the parking lot toward their room.

Fancying themselves amateur detectives but looking more like peeping Toms, the three men now ran for the bathroom. At the knock on the door Chet breathed faster.

"I'd have a little more room to operate if one or more of you would go open that door," said Eugene. "And go tell Berry it's show time."

"Don't you think you should be out there …" Chet caught himself and belatedly stiffened his spine and puffed out his chest, taking up the remaining space. "Instead of hiding in here?"

Eugene ignored him, working.

Larry opened the bathroom door just far enough to holler, "It's open!" They jockeyed to stack an eye along the two-inch gap.

In walked the vampire. Small, very small. And pretty in an adolescent way. She had black, unkempt hair, pale skin and doe eyes.

Lucky recoiled from the door. "She's a little girl!"

The other two came away just as shook. "She can't be more than 15!" Larry whispered hoarsely.

"She's wearing a cute little puffy coat!" Lucky stomped in place and poked his fingers in his eyes to ward off the image.

"We can't kill her," Chet said at a high whisper, trying to pace, ricocheting off men and wall. "Can we?"

"We are *not* going to kill her," Larry whispered. "I don't want to kill a girl. Much less a little defenseless girl who could be my daughter."

Eugene stopped his science project and calmly looked them each in the eye. "Yes, we are going to kill that vampire." He pointed at the door. "She is no one's daughter. She is probably 400 years old." He wagged a finger. "Never ever think of a vamp as a person. They are not people. We are doing the world a favor. We are doing *her* a favor."

As the three men pondered this Eugene returned to his work. Now he raised his head and listened hard. Held out his hand to Lucky. "Your gum."

"Yes." Lucky smacked his gum and reached into his pocket. "You want some?"

"No. Spit it out." Eugene thrust his hand close to Lucky's mouth. "Now."

Lucky shrugged and gently spit it into Eugene's hand. Eugene shoved it in his pocket. "I only have one rule: no eating." He pointed. "Now get out there and stall her. And fetch Berry!"

Three of the Houston Four shuffled out. Eugene closed the bathroom door behind them.

While keeping tabs on the muffled voices from the next room, Eugene spooned his mixture into a tiny latex pouch. He set the pouch on the inside of his wrist and secured it tightly with flesh-colored nontoxic rubber cement.

Eugene was a slayers' historian. This was the way Warren G. Harding met his match. That vampire reportedly fell victim to food poisoning in 1923. Al Capone, he knew better. The gangster had had enough of Harding's meddling and grafting. Sinking his fangs in Capone's mistress was the final straw.

Poisoning a vamp was not the most sporting. But Eugene cared about results, and creativity. Bonus points for recreating the ex-president's slaying in a town bearing his name. The poison was a mixture of blood, sand, liquid silver nitrate, wormwood and liver. And a pinch of cilantro to neutralize the flavor. That had been the hardest ingredient to procure. Warren was a food desert.

Meanwhile in the other room the little girl vamp regarded her audience. "Professor Plum said there might be gawkers." She removed the gigantic coat to reveal her skinny body. She had on a black see-through dress and a black stocking cap. Her army boots seemed four sizes too big. The three men stood looking at her in disbelief and in sadness. "You fuckers can stay. It will cost you 20 bucks though. Each." She held out her hand forcefully. The men were slack jawed. She softened her voice and enunciated slowly. "Since you goobers don't seem to understand what I am saying, I will tell you again. Twenty bucks each on the bed now, or leave. And if you perverts think anything else is going on here you are sadly mistaken."

Chet spoke. "Uh-uh, we just want to watch, uh ..." He looked as ill as the others. "Uh, we just want to watch you drink the blood." The other two nodded in unison.

"How long have you been a va-va-vampire?" asked Larry.

"Long enough to know Detroit is never going to put this on their tourism brochures." She feinted a lunge. They all jumped back. The Very Young Vamp Girl chuckled and watched three twenties hit the bed.

"I'll put in for Jay." Chet pulled another twenty from his billfold, thought twice, then reluctantly tossed it on the little pile.

The vamp stashed the cash in her bra.

Jay walked in. He froze seeing the little vampire girl. Took a step back. Fought to prevent Larry from closing the door behind him.

Larry made the introduction. "This is ... sorry miss, bad manners all around, I didn't get your name?"

The little vampire smacked her gum, arms crossed, shaking her head at the latest arrival. "Petunia."

Jay put his BlackBerry in his pocket without taking his eyes off the adolescent vampire. "Pleased to meet you, Petunia."

"Where the hell is Professor Plum?"

Larry pointed with his thumb. "In the bathroom."

"I don't have all fucking day. You doofs better give me some space. If the Professor takes much longer I'm going to have to start with one of you." Petunia bared her plaque-stained fangs. She did look terribly under-fed.

Eugene emerged from the bathroom and laughed to see the four men pressed against window, wall and door. "Keep your pantyhose on. I was just taking a little extra B-12 to help me recover." He walked over to the bed, beckoned the Vamp Girl to have a seat, and rolled up his sleeve, exposing wrist and a little forearm. Eugene looked at the Houston Four. "You guys paying close attention?"

Petunia eyed the spectators with disdain. "Nice. I get blood, and the three stooges plus one douche bag get to watch."

Eugene knelt in front of her, head bowed and arm extended as if he was being knighted. Petunia latched onto his arm like a turkey leg at the State Fair. She raised her eyes to the four spectators. "You guys aren't going to play with yourselves while I do this, are you?"

Each man was trying to figure out who the douche bag was.

Eugene chuckled. "You said that was okay."

She looked at the four men staring at her in horror. "I changed my mind."

Eugene clenched his fist to pump up his veins. "Suck it so we can be done with this."

"Yes, let's." The vamp eagerly buried her fangs in Eugene's wrist. Went into and through the pouch, into Eugene. She sucked hard and long until the slayer became worried and pushed her away.

The little vampire girl belched. "Not enough! Which one of you is next?" With a spry leap off the bed she was onto Jay, a full frontal assault, legs wrapped around his waist, nails dug through his dress shirt and t-shirt and into his back. Jay screamed, his hands paralyzed into useless claws. Lucky was already three steps out the door. Chet had two handfuls of Larry's plaid shirt.

Eugene strode forward and backhanded the Very Young Girl Vamp. She hit the floor and sprang back to her feet. "You prick! I will devour you!"

"Really?" said Eugene.

Before the little vampire could answer, her neck started to collapse. Her face lost color, lost its white. "Fucker! What did you do to me?" She dropped to her knees, tried to grab the bed to steady herself. "Poison? You dirty son of a bitch." She struggled to her feet, her see-through blouse affording everyone an uncensored view of her skinny body as it melted.

"Damn," Chet whispered.

"Show's over," said Eugene. He looked at the rapidly deceasing vamp. "Keep the 80 bucks."

She reached for him, tried to speak, and fell over. Dead. A shell of herself. Eugene calmly bent down, reached into her bra and grabbed the money, stuffed it into his pocket. As he stood up, the Houston Four were already waiting in the cars.

That night the temperature dropped into the teens. Eugene drove three of the Four into Sterling Heights, another Detroit suburb where the housing crisis had taken its toll. Some areas had a foreclosure rate over 80 percent. The vamps were running amok and houses were prime for the taking. Perfect.

The fourth followed at a distance, as if he were covertly tailing them.

They entered their first neighborhood. Leafy, most of the houses well-lit, with manicured lawns. Eugene drove the Fusion, a crossbow in his lap and a flashlight in his free hand, three GoPros strapped to his head at 60-degree angles. The Three were squeezed into the back seat. Eugene shined the 850-lumens flashlight in their eyes. "I want you to take notes. I want every address of every house with a For Sale sign. Please make good notes about color, relative size, condition, lighting, garages, yard size, fountains, moats, anything and everything that pops into your mind." All the windows were down and the three were freezing.

Lucky hesitantly spoke up. "I thought we were going to kill some more vamps?"

Eugene smiled, a little sneer. "We are going to kill two birds with one stone."

Larry shivered. "Do we really need to have the windows down?"

Eugene's phone beeped; he glanced at the text from Amberly: *When r u back?? Miss u, want u, like this: xxxoooxxxoooxxx*

Eugene started to reply, then pocketed it. "Yes the windows need to be down. Dammit! Where are all the For Sale signs?" He took the next left down Elm. "This street would give me nightmares." Eugene chuckled, alone. He shrugged his shoulders; it would play well on the video.

"What is that noise?" Eugene slowed the car as he looked in the rearview mirror. The noise stopped. He increased his speed. Almost instantly it was there again. A slight ... was it a ... crunching noise? Ice? Was someone back there chewing their fingernails?

Disgusting, the sound was driving him nuts. "Okay, Okay." Eugene jammed on the brakes in the middle of the street. "That's enough!" He made a move over the backseat. "Which one of you is making all that noise?"

The three were confused. They looked each other over, then shrugged in unison. "Uh, what noise, Professor?" asked Lucky.

Eugene looked and looked. Waited for what seemed like an eternity. There it was again. He swung his head to the right and pointed at Chet. "You."

Chet pointed at himself. "Me."

"Yes, what's in your mouth? Crackers, chips, a TIC TAC?"

Chet shook his head.

"You meatheads know the rules. No food of any kind around me, ever." He pointed at each one emphatically.

Finally Larry spoke up. "M-M-M … Mr. Plum." His teeth chattered. "None of us are eating a-a-anything."

Eugene raised his eyebrows. "That's it, your teeth chattering. Fucking stop it right now."

After driving another block in sweet silence, Eugene spotted a man and a woman walking hand in hand. "Isn't that cute, a vampire couple." He slowed the car to a crawl beside them. "Excuse me … Hi, isn't this Sterling Heights?"

The couple smiled and approached the car. The vamp lady's crooked smile exposed her left fang. "Yes, it is."

Eugene was confused. "I thought the housing market tanked here? Where are all the For Sale signs?"

The gentleman vamp spoke up. "Yes, yes it was bad, but it has really turned around lately. It's become a *safe haven* for our kind." He squeezed his vamp wife's hand.

Eugene stared at the couple. "Well, with all the dead vamps lying around, I am sure the market will tank again."

The couple looked confused. "Whaaa …"

Eugene lifted the crossbow from his lap and pointed it at the male vamp. Plugged him in the chest with a quick pull of the trigger and without hesitation plugged his wife before her husband hit the ground.

The three went into full panic. Behind them Jay laid on the Mustang's horn. "What the hell are you doing?!?!" Chet squealed, wild-eyed.

"I guess we are killing vampires, unless we see some houses for sale." At that moment there was big thud on the roof, and a roar. "Oh boy," Eugene said calmly. The vamp pounded on their roof. Eugene pulled out a gun like a hand cannon from inside his coat and pointed it at the Fusion's ceiling. He pulled the trigger and sent the vamp flying, screaming like Nancy Kerrigan, "Why, why, WHY!?" The hole in the roof was the size of a softball.

Larry and Chet labored to burrow through the backseat into the trunk. Lucky was stiff as a board, butt off the seat, knees locked out in terror paralysis. Only the whites of his eyes showed.

Eugene looked at him in the mirror. "You declined the rental insurance, didn't you?"

The vamps were coming in twos, threes and hordes, bolting out of their freshly painted front doors. Eugene moved his crossbow back and forth, left and right. "Don't anyone roll those windows up." The three were now plastered to the floor.

Eugene fired shot after shot at the oncoming vamps, receiving roars of anger and pain. In the head, in the chest, he rarely missed his target.

Behind them, a howling vampire posse was rocking Jay's Mustang, now onto its side, then all the way over, squishing the roof and a couple vamps. Jay came scrambling out of the pinched, broken windshield. He punched a big woman vamp in the boob, stumbled and bear-crawled a few yards down the street, regained his feet and sprinted for the Fusion, Bostonians slapping the pavement. Chet, Lucky and Larry screamed when he yanked open the back door. He slammed the door and ran around to the front, and jumped in.

Eugene hit the gas, dragging a huge vamp for a block before his superhuman grip gave out. After another three blocks at 80mph, the Fusion lurched, tires squealing onto the main drag that would take them back to the Deer-Horn. The wind whistled across the jagged metal hole in the roof.

Eugene clicked the crossbow safety and switched off the GoPros. "Thank God. Shouldn't be a lot of editing. Sometimes I'm up half the night."

"Holy ..." Chet checked the rear window one more time before finishing. " ... crap."

"Nothing holy in that neighborhood." Eugene wrinkled his nose. "But speaking of which, did a vamp pee on us?"

Larry the Li'l Cowpoke sheepishly shrunk down in his seat.

Lucky looked from Larry's lap to Eugene and back to Larry. "I told you, you need to get that prostate checked."

"David, you're right," said Larry, going with it. "That's the fourth time I've peed inappropriately. I'll set up an appointment tomorrow."

Chet scooched away from him. Eugene nodded knowingly at "Lucky" David. "I really can't over-emphasize the need for rental insurance."

"At least I still have a rental car to return," said David.

"Berry" Jay laid his head back on the seat, the breeze picking up strands of his mussed hair. He released a shuddering sigh. "I'm just happy to be alive."

"How many, how many of ... them, those vampires," Larry stammered. "How many did you get?"

Eugene maintained his icy cyborg-esque gaze on the street, always scanning for trouble. "It's not about numbers, Li'l Cowpoke." He turned on the radio and punched the presets until he found Country. Garth Brooks had friends in low places. Eugene wanted nothing more than to down a few shots of garlic-infused aquavit, sing along with some long-time buds to some good-time country, and forget the job that awaited him in Houston.

But of course he had slain his best bud in New Orleans at their shared 17th birthday party, mistakenly taking his friend's gay come-on for bloodthirst. That was when Eugene lost the last few friends who had loved him enough to stick it out through his years of intensive slayer training. He had desperately explained to everyone how the completion of 17 years on Earth could be a trigger for latent vampirism. It made no difference in his soon-to-be-former friends' eyes. That many of them were still 16 didn't help.

"An Evolved Vamp can turn ten humans in one feeding frenzy." Eugene pulled out his smartphone. He couldn't bear the thought of losing Amberly. That woman had never made a sound Eugene didn't love. "And slaying Evolved Vamps is nearly impossible. Unless society stops worshipping these bloodsuckers, humanity is doomed."

The Houston Four regarded each other, the weight of Eugene's words settling their frayed nerves. "So ..." David was the one to ask. "Does that mean you can't kill Vampire Vic?"

"Oh gosh no." Eugene drove with his knees and texted smoothly without delays, dead keys or a frozen cursor. He was so glad he had upgraded to a *smart*phone.

Miss you more. Home soon. Tell me you love me. No matter what.

"Killing evolved vamps is my specialty. And you're right to want Victor Thetherson dead."

His smartphone blinked.

Nothing can tear us apart. I love you Mr. 4man. Come home and let me show you just how much.

Eugene slid the smartphone back into his shirt pocket. That was all he needed to give him the strength to plan his next move on the charter back to Houston. Starting with getting the CWS to tell him Victor's soft spot. "He's as bad as they come. Badder."

"You're the man, Plum!" Chet came out of his seat to lean across David and shake Eugene's shoulders. "You kicked vampire *ass* back there!"

"You know I did," said Eugene.

Chet belted out a rebel yell. "Give me that crossbow, dude, I want to check that thing out!"

"No." Eugene looked at Jay. "Now that I know it's Vic you want dead, we're going to have to adjust the price."

Jay grimaced. "Alright. We'll give you a ten percent performance bonus for hitting a deadline of—"

"Shh." Eugene put a finger to his lips. "Not now. There are a lot of incidentals I need to consider. I'll have my secretary drop off a contract." He looked at the hole in the roof and the dangling side mirror as they pulled into the Deer-Horn. "One of you call me a cab to the airport. We're lucky the cops haven't pulled us over already."

"On it," said David.

"No, make that Uber. I like to negotiate my price." Eugene eyeballed Jay. Who was of course engrossed in his CrapBerry. "Tell them two hours, Lucky. In the meantime, we're all playing poker in Berry's room."

SHEDDING THE MAGIC CAPE

Looked like Victor picked the wrong time to upgrade to P90X2. Onscreen, Tony Horton dropped onto his hands, elbows bent and feet up in the air for quite some time before he allowed his legs to descend in controlled, powerful fashion, toes touching down to put him at the bottom of a push-up. Victor dropped onto his hands and something in his shoulder popped. He collapsed on his face.

"Oof."

Oh shitanski. I never would have said "oof" before the treatment.

Shitanski ...?

Victor realized that even his internal monologue had changed. Changed *back*, that is.

He impaled Tony with a baleful look before poking the TV's off button, gingerly rotating his shoulder, confirming that something wasn't right inside. Why the hell did Tony need to put that acrobatic crap in there? What was wrong with regular push-ups and pull-ups and curls? Was this a Cirque du Soleil training video?

Victor muttered as he abandoned the garage for the house, even as his hand stole to his gut, and then to his shoulder, assessing not pain but size. Unmistakably, his gut was bigger and his shoulders smaller, softer, depleted.

And that was exactly how he felt, the word that echoed in the background of what was an all-too-constant self-evaluation. *Depleted.* Physically, mentally, psychically. And so the meeting tomorrow had Victor worried.

The last place his hand strayed was to his collarbone, site of the implant, the fount of inhibition. Tony Horton wasn't to blame. He had told Victor to bring his swagger (and to modify the moves as necessary). But Victor's swagger was currently being neutered.

He hoped to slip past Barbara on his way to the bedroom. His ex-wife folded clothes on the front room couch. She put a whip-*snap* on a bath towel and spotted him.

"You're not sweaty ...?"

It seemed as if her every utterance lately stated Victor's problem in a nutshell.

You're sure you want a second helping?

Work was tough today, huh?

You're not going out tonight?

One week ago, Victor had "gone out" for the last time:

For old-time's sake, to reanimate his fading bloodlust, Victor visited the bar where it all started, the Opposite-Striped Zebra. He made a pass through the gothic ballroom, making eye contact with potential victims, before exiting out the alley door. There he waited like he had done many times before when Nikki would facilitate a meeting with one of her nervous, intrigued friends. He stood in shadow against the opposite wall in the recessed threshold to the gun shop, remembering the glimmering interlocked scent of the weapons and ammo on the other side of the door.

He couldn't "see" those smells the way he used to, as a vivid fusion of images and molecules. That was Tripp's treatment at work. Also because the gun shop had closed. The alley was different, too, repaved with speed bumps and planters, cluttered with benches and lit by a safety light on the upper corner of the Zebra.

Victor had been forced to zigzag to reach this hiding place, and in truth he wasn't all that hidden.

Can absolutely nothing stay the same? Can we not have some consistency in life? People must not have enough to do to have time to constantly fix things that aren't broken!

On schedule a woman emerged from the Zebra, announcing herself with a clank from the door's release bar and an inebriated laugh, staggering into the alleyway. Energy and bravery she left behind, reducing her laughter to a nervous giggle and making each step away from the Zebra's relative safety a little more hesitant.

Victor hesitated, too, legs seized up by many great reasons to stay hidden:

He was having lunch the next day with Don Chleber's secretary—she was clearly anticipating being bitten, so he had nothing to prove here.

This particular woman had looked a little anemic.

Tripp would be delighted with a pop-in visit to the blood bank, only a few blocks away.

His pale blue dress shirt was Barb's favorite, guaranteed ruined unless he was extremely fastidious in his bloodsucking.

And there was too much shit in the way.

That dwindling part of Victor—the one that was tired of the excuses keeping him off the prowl—forced his hand. "Good evening to you." Gunk coated his voice box and warbled his words, removing the sinister undertone.

The woman bleated in surprise as her head whipped in Victor's direction. She held her neck. "Oh no, I think I pulled something." She giggled and Victor either saw or remembered the keening note of fear that had always painted his stomach in tickling brush strokes and triggered a desire to overwhelm his victim.

"I'm sorry," said Victor.

Nikki's Obi-wan Kenobi–like apparition hovered

above the woman, eyes blazing in disapproval, dressed not in Jedi robes but a too-small tank top with plunging neckline dragged lower by a two-pound teardrop fishing weight. (Ask the meaning for that adornment and Nikki would lift her shirt to display a brightly-plumed lure hooking her belly button.) Victor imagined ghostly Nikki chastising him: *Stop apologizing and play the part!*

"I'm sorry you picked this night to wander into this alley." He paired his words with a threatening advance on the woman, kicking a bench out of the way. She squeaked in fear and delight, backpedaling with no intention or ability to escape, legs wobbly and hands reaching behind her for the wall a good ten feet away. Victor caught her before she crumpled to the clean concrete.

"Oh, please," the woman moaned.

Victor had become adept at widening his eyes and parting his lips with a little Elvis snarl, revealing the tips of his stiletto fangs.

"Oh, my," the woman purred, eyes fluttering.

At that crucial moment Victor thought about a pear and blue cheese salad, cool and crisp and drizzled with ginger sesame dressing. Maybe some Cajun chicken strips on top. It sounded better than blood.

He bit at the woman with less than full commitment, dragging his fangs across her throat, leaving two red tracks. "Ouch," she said, and Victor tried again, half-hearted, nuzzling and burrowing.

A table tennis professional had once taken young Victor aside at a pro-am tournament in Austin, impressed with his performance, wanting to impart his wisdom. "Visualize not the strike, but the result." It hadn't worked for Victor then, and it didn't work now. He chewed rather than bit, drawing blood that he licked up and slurped, one hand under his victim and the other pulling his shirt collar away from the mess.

The woman's yelping made bad harmony with the

shouts from two men racing toward them.

Victor raised his blood-smeared face, glistening and horrible in the well-lit alley, and snarled at the interlopers. "Leave us."

The first man, clearly there for the Geeks Who Drink trivia contest, slugged Victor in the eye. The second man, who Victor didn't get a good look at, half-carried half-dragged the woman back toward the Zebra. The first man kicked Victor in the chest, not with much force, and sprayed spit on him for good measure.

Standing before Barbara now, Victor's black eye throbbed. "I need to prepare for the meeting tomorrow."

Barbara surreptitiously evaluated his body as she rolled the towel. Victor tightened his butt cheeks and drew his belly button into his spine. "I thought it was just a formality."

"I want to knock EnerGreen's socks off with my construction management app."

That was his epiphany, to broaden his accounting system into a total-company system, one that would always be running in the background, automatically collecting mountains of data, then synthesizing it to tell management what had happened and to predict what was coming.

Victor believed he had something revolutionary. He was eager to test it on EnerGreen. "Larry was supposed to have a PowerPoint mock-up. I just realized I haven't seen anything from him yet."

He was kicking himself for not following up with Larry. After his failure at the Zebra, Victor had driven to Milford to spend two days with his mother. She was so happy to have him there, and took great care of him: cold packs for his eye, a whole stack of *Texas Monthly* and *Reader's Digest* magazines, home-cooked meals, foot rubs (those he had declined). She even had four bags of blood for him—she had convinced the

Jaycees during their blood drive to set aside a few donated ounces for her son, although Victor suspected it was mostly hers.

The 18 days since his treatment began had flown by; the serious depletion of his body and mind seemed to have occurred overnight, leaving Victor panicked over the meeting tomorrow, and not sweaty.

"Amberly is bringing over a friend." Barbara stopped folding clothes. "She was hoping you'd be available."

"I need to spend time on my presentation."

Barbara approached, a slow swing in her hips. She stroked his chest, enjoying the silky feel of the black soccer shirt she had given him. "Before or after?"

Victor was puzzled.

"Do you want it before, to relax you so you can focus on your presentation?" She pinched and twisted his nipple. "Or after, as a reward?"

"I have too much on my mind right now."

Barbara put his hand on her breast. "That sounds like a *before*." Both her hands went to his crotch.

Victor pulled his hips away although he kept his hand on her chest. "I don't want to get beat up right now."

Barbara unbuttoned her shirt like a magician yanking the cloth off a fully-set table, leaving Victor's hand in place. "With your treatment, maybe we can be gentler." She dug her fingernails into the crook of his elbow. "Although I have to admit ... I do like causing you some pain." They both watched her drag pink stripes down his forearm. Victor noticed that it wasn't as veiny as it used to be.

She put wet lips on her nail tracks. "That's not very nice of me, is it?"

Victor's libido rose. "I don't think we should risk it."

"Good." Barbara bit him. Her straight, matched teeth left a lemon-shaped wound.

"Aggh!" He had an urge to cuff her. "Dammit, Barb.

I'm not healing like I was."

"Scars are sexy." She gathered two handfuls of his silky shirt and drove him toward the bedroom. "Visible or otherwise."

"What time is Amberly coming?" Victor worried.

Barbara had her slacks unbuttoned, creating space for her own hand to operate. "You should be more worried about what time I'm coming."

"I just don't want Amberly feeling uncomfortable about being here." He couldn't take his eyes off Barbara's hand, and the workings of the sinews of her forearm.

"Uncomfortable is great." Barbara was enjoying herself. "I don't want her moving back in. Now take my pants off."

Victor kicked the bedroom door shut and obliged.

Sitting across the dining room table from Amberly and her friend, Victor fretted they had heard his screams. "I told your mother my shoulder was hurting from P90X. So she starts giving me a 'treatment.' Let me tell you, your mother is not a licensed physical therapist. Just about killed me. I apologize if my cries of pain were distracting."

"My dad loves P90X," said Kimberly Kieler. Darla's daughter. The two had become fast friends since the pre-Bizco merger picnic. "He never worked out until he divorced my mom. Now he's a fitness maniac."

"Maybe he never felt like your mother supported him," said Barbara. Amberly hadn't told her who she was bringing. From Barb's first reaction as they emerged from the bedroom to find the two girls sitting on the floor of the empty dining room listening to music on Amberly's iPhone and watching a movie trailer on Kimberly's, to the tone of her voice now, Victor was embarrassed. "A lot of women don't understand a wife's duty to her husband."

"He eats squash now, too." Kimberly used her fork

to roll a cooked baby carrot from one side of her plate to the other. "Mom said he used to hate squash."

"It's all in how you prepare it," said Barbara.

"Well, anyway," said Victor. "Sorry about the moaning."

"I'm willing to bet your shoulder feels better now," said Barbara, thick with innuendo.

Amberly directed Kimberly's attention to her smartphone below the table. "God he's so funny," said Kimberly.

"Who are you texting?" said Barbara.

"No one," said Amberly.

"Are you even paying attention to this conversation?" said Barbara.

"Oh, hell yeah," said Amberly.

"Amber," Victor chastised.

Kimberly indicated Victor's black eye by touching her own. "Did you get that from P90X, too? Or the treatment?" She quickly took a bite and exchanged an amused glance with Amberly.

"Mr. Victor was sucker-punched." Barbara sipped coconut water and rubbed behind Victor's knee with the top of her foot. "With Nikki gone, maybe I need to accompany you on your 'dates.'"

"I don't think I'll be 'dating' anymore."

"Dad's taking the cure," Amberly reported. "This time it's working."

"Mom told me." Kimberly slipped Porkie the Morkie a fat-rimmed bite of steak. "She's very happy to have you back at work."

Barbara stared at him. "I thought you were in separate departments now."

"We are."

"Separate buildings," said Barbara.

"Floors," Victor corrected. "You can probably imagine having The Vampire back at work is a topic of discussion."

Barbara passed around the tinfoil pouch of grilled

vegetables and attempted nonchalance. "Have you talked to Darla since you've been back?"

Victor worked hard not to lie. "My cost management model will replace our accounting system. So I need to run it by her."

Barbara could hear the tap dancing. "Is that all you talked to her about?"

Victor cut another strip of flank steak and held it aloft, looking for takers.

"You overcooked it," said Amberly.

"Just trying to transition to your human world," said Victor.

Kimberly tapped Amberly's plate with her fork. "Do you ever wonder whether you're going to turn?"

"That would be *so* legit. Can you believe assistant principal Moreno is a vampire? He just came out," she told her parents, "by biting our drama teacher right before he fired him. Everyone was cheering. Dad, do you have any extra blood lying around? I'll use it like steak sauce."

"That's not the life we want for you," said Victor. He acknowledged Barbara's ongoing stare. She was patient. "I wanted to check on my old staff."

"Oh," said Barbara. "How are they?"

"Great." Victor pushed back from the table. "I better get busy on my presentation. It was good to have you here, Kimberly. Say hi to your mom for me."

"She says hi."

Victor wished she hadn't said it like Darla was in love with him.

Entering the conference room at EnerGreen's temporary offices in southeast Houston, Victor's thoughts raced, yet nothing came to mind. He had finished his presentation to the board at 2:30 a.m. and then tossed and turned another hour, stewing about Larry leaving him hanging on such a high-profile project.

A tar pit sat behind his eyes. He had felt physically degraded since getting out of bed, as if key body parts had overnight lost form and function, lungs shrunken and feet reluctant, back muscles like linguine, and brain cells liquefied to a sticky morass, a permanent speed trap for the thoughts racing for his mouth.

He wanted to write it off to a temporary impairment from the treatment chemicals coursing through his body. But deep down, Victor was afraid he had forgotten that this is what his old life was like before vampirism.

For sure Tripp's treatment had eaten his aura. Don Chleber noticed as soon as he spotted him.

Chleber was a jowly man with a melodious voice. "You don't look ready for this."

"Late night prepping." Victor forced a wink. "Maybe you should be the one with the, uh, the fangs, for this, the presentation."

That line might have given Chleber reassurance if it weren't for the stuttering and slight blush. Chleber glanced at EnerGreen's CEO, John Anderson, who was wild-eyeing them from under bushy eyebrows while rocking on his cowboy boots and listening to one of the EnerGreen board members. "I'll try to keep things moving," said Chleber. "Maybe we don't need your presentation? What the hell did you say you wanted to show everyone?"

They were joined by Jay Hansen. The Bizco chief financial officer had been gleefully appraising Victor all along, and continued to do so now. "You look like you've had a rough few weeks since you were released from solitary."

"It was a research lab."

"We're all familiar." Hansen's full-cut white dress shirt was extra-crisp today, in frozen billow, no material touching his body from neck to waist. "Your color is poor. For a vampire."

Barbara had made the same comment as he kissed

her goodbye. The light auburn hair on the backs of his hands no longer stood out against his flesh, and pink had returned to his cheeks.

"Bend down." Hansen wanted to see the top of his head. "Are you losing your hair again? I think so."

Chleber scowled at him. "Since when does CFO stand for chief fashion officer? Can we make a quick decision whether we need Victor's presentation? Maybe we save that for a future strategy meeting with their senior management."

"Don." On the other side of the table Bizco chief Daniel Fasset beckoned, looking to introduce his strategic development head to one of EnerGreen's board members.

Hansen beamed with his eyes. "We definitely need to put our vampire in the spotlight."

Chleber appeared tortured.

"I'll be fine," said Victor.

"Go get some coffee," said Chleber.

On his way to the refreshment table Victor was met by Carl Yorbo, EnerGreen board president. As they made the acquaintance, a queue formed; Yorbo's peers were eager to meet the vampire. One after the next until Victor was in a full cold flop sweat. And then Fasset asked everyone to take their seats and Victor was steered to sit between the only women on the respective boards. No time for coffee. Caffeine wouldn't have helped, anyway.

"Thank you all for being here." Fasset the Bizco CEO donned reading glasses to check his notes, then removed them. "Thank you especially to the EnerGreen board for giving us the opportunity to tell you about our plans for this project. Another chance for us to get all jazzed up again." Fasset was a trained speaker, pausing to smile at Anderson here and raise an eyebrow at Yorbo there. "We've spent a lot of time together over the past few months. I think it's fair to say we've become very comfortable with each other.

Because we have a shared vision for this project.

"But ..." Fasset leaned forward, tomahawk hand poised over the table. "You need to know that we don't see this meeting as a rubber stamp. Not at all." When no one challenged that position he withdrew the tomahawk, converted his sword back to a plowshare, tidying his papers. "Okay, yes ... we're already hiring sub-contractors." This got a laugh. "And yes we do believe the Bizco name will be on the contract to build your campus. But we are not resting on our laurels. That won't happen at any point during the project. You know us well enough now to expect exactly that kind of nonstop commitment. Today ..." Fasset glowed like a proud father at the team he had brought to the table. "We want you to get to know us a little better."

He looked at Chleber, who stood.

His mouth opened, but another voice sounded. "I see a great danger in how we've gotten to know each other so well." Yorbo the EnerGreen board president sat back in the black padded office chair and pulled out a joint. Lit it and took a double drag. Talked with smoke curling out his nose. "I'd rather ink this deal with someone with a lot to prove."

Fasset patted the table. "Carl, that's beautiful. You really couldn't describe this company any better."

Yorbo was bald but for a trimmed fringe, and given to frowning down his nose as he talked, eyes just shy of crossed. He took another hit. "I'm nervous by nature. I get real agitated at moments like this. Marijuana helps me see things clearly. A few of you had a drink before you walked into this room. I know you did." Yorbo studied his joint. "And yes, booze makes you confident. But it also makes you reckless. Today we need to see all the possibilities; but we also need to see our limitations." He held the joint in his lips as he fished in his sport jacket for a folded lambskin packet, which he tossed to the table, in front of the woman to Victor's right. The top fold languidly slid open revealing a row of bent white sticks. "Take one down and pass it around."

Mallry Smitts was her name. Victor had seen her picture in Bizco's quarterly financial filing; very alert, outdoor skin and smell. Mallry wasn't afraid of the packet. She brought the silly cigs in for a close inspection then laid them before Victor. "I'm not sure ganja would mix well with that shot of bourbon I had."

While everyone laughed with Mallry, Victor slid the packet to the woman on his left. He didn't need to be any more in tune with his limitations.

"Here's to New Energy," said Chleber. "Vic, you don't have to inhale."

Victor couldn't come up with a good retort, so he just chuckled.

John Anderson, the bushy bearded EnerGreen CEO, pointed at the packet. "When your boss gives you the green light to smoke a doobie, you do it."

All eyes went to Victor. Half-formed responses hurried toward the front of his mind. One or two might have had the makings of a good one, if not for the tar pit trap. "I had a drink, too," he blurted out.

The squeak of behinds shifting in their seats could be heard. Chleber looked ill.

The EnerGreen board member to his left cleared her throat and took a joint. "I'm always up for something new." She left her seat and headed to Yorbo for a light. "New for a board meeting, anyway."

While facilitating his compatriot's maiden board meeting toke, Yorbo gave Anderson the high sign. The EnerGreen CEO sent a short text and pocketed his smart phone. He nodded at Chleber. "You referred to us as 'new energy.'" He shrugged. "Maybe. Certainly we're not 'alternative' energy. And we're not 'green' energy, despite our name. We're Big Energy. Which means everyone in this joint venture comes from a place of conflict. From governments to activists to property owners ... nobody likes us. Nobody likes to admit their dependence on us. But they are. And dependence breeds contempt."

"That's the key problem with our society today," Fasset waxed political. "Curing that dynamic would make all the difference for this country."

Anderson smiled. "Daniel, we're the sort of people who thrive on contempt." This was met with nods from the EnerGreen execs in attendance, and smiles from their board members, who came from everywhere but Big Energy. "We'd like to create that same dynamic with you."

Fasset laughed. "Good luck with that. Ever since you invited us to compete for your business, our entire company has been walking around like they just met the man or woman of their dreams."

The conference room door opened. "We can fix that," said Yorbo.

Only Jay Hansen would recognize the first man through the door, Mitchell Harms, Playco Construction CFO. After him a short parade of Playco execs and board members.

And then someone Victor recognized immediately, 30 years since their last meeting. No great feat, because the vampire hadn't aged a day.

Anderson looked around the table, daring Bizco to complain. "Welcome gentlemen, and lady. Find a seat." Yorbo's lambskin packet had made its way to him, emptied. "We're out of pot. But by all means grab a donut."

With a clap that fell short of startling, just a little pop, the Bizco CEO tried to claim the floor. "We're always glad to network with our competitors. Malcolm," Fasset greeted a thick-necked thick-haired barrel of a man, his peer at Playco. "I have to apologize. I didn't even think of you for one of our sub jobs."

Malcolm's laugh was easy if not infectious. "Quite all right, Danny. You're not on our sub list, either. But you can start lobbying as soon as we're done here."

The dumpy, homely vampire brought the same intensity as when he had evaluated candidates for Arthur Andersen & Co. in the armory on the University of Houston campus. He was white as a sheet and gushing malevolence, with great big fangs that couldn't be contained with closed lips. Now he evaluated each person seated at the table.

Looking for the Bizco vampire, Victor realized. He kept his mouth shut.

Fasset searched Yorbo and Anderson for an explanation for Playco's arrival. "What do we have here?"

"Discomfort." Yorbo drew on his joint like he was aiming it at a specific neuron. He looked at Chleber. "I believe you were poised to say something."

Don Chleber enjoyed the scrum, and had won enough times to expect to triumph. Unfortunately, he had also grown accustomed to an early passing of the baton to his vampire. "I was going to open my mouth just long enough to ask Victor to make his presentation." He nodded at his charge, making no attempt to force a smile. "Vic?"

Chleber was counting on him to save the day. Wooden and mechanical, Victor walked to the white screen. He nodded to Mallry, who uncapped the projector, revealing the title slide, "Bizco's Cost Management System for EnerGreen." He looked at the screen with his back to the audience.

"You may not know, my background is Accounting. Unfortunately for everyone here, apples don't roll far from the tree. And so I have an Accounting presentation." Hoping to hear groans, even manufactured ones, he received a cough and some squirming. Victor plowed ahead. "Just kidding. That was just to set the bar low."

He had taken two years of college French. Before he and Barbara traveled to Paris ten years ago, Victor had brushed up, excited to use his skills and impress his wife. But his accent and pronunciation were so poor, the French people thought he was speaking English, and endeavored to translate his words back into French. Barbara eventually took over the communicator role.

It was obvious no one in the room understood he was trying to be funny. So he simply described his brainstorm. "We are proposing for EnerGreen a revolutionary construction management system. The unique feature is how our system collects and utilizes cost information."

He clicked to the next slide. Larry was a wizard with PowerPoint. He would have employed moving graphics and pithy, powerful phrases. Instead the audience was seeing a few colorless flowcharting symbols, boxes with arrows pointing to other boxes. Victor cursed him yet again.

"We'll load it on every workstation in our company and yours. Not just the accountants. Everyone. Every employee collects different information, for different needs. We want all of it. The really exciting thing about this program is that there's very little intentional input required. The program collects information by itself, interfacing with internal and external sources. Big Data, that's the buzzword. Our system collects and uses Big Data to establish correlations and make predictions—"

"Now I understand why I was asked here."

Victor closed his mouth and turned to see Playco's vampire striding toward him, giving Mallry the kill sign. Mallry fumbled with the projector cap, couldn't get it to stay over the lens, ran her hands frantically around the machine, couldn't find the off switch, dove under the table and ripped the power cord out of the socket.

"We were extremely fortunate to recruit X Anthony to our team," the vampire was introduced by Malcolm the Playco CEO. "X is a principal for Metafist, which *Fortune* magazine just ranked the world's fastest-growing consulting firm."

The assembled murmured appreciatively, suitably impressed.

"X has agreed to dedicate himself full-time to the EnerGreen project."

The Playco vamp made brief eye contact with Jay, glanced at Victor and checked again with Jay, receiving confirmation. Victor was made. The pear-shaped, pin-headed vampire squinted up at him with eyes on a close tether to the bridge of a hook nose. "Are you ...?" He snapped his fingers.

"Victor." He saw recognition grow in the vampire's eyes. "Thetherson."

X studied him, a study in confusion, his frown curling to a perplexed smirk.

Victor easily read the vampire's thoughts. *What happened to you? How the hell did the bold up-and-comer I interviewed become this sad sack loser?*

X turned away dismissively to address the rapt audience. "Are you here to listen to *accounting* language? There is nothing worse than an accountant who doesn't know how to talk *earnings*."

Victor pointed at the empty screen. "That, this model, it's meant to save money, which drives earnings—"

"Quiet." X made it clear he would brook no more interruptions. "Our entity ..." He nodded to CFO Harms.

"Playco," Harms chipped in such that X barely missed a beat.

" ... understands your world. With this," he tapped one of his fangs, "or without it." The syntax required to avoid lip-piercing consonants made him sound like a Hungarian imitating a New Yorker. "Yet with this," X again fingered a fang, "you gain connections. I *ex*cel at creating connections."

Victor knew he was in trouble. The EnerGreen contract, his position with Chleber, his future at Bizco … in X's vernacular, he was under an *existential* attack. Victor needed to be in full counterattack, anticipating where the vampire was heading, and preparing Bizco's (and his) defense. But the treatment had left him with scrambled thoughts and tunnel vision; Victor stared dumbly at the greasy crown of X's head.

"We own a tax loss credit that is set to ex—" X chose a safer word. "End. Thanks to connections, we can donate it to EnerGreen. That is instant earnings." He nodded to Harms.

"One-point-two billion," the Playco CFO quantified the carrot.

A current of excitement coursed through the room. The Playco contingent fairly strained to get started building EnerGreen's campus.

X jabbed a finger at Victor, would have stabbed him with a pointed yellow fingernail if Victor hadn't been in slow retreat. "We do not waste energy on accounting toys. Hire us, and we get to work."

Fasset and Chleber were on their feet, each eager to respond. "We'll have our tax experts see if we have anything similar to that tax credit that we can contribute," said Fasset.

X laughed, a wet gurgle. "This transaction requires an act of Congress. Which requires *connections*. You will not get it."

"Regardless." Chleber made for the head of the table, and X. "We all know that in this business, special favors come and go. The quality EnerGreen will receive from what Bizco intends to build will pay dividends forever."

Behind Chleber's relaxed smile and velvety voice, Victor smelled the high-pitched keening of fear, saw it as an elongated note from a musical score, high above the treble clef. He was drawn to it, still, even with the predatory nature of his vampirism inhibited and receding.

One didn't have to be a vampire; everyone in the room heard Bizco's desperation.

"Fifteen years from now," Chleber addressed X, "your tax credit will be less than a memory. But our campus will continue to be a source of pride. And savings."

Now Chleber seemed to get a clearer picture of the ruthlessness in X's eyes. He took a half-step back and addressed Yorbo. "Carl, I've followed your career. I know you're interested in what Playco is handing you. Rightfully so. I also know you appreciate what Bizco has to offer. All the skills and proven history that set us apart. With your permission I'd like to table this discussion for a few more days. Allow us to put our heads back together and sharpen our pencil one more time—"

"You want to go *b*ack and *p*lay with your toys?" X spat, violating his linguistic prohibitions. "Did I hear you right?" Blood oozed from punctures in his bottom lip.

"Forget that junk." Fasset waved at the darkened projector screen and the ghost of Victor's presentation, now haunting Bizco. "We mean to—"

"*P*layco," the powerbroker vampire cut him off, "*m*eans *b*usiness!" X advanced on Chleber, tongue flicking across his wounded lips, a growl revving in his chest, eyes molten yellow.

Victor knew he was no match for the Playco vampire. But Chleber put so much faith in him; and Victor had come to care for his boss. He intercepted X, took two handfuls of his high-thread-count dress shirt and drove him back. "If you want to intimidate someone," Victor mustered every residual bit of bravado, "try me."

X held up his hands and turned away. But one hand stayed behind and grabbed Victor by a fang.

"Hey, awgk, klet go ..." Victor was towed forward, no different than how he had seen the occasional unruly student led out of the classroom by the ear by Mrs. Konrath, Milford's fourth-grade teacher.

"The *b*ullshit you're trying to *p*ass off as *b*usiness is an insult to this *b*oard!" X was over the top on verboten letters now, flaying his lip, splattering the nearest execs in blood. "You seem to think you are *p*resenting to a joint con*fab* of the En*v*ironmental De*f*ense *F*und and *P*ETA! This is the oil industry! We are here to *b*uild this campus! We are here to *p*ower this country!"

Pain bloomed from Victor's mouth and enveloped his brain and gut, leaving him with one maddening, senseless sight, the top of X's head, black strands grayed with grease, attached at the crown like the quills of a mostly-plucked duck, anchored deep in the spongy meat.

And one thought.

Bite him!

Too late. X applied leverage beyond what Victor thought possible, lighting up his entire being with a fireworks celebration of world-ending pain. Then his fang snapped at the gum line. Victor collapsed writhing to the floor. He couldn't contain his moans and then couldn't stop them from becoming cries, gut-wrenching piteous bawling.

For everything he had tasted and lost; for the soul-releasing laugh-out-loud power and respect and energy and purpose that he had possessed so briefly and lost so abruptly; Victor couldn't help but cry.

X the vampire stood over him for a few moments of glory before flipping the broken fang to the conference room table. The skinny tooth bounced once, twice and then ricocheted harmlessly off Mallry's throat. She yelped nonetheless.

Jay Hansen leaned back in his chair, fingers laced behind his head, starched white shirt bending unnaturally to give him an hourglass torso. He nodded at Mallry and the fang that had come to rest in the middle of the table. "What great symbolism."

FREE FALLING

On the Strategic Development side of the 49th floor, winter sunlight beamed horizontally past desks, chairs and employees, through the elevator tube, out the other side, touching nothing and leaving everyone blind and aimless. Victor looked up from his window desk to see Chleber standing over him, hands in his pockets.

"Rough meeting yesterday, bub." Chleber unpocketed a hand to rest it on Victor's shoulder. "I don't blame you a bit. If I lost one of my two best friends, I'd be a little distraught, too."

Victor's eyes darted to the next desk. Larry had his back to him. And so it had been since Victor brought him up from Accounting. One arm was tucked in his lap, phone wedged between the other shoulder and jaw while that hand clicked away with his mouse.

After a miserable night at home, Victor had come to the office with the desperate urge to unburden himself. He wanted that confidant to be Larry. Their lifelong connection suddenly warmed his chest. They came from the same small town, and now all these years later in the big city they worked closely together. That was rare and something to treasure, despite all the rough spots that had tried to come between them.

Especially because of the rough spots. At some point, Larry's decapitation of the Thetherson family dog would be a story they could tell together, and have the crowd rolling. Reaching out in a moment of vulnerability might be all Victor needed to have a breakthrough with his fellow Milfordite.

Larry had been on the phone when Victor arrived and had remained that way for the past 45 minutes.

Chleber bent forward, staring at Victor's mouth. "It'll grow back, I suppose."

Victor shook his head, and raised his lip. "Not yet."

Chleber gaped at the lack of a mate for Victor's single spindly fang. "Hum-Jesus, will you look at that."

All heads (but Larry's) turned, only to be frustrated by Victor's hand covering his mouth. He talked as he bent to open a drawer, buying time as if he were 19 again and taking the long route to class to give the inflamed red of his squeezed zits time to mellow. "I printed out a *pro forma* run of my costing model. Hardcopy like you like." As if his broken fang might bud out from the current jagged ridge inside the swollen weeping gum in the time it took to pull out a thin sheaf of papers. "It shows the adjustment of the initial conditions and a re-forecast of the project cost, based on assessment of the auto-collected data." Victor clamped his mouth shut as he straightened and handed the output to his boss.

Chleber didn't take it. "I don't think we'll be using it, Vic."

"We have to think bigger than EnerGreen." That was what the floor was waiting for—not the words from his mouth, but the window on his teeth. Victor let it happen, let them see the carnage. He cared only about his boss's opinion. "My system is a great marketing tool. It's a huge competitive edge, Don. We need to run this software to prove the value internally and to our customers."

"Hansen can make that call."

Reflexively Victor's face screwed up in disgust. "Trust me," he said quietly. "The answer will be 'no' simply because it's coming from me. This isn't a decision we leave to Jay."

Chleber's face only looked avuncular when he was excited. Otherwise, now, his eyes were unapproachably gray. Victor took a breath and finally asked the question. "Do we still have the EnerGreen contract?"

Chleber nodded.

"Thank God." Rumors were sweeping the office that Playco had won the contract.

This was enough to capture Larry's attention; he hung up the phone and turned toward them, making busy dusting and straightening the pictures of his hunting dogs that had replaced the mini-taxidermy mounts, never unpacked, in a box under his desk.

"Sort of," said Chleber. "After you were helped out to your car, the EnerGreen board asked everyone to leave the room. They were about to vote us out. Jay," Chleber hated the taste. "He saved our bacon. He played off Yorbo's speech about keeping everyone uncomfortable and recommended that Bizco and Playco form a joint venture. A JV to service the EnerGreen JV. The board voted for it on the spot. Everybody from Bizco and Playco was stunned and pissed as hell. Me included."

"Everyone except Jay."

"He did what had to be done." Chleber wasn't pleased to be forced to lead a cheer for Hansen. "He kept us in the game." He looked claustrophobic in Victor's virtual office. "I won't have a role in the JV. There's other business to be won. I know you're excited to contribute to the EnerGreen project—"

"I am. I'll make periodic site visits." Victor talked even as his growing gut eclipsed a swath of his lower peripheral vision, even as he knew he was no longer wanted by EnerGreen, who must have felt as though they were at the business end of a bait-and-switch. "Cameo appearances, while we focus on new business." Even as he recognized that Chleber was in the midst of saying goodbye, still Victor babbled. "I'll perfect my model on my own time—"

"You're back in Accounting."

"Don … I can't report to Jay."

"You won't be." Chleber's tone made this less than reassuring. "Now's as good a time as any. Come with me." He stood to escort Victor off the floor.

Head down, Victor felt everyone's eyes on him as he led Chleber into the showcase elevator.

The transparent doors whisked closed. Chleber's team must have thought it was one-way glass for the way they stared. Chleber pushed 14. "I remember when you first came to work for me," he waxed nostalgic, as if it were years and not months ago. "We really took the market by storm for a while there. Amazing how fast times change."

The doors whispered open on the 14th floor. When accountants out of the corners of their eyes see the elevator arriving from higher floors, they take notice. When they saw who it was, they all left their chairs. Dandelion-head Kirby, Quinten beaming and bouncing, Casey watching everyone for the signal to rush their old boss, beautiful bland Monique, and four other accountants from the former Westchase team.

And Florence, for Victor a goddess molded from golden energy to approximate the human form, her skin the very essence of her, the stuff she was made of inside and out and therefore holy. Florence rose and turned her full attention on him, putting a giddy tickle in his throat and giving everyone else the shivers from the dry clicking of her joints.

Tessa stayed in her chair. Her protest at Victor's arrival was plain. "I really don't think it's appropriate," she grumbled to whoever chose to listen, "to honor someone who killed an employee. Maybe it's just me."

And it was. When Darla saw Victor, her face rounded into a smile; when her eyes moved to the man sitting across from her, her features readjusted into a collection of downward-pointing lines.

"Mr. Don Chleber," Kirby acknowledged the exec with a worshipful lilt. "How are things going in the wonderful world of M&A? Oh wait, you don't call it Mergers and Acquisitions anymore, do you? Strategic Business, right? Which I think is a perfect name, because why would you acquire a business if it wasn't good strategy?"

Chleber winked at Kirby in passing.

"Although now that I mention it," Kirby was now talking to Chleber's back, "the word 'strategic' kind of goes without saying, doesn't it?"

"Business," Casey tried out the revised department name. "I like it."

"Hope we're not interrupting," Chleber greeted Darla.

"Don, Victor." She nodded at her visitor. "I told X you might be stopping by."

The Playco vampire stood. His flexed his hands, otherwise stubby fingers elongated by curved discolored nails. "I waited eagerly." X had wolf-yellow eyes for Victor. "Thetherson. Such a shock that you are here."

His time as a full-fledged vampire was recent enough that Victor recognized the deficiency in how his human mind was reacting. His brain cranked out an onslaught of information, every possible response to what X *had* said piling into candidate answers to what he had anticipated X *might* say, in suggestive fragments like from the note cards of an expert public speaker, except that the note cards were shuffled and then sloppily arrayed before him, all in competition for his tongue's selection.

As an introspective and painfully honest man, Victor admitted that fear was to blame. Fear of the vampire, of course, that was only common sense. And fear of failing to impress his superior—he had been conditioned to break into a flop sweat at that possibility. But long before vampires, away from the boss and among his peers, Victor had always felt this same terror: the fear of saying something stupid.

But who's to say which came first, the fear or the thought-jumble? Who wouldn't be afraid of appearing the fool with that scrambled information overload to contend with?

Hand over his mouth Victor spoke. "You haven't changed, even though it has been, what, 25 years?"

Oh? That's how Vampire Vic would have responded, if at all. Where was that realization two seconds ago? It was too late for it now.

X's eyes narrowed. He stepped closer and brought a couple other senses to bear. "Are you saying I gained your acquaintance a quarter century ago?"

Victor was confused. Where did X's recognition come from if not the job fair interview at the University of Houston armory?

Victor was distracted by Florence. She perched on the corner of Kirby's desk, swiveled her hips to cross her long 95%-lean legs, and parted her blouse to give her fingers room to play at her necklace.

X noticed as well. His eyes glowed brighter as he peered into Victor. "Ah, yes. The hiring auction at UH. I wanted you with us at Arthur. You turned X down." The vampire drifted left, tracing the initial arc in circling Victor, cutting him off from Chleber while moving closer to Florence. "And now I get you ..." He cast a jaundiced eye on his surroundings. "Here?"

"You can take the accountant out of Accounting," came Victor's least-favorite voice. "But you can't make him stop counting those beans." Somehow even with the open floor plan Jay Hansen had escaped notice, startling some of Darla's staff as he seemingly materialized at a nearby desk, only becoming visible when he looked up from his BlackBerry.

"Well, what do you know," Kirby enthused. "Victor, 'This is Your Life'!" He turned to Chleber. "Do you remember that show? I don't remember exactly how it

went, or even whether that was the exact name of it
…"

Hansen gave wide berth to X in order to approach
Victor. "Me? This is exactly where I would have
expected to find Victor."

Chleber laid his hand on Victor's back, heavy with
responsibility for the moment; this loss to Jay Hansen.
It was also the leverage the big exec needed to propel
himself to the elevator. "Pleasure working with you,
Vic. I'd drone on about how X and the EnerGreen
project team fit into the Accounting world, but I'll
leave that to Jay, our *chief* bean counter."

"That's the difference I was alluding to." Hansen
was immensely satisfied with the moment and
reluctant to let Chleber leave it. "There are bean
counters and then there are businessmen. Accounting
done right is truly about business, right?" Hansen
never truly asked questions, but in this case he may
have been looking for X's confirmation.

The dumpy vampire was busy introducing himself
to Florence.

"But Victor is about the beans." Jay's BlackBerry
pleaded for his attention and compelled his thumb to
open a freshly-arrived email, even as his eyes fretted
over X fingering Florence's earrings.

"You gotta be kidding." Chleber chuckled at
Hansen's communication device, his parting shot. "A
BlackBerry? I feel like I'm in the land that time
forgot."

"I loved that show, too," said Kirby.

"It's Accounting's favorite communication device."
Darla held up her own, no shame in being part of
Accounting, just a little embarrassed by their lame
nature.

All across the floor, employees bowed their heads
and held their BlackBerries aloft. Florence reached
into her bra, rummaging. Quinten's eyes bulged.
Florence produced her BlackBerry.

"Florence," said Quinten. "Don't you know that can give you cancer in your, your, uh ..."

"Please don't say it, Quinten," Tessa said from her desk.

"Milk," said Casey.

X the Playco vampire tipped his head back and laughed. The sound reverberated in his stubby neck like a middle-register organ chord. The accountants shuddered at his protruding fangs. He was behind Victor now.

Kirby's blood wasn't curdled. He was puzzling. "Am I thinking of the cartoon, or the one with Will Farrell?"

The chime of the elevator arriving to take Chleber away was a mournful sound for Victor.

Hansen took it in. "Did I mention you'll be reporting to X now?"

Darla was positively gleeful in her reserved, weary way. "I'm glad you'll be sitting on our floor."

The injustice of it all spurred Victor to cry out. Instead he opened his mouth and pointed at his broken tooth. "He did this."

"Oh, no," Darla moaned and came around her desk. She was joined by her staff including Tessa, crowding up to Victor to get a good gander.

"My old tabby cat just lost his tooth, too," Kirby purred. "We call him the saber-tooth tiger. Saber-*tooth*, not -*teeth*."

"Did you bump heads?" Casey wondered, eyeing Victor and X's relative height, deciding it was just about right for the scenario.

"It was intentional."

"So *what?*" Hansen's voice cracked. "You once threatened to kill me."

Victor shook his head.

"Sure you did." Hansen's intensity caused the huddle around Victor to expand but not quite break. "You made it clear that if I crossed you, you were going to kill me. The same way you killed Nikki."

"That was an accident."

"That was no accident," said Tessa. "You can't use that excuse."

"The point is, normal rules don't apply to vampires," said Hansen. "They can do—"

"I disagree," said Tessa.

Hansen had enough of being interrupted and contradicted. "You can't disagree that vampires get away with things we can't. That's simply a fact. But like most things, there's symmetry, right? It's physics." He was master of the floor except for the tic at his lip every time his eyes flickered to X looming behind Victor. "For every action there's an equal and opposite reaction."

X gripped the back of Victor's neck. His voice was guttural and damp. "It's not always equal."

Darla removed X's hand. "Do we need to make Victor's first day back so unpleasant?" She took his arm. Victor felt her trembling as she tried to inject levity. "I've never had to do it, but I imagine returning to Accounting can be a little traumatizing."

"I can't even imagine," said Quinten.

"I'd like to leave this place," said Casey, "for three days. Just to see what it would feel like to come back."

"Jay." Tessa was visibly agitated, outrage creating courage. "If you're truly upset with the special treatment vampires get, why are you compounding it by hiring another vampire?"

X fixed his gaze on Tessa and moved toward her. "What is your name?"

"Tessa."

"Tessa." X tried it out, lovingly, seemingly glad to have a name he could safely work with. "Glad you asked. You all need to understand why X is here." He pressed his hands to his chest. "To assist with EnerGreen, surely. I will ensure you nail it and look good to Jay and the execs."

The accountants stood a little straighter and

imagined a positive reflection in Jay's eyes.

"You and Jay are each correct," X told Tessa. "There *are* two standards. And that is unacce—" He protected his lip just in time. "It is wrong. We," he tapped a fang to indicate the population he referred to, "we are eager to assume a greater role in society. And so we need to show how we can work with you. To *add*, not take away."

He turned to Victor. "Not Thetherson. You all need to understand his history. Who his ancestor is."

Of course. X had seen and bought into all the sensational, defamatory blog traffic about him. "Not Morbius again?" Victor anticipated him. "It's all stories on the Internet," he assured his coworkers. "From crackpot slayers." Blood up, he wheeled on X. "I suppose you're getting that, that *shit*, from that blogger, what's his name, Pubic-coca-cola."

"I do *follow Publicola*," said X. "And what he has to say about *Morbius*." Two beads of blood sprang to his lips, reinforcing his conviction. "Wickedest in history. The reason why centuries ago there was a genocide of the *vampires*." He went for it repeatedly, the self-inflicted pain both fed by and feeding the passion in his eyes. "We can't allow that slaughter to occur again. *For* our sake." X again pressed his hands to his chest, representative for the vampire community. Then he spread his hands to take into account the human race. "And *for* yours."

"I brought X on board because he's a successful businessman," said Hansen. "And because he's someone who can control himself." This didn't align with his discomfort as the chinless, toad-like vampire worked toward frenzy. "But when he told me about Victor's ancestor—frankly I would have brought X in even without EnerGreen. I need him to protect all of you." He pointed at Victor. "From that."

"That doesn't make sense," Darla protested. She saw how her team was looking anew at Victor. "We all know Victor. We know what he's done for our department. For every one of us."

"Does that include Nikki?" X jackhammered fist to palm with each word. "That was just the start. The slaughter has *happ*ened once, centuries ago, on *b*oth sides. I swear to you, I won't let it ha*pp*en again."

"For God's sake," said Victor, resisting the urge to retreat. "I'm taking the cure."

"For fuck's sake," said Florence. "Why?"

Why indeed. Even the threat of a murder prosecution wasn't enough to turn him. Victor knew that as a vampire, he would get around it, through it, past it. At his wildest and most primal, when his fangs were *in* a woman, *in* her blood, when he was wowing Bizco's prospective clients and making Chleber's eyes expand with pride; when Barbara was looking at him, the way he loved—that's when Victor knew the right choice. That was how life should be lived. Chances taken and rewards gained, every move made toward *meaning*, lives touched and the world expanded.

But when things went wrong ... when Tripp worried, when he considered the chance that X and the slayer community were right about tracing his bloodline back to the infamous Morbius; when he tried and failed to recall some conscious moment of decision-making as he had taken Nikki into his arms, a point when he had control, when he could have chosen differently—that's when his viewpoint rotated a slow half-turn and he saw the suffering in his wake.

And then when Victor again looked forward to the future, he saw uncertainty for his family. Uncertainty creating unacceptable probabilities for financial hardship and emotional emptiness. At the altar Victor had accepted the responsibility to provide security to his family, to ensure Barbara was provided for till the end and Amberly equipped to achieve the same.

He also saw loneliness. The terrible spoils of the man who lived for the moment, dedicated to doing what he *would* instead of what he *should*.

X touched a hanky to his bleeding lip, wincing at the pain; then he plowed forward, advancing on Victor and demonstrating the sacrifice he was willing to make. "To save the world from erupting in bloodshed, Victor Thetherson must die!"

"He said he was taking the cure." Tessa hurried forward to show solidarity with Darla. She emboldened Quentin and Casey to do the same.

X came quickly at Victor. His eyes glowed yellow and his fangs dripped his own blood. "Tilt your head back!"

Victor was forced to kneel. X grabbed him by the widow's peak and ratcheted his eyes to the ceiling, and peeled back his top lip for inspection. He let go and considered what he had seen, along with a handful of Victor's hair. "You're not healing, are you?"

The humiliation in front of Darla and the others brought back memories, a flood of moments all similar in this feeling of impotence. How many times had he been symbolically driven to his knees? As he watched his uprooted hair fall from X's open hand to the floor, Victor despaired over a future where he would keep his feet only as long as he was allowed.

"Swear it." X seethed at the tipping point of his frenzy. "Swear here to X and your colleagues that you will take the cure. That this is the end of your days as a ..." He paused and then drove his fangs into his tortured bottom lip. " ... *vampire.*"

Victor was ill. "I don't have any choice. No surgeon would ever remove this implant—"

"Swear to X!" the vampire bellowed. "Swear to us all!"

"*F*ine," said Victor, heavy on the *F*. "I swear."

His former team jostled X aside to hug their old boss. "You made the right choice," said Tessa.

Jay chuckled and tousled Victor's hair. "Finish the cure, Vic."

Victor sat slumped in Darla's guest chair. She had led him there after he suffered through continuing congratulations from the Bizco accounting team.

Tessa told him that Nikki's soul could now rest in peace. And that she suspected numerous other executives of being vampires.

Quinten confided one balding man to another that Rogaine was a bust for his thinning hair, but that the bananas and dates diet was working wonders.

Casey was giddy that she could stop posting hate comments on Eugene the Vampire Slayer's blog and re-like his Facebook page and follow him again on Twitter and Instagram and become a rep for Essential Oils.

Monique: "Congrats."

These were his peers now.

Florence had retreated to her desk, distraught over Victor's impending cure. X followed her, and now they left the floor together.

Darla watched their departure with alarm and struggled to settle on an opening line with Victor. "You know my dream?" He didn't seem to. "That someday we would get to work together. That's since the first time I saw you up on stage at the industry conference."

Victor stared dully at her paper-stacked desktop. "The accounting rock star."

"Sounds funny but it's true." Darla's face found balance at sweet, middle-aged contentment. "Maybe my dream is finally coming true." She watched for a glimmer of hope in Victor's face. "I know the transition is going to be rough. X is ..." The open floor plan forced her to lean forward and whisper. "I really think today was the worst. I have colleagues who worked for him. They say he can be intimidating but that he's really a good boss." She took in Victor's pained reaction. "Please be patient."

Victor's ears rang from the impact of his 35-story

freefall. "I'm really sorry."

"There is nothing to be sorry for ..."

"I'm sorry to be here like this."

"Honey." Darla covered her mouth at the slip. "Victor." She tried to transition back to business by touching a stack of documents and twitching her mouse to light up her slumbering monitor. "*Everyone* wants what's best for you." While her posture remained business-erect, her hand stole between two stacks. "We love you. Either way." She held Victor's eyes to make sure he was listening. "We love you."

Victor put his hand on hers in their secret canyon.

Darla gave a little sigh. She nodded at his mouth and the canine imbalance behind his lips. "You do need to get that fixed."

THE FACES

As we leave the airplane I wonder sleepily to myself why I have a hood over my head. Again I ask Eugene. "Can you please tell me why I am blindfolded?"

Eugene holds my hand tightly and squeezes it with excitement.

There are three places that Eugene has always wanted to visit, and Guantanamo is one of them. I am a little concerned waterboarding is about to ensue.

"Sweetums, you are going to be so surprised." Eugene hurries me through what he has described as a small airport and to a car waiting outside. As he shoves me in, I bang my head against the doorframe. "Oops, watch your head."

I'm scared, frustrated, and excited. Eugene always has a plan and I love him so. "Eugene, honey, what is going on? Why did you drug me and put this hood over my head? I love to fly. It would have been nice to be awake for the flight."

I'm coming out of my daze. Last thing I remember is the champagne brunch and Eugene with big news. The brunch was nice, the food and the drink delicious. Even though I am almost 17 I look 25. Eugene said to pack for a getaway weekend. I had my duffel bag under my chair. I was expecting the Motel 6 a few miles north.

Still I was giddy with excitement thinking this might be the weekend that Eugene and I go all the way. So romantic, but I was and am so nervous. Am I ready? I think so.

While I was in the restaurant bathroom Eugene must have slipped something in my drink. I hammered down my third mimosa and that is the last thing I remember.

Eugene lets out a big sigh as we accelerate onto a highway. "Honey, you make me sound rotten. I did not drug you. I slipped three Advil P.M. into your champagne so I could surprise you. I was Melaleuca's partner of the quarter and I won a trip, anywhere in the U.S. I wanted to make this a special trip for us and a great surprise for you. Boy, was I surprised when the sleeping meds hit you while you were eating your eggs Benedict. Bam!" He slaps his hands together. "Face first into the Hollandaise sauce. I had to pretend to give you mouth to mouth." He laughs. "I did not mind. Then I put you over my shoulder and brought you to the airport. Getting you on the plane was no small matter."

"Eugene, tell me we are not in Gitmo."

"No, the S.O.B.s would not give us a tour. National security, ha! I am the nation's most secure person. But I do have for us a behind-the-scenes look at the underbelly of the government. I had to swing a lot of favors but I got us the trip of a lifetime, baby."

I try to guess where we are. I wonder if it is New York, L.A., Tulsa, the Smithsonian, world's largest ball of twine, NORAD, Washington D.C.? Eugene can be a bit rough around the edges and a bit extreme, but he is really a special romantic person who has captured my heart.

We've been about an hour on a winding road. "Honey, can you take this bag off my head please? I really want to see the sights and I am getting quite claustrophobic and a bit carsick."

Eugene pats my head through the bag. "Sweetie, ruin the surprise? No way."

"It wouldn't ruin anything, I promise." My voice rises.

Eugene stops patting. "Don't make me gag you, honey."

I go limp. "Okay, but this better be worth it."

"It will be the most amazing trip. Almost as good as Guantanamo, I think."

I sigh deeply. It's nice that he thinks this is romantic. I am going to have to train him a bit, the way Mom trained Dad. Except I won't break Eugene's spirit.

"Honey, what are you doing?" Eugene asks.

"Nothing, just sitting here with a hood on my head."

Another minute goes by and Eugene erupts. "Amberly, stop it."

"What? What am I doing?"

Eugene slows the vehicle to a crawl. In silence he listens intently. "That. That noise. Are you singing, whistling, crying? Stop it, you know how I am about noises."

"Eugene, I was humming a bit. Softly to myself, to pass the time. It's frightening with this hood on and it helps me calm myself. Besides, I thought it was food noises that bothered you."

Eugene slams his hands on the steering wheel. "Food noises are the worst, but anything that's soft and repetitive drives me nuts. Besides, I don't determine what bothers me. If it does, it just does. Sing or something."

"Okay." I take a deep breath and belt out one of my favorites. "SWEET CAROLINE, DA DA DA!!!"

"Stop!" says Eugene. "That's worse, go to sleep."

I weep softly a little. Then before Eugene can freak out again I fall asleep.

***

While Amberly naps in the car, Eugene walks into a KOA campground and rings for the clerk. As an elderly gentleman approaches the counter Eugene sizes him up. Eugene sizes everyone up, surmising their weaknesses. This guy has a few. Age, limp, scoliosis, Coke bottle glasses, really tight shorts. Just to name a few. "Sir, I have a reservation for a cabinette under George Jefferson."

The old man smiles wide. "Like the TV show?"

Eugene looks at the man, resizes him. "Sure." Actually, he took two Presidents' names.

***

We drive a bit farther and park. Eugene picks me up and carries me like he's carrying me over the threshold. It's very sweet but I wish I could see where I am so I can fully enjoy the moment. Eugene sets me down on a bed and takes off my hood. My eyes take a moment to adjust. It's a cute but small cabin. Antler lamps and a bed made out of big pieces of rough lumber. Stuffed squirrels on the mantle. Rustic but nice. "Eugene, can we go out for dinner?"

"Nope. We can't. I brought us rations and we can eat those." He swings the duffel bag off his shoulder and shakes out the contents on the bed. Two cans of Spam, two cans of smoked oysters, one package of Ritz crackers, a can of pigs feet, two bottles of water, a bottle of wine and some beef jerky. He looks at me intently. "Wow, I can't believe the Hollandaise sauce did not burn you." He gently brushes my hair back from my cheek. "I will let you take a shower now."

I smile. "Join me?"

Eugene walks into the bathroom and comes out shaking his head. "Too small. You go ahead."

I shrug. "Okay." I walk to Eugene and stand on my tip-toes and kiss him on the nose. "See you in a bit."

I get out of a long hot shower and into one of Eugene's t-shirts. He's cooking Spam and has the bottle of wine on the table with two Dixie cups filled, next to the opened can of smoked oysters and the Ritz crackers. I put an oyster on a cracker. "I hear these are an aphrodisiac." I eat the cracker and wash it down with a Dixie cup of wine.

Eugene turns to me. "Perhaps but what I do know is that they are a great source of protein and iron. We are going to need energy for our adventure tomorrow." He sets a plate of pan-fried Spam on the table. "Eat up, then to bed for a big," he pauses for effect, "big day tomorrow."

"I have enough energy for a big day *and* a fun night. Eugene, can't we just go for a walk and then fool around?"

He kneels next to me. "Babe, there will be plenty of time for that." He kisses me on the cheek. "But seriously, we both will need rest."

"I don't want to go to bed ... and sleep!" I'm getting upset. I feel a yawn coming on. "Eugene, tell me you did not spike my wine with Advil P.M."

"Amberly, I knew I was going to have a fight on my hands putting you to bed. Now eat up quick before you pass out in your oysters."

A few minutes later I am exhausted. I'm too upset to even talk to him. He rubs my back and tries to explain over and over, each time slower and more sweetly than the last, that this will all be worth it. And that it is good practice just in case a hostage situation arises. After I eat all my dinner, Eugene pats me on the head and slings me over his shoulder like a sack of potatoes and tosses me on the bed.

I'm just hanging on now. "Well at least take advantage of me."

"Sweets, I want you so badly. But when we do it, we need to be in control. You are not in control of yourself." He kisses me softly on the lips as I fall asleep.

The next day does not start any better. When I wake we're stopped in the vehicle and the sack is back over my head. "Eugene, I have to pee."

"We are here. I was worried you would not wake in time and I would go on without you." He jumps out and runs around to my side. Opens the door and grabs my hand. "My lady, a day of adventure awaits."

He walks me about three minutes up a rocky hill. "Eugene, take this hood off and get me to a bathroom."

"There is nothing to see, it is still dark outside." A moment later we stop and Eugene knocks on a door.

A man on the other side of the door: "Who is it?"

"George Jefferson," says Eugene.

"Very funny. It's 4:30 in the morning, this better be good."

Eugene lets out a big sigh. "It's Eugene."

I can almost feel the man behind the door straighten up. "Yes, right away sir, sorry about my delay." The door opens and releases the musty scent of wet dirt. "Who's this? A prisoner, the undead, a vampire? I don't know if you can keep ... it, here. You said you wanted a special tour, not a place to store a body or hostage."

I am really going to pee my pants.

Eugene chuckles. "No, no this is my girlfriend, Amberly. She needs a restroom."

"Right this way." The man seems reassured and dubious at the same time. He grabs my hand. "Eugene, I did not know you were going to come so early. This should only take an hour or so. Why are you wearing such a big backpack?" He opens a door. "There you go, ma'am. Can I take off your hood?"

"Leave it on," says Eugene. "I want to take the extended tour, see the underbelly."

I shut the door and feel around for the toilet. Find it, and sit. I can hear Eugene and the man outside the door.

"You are going on the extended tour, but it still only takes an hour, two tops. And it's 4:30 in the morning."

"Look, you owe me. I helped you with your little problem and I intend to collect. I want the extended access you promised."

"I do owe you, V.S., and this is the extended access. I just think you are looking for something we don't have."

"Fine. When my girl gets out of the bathroom we will take our tour unguided." Eugene rattles the door knob. "You ready sweets?"

I wash my hands and join the two men. "Is there any coffee, breakfast? I'm a little hungry." I am starving.

Eugene rustles in the pocket of his jacket. "I brought a 5-Hour Energy and a Power Bar."

I have had it. I tear off my hood in disgust. "Damn it, Eugene, I am not eating ..." I take a good, long look around. "Where are we, some kind of dungeon?" It looks like the half-finished basement of a cave. Lights are strung across the dirt ceiling into side rooms. Caverns of some sort. "Caving, you took me caving?"

"Whoa, V.S., your lady is hot," the cave dweller says.

Usually I take compliments well but I am running in the red. "I am leaving." I spin around and start to storm out.

Eugene blocks my exit, arms raised and restraining me at the same time. "Honey, this is it. We are about to embark on a great adventure. Secrets and mystery surround this place. Dark caverns and caves with the secrets of the government."

The cave dweller looks around as if he's curious where the secrets are as well. "I don't know what you're looking for here. There's not a lot of mystery or hidden treasure. There is a lot of fun history."

"Nonsense!" Eugene raises his finger high and strides forward. "On! On to the *chamber of secrets*."

I trail behind him. "Give me my damn energy bar."

"That's the spirit, babe."

The dweller stays put. "Guys, there is no chamber." He shrugs his shoulders and grabs the sports page and enters the bathroom.

I look out the eye of Teddy Roosevelt. It really is a sight to see, even if there is no hidden treasure or secrets. I love the movie *North By Northwest* and I want to pretend that Eugene is Cary Grant and I'm Eva Marie Saint. We are about the same age apart. They were a dashing couple. My anger has subsided and I know that misguided as Eugene can be, he truly has a great heart and has tried to plan a great trip.

"Damn it!" Eugene shouts. "Nicolas Cage found the secret door right over there." He points toward the backside of George's head.

We have walked in circles for hours. We have found cleaning supplies and drawings of The Faces. I wave Eugene back to me. "Honey, come look at this view, it's spectacular. This trip has turned out to be great. Really, stop beating yourself up." He reluctantly joins me. "Kiss me, please kiss me."

Eugene kisses me. "Amberly, I am so sorry and so mad."

"Eugene, shh, calm down. Let's just enjoy each other." I hold my finger to his lips until his face relaxes. "This is the best adventure ever. You're my Cary Grant and my Nicolas Cage all rolled into one."

He kisses me passionately. I found the most interesting, heroic man in the world. And he loves me with all his heart.

Eugene rests his forehead against mine. "I'm glad you are happy. But I am still going to have the guy who promised me national secrets dropped from Amway."

JAY HANSEN

Perhaps some chirping crickets would have settled Jay's nerves as he walked up Florence's sidewalk. Her house was dark and somehow foreboding despite sitting safely in this working class neighborhood, lit up with warm lights and lively children, lawns well-groomed if still dormant, scented with swimming pool chlorine and charcoal from old-school grills.

From the rundown Acres Homes district to his gated community, Evil settles where it chooses, in pockets, infesting a house here and a crazed mind there. Always has, Jay acknowledged. But back in the day, he ranted to himself, you could reasonably assume going your whole life without encountering It.

Because of vampires and the country's refusal to label them as Evil, such an assumption could now leave you permanently impaired or worse, and without legal recourse for you or your next of kin.

Jay's wife Madeline worried about this. She also worried about him driving on Houston's narrow highway lanes. This was stupid; he drove an Audi, and he drove it well.

She worried about Jay having two vampires under him. This was valid. She considered her husband's approach to "managing" Victor—bringing in X—equivalent to importing Tasmanian devils to lower the prairie dog population. In Madeline's words, "Now what do you do with all those Tasmanian devils?" But Jay really hated those fucking prairie dogs.

Reaching for Florence's doorbell, Jay understood that Madeline would consider this another Tasmanian devil treatment. And so it could be—replacing Vampire Vic with Fanged Flo might turn out to be a serious miscalculation. Florence in her human state possessed an edge that could be terrifying as a vampire.

Regardless, Victor would be dead. That thought made Jay warm inside.

And he might have reminded his wife that, as a businessman he was also looking beyond immediate results; he was very focused on how his machinations would be interpreted. Every action sent a message.

As X had alluded to the Bizco accounting team a few days ago, vampires were increasingly popping up in positions of power. On their school board. In their suburban administration and their congressional delegation. And everyone believed the lie X had told: "We just want to fit in. We just want to contribute." Rumors were flying that Houston's district attorney was a vampire, and the *Chronicle*'s editorial page had cheered: "In a role that requires cold-blooded evaluation, we can't think of a better fit."

(*Cold-blooded.* That's how D.A. Goodnight's voicemails left Jay. He received them at work and at home.

How is Thetherson's cure coming?

That was the recurring theme, the threat that was no longer veiled. And so Jay was paying it forward to Dr. Regnald Speer at the Longevity Labs, making sure the scientist was aware of the terminal liability the Labs faced with another failed cure.)

None of these monsters gained office or appointment as vampires; they always came out after. Yet the public didn't object. If these so-called leaders were revealed to be philanderers, tax evaders, or résumé embellishers, the press would have been howling for their resignations. Worse yet, the humans in position to stop them were letting it happen. No one was setting a forceful, message-rich example.

Like D.A. Goodnight and the others, X was a problem. EnerGreen was always the topic when he talked to Jay. But clearly the vampire had bigger plans. Victor's death would be an example for X. Sort of like the English "overkilling" William Wallace: dragged by a horse, hanged, emasculated and eviscerated, beheaded and finally quartered so that his remains might be placed at each corner of the rebellious province as a warning to his ilk. Unlike Tasmanian devils, Scots and vampires were capable of understanding a good example.

Was it a stretch to compare what Jay had in store for Victor to the mortal indignity visited upon Braveheart? In the Labs' file notes Jay had found a description of the death of Victor's predecessor, Agnes Schmitz, an executive secretary with Bizco's parent company, Verrstagg. Agnes' path to death—one of the three Jay had planned for Victor—was grotesque and message-rich.

The other two weren't bad either. Death by slayer— after the show Eugene had put on in Detroit, Jay actually believed in the bizarre young man. He took his craft seriously. And he was a businessman to boot—that Detroit REIT was really taking off.

As was Jay's idea to bring in X. He couldn't take full credit; he had never heard of this dread vampire "Morbius" or the ridiculous rumor that Victor was his descendant. He had no clue that X would see the fat schlep as such a threat.

But X didn't know that. He was going to believe he had been manipulated by a ruthless strategist. Once all three plans came to light—and regardless which one accomplished the goal, Jay would make damn sure X knew all three had been in process—in terms of the *message*, Victor's demise would be the equal to what had happened to the famed Scotsman.

Three separate plans to kill Victor Thetherson! Who

could match that kind of redundancy?

Jay knew that Madeline didn't really worry. Not the way most wives worried. She knew she had landed an alpha male who brought home the bacon. She had witnessed her man in primordial battles with men and women who loved to send messages, and had thrilled to see him always come out on top.

That included the war with vampires. When Victor and Mellow Larry Cocachello got the better of Raj in his attempted coup, Jay had quickly sacrificed the slick-tongued accountant and moved on. Not only that, he had slugged "Vampire Vic" and lived to tell Madeline the tale, if slightly edited from the actual event. He was his wife's hero.

Still, Jay had a terrible feeling when no one came to Florence's door; when he tried it and found it unlocked.

"Knock, knock?" In the gloom Jay saw the outlines of a formal dining table, piano and china cabinet to his right. He smelled Swisher Sweet smoke embedded in once-overstuffed furniture in a sitting room to his left and felt gentle puffs of air coming down a staircase immediately before him. There was a hallway a few feet to the right. Jay left the door open to ensure unimpeded egress—then chuckled at his lack of commitment and fairly slammed it shut.

He was halfway down the hall when Florence called from the sitting room. "I'm in here."

Jay retraced his steps and paused at the threshold, waiting for his eyes to adjust, hoping some of the fresh air he had felt would precede him and dilute the room's sour warmth. He only spotted Florence lying on the sofa when he banged his shin on the adjacent coffee table. "Okay if I open a window?"

"Buddy doesn't like to turn on the heat."

Jay rubbed his shin while trying to get a bead on Florence's condition. Her voice was a wheezy rasp. "It's like a tomb in here. Like being in the tower on the weekend, right?" Bizco's new "smart" building dimmed the lights and switched off the HVAC at 6 p.m. sharp every business day. By 6:05 Jay could barely breathe, and even with an ample supply of oxygen wouldn't have been able to focus in the absence of white noise, the floor deathly silent so that every sound found him.

"I don't work overtime." Florence sat up. "What are you doing here?"

The only light was from the front window behind her, from a streetlight down the block, leaking through lace curtains gauzy with dust. Still he blanched at the sight of her. In the week since he had introduced X as department manager, Florence had become severely gaunt, cheeks sunken, skin lined and loose. Her hair had thinned. She picked at it now to pouf it. She wore a housecoat for Christ's sake, no one looked good in a housecoat, especially not if you were already bone-thin and bloodless.

And she smelled. Jay recoiled a step and then another until his nostrils stopped filling up with her. "I was at the television show. I know how you want what Victor had—"

"It's too late," Florence rasped.

"I know he's taking the cure. But I have it on good authority his vampirism is still transmissible."

"I mean I'm already getting it."

Jay wasn't much for measuring his words. He cooked without a recipe, so to speak. "I know you weren't expecting company," he referenced her appearance. "But I don't think this is what you were looking for."

Florence reached for a bottle of eau de toilette on the coffee table. With a hand clamped over the left side of her throat, she spritzed herself top to bottom. "You dumb fucker. It's a process." She reached for cigarette and lighter. Now Jay saw the bite, raised and festered.

"One step forward two steps back, that sort of thing?"

Florence checked her watch and threw a nervous

glance toward the door. "Something like that. You better go."

"Your 'buddy' coming home soon?"

After a deep drag on what the cigarette had to offer, Florence snuffed it and waved away the smoke she hadn't been able to absorb. "My husband Buddy's upstairs. Too lame to go out, too gotdamned scared to come down." She scooted laboriously sideways to enlist the sofa arm's assistance to gain her feet. "X'll be here any moment. He gets himself in a lather before he comes. You don't wanna be here."

Jay ignored the cold flush across his scalp. In fact, he decided to enjoy it, a nice cool-down from the room's fetid humidity. "X reports to me."

"So?" Florence shuffled to the mantle rimming the artificial fireplace and picked up a butane wand. "What are you gonna do when he bites you? Give him a poor performance appraisal?"

"Vampires do what they want, right? At least the powerful ones." Despite the ingrained bravado that came from being on top of his game and one step ahead of everyone around him, Jay hurried his words as he watched Florence shakily lighting candles. "Listen, from what I understand not every vampire transmits his curse. And for those who do, it happens differently, depending, right?"

"Yep." Florence did not multi-task. She was absorbed with creating the atmosphere her vampire demanded. She had many candles to light.

"How do you know X is going to give you what you're looking for?"

Florence paused to study him. "Do you like getting older? Older and lesser? Even you, Jay. In the seven years I've known you, your hair has thinned and your gut has sagged. You've got crow's feet walking on age spots. You clear your throat all the fucking time." She cleared her own throat as she walked past him. "Yep, you got a high-paying job. But I know what's really important to you."

"Mm?"

Florence put on oven mitts. "Being noticed." She extracted a block of dry ice from a portable cooler and tucked it under an end table shrouded in lace. White smoke oozed out, rolling along the floor as if in a chute. "By women especially. For what you do, of course. But also for what you look like. But you're pushing 50. Another ten years and I guarantee you won't be making nearly enough money for women to get past your looks."

"I've never been much of a looker."

Florence chuckled, and then launched into a harsh coughing spell, holding her stomach and her bite wound throughout. "Got-dammit, he told me to stay hydrated." From the cooler she retrieved a wide-mouthed water bottle that looked to contain orange juice, and drank and drank, liquid trickling down her chin, each swallow audible. She toweled off with the housecoat sleeve. "You're aging. Fast. Take all the testosterone you want. It won't make a difference."

"Do you want to hear what I have to say or not?"

"Not particularly." Florence's eyes jumped to the window, swept by the headlights of a car pulling into the driveway. "To get younger and to stay young? I'll suffer whatever I have to." The lights went out, and Florence gave him a wild, frightened leer. "I think you would, too. Maybe you should stick around."

"You sound like a desperate gambler with a bad hand." Pulling an envelope out of his blazer pocket, Jay felt his heart hammering against his ribs. He tossed the envelope into the lap of a Barcalounger. "This tells you exactly how you can have what Victor had. No suffering involved." He considered the Labs' description of the curse's sexual transmission. "Okay, maybe a little."

Florence only had eyes for the front door. She pointed him to the kitchen, her body curved and contorted defensively. "Get *out* of here."

Jay's legs went to jelly, forcing him to slog through nightmarish gravity. "Make the right choice, Florence." That advice was less self-serving than it would have been when he arrived. Jay was genuinely concerned for the Bizco accountant.

"You think I have a choice?"

Jay was briefly visible from the front door as he hurried through the kitchen on his way to the laundry room and then out the back door, which he left open to avoid making noise. The yard was dark. Going left meant skirting the sitting room wall so Jay went right, creeping forward, meeting a shed that was linked to the house by a seven-foot high, 90-degree elbow of wire fence. He could scale it under optimal conditions, when his muscles weren't sapped by paralytic fear.

He went left, crawled below window level on a narrow path of sunken paving stones, ever-so-carefully through a gate and around the back corner of the house, crouched and shuffling forward. As he cleared the front corner he heard Florence scream, separated by the wall but only a few feet away.

There was a heavy *thunk*, the fracture of glass and wood. The coffee table, Jay guessed. More screaming from Florence, now further away. Maybe she was fleeing upstairs to her husband—who would surely be calling the police, Jay consoled himself as he ran low across the lawn.

Jesus Christ! It was both an epithet and an invocation for assistance. Jay forced himself to reverse course. *What am I doing? The man reports to me!* And regardless, there was a woman in trouble in that house and the hero Jay was to his wife would not turn his back.

Underneath the high tones of Florence's awful cries there was a tortured howl. Perhaps Jay's ancestors had been more gatherer than hunter, for he recognized the guttural emanations from a predator's chest, the frenzied anticipation of the kill.

His hand hovered at the door handle, a graceful golden swoosh. On the other side of that door the vampire had caught Florence and was dragging her back down the stairs, her backside and maybe her head thumping on each step—duh, duh, duh, duh, each thump accented by her ragged breath.

Florence protested and Jay heard X's response, a blow that reduced her plea to a weak babble. Jay pictured Buddy listening upstairs and had never hated another human so. *You fucking coward!* Jay screamed, in his mind. *It's your wife!*

One more attempt to grab that door handle. Inside, Florence was no longer calling for help. Jay put his ear to the door, straining to hear ... what? A sort of snuffling, almost erotic. Tears streamed down Jay's cheeks and he was screaming again, out loud now as he got in his fine little Audi.

From the "Ask the Slayer" fan page on the *Sage Slayer* website

"Your emails have been flooding in, a sure sign that the vamp problem is only getting worse. And that you haven't been reading Dear Abby.*"* – Eugene the Vampire Slayer

From: Jean
Posted: Wed Feb 12, 2:56 a.m.
Subject: Vermin and stale love

Dear Eugene,
I really hope you rid the world of the vermin that have become an extreme nuisance on this planet. I have been following you for quite some time & find your tactics and your advice very helpful.

The issue I have is with my fiancé Walt. We have been together for 7 years now. The last three we have been engaged. We have no real plan on when we are to be married. When he first proposed, he had all these grandiose plans on where, when & how we would be married. But it has been three long engaged years. Walt keeps telling me it's not time yet, that he wants our finances & our circumstances to be just right. Also, he never takes me out. His idea of a romantic evening is ordering in Domino's and playing Halo online. Never tells me he loves me. He stays out all night with his buddies. What should I do? I am at wits end! I love him so much, but I feel like we are in a permanent holding pattern.

Your servant and admirer,

Jean

—

Jean,

Walt is playing you like a three-dollar fiddle. He knows he can keep you around. Dangle the idea of getting married and keep you around even longer. Confront him, talk to him in very plain terms. "Walt, you know I love you and I know you love me, but we need to make a plan, a date to get married. If we wait for the perfect time, we will never be married." I am sure that when Walt understands that you are not waiting for the perfect time, moment or finances, that you love him and want to be married, he will come to his senses and make a date.

As for the Domino's and the Halo. You are way off base, way off.

Did you also mention that he stays out all night? He's probably a vamp. Since you love him, a stake through the heart is the most painless death. But truly. Kill him, kill him now.

Yours,
Eugene > The Vampire Slayer <

From: Samuel
Posted: Wed Feb 12, 11:22 p.m.
Subject: Not ready to "retire"

Eugene,
I have a life problem I need to discuss with you. Any &
all advice is welcome. I have recently moved to a
retirement home. I am single and feel like I am ready
to date again. I have not been on a date in a long time
and would like to know how to approach a cute little
chicka on my floor. She is also taking a painting class
at the home & I was thinking about joining that class
in order to get close to her. I have asked her out a
couple of times, but she is always busy. I am thinking
about giving up. Do you have any suggestions? Also,
there are two new guys on the east wing. They look
way too young to be here, and they go out almost every
night. What do you think, Vamps?

Really like the good your doing out there, thanks.
Samuel

—

Sam,
Don't give up, you probably don't have much time, so
you gotta get to it. Did I give up when a Vamp tossed
me off the cliff? Did I give up when I was accosted by
the Vampire mob in the dark alley? Did I give up when
all I had was one good arm and a wheelchair?!?! No!
No! No! I did not. You will not give up. Figure out her
schedule, follow her. Take every painting class she is
taking, watch Wheel of Fortune with her, crochet.
Whatever she does, you do. Wherever she goes, you go.
Get her, Sam! Fight for her!

Just because the two new guys on the east wing are young-looking does not make them Vamps. Here's what I would do: About midnight, send out a code 9 from the new guys' room. Make the employees check on them in the dark of the night. If the employees don't come back, then and only then, kill the young dudes. Kill them. Kill them.

Good luck out there, and go get her, you may die soon.

Eugene > The Vampire Slayer <

BACK TO EVEN

For four days Victor holed up at home. He kept to the basement, embarrassed for Barbara to see him, demoralized by the way she had reacted when he described his encounter with X. She had deflated. After listening to one-fanged Victor make no attempt to rationalize his demotion to Accounting, Barbara had gone into mourning. For the man she had lost.

Two days at home was enough to recover sufficiently from X's psychic beating, so that Victor began to feel guilty for missing work. Two days was enough to reach his limit breathing in the dismal air of Barbara's waxing depression, which was undoubtedly deepened by the poison of his own malaise. But his broken fang had teased him, growing a spindly root like a needle-pointed stalactite. The tepid regeneration hadn't given Victor hope as much as frozen him in suspended animation in the basement for another two days, his transition to humanity arrested.

He couldn't let go of that tooth. On day five Victor returned to the prosthetics artisan who had crafted the falsies for his *Xtreme ReVamp* outing and threw down a grand on a tailored mouthguard to protect the fragile proto-fang, only to snap it off flossing. Fell into the sink and shattered, the fragments caught up in the trickle coming from the faucet and the droplets clinging to the bowl, and down the drain. Victor made a dental appointment for that afternoon.

"So you finally put a trigger guard on those

weapons, huh?" Dentist Mulvane greeted him in a turtleneck, eyeing Victor's mouthpiece.

"I'm down to one now." Victor removed his mouthguard. "I want normal teeth."

"Would you look at that?" Dentist Mulvane rushed forward and forced open Victor's mouth. He fingered the gap and tugged on the remaining fang. "Oops, better wash up. Hop in the chair."

Over the whine of the grinder Victor's nose filled with hot powered tooth, to the point he couldn't take the smell, the remnants of his vampire olfactory system painting a picture of gray spicules with steaming blood-red roots, waves of them billowing from his mouth and saturating the room. "Stop ..." His plea was lost to the deafening squeal of the overworked grinder and the dust coating Dentist Mulvane's goggles. Victor finally knocked the power tool aside and hustled to the little bathroom to throw up.

The remaining fang looked like a pencil chewed up by a dull sharpener. That helped; Victor survived the rest of the session by imagining the sound and smell of the old wall-mounted sharpener in Mrs. Konrath's fourth-grade room. Oh, how Victor had loved to keep his pencils sharp.

Monday morning heading to work, Victor lied to himself. Lied about having come to grips with everything that had happened. *Vampirism excavated the Real Me*, he told himself, *finally bringing Him to the surface. The trick is not letting the world bury Him again.*

Lying had been necessary to drag him up from the basement and out of the house. Now, stepping off the elevator, Victor's delusions dissolved with the transparency of the open floor plan. Everyone saw him just by raising their eyes. He couldn't feel any more revealed.

"So let's see the teeth." Tessa marched on him,

hands subtly out for balance on her tiny feet. The other accountants followed suit, crowding around Victor.

In truth of course, the "Real Victor" was only a mask, a pair of fright fangs giving him the confidence to play a role. He couldn't remain in character forever. And there was no sense trying any longer because everyone could see right through.

He showed them his teeth.

"Oh that's a shame," said Kirby. "You're just like us now." His sadness earned a scowl from Tessa.

Quentin returned dejectedly to his desk. "So what are we supposed to do with all of this?" He untucked his dress shirt to reveal his white "Team VV" t-shirt and held up his "VV" coffee mug and scissor holder.

"Get rid of it," said Tessa. "It's like owning Nazi memorabilia."

Quentin hung his head and pushed the paperweight with Victor's holographic hissing face into the trash can.

"VV was a Nazi," Casey lamented.

"Which means they're collectors' items now," said Kirby.

Quentin raced Casey to retrieve the paperweight.

Tessa took a challenging stance. "Does this mean the cure is final?"

Victor pointed to his clavicle. "I have an implant delivering a chemical treatment that shuts down the vampirism. The cure won't be final until they perfect the genetic treatment."

Tessa wagged a finger. "Just remember your vow."

Darla watched from her desk, face stern but eyes warm and pleased. "We should all get back to work now." She sent a wary glance down the aisle to a set of black drapes hung floor to ceiling. "So Victor can do the same."

He joined Darla at her desk and pointed at the black tubular enclosure. "What is that?"

"His office," said Darla. "He isn't a fan of the open floor plan." She looked apprehensively at Victor. "I hope you're not either. Your desk is in there, too."

"You have to be kidding." Victor suddenly had trouble breathing. "I don't know if I can go in there. He's insane."

Darla hurried around the desk and knelt at his side, in plain sight, accepting any stir she might create. "He's actually been very good to the team," she said quietly. "He already studied our salary structure and determined we're all under-compensated. He hasn't announced it yet but he's going to get everyone a raise."

Victor could only nod. "Happy for you."

"Honey." Darla found his hand and looked for his eyes. "I just want you to give it time. This will be better once your cure is permanent." She smoothed his long forearm hairs. "You're such a gentle soul. First Jay, and now X. I know this isn't easy for you."

"It's one thing to be gentle through strength." Victor couldn't bear to hide his weakness from Darla; someday she would see through him, see him as others did, and be disappointed. "There's nothing impressive about a man who's gentle by necessity."

Darla shook her head. "I don't care. By choice or not, I love how you are."

Victor let her eyes soothe him. He imagined his head resting on her lap, her hands on his face, caring for him.

The elevator arrived bearing Florence. While everyone stared she stood half in and half out, dazed. The doors tried to close twice, the elevator finally honking in distress before Florence walked onto the floor. She was deathly white with red-rimmed eyes. Her hair was disheveled, straggly, thinner. Her blouse hung a size too big on her bony shoulders. Even Victor thought she looked a little under the weather. On the left side of her throat was a bandage.

Darla hurried to meet her at her desk. "Where have you been? Florence, you've been out a week without a word."

"Sorry I didn't call." Florence sounded like she had laryngitis.

Darla lowered her voice but everyone could hear, and they were all listening. "Are you okay?"

"Never better," Florence rasped, and bared her fangs.

Only Darla looked shocked, although the rest of the team and a few from the adjoining Accounts Payable department did leave their desks to get a better look.

Victor was mesmerized. Florence truly had perfect teeth to begin with, and her fangs followed suit. Gently curved and symmetrically tapered, neither long nor short, pearly white with glistening spittle threads spanning tips to tongue.

"This is unbelievable." Darla might as well have been swearing a blue streak for the bite in her words. "Who did this?"

She could be a little naïve and unaware of pretty much everything outside her accounting role, Victor admitted.

Florence nodded toward the black drapes.

"Really?" Darla mouthed more than spoke it. Now she looked at X's "office" and found her voice. "He can't do that. That isn't appropriate. Did you go to the police?"

"Wake up, Darla," said Tessa. "She was asking for it. No offense, Florence."

"None taken."

This was the first time Victor was jealous of another man with Florence. He had always accepted she was unattainable in the traditional sense. But that she had let another vampire bite her .... He knew the jealousy was irrational. Florence wasn't promised to him in any sense of the word, and his bite could never give her what she wanted. But this felt like the worst kind of cheating.

His anger boiled over on Tessa. "What about Nikki? She wanted me to bite her!"

"That's different and you know it."

"Tessa," Kirby meekly objected. "You said you didn't want a double standard here at Bizco. This seems like a double vampire standard."

Tessa's eyes widened and her face grabbed a disproportionate share of her body's blood. "X isn't heir to the most evil vampire in the history of the world, is he!? He didn't *kill* Florence, did he?!"

"Maybe next time he will. Bite her," Quentin acted it out on some invisible Florence, "and suck on her, and lift her off the floor ..."

Quentin became borderline hysterical. Victor realized he was reenacting Nikki's death.

" ... and hold her so tenderly in his arms while he drinks and drinks—"

"*No.*" Tessa raised her hand to slap Quentin. He snapped his mouth shut. "No," Tessa repeated. "You *know* where X stands." She pointed an accusing finger at Victor. "Did you ever know where *he* was coming from? Who *he* was going to bite? *X* is all about communication and certainty. First and foremost he's a businessman. And a damn good one as far as I can tell."

"It's true." Monique startled everyone. "He already suggested cutting out half the reports I prepare so that I can focus more time on cost analysis." Victor was amazed to learn she had a beautiful voice.

Tessa rested her case. "Sorry, Darla. X is a great manager. For all of us."

Darla seemed to hardly register the conversation, distraught over Florence's vampirism. "Why, honey? Why would you want to be ..." She looked at Florence's appearance and struggled for the right word. *Drained* was the best description. " ... like this?"

"*This* is just the beginning, you st—" Florence

checked her advance and held her tongue, turning away and looking for a moment as if she wanted to go visit the vampire behind the curtain, to double down on her bet. "If you're fine getting old and dried out and disgusting, be my guest. I've heard the fountain of youth isn't for everyone. Which I sure as shit don't get." Florence sat at her desk, stabbed the monitor's on button and logged onto the network with a clicking flurry. She looked up at the little crowd. "Doesn't anyone else have any work to do? Or are you shitheads competing to be my first victim?"

While everyone dispersed to their desks, Darla stood with tensed neck and tight lips while Florence read her email. Finally Darla gave Victor a helpless look and walked away.

Victor saw a bruise on the back of Florence's neck. Telling in two ways, as it previously wouldn't have been visible through her hair. He moved to stand close beside her so he could talk quietly. "Is he abusing you?"

Florence said nothing for some time. Then she shook her head—not in denial, but conviction. "I know what abuse is. This is part of the process. It's worth it." She stood, very close to Victor, making his pulse race. "Are you going to pretend you don't agree?" Florence put her perfectly crafted fingers to his lip, lifting it and sliding her thumb up into his gums, still tender from the occasional slip of Dentist Mulvane's chisel. Victor didn't mind the pain.

Florence gave him a sad smile. "Two ships passing in the night, mm?"

Years ago as Gale, Florence's eyes danced at the delicious ironies of life. Those eyes were always drawn to someone more thrilling than he.

"I knew you were too soft to stick with it."

"That's not it," said Victor. "I don't have any choice."

She patted his cheek and sat down to again address her computer.

"Florence." Victor stood awkwardly above her. "Please let me know if you're in trouble. I won't let him—I won't let him hurt you."

She snorted, immediately absorbed in an email. "Don't be stupid. And don't worry. I'm past the point of needing anyone now."

Victor finally drifted away from her desk. So badly he wanted to continue drifting, to the elevator and out of Bizco for good.

To what? He was 50 years old. A demoted former manager. Starting afresh was a term that could never again apply to him. And how could he assume his next boss would be any different? It was impossible to avoid vampires these days. They were popping up everywhere.

"Thetherson!"

X, calling him into the black tube. Victor had already been on his way there.

Felt like a mere pause to Victor, his hand hovering at the curtain. For anyone watching, and there were a few, it was a good ten seconds of Victor's shoulders rising and falling. He pulled the heavy drapery aside and entered.

X's lair. And Victor's office. The velvet theater curtains encircled X's big desk and Victor's smaller one.

"You're late." X's business voice could be musical, an alto. He leaned back in his chair and stroked the velvet. "It's nearly 8:30."

Victor looked at his desk as if at a firing squad. "I can't work like this."

Behind Victor's lips X saw what he was looking for. "We are going to work closely together."

His backpack heavier by the second, Victor set it on the floor. Overheated, he shed his jacket. "Florence doesn't look good."

"They always look that way." A touch of mirth tugged the corners of X's mouth. "Tell X: Now that you decided to show, what do you intend to work on today?"

"I suppose I can start reviewing the Playco procedural manual to see whether we want to adopt—"

X slapped his desk. "Liar. You're going to work on your little *thing*."

Victor colored. "My ... my program? No. Not unless you think ... No. I wasn't planning on working on it."

X shook his head. "I don't trust you, Thetherson. I can watch you here, yet how do I know you don't work on it at your house?"

Victor frowned. "Of course I do." He did, intermittently, when he wasn't too depressed, when he could force himself to focus for longer than a few minutes. "It's my system, on my own time."

X looked positively puzzled. "I thought you were salaried?"

"Sure."

"Then you don't own anything. Do you? Are you punching a clock on me?" Blood beaded on X's lip, blood in the water, his own blood, beckoning him toward frenzy.

"No. I'm sorry."

"Hand it to me."

"What do you mean?"

"Your ..." X snapped his fingers five times fast.

"Program?"

"Yes. I want it. All of it. Either you work with X and with EnerGreen or you don't. I want it on a CD and then I want it deleted there." X pointed at Victor's computer. "And at your house." He watched Victor slump in his chair, saw the shadow darkening his eyes. "Don't let X need a reason to go to your house."

Victor drove his trimmed top teeth deep into his lip. "Fine." He rummaged through his backpack and found a blank CD, popped it in his machine and copied over his program under X's watchful eye.

For a second Victor was actually embarrassed—his vision for this product was far from realized.

Substantial programming remained to perfect the interface with the user's data files. He wasn't up to the task for his software's more sophisticated requirements. He had planned on enlisting support from a freelance programmer he had stayed in occasional contact with since college.

Victor berated himself for feeling guilty about falling short of a thief's expectations. He wished he had built in some malware.

He handed over the CD and nodded at his computer. "I deleted it. I'll do the same at home."

X held up the CD. "Could I get a case for this?"

Victor reddened and returned to his backpack while X spoke. "I heard you say you wouldn't let anyone hurt *F*lorence. That was in regard to ... who?"

How could he have heard me? Fear chilled Victor's gut as he handed X the jewel case. A malevolent musk poured off the vampire as he leaned over the desk, which bowed under his weight, making it obvious nothing could stand between them.

Victor pictured Florence and held onto the case for an extra beat. "You."

X's eyes narrowed. "Continue your cure, Thetherson. Stay a threatless joke in X's eyes." He took the case.

Victor remained in front of the freight train. He wasn't feeling brave, just reckless. "Are you really so worried about me as a vampire?"

"X worries on nothing."

If Victor had more self-confidence he might have decided X's smile was forced. If his vampire "hearing" was still working, he might have smelled fear.

"You should worry unless you start taking our work seriously," said X. "Regarding her," He nodded in Florence's direction. "I will not darken her door again."

"I guess you both got what you wanted."

"Sadly, she will get let down. This," X pointed to his fangs, his head, his essence, "cannot *go* to others. You understand?"

Based on the good news/bad news transmission of his own curse, Victor had some idea. "Florence just wants to be young again."

X's eyes glowed like candles' flame against pale skin and the black backdrop. "What she got, is truly a curse." He checked his watch, a gaudy gold behemoth. "Go. I need to call associates."

Victor left the tube and wandered into Accounts Payable looking for a spare desk. He should start making his own calls, to Playco's and EnerGreen's accountants, to gain an understanding of their daily processes. After spending his days working for Chleber and talking to executives about *their* jobs, this prospect was incredibly mind-dulling. He didn't have the heart for it.

Besides, Victor realized it had been too long since he drank blood.

He occupied a donor seat at the Good Sisters blood bank. A needle drained blood from Victor's left arm while his right hand held a quart-sized sippy cup cocktail of tomato juice and blood.

"Drink faster." Tripp sat in a folding chair pulled up to face Victor. "Net-net, you're falling behind."

Victor sucked and blanched. "I forgot how bad this tastes."

Tripp produced a flask from an interior pocket of his fringed leather jacket, theatrically looking furtively left and right. "Allow me to pop Bloody Mary's cherry." He pried the top off the sippy cup and spiked Victor's beverage with vodka. He twirled his finger to suggest a good stir.

After using the sippy straw to do so, Victor sampled. "Better. How much longer will I need blood?"

After another dramatically surreptitious check for peeping eyes, Tripp took a pull from the flask and winked. "You're going to need to stay on the red sauce for the time being. The treatment only keeps your vampirism comatose in the attic. We need the full genetic cure to put it in a coffin and carry it out of your house."

"Somewhere between lab-speak and that picture book description there must be a workable layman's explanation."

"Unless I'm being grilled by Dr. Speer, I refuse to use the terms 'lentivirus vector,' 'universal tropism' and 'restriction enzymes.' Much more straightforward to report that I'm working on designing the coffin and the coffin movers. As quickly as I can."

"You're talking to Speer about my cure?"

Tripp's nod said, *Can you believe it?* "Suddenly he's all for it. Out of the blue he came to me—caught me red-handed actually, working on the protein sequence to target your vamp DNA. 'Right on,' he said, or something to that effect. He acknowledged that understanding your longevity and working on your cure can go hand in hand. 'Strides in one means strides in the other.'" Tripp nailed Speer's pompous certainty. "Which means I can finally keep my boss happy and take care of my buddy at the same time."

The term of endearment didn't do much for Victor. He felt their relationship returning to its old imbalance: Tripp as savvy counselor for his older, timid friend. Tripp was steering their dynamic in that direction, Victor was certain.

As goofy as a single fang must have looked, losing it was an emotional blow. Victor had forgotten what he looked like before vampirism. Dumpy, he now remembered. He still couldn't recall how had he *felt* back then. What was his self-image?

There was a more telling way to get to the answer to that question: *How did I picture my future?*

And now he wondered: Had he ever been brave enough to look ahead? Had he ever tried to peer into the distance, to envision his old age and imagine his state of mind decades down the road? What had pre-vampirism Victor looked forward to? Had there been any *anticipation*? Because there wasn't now.

I need to turn this around. I have to find a way to tap my potential. The abilities were *there*, buried under muddled insecurity, dormant until awakened by the vampire. They *had* to be.

"I have to tell you ..." Victor worked hard to strip the weakness from his voice so that Tripp would talk to him as an equal. "The transition away from vampirism isn't easy."

Tripp winked. "It's a relief to see you without fangs, Viccy. It was like looking at a ticking time bomb. I think we defused you just in time." He picked up a package of Fig Newtons from the adjoining table. "Newton?"

Victor took two. "It's just ... I'm having a hard time feeling like I have something to look forward to."

Tripp swigged from the flask and then popped a Newton in his mouth. "That's how it is after you end an affair."

Mouth full, Victor frowned his confusion.

"Your dabbling as a vampire. That was an affair."

"It can't be an affair if your significant other approves."

"Broaden your analogical boundaries with me," said Tripp. "Your *humanity* was your spouse. You were cheating on your humanity."

"Was my humanity hurt by my cheating?" Victor was sarcastic.

"Crushed. Feeling inadequate and blaming itself, no doubt. And sure, being with your humanity can be a drag. No superpowers. Loads of accountability. So of course when a seductress whispers in your ear, 'Victor, you sexy beast.'" Tripp swallowed Newton as he whispered breathy and husky toward Victor's ear. "'You're better than that, you deserve more than what your humanity is giving you. Come lie down with me and let me stroke your—'"

"Hey."

"'Ego.'" Tripp paused for a pull from his flask. "That's what adultery is all about. Stroking the ego."

"So you're saying what I got from vampirism was all about vanity?"

"I'm saying you don't need a mistress. You can learn to be the best you with your spouse. With your humanity."

Victor wanted to lash out at Tripp; but wasn't that the argument he had been making to himself? It wasn't vampirism he wanted, not really. His deepest desire, his only real yearning was to be his best self.

But having the challenge come from Tripp was extremely aggravating. "Your analogies suck."

Tripp clucked. "Dr. Linciome …" He soured, angry at himself for recalling the disgraced scientist. "He hated that word. 'Suck.' This or that 'sucks.' He said it was vulgar and indicative of a poor vocabulary. I think I'll start using it again." Tripp nodded while thinking. "You had your dalliance, Viccy. Now it's time to suck it up. Accept your responsibility to your humanity. And Barbie. She's excited to have you back, I'll guarantee you."

"I wouldn't bet the lab on it."

"For starters," Tripp said while munching Newton and nodding at Victor's lap, "she can get back in the saddle without worrying about killing her trusty steed. Not yet," he quickly appended the caveat. "Not until I have the gene therapy cure perfected. In the meantime …" Tripp hooked a thumb in the belt loop of his gaucho pants and leaned his chair back on two legs. "Her steed will have to remain in the barn eating hay. Or whatever. Sorry. Couldn't come up with a good metaphor."

"Great." Victor washed down cookie with a swallow from his tall cup. "Barbara and I can look forward to resuming the passionate love life we enjoyed before I was a vampire."

"You're a changed man, buddy. I saw how Babs looked at you."

"As a vampire."

"The fangs had nothing to do with it. Babs grooves on you."

Victor scowled. The IV site hurt. "You're being intentionally naïve. Get this out of me."

Tripp waved for assistance. "Here's what you do, Viccy. You begin as an actor. If you don't feel it, you act it, and eventually it becomes your nature. Chicks dig dudes who give great performances."

"I'm not an actor."

"So then just be great. You've proven yourself. You're at liberty to strut your stuff."

"I was demoted back to Accounting."

"Office politics. That's like a bad review from a cheap hack taking bribes from your competitors," Tripp returned to his acting metaphor. "It's no reflection on your work."

"No matter what I say, you're going to make it fit your opinion, aren't you?"

Nurse Collette arrived. "Done already?" She had an engaging, amused professionalism.

"We're done when Vic says we're done," said Tripp, while Victor stewed.

"Some deal." Nurse Collette disengaged Victor from the IV. "We do all the work and Tripp gets all your blood."

Tripp nibbled a Newton and appreciated Nurse Collette's well-proportioned body. "I promise to put Vic's juice to good use back at the Labs. Won't be long before he can start working toward another ten gallon hat donor pin." He nodded at Vic's cup. "Tell Perry we appreciate the facility and the reverse donation in the meantime."

"Perry loves you both." Nurse Collette tweaked Victor's cheek. "So how's it feel to be human again?"

Victor gave Tripp a baleful look. "Magnificent."

"I don't know." Nurse Collette handed Tripp the blood pouch. "Seemed like you had a great thing going there."

Tripp enjoyed watching her walk away even while disagreeing with her parting remark. "Medical professionals should know better."

"Maybe she does know better." Victor took Newtons for the road. "Better than you." Criticizing Tripp was risk-free, Victor's barbs carried no sting. "So you never told me what happened to Dr. Linciome."

"I have no idea where he is." Tripp brushed crumbs off his wet suit shirt and stashed the blood in his Hello Kitty backpack. "He left town that same day. It made all the industry gossip sites. Dr. Speer isn't reluctant to tell anyone who asks why he gave Linciome the boot. Neither am I." He led the way out of the blood bank and stopped on the busy sidewalk. "But the outrage isn't there. People are idiots. Scientists included. The head of the gene therapy division of the NIH was just outed as a vampire. And he's being allowed to remain."

The disgust in Tripp's voice was too much for Victor. "Maybe because what he does on his own time is his business."

Tripp's eyes bugged. "Drinking people's blood has now become a privacy right?" His gaucho pants snapped in the breeze for extra emphasis.

"If those people don't care, then *yes*."

Tripp's face relaxed into a gentle grin. "Do you think you might be a little biased on that topic?"

His composed certainty was infuriating. Victor had to walk away. "Do you ever think you're a prejudiced jerk on the wrong side of history?"

"All the time, and I couldn't care less. Hey," he called after Victor. "Still up for a beer later?"

Victor shook his head without breaking stride down the sidewalk, unconcerned whether Tripp could hear his reply, startling a mother and her baby in a stroller.

"You and I are *not* going back to the way it was!"

BARBARA

This is Amberly's 17th birthday party and you're delighted to have for once talked her out of playing Apples to Apples. "Left hand, blue," you announce.

Contorted on the Twister mat are four teenagers including Amberly. Victor, too, overly dedicated to being a good father, belly getting in the way of his right knee and his sweat getting on Amberly's friend Jasmine.

In it to win it is Eugene the Vampire Slayer. The young man is strong and flexible, holding stoic poses while the other teenagers' arms shake and legs cramp. Right now he's in bridge, belly to the sky, upside-down and locking eyes with Amberly. Your daughter is beaming.

"Mrs. Thetherson," Cale Bridgeport begs, his muscular arms quivering. "Next position, please!" This makes his girlfriend Jasmine laugh, while Amberly—suffering no less—grins at Eugene, who winks at her.

"Just a second, I need to change my Facebook status to Highly Amused."

Jasmine: "Mrs. Thetherson!"

Amberly: "Mom!"

Eugene: "I don't believe such a category exists."

Cale: "We beg of you ..."

"Oh all right. Left foot ..."

"Ahhg! Hurry!"

" ... red."

"No!" Cale struggles to transfer his foot to the

nearest red circle.

Eugene sees it; he lowers himself, head touching the mat for a second, then springs into a handstand, controlling it for a full two seconds, arrow straight and black clad from skullcap to socks, before carefully, powerfully lowering into the splits, right foot returning to yellow where it started, left foot on Cale's coveted circle.

"Good Lord," says Victor, whose own journey to a red circle is easy. He sees buffoonery in Eugene's every action, an opinion that seems unlikely to change.

Cale is seeing red, as Eugene's thigh presses down on his knee. The 16-year-old's whole body shakes as he searches desperately for an available, feasible circle. Upon collapse he instantly protests. "He lifted his right foot!" Cale hasn't addressed Eugene directly or called him by name all evening. Eugene is a little taller, but Cale must outweigh him by 50 pounds. Eugene has the look but not the style to be bullied, and Cale doesn't seem to know what to do with that. "That's a violation! He's out!"

"You're out, Cale," says Amberly, with Jasmine laughing affectionately at both her friends. Eugene scratches his nose and replaces his hand.

"There!" Cale points. "He did it again!"

"Slaves to the rules of life," says Eugene, "lose every time, Cale."

"This isn't life!" Cale rails, a little squeak in his stout neck. "It's Twister!"

"Let's play Life next," says Amberly. "We haven't played that for years. Cale, you're out."

"You're out, honey," Jasmine seconds.

"Perfect example," Eugene continues, waiting for Cale to extricate himself from the entanglement. "From a recent trip to Cassis." With most of his 160 pounds borne by his arms, Eugene breaks a sweat, a trickle running out from under his skullcap and down his temple. His voice remains even. "French village on the Mediterranean. Prime real estate, but prices were in the tank. Golden Rule of Real Estate: You never buy until prices are on the upswing. You can't predict a bottom."

You spin the dial. No one is watching, so you call out whatever you please. "Right foot blue." This allows Eugene to bring one foot underneath him and take the weight off his arms. You hadn't considered Victor, who now has to cross his legs.

"I broke The Rule and picked up a few properties," says Eugene. "Prices sank for a bit, but now they're rising. I've already gained 20 percent. Of course, it didn't hurt that Slayer Sven and I offed all the vamp occupants first."

Cale stares at the floor, trying to make sense of what he just heard.

Jasmine drops to the mat. "I'm out." She reaches for Amberly, digs her finger between the sixth and seventh ribs until Amberly collapses giggling.

"Jasmine!" Amberly is on top of her friend and they briefly tussle, squealing and laughing.

"Fine, you're still in," says Jasmine. "Happy birthday." She jumps in her surly boyfriend's lap, even though there are plenty of places to sit now—you've brought most of your furniture back from storage. You haven't yet canceled the closing on the house you had picked out up north, but you need to.

Amberly declines. "I was ready to fall. It's between Dad and Eugene now."

It breaks your heart a little to see Amberly's face. She's at boarding school most of the time, so she doesn't yet have an appreciation for how much Victor has changed.

Reverted.

When she looks at her father, her eyes still shine with high expectation.

It's awful, isn't it, that Amberly only started looking up to her father when he started drinking people's blood. Awful, too, that you enabled it. In fact you encouraged it. You had been praying for that bond to develop for so long.

Are you that kind of woman? Of course we all want our men to win, to be the alpha male. But the victories are supposed to occur within bounds, within the rules. Amberly had said it best when she was 12: *I don't want a bad boy. I want him bad-ass.*

Victor had chastised her. Thankfully no one had taken your temperature on the topic, because you would have had to lie to Amberly and side with Victor. There was no pretending he was bad-ass.

That's a little revisionist, isn't it? Think back—you were hoping Victor would ask so you could second your daughter.

You haven't been wonderful to your man. You haven't been a good wife.

"Try to make it fast, will you, Mrs. T?" Cale pretends to be good humored. "Watching two grunting dudes intertwining their sweaty bodies isn't my idea of a great Saturday night."

"To each his own."

"Mom," your daughter chastises.

You grin lasciviously and spin the arrow. "Left hand red."

Eugene could take the dot under his leg but instead selects the one to his left. This leaves Victor with the dot underneath Eugene. Choosing it will be a stretch for the big man, the increasingly inflexible man whose muscle tone is softening at an alarming rate. That dot will bring the two in contact with each other. Eugene seems to hate and relish the thought all at once.

Victor makes a half-hearted attempt and drops his butt to the mat in defeat, smiling. Dentist Mulvane whitened his teeth when he filed down the last fang, really made a nice difference. He gains his feet in three stages: hands-and-knees, one knee, and then a big push to stand. "My turn to spin."

"That's enough Twister." You fold up the mat. "Let's play Cards Against Humanity."

"I don't think that's appropriate," says Victor.

Of course it's not, you think. *That's why it's fun.*

"Let's leave the kids to themselves. We can watch TV in our bedroom."

"Cards Against Humanity, we gotta play Cards," Cale brays. "I kick ass at that game."

"It's not a game of skill, Cale," says Amberly. "And I really don't want to play that game with my parents. Awkward. How about Apples to Apples?"

"No!" Everyone is a little surprised by the vehemence of your veto.

"We're playing Cards with Mrs. T." Cale finds you attractive. Cale would like Victor and Eugene to leave, or die, whichever is quickest, and unfold the mat again for a game of Strip Twister.

Eugene has been studying Victor all night. His teeth mostly. "You made a very wise decision," he tells Victor, seemingly out of the blue. "You know that no matter how I feel about your daughter, I won't coexist with a vamp."

"Taking the cure had nothing to do with you." Victor glances unhappily your way. At least he acknowledges that things aren't good. He hasn't come out and said it, but you can tell he's that close to apologizing. How unattractive would that be? Better he leaves it unsaid.

Better yet would be some indication he was interested in trying not to backslide.

And why was he regressing? You can't figure it out, because you know what he's capable of. You knew this was the man you were born to love at your first meeting, at the University of Houston job auction. Vampirism had nothing to do with it. Victor was bad-ass. Amberly should have seen her daddy then.

So it's there—the attitude, the aggressiveness, the confidence. It's all in there. You wish you could believe Victor had the desire to access it.

You want to be supportive. You want to be a good wife.

You're lying. Being a "good wife" suggests denying the heart's true desire. Loving Victor back at UH and then later as a vampire was no effort. The challenge was convincing him you were worthy. And you like that challenge. You want to be the wife chosen by an alpha male.

You aren't going to revert with Victor. You have no idea how you ever let it get so bad, living together divorced and unhappy, engaged in a battle of wills for ten years without realizing the other side wasn't trying.

Never again.

So why not escape this terrible situation tomorrow? Because in moments like this where you are insulated from the stressful details of leaving and your soul is free to express its true desire, contemplating walking out on Victor doesn't leave you giddy. It only makes you feel sad.

But think of what you are giving up by staying. You haven't painted in a month. After his failed cure, Victor's crackling aura colored your world; you couldn't leave the easel. In large part it was the anticipation of seeing your man gaze at your work—you painted to inspire him. You painted for the immersion in the vivid, perfect representation of everything you love about the world. But more than anything you painted to make Victor proud, lustful, and more determined than ever to succeed.

Stay on principle, blindly refuse to give up, and so give up on making yourself or any man feel that way ever again. True to Dr. Linciome's assertion, the local gallery will be featuring one of your paintings at an upcoming benefit cocktail party. Stay on misguided pride and accept that this exhibit will be your last.

Stay because in that protected corner of your soul, there is faith. An intuition that Victor still has the ability to turn things around, to stop his slide toward irrelevance.

Intuition, you're afraid, is actually *delusion*, and you wouldn't be the first woman to throw her life away to it.

"I guess that's good news, honey," Amberly says to Eugene. "Now you don't have to kill my dad." She has had such a smooth, wry delivery, basically since birth. You have marveled, been driven to the brink of madness, worried constantly and enjoyed it immensely. With a single comment your daughter has the ability to highlight the ties that bind and keep everyone on edge. No wonder Eugene is crazy for her.

Smoothing a path for the two of them might be the only benefit from Victor's cure.

Although wouldn't that have been an interesting confrontation? Eugene, young and vital and cocksure. How would he fare against Victor, ageless and at the height of his power? These two men in your living room have killed people. They wouldn't mind killing each other. That would be some battle to witness. You really are a bad girl at heart.

Cale challenges Eugene without looking at him. "You're killing vampires? That's a load of b.s."

"I'll pull up the videos right now," says Amberly. "Mom, where's your iPad?"

"I wear GoPro," Eugene informs Cale. "They're a sponsor."

"It's in the bedroom." You've seen the videos, and they are something else.

Victor talks loudly while he collects used glasses and nachos plates. "In case anyone has forgotten, Eugene already tried to murder me. Many times. And failed."

"It's called slaying," says Eugene. "Vampires murder people, and I slay vampires. And you know what they say, the last time's the charm. Let me help you with that." Eugene tries to lighten Victor's dirty dishes load.

Victor plays keep-away. "I would love to knock you out right now."

"You've already tried that, many times." Eugene continues trying to take dishes from Victor who strives to prevent it. "And I always wake up."

"Okay, you can't date him," Victor calls to your daughter in the bedroom.

Knock-knock.

You ask Jasmine to get the door, assuming other kids have been invited to Amberly's birthday party to hang out and play games, slurp down spiked energy drinks and crash en masse in the wee hours around the television. You love being that house.

Jasmine yanks open the door. A vampire stands there, his curse obvious even without the overbite exposing the tips of his fangs. He's short and homely, immediately repugnant, clearly dangerous. Jasmine yelps and backpedals.

Victor is unsure what to do with the armful of dishes. "Why are you here?"

"I'll take that as '*entrez.*" The vampire enters your house.

Eugene's eyes bulge. He steps in front of Amberly as she returns from the bedroom. One hand goes to the small of his back where he expects to find, what, a stake? He comes up empty.

The greasy, stumpy, fanged thing saunters up to you. "The lady in the house? Sorry to knock unannounced." His speech pattern is bizarre, a foreigner without an accent struggling to find the right English word. "I was curious to see where the Thethersons reside. X," he introduces himself, looking to receive your hand.

You turn to Victor and affect indignation. "Honey, you didn't tell me your boss was a vampire."

"Oh, you know ..." Victor looks ill as he dumps the dishes on the dining room table. "It's what's on the inside."

X smiles. "Did he blame his cracked his tooth on a nectarine ... seed?"

"You mean a *pit?*" Cale offers.

X brushes aside your shoulder-length hair to inspect your throat. "No tracks." He shakes his head at Victor. "Your ancestor would not understand." X looks to the teenagers who have corralled themselves in the front room. "Your daughter ... ah yes."

Amberly shrinks behind Eugene as X advances.

"You're up, slayer," Cale hisses in Eugene's ear.

If the vampire heard he ignores it. He waves the other three away. Cale and Jasmine take him up on the offer. X extends his hand to Amberly, shielded by Eugene. "Here, young lady."

"X." Victor in roundabout fashion moves to intercept his boss. "What do you need from me?"

"X takes what he needs. *B*ut, you could gi*ve* me your disc. Your *fab*ulous *p*rogra*m.*" The emphases gash his lower lip. Blood runs down his chin and he licks at it, growling.

"He's creating a frenzy." Eugene widens his stance. "That's close enough, vamp."

"I told you I don't have any more copies," says Victor.

"Shit." Amberly makes a move to get to her father. Victor lunges for her and X palm-strikes him in the chest and snags Amberly's sweater; with the other hand he takes Eugene by the throat, lifting him off the floor.

Eugene turns purple and kicks X in the crotch. You hurry forward, too late to stop X from slugging Eugene in the stomach but able to pull Amberly out of the way even as she wants to aid her boyfriend. X has the young slayer in the air, gagging through a flattened windpipe.

"*Go.*" You shove Amberly toward the door.

X heaves Eugene into the wall, slamming him into one of your pieces, the one Linciome loved, Victor as renaissance man astride the ages. You created it during an overwhelmingly spiritual sensation of Victor folding eras together like an accordion, shortening the intervening distances until time became meaningless. The painting lands angled against the wall and Eugene upon it, cracking the frame and tearing the canvas, leaving Victor isolated at his early colonial writing desk, trapped in the past.

The vampire summons Amberly with a stubby, yellow-taloned finger. "Here, girl."

A glance at Victor tells you he's thinking the same thing. *Never again.* Never again will you allow Amberly to be bitten in her home.

If Victor can hold his own with X for just a few seconds, you will return with the carving knife and we'll find out just how much destruction a vampire can live through.

The vamp reads your minds. "No worries. X is not here to drink." He licks his fingers to wet-wash the blood from his chin and then sucks them clean. "Nasty, I know. Can't waste it though."

Amberly shrinks as X approaches her. "Oh God." She's more disgusted than frightened as his spittle fingers comb through her hair.

"Get your hands away from her," says Victor.

X sees the ever-so-faint tracks left behind by Bob the appraiser vampire. "I see there is one who knows how to treat a lady."

Eugene struggles to his feet. "Hands off, vamp." X stomps him in the face.

"Stop it!" Amberly screams into the vampire's face before collapsing protectively over Eugene.

X points at Eugene through Amberly. "You don't know how lucky you are ..." He debates for a moment. "*Fore*man." Blood wells anew from his mulched lower lip. "Dammit." This gouges his lip again and there might be tears in his eyes as he heads for the door.

"I look forward to hearing my name again on your

dying lips," Eugene rasps, lying on his back looking up at the ceiling.

The vampire chortles on his way out. "I will take your word on the disc, Thetherson. Your word or your daughter. Okay? See you at dawn." X likes him in the office early.

Cale for some time has been in a wrestler's crouch, a frozen state of readiness. His knees quiver as he stands up straight. "What an a-hole."

Amberly clucks over Eugene's mashed lip and possibly busted nose. "You are so brave."

You hold the curtains ajar to see X's disappearing taillights. "When are you quitting Bizco?"

"It wouldn't matter." Victor's voice is flat. You don't want to look at him right now.

"That guy was more of a jerk than a threat," Cale decides.

"Go home, Cale," says Amberly. "Jasmine, I'll see you tomorrow."

Jasmine leans down to hug Amberly. "Happy birthday, huh?" She gives Eugene a gentle touch on the knee and pulls Cale out the door.

You need an explanation from Victor. "You gave that creature your program?"

Victor looks ready to cry. There is absolutely no fire in his eyes. "He's intimidating me. That's all this is about. I'm sorry, Barb." At last the apology you didn't want to hear.

Eugene sits up. Amberly gives him a wad of tissues from the box on the coffee table to staunch the bleeding. "I returned to Houston to slay you," Eugene says to Victor. One of his eyes is developing a shiner, the other one obscured by tissue. "This is your lucky night. Because now I'm going to slay your boss instead."

JUST A NIBBLE

"*Victor!* Get in here."

Victor wanted to miss Nikki on her own account. To mourn on her behalf, for everything she was missing.

But her absence had instead become a depressing reminder of how things had changed for him. If Nikki were here he wouldn't be taking the cure. He wouldn't be sitting outside a black tubular teepee in Accounting, listening to his vampire boss really digging into the "V" in his name, drawing blood to work himself into a preemptive frenzy. Missing Nikki was inextricable from Victor's yearning for what could have been.

Things were so bad now that he looked fondly on the time he had managed this department, before vampirism had really kicked in. Maybe his staff hadn't respected him the way he would have liked but they had still considered him their boss. Although they never would have said as much out loud, Victor had been their leader.

He would never lead this or any department again. *You did it once, you can do it again*, Barbara had encouraged. *How?* he wanted to respond. There was no roadmap to follow, no highlighted route to help him retrace his steps. Years ago, he hadn't consciously pursued a leadership role, hadn't won it by a series of intentional steps and achievements. He had become manager by default, sliding into the role as Bizco's predecessor had grown.

That wouldn't happen again, not here or anywhere

else. Not as a defanged, aging 50-year-old. No one would look at him and think, *This guy has potential.* It was too late for that. Barbara knew it.

That moment on the *Xtreme ReVamp* stage when he took Nikki into arms, when he gave in to what they both craved—how did he fail to see the future he was destroying for them both? Nikki had buffered him, facilitated him, thought about him. Led him into temptation. The "date" nights she arranged were nerve-wracking and thrilling. Sitting at her desk outside his office, polishing her toes and smacking her gum, Nikki was a spark of *what if* that made the future worth living for. Victor's heart ached in mourning for her, however selfishly.

Florence cringed when X's voice rang out from his dark enclosure. She too was occasionally called into his "office," despite the fact she reported to Darla. They looked at each other now as Victor got to his feet. Florence tucked a strand of black silken hair behind an ear that was perfectly curved to receive and gave him a solemn nod. Like the memory of managing these accountants, Florence's presence was an unlikely blessing. No *what if*, just an otherworldly touchstone to an earlier time with an unremarkable but palatable future. For that, anyway, Victor was grateful.

Florence coughed. These days the rattling in her lungs made everyone think of residual blood rather than smoky gooey tar. Her fangs were still a novelty for her tongue, always assessing the points.

"Florence?" Darla called from her window desk. Her frustration with Florence's lack of productivity as a vampire was in her voice. "Are you done with the reconciliation to test the XFP?"

"Xtensive Feedback Predictor" was the name X had given to Victor's creation. On a small scale, on the workstations of various Bizco and Playco senior managers, the EnerGreen joint venture was running the XFP parallel to the regular accounting and forecasting systems. Darla's team was charged with reconciling and comparing the data captured in the traditional systems to what was automatically being collected by the XFP. This was in addition to their regular Bizco tasks. They were swamped. Florence had picked a bad time to become a vampire.

Rather than answer, the senior accountant manhandled the XFP and general ledger applications on her touchscreen monitor. The onscreen data representations didn't respond efficiently to the cold stroke of her fingers, heating Florence's bile. She grabbed her mouse and slammed it on the desk, the bow in her spine becoming more pronounced as she squinted at her screen.

Even Victor would have to admit that vampirism hadn't done anything for Florence. In the three cursed weeks, the flesh around her eyes had deteriorated, hollowed to the sockets. Liver spots had sprouted on her hands, standing out against white skin. And she had returned to wearing denim shirts cinched tight with bolo ties and blue jeans with big brass belt buckles, to mask the extent of her body's shrinkage.

Luckily for Victor, he hadn't donated his old wardrobe either: Extra-large dress shirts with short sleeves to vent the heat, and fat pants—still too big for him, but he was too cheap to purchase transitional clothing.

Why was he allowing himself to get fat again? It was just as obvious to Victor as to those around him that his confidence would be greater if he could maintain the robust physique he had enjoyed as a vampire. He was no less committed to exercising—but the intensity of his workouts had diminished. Same for his consistency. His back and feet hurt … he spent afternoons vowing to turn on Tony Horton as soon as he arrived home, simultaneously battling nausea over the thought of the suffering he would endure, suffering that Tony just didn't understand.

It's very possible Victor had as much control over his physique as he did his hair. His widow's peak was now an eroded hillock. Good news, the hair around his crown was growing strong, leaving him only a few weeks from a respectable comb-over.

When he caught Florence looking at him these days, her expression was that of a mirror-gazer unhappy with her reflection but peering deeper in search of some inner beauty that would give her the strength to carry on. Maybe Victor was projecting his own emotions, for surely that was his goal every time he reflected on his current life.

He parted the flap and stepped inside X's domain. The air was tainted warm with decay that had precipitated out and settled to the floor, disturbed by his entrance.

"I hate open floor plans, don't you? It's why cubes were invented." X spoke without looking away from his computer screen. "Do you have the framework for the weekly XFP reporting package ready for my review?"

Blood should have been spouting from multiple puncture wounds. X's lower lip remained intact.

Victor sat at his desk facing the vampire. "Almost."

"That was your progress report this morning." X's beady eyes were so close to the bridge of his hooked nose that a slight turn of his head hid one or the other. His right eye glared at Victor, while the left for all Victor knew continued to study his computer screen.

"I should have it done tomorrow morning."

"You're wondering about my fangs." X tugged at one and came away with a little clear plastic cap. He reattached it, nearly invisible on his tooth, before speaking. "Prophylactics. Kirby made them for me. Frankly, I love them."

"Why don't you marry them? And give Kirby another big raise. Everyone else, too, while you're at it."

X clearly didn't like Victor's tone. "You're jealous

that you haven't earned a raise?"

"You mean a bribe. Like the free parking in our building ramp, and the free weekends at your Galveston condo. I don't expect any of it from you. But at least now I know how you made your reputation as a great businessman."

X resembled a high-pressure geyser field, every vent capped and straining for release. "At Arthur Andersen we had a saying. Under-promise and over-deliver. You are a walking under-promise."

Victor sulked.

"I want that reporting package first thing Thursday." Two days out. "I also have some programming changes for the XFP." X slid a sheet of paper to Victor; his yellow nails tacked it to the desk. "By Friday. Chleber doesn't want Larry so I'm bringing him back as your assistant. Now you'll have no excuse for missing deadlines."

With a quick tug Victor claimed the paper. He frowned reading the numbered to-do list. "Some of these modifications would capture personal data we don't need."

"*You* know what *I* need?"

"Phone numbers, addresses?"

X ripped the endcaps off his fangs and stood. Victor heard the creak from the engineer's boots X had been wearing, thick leather with steel capping the toes and wrapping around the heels. "Did I ask what *Bizco* needs or what this joint *v*enture needs?" Now came the blood. It ran down his chin while he drew in the scent. "Who do you think you work *f*or, *V*ictor?"

Despite the malevolence engulfing him, the very real chance X meant to physically tear into him or perhaps stomp him to death with those boots, Victor submersed into numbness. It was nice not being afraid. Not the same as the electric boldness that had suffused him as a vampire. But better than the fear he used to feel with Jay, with anyone who held or claimed the power to judge him.

"You work for *me*. Not *Bizco*, not EnerGreen. *Me*." Every staccato sentence was accompanied by X's fist jackhammering his desk. Splinters flew. "You are *mine*. The X-*F-P* is *mine*. If you try to lea*ve*, if you try to take what's *mine* ..." X's face was purple. His jaw unhinged to reveal a maw that could have swallowed Amberly's little Yorkie cross. It snapped shut, fangs embedded in his lower lip and protruding like yellow-ivory piercings. X's scream filled the tube as he extracted the daggers with his fingers. "Thetherson ..." There was true hatred in the naming. "I know where your daughter resides."

The damaged desk collapsed. X was unable to prevent his computer from crashing to the floor. The vampire vibrated in rage as blood filled the network of arteries and capillaries in his cheeks.

Victor contemplated the red spatters on his plaid dress shirt and blue-and-green striped tie as he emerged from the black tube. Tessa commented without looking up from her work. "When is Victor going to learn how to adapt his style to the boss's?"

"X is an ENFJ," Quinten offered.

Victor stared blankly.

"Extraversion Intuition Feeling Judging," Quinten defined the acronym. "Myers Briggs."

"What are you talking about?"

Kirby chimed in. "We spent the weekend in New Orleans with X, doing personality inventories." He turned to Tessa. "Were you surprised that X is a Blue?"

Tessa pushed back from her computer. "Do-Gooder? Why does that surprise you? We were staying in the Maison Dupuy on his dime so that we could learn about each other's work styles and build a more cohesive team. X is all about altruistic commitment."

"Hartman color palette," Quinten explained. "I'm Yellow."

"We missed you, Vic," said Casey. "I'll bet you're

Intellection, because you're smart."

"That's StrengthsFinder," said Quinten. "First, discover your strengths."

Tessa took in Victor's confusion and the hurt that he didn't want to feel. "You can't expect him to include you. Not until you commit to the cure."

"I don't know how much more committed I can get."

"Are you still drinking blood?" Tessa confronted him as if this were an intervention.

"I have to."

Kirby sighed. "X talked about your inventory. You constantly need blood to maintain your desired status as a Power Wielder."

"That's Red," said Quinten.

"I don't give a shit," Victor spat at them. "I don't want anything to do with X or his team-building! And he doesn't give a shit about any of you!"

Darla stood at her desk silently asking him to stop.

"He just wants you to hate me! Don't you see that?"

Casey was near to tears. "He doesn't hate you. He wants to save you from becoming ..." She looked around for help.

"Morbius," said Tessa. "And I have to wonder ..." Her words were ominous. Everyone found a way to move a little farther from Victor. "I just hope that's not what you want."

The numbness protecting Victor in X's black chute was gone. He was feeling again. "Anymore, I just want to be left alone."

"We care about you," said Tessa. "You know we do. But can you really expect us to *trust* you? You need to do the right thing. Give up your inheritance, Vic." Looking tired of standing on her little feet, she headed back to her desk. "Humanity or bust. That's your choice."

Everyone paused in glum reflection before likewise returning to their jobs. Only Kirby lingered.

He was assessing the blood spotting Victor's front.

"Did he poke himself? Didn't my safety caps work?"

"They worked great."

"Oh, oh good." Kirby looked at Florence, in a winter jacket and arms wrapped around her torso, shivering in her chair. "If you'd like, Florence, I'll make you a pair, too."

Florence flipped him off, sending Kirby back to his desk. She glanced up before Victor turned away. "Stop by when you're ready to leave, okay?"

Victor nodded and headed for Darla. He needed her. Needed the unconditional love she offered, to be enveloped in her warm peaceful bubble and find some way to stay enveloped from that point forward.

The elevator opened and Sally Bornel stepped out. She too made for Darla and only noticed Victor as they arrived at their common destination.

"Hi, Sally. It's good to see you."

"Same here." The HR director gave him an empty smile and turned to Darla. "I want to talk about getting your team's assistance on a medical liability accounting issue."

Victor loitered. He had nowhere else to go and he expected Sally would want to catch up.

When he didn't withdraw, Sally did. "I'll come back. It's not urgent."

"How have you been?" Victor stammered.

"Great. Darla, ping me when you're available. Or just come to my office if that works." Sally gave Victor the briefest of glances. "Bye."

Victor sank into Darla's guest chair as Sally left the floor. "As if I needed any more proof."

"She isn't the cuddliest person in the company." Darla raised her eyebrows. "And you shouldn't be looking for any 'cuddliness' from her." She quickly clarified. "Now that you and Barbara are moving to a new house and all."

Victor slowly nodded. "We're not buying it."

"Oh?" Darla looked for some preoccupation on her

desk. Found a paperweight, an I-beam embedded in a stone. Victor imagined she was waiting for a hero to stride up to her desk, pluck the steel free from the rock and use it to start erecting something amazing.

That would describe Barbara. Not Darla.

She lifted the paperweight to tighten the underlying stack of papers. "I know rates have been rising again ..."

"It has more to do with my stock falling."

"I don't understand that."

"Yes, you do." Not only did he have to live small and inconsequential, he was constantly required to call attention to it. "I'm not the same person."

"That's ridiculous." She raised her head to check for prying ears. "I hate not having an office."

They watched X leave his "office," laptop over his shoulder and briefcase in hand. He thanked everyone for their hard work as he walked to the elevator in his cruel shoes. "I'm sure he wouldn't mind if you borrowed his," said Victor.

"No thanks." Darla's pulled a packet of baby wipes from her desk drawer, came around the desk and daubed at the stains on his shirt and tie while striving to deny eavesdroppers anything juicy. "You are the same man you have always been. I don't feel any different about you."

"You're attracted to fat mental deficients." Victor watched her mop at X's blood. "Fat, messy idiots."

"No, to you. Who you are hasn't changed." She moved closer. "Your essence is the same. And I love ... that."

Victor challenged her with his eyes while his voice remained flat. "What I accomplish—or don't—that doesn't make a difference to you?"

"Yes and no." Darla stripped away her crisp professionalism, leaving her voice low and soft for Victor's ears only. "What you achieve might be conditional on what you do. But who you *are* isn't." She leaned in and spoke just above a whisper. "I have loved ... everything about you for a long time. Not VV, not the office manager or the heavy hitter. But yes, all of them. You. Through your ups and your downs."

"Darla ..."

"I know." Her voice was hoarse. "I know I'm going too far. I know this is inappropriate. But you need to know that you're important. That how you feel is important." She swallowed and continued. "I don't care how good or how bad things are in your life. I love all of it."

Victor was taking her hand before he realized it, grabbing it and squeezing it. He let go as soon as he was able, when Darla became uncomfortable, even as her eyes continued to glow.

She returned to the business side of her desk. "Maybe we can do that after work."

He wanted that, to leave with Darla after work, check into a hotel room and hide out with her. Let X's deadlines come and go. Victor didn't care if he pissed off the vampire, no longer cared what Jay thought of him.

Except that X would take it out on his family. On Barbara and Amberly.

And when he finished hiding, then what? What was waiting for him when he came back?

He didn't want to think about it. Right now he wanted to enjoy Darla's love without analyzing it, without the future getting in the way.

"I have to pick up Kimberly from dance lessons at 6. Maybe we could meet for dinner afterward?"

"I'd like that," said Victor.

Victor worked on the EnerGreen reporting package for the next two hours, then realized he needed to talk to the programmer X had enlisted to design the XFP interface with the company's workstations. Four floors up he sat at the programmer's desk discussing the additional data-capture features X was looking for.

"A little intrusive," the programmer observed dryly.

"That was my response."

"Fucking vampires, they think the rules don't apply to them. They should all be exterminated." The programmer glanced at Victor. "You used to be one, didn't you?"

Victor ran his tongue over his smooth, even teeth. "I did."

The programmer didn't apologize or qualify his statement. It was that kind of meeting, four hours of uncomfortable, grinding progress. Victor texted Darla he was running late as he entered the 14th floor to shut down his computer and pick up his briefcase. Everyone was gone, the floor dark and dead-silent with the lights and HVAC system turned off for the night in Bizco's green commitment. The sun had long since set. The "office" he shared with X was a black hole against nighttime Houston.

X owned him. Victor had already handed over the title to his creation, and now he was forced to detail it for his master. His enslavement was never so obvious as in the vampire's absence. He should have stomped on X's computer, pissed on the cardigan he kept in his file drawer, enjoyed a moment of rebellion. Instead he fled the floor as fast he as could.

With the demotion back to Accounting, Victor had given up his parking lease in their tower for an economy lot seven blocks away. How thoughtful of him to open up a spot for the rest of the Bizco accounting team. The night was damp and cold. A penetrating wind rushed through the high-rise canyon. He hurried for the partial relief that would come when he turned the corner at the end of the block.

Someone stepped out of the shadows. Victor stumbled to the side. He had never felt so vulnerable.

"You broke your promise."

In his first skipped heartbeat Victor saw only

glowing red eyes and fangs and decided this was a fitting end for him.

Florence took his arm to steady him. "You said you'd stop by."

"I'm sorry."

She maintained her grip above his elbow and stood close, leeward with Victor's back to the wind. Florence's scent set Victor's head aswim, no different than the first time he had brushed past her, a momentary jostling as each of them were swept in separate directions at the entrance to the UH business hall during class changeover. One o'clock on a Wednesday, leaving Marketing 201. Victor harbored a reverential glow for that moment, that memory.

Florence took it all in. "You still like me, don't you?"

If he was still her manager, Victor might have done the right thing and lied. Knowing the truth was coming, his vocal chords constricted. "That's never changed."

"No matter what I look like?"

"You look good, so ..."

Florence backed him into a small recess. "Come here." She touched Victor, neck and back of his head, her back arched just so, elbows tight to her side, shrinking her body and the space between them. She put her lips on his.

Victor had to stop a whimper of pleasure trying to burst from his head.

I'm kissing Florence.

He resisted the urge to put his hands on her, pressing his fingers into the smooth concrete wall behind him. Victor didn't want to make a misstep. His restraint prompted Florence to kiss him more passionately.

She broke their kiss after a short while. Victor was satisfied and would be forever thankful for the moment. The taste and texture of Florence's lips was timeless.

Her face stayed close to his and blurry—not that he would have put his readers on given the situation, but vampirism had broken the habit; he didn't have them along. So he sensed more than saw the gleam of fangs as Florence smiled.

"I didn't imagine that would ever happen," she said with a husky rasp.

"I know you never thought of me that way."

He expected her to move away, but Florence settled in. Her thumb pressed into the meeting place of his leg and hip. "Maybe I never allowed myself. Lately I've been feeling so connected to you. It's hard to explain because I don't really understand it."

"I've been feeling it, too." Victor allowed one hand to rest on Florence's waist. Electric emotions coursed up his arm to stymie his lungs and expand his head. "Lately our past has meant so much to me."

"Do you think it's because I'm a vampire now, too?" She kissed his chin with impossibly soft lips, lips that had yielded so sweetly against his.

It was hard to draw enough breath to speak. "I think it's more than that."

Florence searched his eyes. "Especially since you're all but cured now. Hmm?"

"Treated but not cured."

Florence kissed him again, full and wet, sliding to the corner of his mouth and making her way to his ear. "What we have is very special." She wrapped her fingers around him through his dress pants. Victor moaned; Florence's breath quickened. "Victor," she whispered, making him shudder with pleasure. "I want to bite you now. Just a little. I want to know what it feels like to taste you. To be inside you." She pulled him gently, kissed him behind the ear, felt him nod, and slid down to his throat.

The sensation was incredible. Victor felt every bit of her lips pressed to his skin, a ring of pleasure around a lance of wild fearsome horror. Death was in her fangs;

Victor understood it now like he never had when he had drank.

"*No.*" He shoved Florence away and bounced his head off the wall in the recoil. Through a smattering of stars he saw Florence gathering for the attack, fangs bared and eyes on his throat.

"You're denying me, hmm?" She took a settling breath, pulled out a Harley Davidson hanky and wiped his neck while he leaned against the wall for support, knees shaky. "We'll see how long that lasts. Walk me to my car?"

The overwhelming aversion to Florence's fangs was much the same as his physical reaction to sexual climax. His curse seemed to come with a mind of its own.

One more reason why the cure was his only option.

At the entrance to their building's parking ramp Florence swiped the card entry and they descended to the second level. A gaggle of unhappy men's voices prompted them to proceed quietly onto the floor.

"What the F is taking him so damn long? It's been a freakin' month!"

Victor recognized Teddy the construction foreman from the four-legged race. He had lost hair, put on pounds, and still shouted everything. He was berating Larry and some poor fellow with a hunchback.

"I did see him tweet about an Amway seminar he's conducting at the convention center," Larry drawled. "Why don't you attend and ask him."

"We made a mistake hiring him," said the hunchback.

"You have to admit our real estate investment is doing well," said Larry. "And Ma loves the Mary Kay."

Teddy chested him. "Why do I keep getting the feeling you're not all in?"

Larry squinted at him. "I told you I don't think it's necessary anymore."

"Berry doesn't agree," Teddy barked in Larry's face.

He laughed raucously. "Berry! That's perfect! That douchebag slays me."

The hunchback wasn't laughing; he was sensing trouble, scanning the ramp.

Teddy soured again and poked Larry in the forehead. "You think we're getting a refund out of this guy? I don't wanna invest in makeup. I want the slaying he agreed to."

The hunchback made Victor and Florence and dumped himself on the hood of a Mazda Miata. "What are you doing here?!"

For God's sake it was David Copperfield—or his twisted imitation. Beyond the physical deformity, his demeanor had decayed, a man poised to flinch.

David slid off the hood and shaded behind Larry, who looked extremely uncomfortable.

"Dammit anyway," said Teddy.

Victor recalled the group text he had glimpsed on Jay's BlackBerry. Project Well Done. "What's going on?"

"It's none of your business," Larry muttered.

"Then why do I feel like it's all about me? Are you working with Jay?" Victor drew up his collar to hide Florence's nicks. "What is your problem with me?"

"You have to ask?" The bowlegged accountant looked cornered and ready to fight out of it. "You can't just go around *biting* us. Maybe you can make all the rules at work. But out here, goldammit, here in the real world there are repercussions."

"I only bit one of you."

Teddy took a step toward Victor, sideways in a fencing stance to minimize his profile. "I lost my job after that picnic. I told you I was *injured*. But you made me keep running. Parish fired me. Said it was part of the merger but I saw the way he looked at me after that race. I lost his respect, man." The former foreman's voice cracked. "I have exercise-induced asthma! Of course I looked panicked! I thought I was going to suffocate!"

"I think your exercise-induced asthma is kicking in again," David cautioned.

Larry grimaced. "Both of you can shake out your exercise-bunched undies." He pointed at Victor's mouth. "Like I said, we don't have anything to worry about. Vic's neutered."

David and Teddy crept forward in the dim ramp to get a better look.

Victor bared his teeth.

Teddy burst out laughing, kept laughing until it grew a tinge of hysteria. "Ha-ha. You stupid dumbshit."

They heard the metallic echo of a door closing. Seconds later a car started, the rounded hum of a high-performance engine. Headlights flashed them as the car came around the corner.

X was at the wheel and he drove by slowly, window down, eyes hooded and mouth open like a cat copping a smell. He registered their identities. Victor's face was kept for last, held longest.

The Maserati accelerated away from them. It braked with a squeal of tires at the far end of the floor, turned sharply and laid rubber into the spiral ascent to the street.

It took Victor a second to realize the continued squealing now came from another car. A Honda Civic retraced the Maserati's path at higher speed. The driver worked the manual transmission up and down the gears, flying without braking through the U where the five of them stood, tires screaming nonstop over a bass thump from speakers vibrating the hatchback window.

Eugene's wild eyes swept over the bystanders. The sight of Victor made his eyebrows shoot up. Eugene accelerated down the row and then power-slid around the final turn, not a brake light in sight, the back end straightening out as he entered the spiral exit.

"He drives like shit," said Victor.

"Idiot's after the wrong vampire," said Teddy.

Victor turned on the crew-cut polo-shirted boob. "Did you hire Eugene to kill me?"

Teddy tried to make contact with his puffing chest but their guts touched first. "Why would I need someone else to do my dirty work? If I want you dead there'll be a stake with your name—"

Florence stuck her finger under Teddy's chin and throttled his words to a squeak. She flashed her fangs for the first time.

"Dude." David quailed, hunchback swelling.

"Get your greasy behind out of here," Florence threatened Teddy.

Teddy slapped her hand away. "You scaggy vamp bitch."

Florence punched him in the gut, fast and hard. The blow was debilitating for Teddy, disturbing for the onlookers. While his lungs waited on his diaphragm for permission to inflate, Teddy scavenged enough oxygen to beg not to be bit.

Pheromones poured off the senior accountant vampire. "I wouldn't bite you if you were the last sack of blood on this rotten earth." Her eyes went to David. "You, on the other hand."

"Oh no," said David as he backpedaled.

"Flo," Larry chirped. "The boy's had enough punishment for a lifetime of transgressions."

"There is no causation between transgression and punishment." Florence aimed her fangs at Larry to hold him in check. "Not in this life. Otherwise Victor would be a saint and you'd be a fucking goat." She turned back to David. "And I wouldn't be so gotdamned thirsty."

David Copperfield couldn't disappear fast enough. He ran good for a hunchback. His sneaker soles squorked on the glazed concrete. Florence flew down the next row, in parallel, in her dress shoes, making great time and nary a sound.

Halfway down the row, Florence ran up and over a sedan in a crouch that became a four-legged leap onto David's back. The squeak of his face across the floor melded into his squeal for mercy.

Buffeted by Larry's hollering as he hurried to David's rescue, Florence only took a moment before she stood, mouth wet with blood. "That boy wasn't nearly as sweet as I imagined."

Victor arrived to find David in fetal position, his humpback like a self-contained, useless sac of amniotic fluid.

Larry squatted on rickety knees to assess the latest damage done to his former direct report. "You didn't need to do that, Flo."

"Real world repercussions," said Victor. He was glad he hadn't let her bite him.

Teddy the foreman drove past them in his two-door Impala. Through the tinted windows they could just make out the bird he flipped them.

EUGENE

Do all old folks' homes smell the same? This Eugene wondered in his blond wig and fake peach fuzz mustache leaning on his fake mop and shooting the breeze with the faux security guard he had installed here at the Cool Breezes retirement village.

"Everyone thinks we're in it for the strip searches," said Kyle, a muscle-bound TSA agent. "I'd rather not take anyone's clothes off. But if I need to I'm going to do it with all my heart. *Single-pointed* is how the Buddha described it." He briefly took his eye off the Cool Breezes entrance to give Eugene an intense once-over. "Something bothering you, Rupert?" For a musclehead he was really very perceptive.

"Having a moment," said Eugene. "Like I've been here before."

"Déjà vu."

"Déjà *phew* is more like it. Already smelled it. Nothing looks familiar, though, so I must be thinking of the nursing home Father stuck Granny Foreman in back in New Orleans."

Kyle resumed staring through the front door. "A fellow in your line of work, Rupert? You should listen to your hunches."

Siena the receptionist sitting five feet away frowned. Nursing home janitors needed to listen to their hunches?

She had also frowned when Kyle showed up for work that morning, and frowned some more when he hauled in a white metal door frame with LED lights strung along the sides and a red light screwed into the top and announced that anyone entering the building must pass through his checkpoint.

Her very first frown had been yesterday, catching "Rupert" re-tucking his hair into the blond wig when he thought no one was looking. Siena had reported the troublesome occurrence to the nursing home administrator, who told her to mind her receptionist duties.

If she like the administrator had been privy to Eugene's mission to kill the dragon terrorizing the villagers, the vampire who had become the facility's de facto administrator, Siena would have been smiling.

After following X for the past three weeks, Eugene knew the Vamp liked to park in the east lot for easy access through the employee entrance to his ground-floor room. Today X would bypass that side entrance and enter Cool Breezes through the front door. Eugene had changed the locks.

Never had he taken his time on a slaying like this one. His investment had nothing to do with the humiliation at the Thethersons. Eugene had lost battles before. Just that morning he had been aced out on an apartment complex. Eugene had outbid and yet was outmaneuvered by a broker working for the Houston district attorney. Eugene had accepted the defeat and moved on. Although rumor had it the D.A. was a vampire, in which case Eugene would slay him and pounce when the apartment complex came back on the market.

X had stumbled upon Eugene breaking a cardinal rule in the Slayer code: Never fall in love. Or at least do a better job hiding it.

The images that blossomed in Eugene's mind when he thought of Amberly ... she was The World. Simply looking at her cheeks made Eugene's heart melt. Amberly's tears or a vampire's claws, if either touched those cheeks, The World ended. Thanks to an imprudent game of Twister, X had seen how much Amberly meant to him. X knew Eugene's soft spot.

And so the vamp had sealed Eugene's commitment to slaying him.

The CWS was going to throw a Southern gentlemanly fit when he realized how much time Eugene had spent on this vamp while Morbius's supposed reincarnation scurried about the earth. Make no mistake, Eugene preferred Victor dead too—once a vamp, forever on the list. But the CWS was wrong; the fat slob was no longer a threat. Eugene would continue scoring big points with his sweetie-pie by showing forbearance to her father.

And slaying his tormentor.

Two nights ago he had peered through the window of X's room here at Cool Breezes and watched the vampire remove his steel-heeled boots and tenderly, protectively rub his Achilles tendons. Eugene had found the sweet spot. When Amberly canceled their date, he had time to dream up this plan.

X's boots crunched the gravel bordering the building. The vamp came at a stiff march.

"Look lively, Kyle."

Kyle popped his knuckles one by one. That sound really didn't bother Eugene.

"Keep it by the book," said Eugene. "I don't want you losing your license. Leave the rough stuff to me."

"The book is flexible," said Kyle.

An old person entered the lobby. "Girl," the old dude barked at Siena.

"Hi Mr. Grivens. What's bothering you now?"

"Inmate, you should return to your quarters," Kyle advised.

The geezer shouted at Siena. "The cable broke!"

Siena sighed to Kyle. "Poor old guy. He was a bridge engineer. He's still haunted by the men who died on one of his faulty designs."

The wrinkle-faced old man stomped his foot. "The cable TV, you dumb broad!"

"Samuel, honey, we don't have cable. It's Dish."

"Sir," said Kyle.

"It's go time," Eugene hissed, head down and swabbing the floor.

Through the front door came X, bottom lip sucked in to spare it from his ice pick fangs. Ugly as sin, evil eyes embedded in puffy eyelids. Short arms, stubby bowlegs and a jiggly paunch. Awful acrylic sweatsuit. "The side door is locked," he told Siena.

"Oh it is, I didn't know, I'm sorry," Siena stammered. "Let me get somebody—"

"Sir, everyone comes through me now." Kyle motioned to his door frame. "New policy."

X got as close as Kyle's massive chest would allow and huffed in his face. "I don't like your rule."

Kyle was expressionless. "Visiting one of the inmates? Please sign our guestbook."

X growled. "I reside here."

This genuinely surprised Kyle. Eugene hadn't fully filled him in—because he couldn't explain why the practically ageless vampire rented a room in a nursing home. "A little young, aren't we?"

The vamp leered. "X is older than you know."

There came a crash from Samuel's direction. The geezer had tried to slip away unnoticed and now writhed stiffly on the floor amidst the shards of an Egyptian-style vase and a bundle of silk flowers. He picked up a piece of pottery painted with hieroglyphs. "Oh no, how much was that worth?"

Kyle reclaimed X's attention. "Well, sir, you are to be commended on your youthful appearance." He moved to stand before the "metal detector," flanked by the receptionist desk and three potted bamboo trees. "Unfortunately, unlike the TSA we don't have an age exemption here. Everyone gets scanned." His eyes dropped to X's armored boots. "And removes their shoes."

X surveyed the room. Siena was debating whether to help Samuel. "Rupert" was committed to doing a quality job on the six tile squares under the water cooler. The vamp turned mesmerizing eyes on Kyle. "The shoes stay on."

"Then they'll have to walk you right back out that door, sir." Kyle rested a hand on his revolver, biceps engaged as a backup. "Company policy."

X pondered his options. "All right then." He looked for a place to sit. "These aren't easy to, uh, to get ..."

"*Off?*" Kyle offered.

"Uh-huh." X perched on the receptionist desk. He leaned back and stroked Siena's cheek. "Sorry to create an uneasy situation, dear."

Siena worked not to shudder. "No, no, not at all. I'm here to assist the residents."

"Good to know." X tugged and grunted at his boot. "I'll ask you to assist X later."

Siena could barely nod.

"Need some help with those, sir?" Kyle offered. "Rupert!"

"No-no," X refused assistance. "Rupert" polished the fountain chrome.

After some effort X stood in stocking feet. He held up the boots. "These are dear. I can't stand to let them get too long away."

"Too long away, huh?" Kyle shook his head at the convoluted syntax and reached for the boots.

X pulled them out of reach. "Too *far* away, then." Two blood droplets formed on his lower lip. "You *promise?*" Stabbed again and again, the holes bled freely down his chin.

"I do," said Kyle.

Only Samuel noticed Eugene unscrew the mop top from the handle and from his suds bucket produce the steel head of a medieval pike, a dagger-like lance trimmed with a curved scythe on one side and an axe blade on the other. Eugene calmly screwed the cruel weapon onto the handle.

On cat paws Eugene padded forward. Over the last three steps he twisted at the waist, back arched—his core flexibility was something else—with the pike at full extension overhead. He brought it whistling down. No words, no delay.

X threw his hands up but Eugene attacked low and drove the dagger-lance into the vampire's heel. The steel entered where the Achilles' tendon fastened calf to foot and exited out the bottom of the foot, staking X to the floor.

The bloodsucker unleashed a hellacious howl. Music to a Slayer's ears.

X seized Eugene by the throat. "How could you?"

His grip was weak. Eugene's skin crawled under his touch but he wanted to be face to face to deliver his final *adieu*, a line that would circulate through the vamp world as a word to the wise. Something he could quote to the future Mrs. Foreman later tonight.

X was terrified. "How could you, how could you ... *be* so stu*p*id?"

His grip became a vise. Eugene's windpipe buckled like a thin straw. X removed the pike from his heel and whacked Kyle's head with the flat of the blade. The brawny security guard buckled like Eugene's windpipe.

X tossed the pike into the bamboo and pointed at Siena, compelling her to put down the phone. He retrieved one of his boots. "Did you really think my Achilles' tendon would be my Heel?"

How had he failed to recognize the trap? Eugene kicked himself, figuratively, literally, his legs jerking spasmodically as he writhed in the vamp's death grip. He should have realized X was girding for battle when he drew his own blood. Now the frenzy was in full bloom.

Thunk. The six-pound boot slammed into Eugene's

ear. Over the ringing in his head he had a hard time hearing X's speech.

"We understand that with great *p*ower, we *m*ust endure *p*ersecution. Like the X-*M*en." X chortled as he re-gripped the boot. *Thunk.* "We understand the *f*ear. *B*ut we want to send a *m*essage of *p*eace. I want you to *be* that *m*essage." *Thunk.*

You were supposed to be my *message*, Eugene thought as blood fountained up from his ear and rained down from X's lip, the two spattering each other.

The vamp arched his back as if to howl at the moon. *Thunk*! landed the boot with a grunt as he poured on some extra sauce. Now his expression mellowed. "Actually, let's call it a contract: Quit hunting us, and we won't annihilate you." *Thunk.* That one was less vehement but targeted to split open the blood-rich flesh above Eugene's eye.

X chucked the bloody boot to the floor. With adrenaline-jittery blood-slicked fingers he fumbled fitting a pair of plastic caps over his fangs. He pierced a finger—"Aggh! Are you kidding me?"—nearly launching a new frenzy. After a couple deep breaths he was able to place the prophylactics. He smiled at Eugene, who was unconscious. "Thank God I can stop wearing those shoes. They were killer on my ... *b*unions."

With a wink at old Samuel and a leer for pretty Siena, X got down on hands and knees and lapped up the blood oozing from Eugene's wounds.

WHEN DOVES FLY

"For the last time, don't help me if you don't want to."

They carried food from Barbara's car toward a canvas canopy pitched on the lawn of Houston Presbyterian Hospital. A wet breeze had the canopy popping, had Boy Scouts from Troop 813 jury-rigging a crisscross, mishmash, sailor's nightmare of stabilizing guy lines.

Against that stiff wet wind the Scouts had pounded deep into the ground the poles supporting the vigil sign:

Houston Loves Eugene!!!

Victor didn't want to help Barbara, didn't want to assist any effort that might hasten Eugene's revival. He couldn't bring himself to wish for Eugene's death—nothing these days triggered that much passion. But some brain re-circuiting would be great. Nothing traumatic, just enough shuffling of the connections to alter the young man's essence. Victor no longer cared whether Eugene was a slayer. He just wanted the irritating punk to develop a personality his daughter didn't like.

"No worries."

"I hate that phrase." Barbara spoke conversationally as they fought through the crowd that sipped piña coladas from coconut shells and eyed the passing food. "From you especially. You can't pull it off. You look worried all the time."

"Shouldn't we be worried? Amberly is in love with a vampire slayer. A terrible one with all kinds of loose screws. This vigil will just feed his psychosis. Eugene is a menace, a misguided do-gooder. He's worse than Ralph Nader at a pep rally."

Barbara waited out his screed.

"He's worse than Voldemort."

Barbara sighed. "Like I said, no one asked you to help." She hurried ahead to deposit the casserole dish of three-layer dip on one of the five card tables lashed together with twine about the legs and a paper runner over the top. She was careful not to cover the message someone had written on the runner in pink and red:

Get well soon, Eugene!! ♥♥♥

The pan of smoked ribs Victor carried wasn't as respectful. "You'd think at some point everyone would start packing lunches." This was Vigil Day Four. "Or at least consider this a potluck."

"It's the least we can do for all this support."

Victor struggled to keep pace as Barbara returned to the car, buffeted by a horde converging on the food table's new arrivals. Five hundred plus was the fire marshal's latest headcount, presented to Victor with a warning that city hall was considering shutting them down for lack of a permit.

"I dare you," Victor had said.

Ten minutes ago the marshal had returned to tell him not to worry, everything was taken care of. And that Waste Management had donated port-a-potties which should be arriving any minute.

Victor was accosted by Mary Roe, a neighbor from their block whom he never had the inclination to bite. She nodded at the food tent. "Did you see my cobbler?"

"In the little 6-by-9 pan? It's gone."

"It's always a big hit. I feel so bad for Barbara cooking all day for everyone. You know Qdoba does a great job catering."

"Thanks, Mary Roe. I'll remember that for the next

vigil."

"Comas? Hello? We could be here for months."

"Let's pray something happens tonight, one way or the other."

"Really, that's a terrible prayer. What time are we releasing the doves?"

"The what?"

"The 46 white doves?" Mary Roe was stunned Victor wasn't aware of this particular tribute and pleased as punch to tell him. "Two for each year of poor Eugene's crime-fighting life."

"Sucking blood isn't a crime, Mary Roe."

"And isn't that a crime?" Mary Roe crossed her arms and cocked a hip and shook her head at Victor. "So I heard it was Eugene who counseled you to take the cure."

"Eugene's preferred cure was to drive a stake through my heart. Excuse me, I need to make sure nobody skipped breakfast and lunch in vain."

"Everyone," came Amberly's voice over the loudspeaker. "If I could have your attention for a moment. And your prayers."

Victor's daughter stood on a crate that had contained the coconuts donated by Maui Jim. Bert's Hardware Hank had provided the drill to drain the coconut water and replace it with the rum and/or pineapple juice donated by Gulfer's Liquor. Today's allotment of rum had run out 20 minutes ago so that many of the coconut shells were empty and now being banged together in approval of Amberly's announcement, and in protest of the Scrooge-like supply of booze.

Amberly looked up at Eugene's window on the hospital's fourth floor. Turning back to the crowd her eyes were wet. "I'd like you to pray for a man we all admire." She was so young; this girl on stage wasn't far removed from the 10-year-old who smiled through her tears when Barbara announced that her pet iguana had heard the call of the wild and was now living happily in the desert as the leader of a pack of Gila monsters. She was so young and yet so composed and mature, and flat-out gorgeous.

"I've come to know Eugene on a deeper level and I can tell you ..." Tears streamed down her cheeks. "He is worth your prayers."

The crowd cheered. Young girls, grown men and old ladies called up to his room, "We love you, Eugene!" "Wake up, Eugene!" "Amway's here for you, Eugene!"

This allowed Amberly to collect herself. She took a shaky, lovely breath. "As you know, Eugene continues to rest peacefully in a coma. In the meantime, we're eagerly awaiting the results of his latest CAT scan." She held her hands aloft, four fingers on each hand crossed. Victor waited for the cold, damp wind to force her to don a wrap over her tight shirt and put a damper on the lustful gazes cast upon his barely-17-year-old. "And we're also hoping the police will finally decide Eugene's life is worth something!"

The police were being accused of reverse discrimination for failing to arrest X for an assault in front of multiple eyewitnesses. But the eyewitnesses were reluctant to speak and the D.A., recently confirmed as a vampire, had decided that Eugene's unlawful detaining, searching and spiking of X had made successful charges unlikely.

Human district attorneys around the country had largely agreed. But that hadn't stopped the local outcry or the formation of the nation's first serious vampire protest movement, Stop The Attacks Killing Everyone. (According to the group's spokesperson, a working group had been formed to come up with better words for the acronym.)

Five women standing shoulder to shoulder started a chant. "Justice for Eugene, the stake for X!" The two phrases were printed front and back on their t-shirts. The women rotated in choreographed half-turns, facilitating the read-along chant-along, clacking their coconuts. "Justice for Eugene," *clack-clack*, "the stake for X!"

The crowd got into it. Amberly waited out a few boisterous repetitions, nodding thanks to the women. "You know that Eugene was brutally attacked by a vampire, X Anthony. But you may not know why. This vampire personally threatened my family. Eugene was trying to protect us."

"That's a load of baloney," a woman hollered from the other side of the crowd. Victor couldn't see her but it sounded like Tessa.

The great majority of the vigil-goers disagreed. "You shut up!" was their composite request.

"X was defending himself!" the woman who could be Tessa said. "How would you like it if someone tried to put a stake in your heart?"

"It was his foot!" quite a few responded, some quite angrily. A minor scrum ensued.

"Everyone, please," Amberly called for restraint, on tip-toes and back arched, trying to see the commotion. Victor's vision had deteriorated with the loss of his vampirism, but he could see his daughter's nipples from 30 feet. He headed for the stage amidst yelling and chanting, as Amberly called for the release of the doves.

Below the makeshift stage were two dove handlers who looked like carneys, each with a bottle of the free rum lying next to the cages. They were eager to release the birds so they could resume drinking and ogling Amberly. They opened the hatches. The doves were loath to leave so the carneys shook the cages, turned them upside down and then extracted birds by hand. After the first couple took wing the rest followed in a rush that surprised the two scruffy gents, who energetically defended themselves, knocking a few doves to the ground.

The "doves," mostly pigeons, were swept sideways

by the aqua-wind. They sought shelter and found it under the canopy. The birds settled onto the ribs, bogged down in the three-layer dip, cracked the corn chips, ignored the coleslaw and rabidly pecked at the caramel corn.

Horrified, Mary Roe chugged toward the food table hollering, "Shoo!" Her husband Dennis grabbed her, caught her right before the web of guy lines claimed another victim. The birds gorged and chortled while Dennis held his wife and cooed, "Too late, too late, let it go, let it go."

Victor stood before the crate to offer Amberly his jacket. She declined. "I can't be comfortable while Eugene suffers in there."

"Honey, believe me: He'd want it this way."

"Hey!" A tall man holding a *John 3:16* sign pointed at Victor. "You're the son of a bitch who bit my wife!"

The crowd gasped and recoiled before realizing the accused was the big balding fat schlep dangling a tent-sized windbreaker. That's how Victor mentally narrated their reaction. Now the sea of vigil-goers parted to reveal a short stocky man in a jogging jacket over a compression shirt from Under Armour's Captain America collection. Around his wrist, a rubber red S.T.A.K.E. wristband.

Despite the wraparound Bono bubble glasses Victor recognized him from the only time they had met, in front of the Thetherson house when he had fraudulently picked up Amberly for the school's Father-Daughter Dinner.

"You bit *my* wife, too," said Jasmine's dad. His voice was deeper than Victor remembered.

"I don't think so," said Victor.

"You bit Jasmine's mom?" Amberly was mortified and amplified. "Dad, you promised!"

"If I did," said Victor, "she must have been a regular in the downtown club scene."

"Liar!" Jasmine's dad squawked. He quickly

squeezed his lips together and reestablished a persona
of barely-contained righteous rage, and a deep throaty
growl. "The attack happened behind the Salvation
Army store. Mitzi was dropping off donations for the
financially-disabled."

Victor shrugged. "Those days are behind me." For
the benefit of Jasmine's dad and everyone watching he
bared his teeth, newly rounded and already a shade or
two dimmer after Dentist Mulvane's whitening.

"I'll never forget overhearing my wife describe the
attack to one of her friends," said Jasmine's dad. "It
was traumatizing. Because of you, she is no longer
charitable. Because of you, I became …" He removed
his jacket, displaying a bandolier strung across his
back sporting seven silver stakes and a pistol. "A
slayer!"

People craned their necks and jumped up and down
to see the 5-foot-6-inch slayer.

"I was reluctant to give up my comfortable lifestyle
for the dangers of slaying. But Mitzi and I have been
financially blessed by my career as a private equity
fund manager. We're debt-free, praise the Almighty!"
This earned him a muted *amen*.

"And then some, actually," Jasmine's dad qualified.
"So we had a sit-down family conference and decided I
can afford to devote myself full time—to slaying!"

He received polite applause. The pigeon carneys
hoisted their rum bottles and toasted, "Good for you,
Bruce Wayne!" Jasmine's dad reached as if to scratch a
hard-to-reach itch and finally extracted a stake. He
thrust it aloft. "Good people of Houston! It's time to
take back our neighborhoods! Our fair city! Our lives!"

That got the crowd into it, ramped up to a wind-
dulled roar. They pressed forward and flowed around
Amberly's stage crate.

Jasmine's slayer dad pointed the stake at Victor and
a finger at Eugene's fourth-story room. "No matter
what happens up there, know that Eugene's good work

will be continued down here!"

"Eu-gene! Eu-gene! Eu-gene!"

"Stake X! Stake X!"

"Stake the vampire!"

Victor donned his windbreaker and retreated. His teeth ached all the time these days.

Ditto for the rest of him. He had resumed aging. Victor didn't mourn the loss of longevity. Gladly he would have grown old as the man vampirism had revealed, the man Barbara had fallen in love with; he could have asked for no more. But that man had only been revealed through some kind of magic— Legionnaire's disease when he was 22 and then vampirism. No magic remained and he couldn't conjure up that man on his own.

Victor reminded himself that he was no worse off now than before vampirism. He recalled Tripp's assurance that his despair was just a transitional phase. And he heard his mother's voice: *This too shall pass.* That had given him comfort as a boy, prompting young Victor to look past his present misfortunes to a better future.

That's the way his father had taught him to drive across the endless Texas plain. "Pick up your eyes, Victor. You're looking right in front of the car. Raise your gaze to the distance." One simple step and young Victor would instantly relax behind the wheel of that Chrysler K car.

Lift your eyes, this will soon be over. Raise your gaze, and see yourself in the future.

But there was nothing out there. Nothing he wanted to picture, or experience. From a great distance, as a young boy, the future must have looked good. It was much closer now, much easier to see. Good from afar, but far from good.

Why would he mourn his loss of longevity? Victor couldn't stomach the thought of an older version of this.

Florence. Now that was something to look forward to. She had been taking him out to coffee and for drinks after work. They reminisced and even though Florence's college stories didn't involve him, they evoked for Victor that slim moment in time when he had been wonderful.

Yes, the two of them were growing closer in a way Victor never dreamed possible. But the relationship was a memory lane charade. Florence kissed him and touched him and made his head swim, but she didn't like him or herself as they were now; she was picturing them as they were back then.

What about Darla? Yes. Yes. Darla gave him comfort whenever he thought about her, including now. Darla loved him and Victor understood that no matter what, she would love him forever.

Barbara stood at the edge of the throng, arms crossed. She was staring at him, a rare occurrence anymore. Victor wished he could give her something to see.

"Where are you going, *vampire*?"

Jasmine's slayer dad had forced Amberly to bend down so he could yell into her mic, right as the wind died. His epithet echoed off the hospital and startled the birds, which rose protesting and then returned as if tethered by rubber bands to the serving dishes. The carneys waved their bottles of rum in moral support. "Do him, Slayer Batman!"

"You think you can just walk away from what you started?" As Jasmine's slayer dad approached, the crowd closed ranks behind him. "Were the Nazis allowed to remove their swastikas after the war and rejoin humanity?"

"I suppose it depended—"

"The answer is no. So what makes you different than the Nazis? You think you can terrorize us, then file down your fangs and pretend it never happened?"

"No, of course not. Well, yes, because I didn't

terrorize anyone."

"You effin'-A right you did," said John 3:16. He jabbed the pointed sign at Victor. He wasn't alone: A growing gaggle of men and women were primed for confrontation.

"You see no reason to atone for your sins?" Jasmine's slayer dad played to the audience, brandishing the silver stake. "You think we're all too afraid to say anything? You're a New York City gang-banger terrorizing a subway full of innocent passengers. Aren't you?"

Victor squirmed under the analogical onslaught. Jasmine's slayer dad seemed to be seven feet tall. "That's not it at all, Mr., uh ..."

The newbie slayer bumped Victor with his carved chest. The individual pecs jostled Victor's rib cage. "Let's just say I'm the guy who should have put you down when he had the chance."

"That's perfect." Tripp ambled out of the crowd, spurs jingling and sucking on a piña colada. "We'll call you Shoulda." He pointed at Jasmine's slayer dad, John 3:16 and an outraged woman. "Shoulda, Woulda and Coulda."

Amberly ran to Tripp and gave him a hug worthy of a hero saving the day, in the shadow of the slayer and his fellow belligerents still leaning toward confrontation. "Thanks for coming."

"Wouldn't miss supporting your sweetheart, sweetheart."

After a brief brave smile, Amberly couldn't hold back tears.

"What's wrong, little Thethy?"

"We're not sweethearts anymore."

"Why?"

"Because it can't work." Amberly shook her head angrily. "A slayer and a bloodsucker." She struggled for composure. "Have you forgotten my father is a vampire?"

"Who's almost cured."

"Tripp," said Victor. "Let her make up her own mind."

"Vampires have ruined enough lives," said Tripp. "Do they have to ruin love, too?"

Amberly glared at him. "Don't you think it's a little more complicated than that?"

Tripp winced. "That was uncalled for, wasn't it." He glanced at Victor. "Your pop knows I man-love him."

Amberly shook her head, refusing to look Tripp in the eye. She swiped away tears and collected herself. "I better get this crowd's mind right."

"Not until I give you a make-up forehead kiss." Tripp did so, hugged Amberly through her stiffness, while Victor suppressed the desire to cheer. Now he could honestly say he was fine with Eugene surviving.

"You're something special, little T-h," said Tripp. "'Nuff said."

Amberly pecked Tripp's cheek and took Jasmine's slayer dad by the arm. "Mr. Alioto, how's Jasmine enjoying her mission trip to Russia?" She led him away as he threw dirty looks at Victor and worked to holster the stake.

Tripp likewise towed Victor away from the hotspot to join Barbara. "Barbie." The warmth in his greeting wasn't reciprocated but Tripp continued as if he had just scored another Thetherson hug. He bobbed his head toward the hospital. "The kid isn't afraid to stick his nose in a scrape."

"Someone had to stand up to that disgusting little prick," said Barbara.

Victor reddened with the unstated comparison.

"And when he wakes up," Barbara continued, "I'm sure he'll go back and finish the job."

"I'd like to think we're doing our part," said Tripp. "Last week we published the results of Victor's implant treatment. Just one unverified success, which means no scientific credibility. But we've already had 20 calls from courts, cops and corrections officials, looking to use our treatment on their incarcerated vamps." He sucked his piña colada dry, eyes eager for the future. "Wait 'til they see what's next."

"For everyone who entered the drawing for a gift basket of Mary Kay cosmetics," Amberly announced over the loudspeaker, her emcee face restored. "We'll draw the winner now."

The crowd continued to grow. People filed in from every direction, disembarking from their vehicles on the bordering streets, hopping off the local buses and leaving the hospital on break, whether from their jobs or their own loved ones' vigils.

Tripp continued when no one nibbled. "I think we have it. The cure, Viccy."

"Okay," said Victor.

Tripp pushed his hat back to contemplate Victor's reaction. He chuckled. "Not too long ago you would have chewed me a new one. I'd call that progress." He gave Barbara a wink. "It's good to have the real Victor back, isn't it?"

"I get confused with all the comings and goings." Barbara scanned the crowd and looked inward. "I honestly don't know what's real anymore."

Amberly's announcement of the lucky name was greeted with coconut shell clacking and an old Hispanic cowboy's sheepish receipt of the cosmetic gift basket.

Barbara excused herself. "I have dove doo-doo to clean up."

"I'll finally have a little leisure time after we get Vic cured," Tripp called into Barbara's wake. "Why don't I have you guys over for dinner? Or vice versa."

Barbara answered without looking back. "I'll let you entertain Victor, just the two of you. Like the good old days." She stepped through the guy wires to reach the food table, surveyed the damage and ordered Troop 813 back into action.

Tripp whistled. "You two having a little spat?"

Victor cocked an eyebrow.

"I know it doesn't help that you're in limbo, stuck in mid-cure."

"That's not it at all."

"Trust me," said Tripp. "You'll be happily surprised once it's over, as soon as we can actually cure you. We just need to run a final safety protocol. Sort of a 'What would the FDA have us do if they had any idea we were planning a gene therapy treatment?' I think I told you there's a vamp in charge of the gene therapy section of the National Institutes of Health, for crying out loud. So we're keeping our progress under wraps. Three weeks and we'll be ready to roll."

Tripp noticed and ignored a knot of vigileers edging closer, including John 3:16 and his outraged woman. They were offended by Victor's presence and working themselves into deeper, actionable anger. "If Ol' Doc Speer has his way it'll be sooner. Now I understand why he's suddenly keen on this cure—I witnessed one of our investors busting his chops to perfect it. They obviously see it as a profitable treatment. Too bad I'm just a lowly employee. No profit-sharing coming my way."

Tripp talked on like Victor was attentive, like he wasn't concerned about the small band of vigilantes. "Speer used to chew my ass when he caught me working on the cure. Now he chews my ass double when I'm not."

One of the men took off his coat, revealing big, padded biceps. Turned out Tripp had been paying attention; he executed a flairful 180. "Ladies and gents, why don't you all go find a real vampire to torment?"

Paddy Bare-Arms pointed at Victor. "Someone needs to make an example of them!"

"That's my preferred teaching technique, too," said Tripp. "But it's not how vampires learn. And this fellow here, this friend of mine, he's not a vampire. That's a distinction I'm going to make for the cops. When they review the video." He nodded at the Channel 7 television cameras drinking it in, a reporter poised to add his voiceover to the potential violence.

The vigilante vigileers retreated. Paddy Bare-Arms shrugged off his woman's attempt to protect his exposed but insulated pipes from the elements. He cast away his straw and drank straight from the coconut, then spat away the dirty coconut hairs on his lips.

Tripp gave Victor a friendly backhand. "Tell me I didn't miss the housewarming party at your new digs?"

"We're not moving. We're not getting married."

He let it sink in. "I'm sorry, buddy. But don't get too down, promise me? You're just getting started in your new life."

With Amberly surveying the steadily swelling crowd with apprehension, a long-haired dude ran to the little stage and whispered in her ear. *Thank God*, her lips could be read. "I've got great news," she spoke into the microphone.

Victor marveled how natural his daughter looked onstage. Wired, confident and engaging. He looked at Barbara to share the moment but couldn't make eye contact.

"You'll be very happy to hear … we're turning this into a benefit concert!"

This received a raucous roar.

"We hope you'll stay with us all night and donate to an incredibly worthy cause. The entertainment will be here in about an hour. Some of Houston's own to comfort and serenade our Eugene." Amberly received a piece of paper from the long-haired dude. She stomped her foot in excitement and disbelief. "Beyoncé will be here!"

After pandemonium died down she read the names of the other entertainers, shrugging and looking puzzled. "Also, there will be a Kenny Rogers and a Zizz

Top ...?"

"Here comes the doctor!"

All eyes went to a man in a lab coat making his way across the lawn in what had become a decent evening, marred only by the sound of sirens. He accepted a hug from Amberly and the microphone. The doctor stood in front of the crate stage to address the crowd. He did not look pleased to be there.

"Hello, everyone. I'm Dr. Cravits. On behalf of the hospital, thank you for your concern over these past couple days."

"It's been *four*," someone hollered. "A couple is two!"

"I have some information on Mr. Foreman."

"Tell us about the CAT scan!" demanded one of the women in the "Justice for Eugene" t-shirts.

"I'm not at liberty to share confidential information, but I can tell you our tests have been mostly encouraging."

The crowd was mostly relieved.

"More to the point ..." Dr. Cravits was distracted by the sirens, which turned out to be police not ambulance. "I do need to get back inside. But in a nutshell, Mr. Foreman is no longer a patient at Presbyterian."

"You let him check out?" said the "Justice" woman. "In a coma?!"

"Not officially." The doctor looked for someone to hand the mic to as Amberly was running toward the hospital. "We believe Eugene was abducted. At least no one informed us they were taking him." Dr. Cravits set the mic on the crate and hustled after Amberly.

A complete and eerie silence settled over the thousand-plus crowd.

A man near the front raised his hand, looking for someone to call on him. "We still get Beyoncé, right?"

THE GREAT ESCAPE

"Chim chim-in-ey, chim chim-in-ey, chim chim cher-ee," the CWS quietly sang. He stifled a sneeze.

He was wedged in the crawlspace above the fourth floor of Houston Presbyterian. Shimmying away from Eugene's room with a body bag in tow. He had a rope tied around his waist, the other end tied to the body bag, plowing a furrow through the dust.

A few minutes earlier the CWS had crawled alone to Eugene's room. He had waited somewhat patiently in the ceiling until shift change, then lowered himself into Eugene's room, produced a syringe and jammed the needle into Eugene's thigh. Yes Eugene was in a coma, but the CWS did not take chances.

The hospital was crawling with police, crowd-control for a thousand vigileers. Cramming Eugene into a body bag, the CWS marveled that the young slayer was so loved. He could not fathom why. Abducting Eugene would have been much more straightforward without the heightened security. Although truth be told, the CWS enjoyed circumstances that called for an elaborate plan.

Hilda waited below behind the wheel of a hearse in the morgue pick-up and drop-off zone. Two orderlies had been paid to look the other way and to convince the police to do the same. One other accomplice waited for the CWS in Room 410.

Eugene kept wasting time on the wrong vampires. This time he had almost paid the ultimate price. It had given the CWS quite a scare. He thought they had applied ample heat to Eugene to get him to slay Victor Thetherson. It was time to sit the slayer's arse squarely on the burner.

He had rolled and bent and stuffed Eugene into the body bag, tied the rope around his feet, and then removed his oxygen and monitors. Bells and whistles went off. Yelling and footsteps ensued. The CWS was in the ceiling in an instant, hauling up the comatose and sedated Eugene with deft precision and a grunt. As the CWS replaced the ceiling tile the door was forced open.

"Where is he?" demanded a masculine nurse. The male nurse who came in behind her started to panic. He looked out the window, under the bed, and then ran out the door. "Doctor, doctor!" he said. "Come quickly!" The masculine nurse stood rooted dumbstruck.

The CWS laid in the crawlspace as motionless as his body bag. Doctors, nurses and security guards ran in and out of the room. The CWS heard them trying to surmise what had happened and trying to come up with plans. Plans on what to do and plans on what to say to the mob outside.

After ten minutes of this they posted a security guard outside the now-empty room. The CWS towed the body bag to Room 410 and untied himself from Eugene. He pulled back the ceiling tile. The young man in the hospital bed was startled, then happy to see the CWS, motioning him to come down. The CWS dropped to the floor like a gymnast cat.

The young man was clearly in some pain but smiled at the CWS nonetheless. "How did it go?"

"Fine." The CWS let out a huff. "Fine."

"Now what?" the young man asked.

"I told you what comes next." Smiling, the CWS approached the young man's bed. Reached into his pocket and pulled out a Ziploc bag. The bag contained a rag. The CWS gently put the rag over the young man's nose and mouth.

The chloroform worked fast.

Hilda had scoured the city for appendectomy patients without insurance, found this one at Houston Methodist, and had him transferred to Presbyterian. The CWS told the young uninsured man he was part of an elaborate caper to smuggle out a relative who was also scheduled for an appendectomy, which was against their religion. The young man was reluctant at first, but the persuasion of religious freedom and a free surgery made for a willing accomplice. Methodist had been all right with the transfer, too.

The CWS had warned the young man about the need for chloroform. "Some people do feel nauseated when they wake up." He had told the young man his body would be swapped for Eugene's and that he would awaken in post-op, sans appendix. And that maybe he would find a small token of their appreciation in the pocket of his dungarees. He had lied. The CWS took the pillow from beneath the young man's head and placed it over his face. Applied pressure for nine and a half long minutes. Then he scampered back into the ceiling.

More alarms, more nurses and doctors. They tried valiantly to save the young man. He was pronounced dead, with an autopsy scheduled to confirm a burst appendix. They had lost two patients today—one to an apparent ruptured appendix and one to the wind.

When the coast was clear the CWS lowered Eugene into Room 410. He took Eugene out of the body bag and put the young man in, and then hid him up in the crawlspace. The zippered bag would suppress the smell for a day or two.

He put Eugene in the bed and covered his head with the sheet. As the CWS walked out of the room, one of the paid-off orderlies walked in. The orderly put Eugene on a gurney and whisked him down the hall to the service elevator and then down to the morgue. He bypassed the check-in window, rolled the gurney to the pick-up zone and loaded Eugene into the waiting hearse.

The CWS emerged from the hospital as the hearse roared up and out of the ramp, tires squealing as it left the premises. The first police cars were arriving, sirens winding down, lights flashing. The CWS admired the pretty girl standing on a crate addressing the huge throng trampling the hospital landscaping. He strolled down the sidewalk to a waiting cab, hopped in and asked the cabbie to follow that hearse.

THE WOMAN HE CHOSE

Hard-sided suitcase in hand, Victor stood on Darla's doorstep. Her townhome. He wasn't sure whether he was expected to ring the doorbell or just walk in like he lived there.

Darla must have been watching for him. The door opened before he had to make a choice. "Hi." She beamed. She sighed. And then broke down crying.

Victor wrestled his large suitcase past her in the cramped hall. He knocked over a pedestal holding a painted wooden basket that spilled keys, ChapStick, sunglasses and spare change across the composite hardwood floor.

"It's okay," Darla sobbed.

"Are you okay?" Victor abandoned the mess to embrace Darla through her nodding.

"I'm great. Really. I can't believe this is happening."

"I know."

"Sorry about my outfit." Darla was in a sleeping shirt and slippers.

"I'm sorry for showing up so late."

Darla refused the apology. "I'm glad you're here. I didn't think this would happen. Even though you were having problems, I didn't think you'd leave her."

"I know."

If he said more than that, Victor might be the one crying.

Three hours earlier he was at his dining room table working on his laptop on which X had allowed the programmer's copy of the Xtensive Feedback Predictor software. Barbara descended from upstairs to stand arms crossed looking at him.

"I can't take this."

When Victor didn't respond or even look up from his laptop, Barbara's voice sharpened. "It's every night. And weekends."

"I don't have any choice." Victor still refused to look away from the programming on the screen, his program, the one he didn't own any longer. As if his focus was so intense that there was no room to consider Barbara's protest. Except that for the past half hour he had been staring blankly, unfocused, each eye separately capturing and making no attempt to integrate floating images of the coding. His mind wandered all the time. "I have to get this done."

"You're not getting paid for this."

"I don't punch a clock. I'm salaried."

"This isn't Bizco work. Is it? It's for him."

Victor shook his head, not denying his enslavement to X but Barbara's accusation that he had a choice.

"Amberly can't take it. She can't take your sighing. The sounds you make."

"I know she hates me."

"That's not true." Barbara's chin trembled. "She said when they find Eugene she's going to tell him it's over between them."

"Thank God."

Barbara's bitterness dried out her eyes. "That's so easy for you to say. She loves Eugene with all her heart."

This pained Victor to hear. It almost wasn't enough that she was ending it with the slayer. He wanted Amberly to have seen the error of her ways. "She's barely 17."

"Which means she loves him all the harder. She's leaving Eugene for you, do you understand that? You've broken her heart, Victor. God she looks terrible.

She wants to leave. She wants to finish high school somewhere else. She wants to get away from everything that's happened and everything that reminds her …"

In a twisted form of empathy Victor saw himself through his daughter's eyes. "I don't want her thinking of me anymore."

"You don't get to control that, do you? You can only control how you act—"

"I thought she was heading to the police station tonight," Victor talked over her, "for the hunger-strike sleep-in." The ridiculous slayer had been missing for almost two weeks now. Three thousand people were willing to starve and sleep on the concrete in dismayed protest at the cops' lack of action.

"She won't leave until they find him." Barbara's voice quavered. "It's disgusting, you sitting there. I know you have to," she cut off his protest. "I know what X would do to you and to us if you don't. But I don't care. I think about you," the tiniest amount of pleading bled into her vitriol, "at that Accounting job auction."

"If only I had known I wasn't winning a *job*, but a *career* in Accounting."

Barbara ignored the sarcasm. "How you walked into the interview with X like you owned the armory. And when you walked out that job was yours if you wanted it."

"That was …" *Different*, he was about to say. And it was. But it wasn't X that was different, or the circumstances. It was him. He was a different man back then. A better man. That was Barbara's lament and she was right. Now his diminished self was holding her and Amberly hostage. He needed to let them go.

Barbara saw excuses in his face and posture. "I can't take listening to you complain. I can't take listening to you. I can't stand looking at it. I'm leaving, too."

Victor understood perfectly but shook his head. "He won't let you."

"I don't care." Barbara's fine fingers were knotted, intertwined with each other, and now shakily reaching for her phantom ponytail. She let out a frustrated cry. "I should, but I don't." She looked upstairs, tears in her eyes. "Neither does Amberly. Right now all she can think about is Eugene. And your gutless sounds."

Victor slammed the laptop shut and stood, for the moment imposing. "Tell me what I'm supposed to do."

Barbara shook her head, eyes on the stairwell.

"Tell me how I'm supposed to think." Victor gripped his skull, digging for his numb mind, unable to get through loose flesh and thin hair, fluffy between his fingers, too insubstantial to tear out. "Tell me how I'm supposed to act when nothing works!"

"I don't want to tell you what to do." Barbara refused Victor's desperate need for her to look at him. "I know it seems like it sometimes and that makes me angry with myself. Because I honestly don't want to."

"Barbara!" Victor stood by himself in the middle of the room. "Tell me how I'm supposed to live like this!"

Her response was to go upstairs. Victor had the laptop in his hands and he started to spin, Barbara's paintings revolving around him, one revolution, two, he was a discus thrower building momentum to hurl the machine through the window.

Instead he rammed it against his high, high forehead and headed for the bedroom.

Twenty minutes later he was packed and at the door to the garage. Barbara had materialized in the kitchen doorway.

"I'm amazed." She nodded at his suitcase. "This is the most decisive thing you've done in months."

So he had surprised two women tonight.

"I like your townhome," he told Darla as they entered the combination living room-dining room-kitchen.

"It's detached. It's a house."

"Town *house.*"

"Townhouses share walls. I have my own walls. Please call it a house. Let's bring your suitcase up here."

They climbed the stairs. "I really should be staying in a motel."

"We know each other well enough for this," said Darla. "If you want to be here ... you do want to be here?"

"This is the only place I thought of coming to." Victor realized he was talking too loudly in the short upstairs hallway. "Kimberly home?"

"Of course."

"Of course. Not everyone's 17-year-old daughter rents a place and comes and goes as she pleases."

"Amberly isn't exactly 'renting a place.'" Darla enjoyed the humor in his pathos. "And I doubt the school lets her come and go as she pleases." She looked at Kimberly's closed door in passing. "For as much time as she spends in there, it's kind of like she's not here. Meanwhile my son decided he'd be better off living with his father." She led Victor into her bedroom and closed the door behind him. "I don't want to think about how little structure he's getting over there. You can have that dresser. I cleaned it out for you."

"I can just use the suitcase for now."

"Nonsense." Darla put his suitcase on the bed, popped the clasp and started unpacking him. "This isn't a commitment—although I'm sure about it. You don't need to be in a motel room feeling awful. You could use someone being nice to you. Full time. She only seemed to love you when you were a vampire."

Victor watched how lovingly Darla carried his clothes from suitcase to drawer, occasionally setting aside dress shirts and pants to be hung up. "It was how I acted. That's what Barbara loved."

This brought pain to Darla's face. "That's not the

way love works. It's not supposed to be conditional—'You do this for me, and I love you. You act this way, and I love you.'"

"But I don't love myself, either, the way I act. The way I am."

"That's awful." Darla stopped rolling his socks and crossed the bedroom floor to where Victor stood a couple feet inside the room. "I don't want to hear you say that anymore. I don't want you to go back there. Jay and X, maybe there's not much you can do about them. But you have to receive love at home. Unconditional love. For who you are, not what you didn't do."

Victor's voice was husky. "It's what I *can't* do."

"Then that's even worse." Darla kissed him. "Oh, sweetie. What you've been through." She kissed him again, soft and somewhat chaste but offering something deeper if he was ready and wanting. "I love you, Victor. Do you know that? Not for anything other than who you are. I love *you*."

He tried to leave the words unexplored as they kissed, to simply take refuge in Darla's love. Without wondering whether he deserved it.

"This is better without your fangs, I have to say."

Victor pulled his face back until he could clearly see Darla's eyes. "Why? I have to know why, Darla. Why do you love me?"

"Because—"

"At my age, with the job I have? With the marriage I've ruined? With a daughter who doesn't respect me?"

Darla bristled. "If that's the measure then I don't deserve your love either. I think I've done everything I can to be a good mom but it doesn't seem to matter to Kim."

"Then we're not the same. It's different for me because my daughter is right. Amberly is right. Kids don't have to love their parents unconditionally. And I haven't done what I need to do to earn her love."

"I'm sure that's not true, you love her—"

"Of course I do. But that's not enough."

"If that's true, honey ..."

Darla wouldn't let him leave her embrace, to lie down on the floor, just lie there and take the weight off his mind, close his eyes and let the ringing in his ears grow and grow until that was all he knew.

"If our kids can't love us for who we are and for the love we give them, okay. I don't agree, but if that's true then it's up to us to teach them how to love unconditionally." She tried to smooth the sorrow from his forehead. "That's what I'm offering you. I know it's what you need."

Her touch was wonderful. Her fingertips did release the tension in his face. Victor drew her into a long hug with all the strength he had left. He felt her own angst melt against him and was glad for that. Darla deserved it. Being here was right. For everything Darla had done for him and for everything she promised.

"I'm tired," Victor told her.

"So am I."

In the closet Victor changed into a pair of shorts he used to wear for his P90X workouts. He kept his t-shirt on and climbed into bed with Darla. He was barely able to hold his eyes open long enough to wish and kiss her goodnight.

I'm lucky to have found you, Darla.

Sometime later Victor's eyes opened.

Darla loved him the way he was. But Victor didn't.

Here he was and here he would be, in a miserable, slow-motion sleepwalk through meaningless days and decades for the rest of his days.

He got out of bed and heard Barbara's voice.

This is the most decisive thing you've done in months.

Darla was awake. "What's wrong?"

"I'm sorry." Victor dressed quickly, jammed sockless

feet in his shoes and made for the door without tying them. "I can't stay here."

"Why?" Darla chased him, biting her tongue in the hall past Kimberly's room and down the stairs, catching him at the front door, hands shaking and heart breaking all the more for having just been there three hours ago, deliriously happy. "Victor, no. Please. Why? Where are you going?"

He wouldn't tell her. Victor couldn't do that to her. He only hoped he had enough vampire left in him to get this done. "Just out. Thank you, Darla. For everything." He held her up to kiss her forehead, knowing she would be collapsing behind the door after he left.

In his car, the Charger, now like an overdue lease, Victor called Florence. She answered before the second ring.

"Is it too late?" said Victor.

Florence cackled. "You think I sleep at night?" She coughed. "That's for my desk at work."

"I'm coming over."

"Please."

"Tell Buddy to leave the house." Victor drove recklessly through the city, through yellow and red blinking traffic lights, the car dipping and nearly coming off the pavement through the humps of the intersections. "I want to be with you, Florence."

"Yes." Never had he heard that kind of lust for him, and in a single word. "I am so ready for this."

The house smelled as if a wand of Glade air freshener had been waved through the baked-in smoke. Victor was turned on. He had never been a smoker but his father was, and his mother had loved Glade's products. Smoke-scent meant a girl who flaunted the Surgeon General's and her daddy's wishes, a girl willing to surprise and do more than one might have assumed.

Not for a second had Victor ever believed Florence wanted him. So why was she so hot for him now? Vampire hormones? Vampirism had depleted her in every way. Florence's curse did not resemble his.

Had she learned how his curse was transferred? Victor would be shocked. Tripp and the Longevity Labs had their ethics on straight, committed to keeping that knowledge under wraps.

Chalk it up to Smoker Girl Surprise. All Victor needed to know was that Florence wanted him to fuck her—yes he was uncomfortable with that word but no other term or euphemism accurately described the vibe Florence was sending. She wanted to fuck him, which meant he was going to get what he came for.

But now as she led him up the stairs to her bedroom, the moment overwhelmed him: He was finally, actually, truly going to have sex with his ultimate crush. His most unattainable woman now wanted him. And even though his mind would only benefit from the knowledge for a matter of minutes, the *why* suddenly became important. He had to know her desire.

"Is Buddy gone?"

"As good as." Florence's fingers were interlaced with his. Her hand was a perfect construction of bone, sinew and skin (if a bit cold). "I told him to stay in the basement until I said it was okay to come up."

She wore a shift of a shirt, barely covering her hips, revealing every inch of her long legs, the filmy garment clinging to her. Her body was too skinny but that was irrelevant; that body was Florence's, so it took his breath away.

The bedroom was close to stifling. No air conditioning, a thick blanket hung over the window, the only light from candles on nightstands on either side of a double bed.

At any other moment Victor would have instantly burst into perspiration, panicked at the thought of trying to breathe in this hothouse, fearful of Florence seeing and smelling him sweat. Now he couldn't wait to get his clothes off and get Florence on that little bed and feel his skin sliding slick against hers.

"I never thought this moment would happen." Victor watched her dabble at the hem of her shift, giving him a glimpse of her skimpy panties. Behind her stood a potted plant, her height, a slender woody stem sporting clusters of spiked leaves. He expected some version of that when Florence removed her shirt and couldn't wait to put his hands on it. "I couldn't even try to picture being with you. It was too far-fetched."

"You thought you'd have to be some stud? Like Buddy?" Florence gave a self-disgusted chuckle and watched her own fingers make a slow exploratory journey up her garment. "Do you know how blessed I feel that you still want me?"

With his fingertips Victor traced the prominent bones from her wrist to her knuckles, following her hand as it rose above her head, rustling the plant's thin fronds. He let his fingers trail down her forearm, through the inside of her elbow, over her stringy biceps and across her armpit. He barely breathed as he dragged the patterned linen across Florence's breast. He looked at her parted lips, sucking oxygen, small triangular fangs revealed.

"How do you want me, Florence?"

She tilted her head back as Victor touched her through the shift. The garment absorbed her sweat and caught on her skin. "Like this."

Some vestigial impulse brought Victor's mouth to her throat. He pressed his teeth to her flesh, felt her blood coursing beneath. He stayed there to breathe her in and saw Florence's skin and hair as they had existed decades ago. To the beat of her pulse Victor mourned the impending tragedy that had brought him here. He whispered in her ear. "*What* do you want, Florence?"

"You, Victor."

"You'll have me." Victor put his arm under her butt and lifted her off the floor. Not without some effort—his back had been in and out lately and with his gut in the way, Florence's center of gravity was a little too far away for comfort. He moved quickly to the bed and the mattress knocked his legs out from under him. He slammed down upon her.

Florence's desire only increased. She mashed her mouth against his, opened wide to let him in, her fangs slicing his lips and tongue.

"You'll have me." He ran his hand underneath the shift, exhilarated by the feel of her skin, stomach, ribs and breasts.

I wish the last time had been with Barbara.

That thought appeared from nowhere. Victor had already said goodbye to Barbara, out loud to himself as he drove to Darla's, and then out loud on her voicemail as he traveled this last leg. That Barbara wasn't in his arms now, wasn't the chosen one for his final embrace, brought a deep melancholy.

It did nothing to derail the physical pleasure of Florence writhing and moaning beneath him, tangling the bedding, their heads becoming wedged under pillows.

Sex with Barbara was impossible, of course. He couldn't curse her with his vampirism. She didn't yearn for that power. Not for herself, anyway. And of course, she no longer yearned for him.

"Take it off," Florence rasped. "Tear it off me."

With a snarl of angst and desire Victor took the shift in both hands and pulled unsuccessfully.

"Here." Florence stabbed the collar with a fang, separating a few strands of the fiber. Victor finished the job and moaned softly to see her body uncovered, skin glistening in the candlelight, bare but for her panties, the lace band barely touching her abdomen between the high ridges of her hips, a small triangle of silk clinging to her wetness.

There was magic for Victor in slowly, fully revealing Florence. He wanted mouth and nose on her, to know her taste, scent and texture. But Florence held him in place, undoing button and zipper and pushing his pants and underwear to his knees, her foot finishing the job.

"Do you want me?" she purred, taking him in her hand, surely answering her own question.

"Florence," said Victor, guttural, finger sliding into her, his mind spinning with that knowledge of her and of what he was about to do, a slow-motion tornado that picked up images of his family and scenes and memories from his job, none of them pleasant. None except for the presence of Florence and the idea of finally making love to her. "Do you understand what you're doing? Do you know what you're about to receive?"

"I do. I do, Victor." Florence kissed him and tugged at him, maneuvering and tilting her hips to accommodate him. "I want it, I want *you*, so badly."

"Oh God." The acceleration, Victor now remembered how fast it happened. There was no stopping it. "Do you understand ..." She deserved to know what was about to happen to him. The nature of his selfish act; why he was truly there. " ... that I don't want to go on."

Like breaking a fever, sweat burst from his every pore. It lubricated their coupling and made every angle permissible. His soul was departing—the room lost warmth, lost color, lost smell as a vacuum formed in his skull, expanding, calming the tornado and dissolving his memories, accelerating the emptiness, replacing the angst.

He was dying; Victor was afraid. "Tell me how you feel about me! *Tell me why I should go on.*"

"Oh Victor." Florence moaned as she took him inside her. "I want what you want." She rose hard against

him, latched on with a death grip as tremors rocked
Victor's body and soul. "Please God," Florence cried
out, "don't let it be too late!"

And so Victor Thetherson had his answer.

Mom, I'm sorry you didn't go first.

His mom was the type who liked to tidy up. Her
son's discombobulated life caused her stress, he saw it
in her face and heard it in her words every time he
visited little Milford where the squeaky wheel that
was Larry's family got all the laughs and attention and
respect. Victor's only regret was not rampaging
through those dusty streets and little bungalows as a
vampire, making the men quail and the women moan.
It would have given his mom some relief to know that
her son could make messes for others to clean up.

Florence didn't care about him. Despite their
connection before she ran off with her New Zealand
sheep rancher and despite him being there for her
when she returned. None of that meant anything to
her—and why was he surprised? He had given the
same to every woman in his life, from his mother to his
daughter to his wife.

Barbara! Sirens screamed and bells rang for her, a
wail and a peal for every way he had failed his wife.
Victor remembered and relived word for word the
voicemail he had left.

*I love you Barbara, I love everything about you. I
am so, so sorry I couldn't live up to what you expected.
What you trusted you had. I gave you what I could ...
but it's not what I give you. That's not the measure of a
man. It's what I create. Laughter, awe, envy,
inspiration. I feel like it was there, I know it was,
inside me, locked away. The man you expected me to
be. I simply couldn't break him free. You believed in
me and I failed you.*

*Please don't feel guilty. I love the way you wanted
me. I hate the way I am. I blame you for nothing.
Another 30 years like this, like I am, is meaningless, is*

madness. Barbara, Barb, my lady ... I can almost see your face relaxing now that you can stop kicking yourself for your inability to compromise. I can feel your relief, now that I'm gone.

As Tripp's treatment had done its work Victor's streaming thoughts had become a waterfall cascading down as a million whispers and arriving as a single thunderous deluge. Death was the only way to dry off and quiet the roar. The promise of Heaven or the possibility he would no longer exist was just more onrushing overwhelming meaningless thinking.

Deafening were the sirens and bells as Victor worked into his last push. The bed lifted and spun him through the air. Victor remained in his body but left the room, soaring as the Earth repelled him, flinging his corporeal form heavenward, stripping out his soul and mind, snuffing them, sick of his act like everyone else.

One more push, a voice commanded. His last thought in this realm.

Victor pushed and his squishy dick fell out.

"I'll never forget you!" Florence cried. That was the oath she was set to utter upon receiving Victor's vampiric seed. It was premature.

Victor fell off the skinny bed and whacked his head on the nightstand on the way down, knocking over the candle and receiving a fast few drips of wax in the middle of his expansive forehead.

Florence felt herself, felt around, and then leaned over the bed and saw Victor's limp penis. "Did you do it?"

After a brief self-assessment: "No."

"Why?" A tinge of panic in her voice.

My God, Victor thought. *It won't let me.* "I wanted to."

Florence pulled Victor to a sitting position. "Get back up here and do it again. Do it *right* this time."

Victor was numb in the brain, numb to the bone.

"*Victor.*" Florence brought forth the demons X had implanted. "*Get in my bed.*"

"I don't have the strength to stand much less fuck you."

Florence yanked open the nightstand drawer, smacking Victor in the skull. She rummaged without success, pulled the drawer out, fracturing the runners, spilling the contents. Amidst loose change, a fingernail clipper, paperback books, a tube of petroleum jelly, crackers and a previously full ashtray she found a bottle of purple pills.

When the cap didn't cooperate, she bit it off and dumped the pills in her hand. Victor couldn't escape. Florence pounced on him and forced the Viagra into his mouth.

A massive gag reflex turned his stomach inside out, ejecting a horrible stream of bile along with the pills.

Florence screamed.

Disobedient Buddy with his hand on the basement door handle turned right around and went back to what he and only he would call his man-cave.

Her scream boiled down to a deep tortured howl. Hands became claws. Her neck elongated and her ribs protruded, skin stretched over sinew and bone like gray parchment. She was a monster and Victor would never again see her otherwise. The vampire clawed her face and pulled out her hair then did likewise to Victor and yanked him to his feet by his head. She led him at a fast clip across the room, lifted him pro-wrestling-style and threw him out the bedroom window. Victor bounced once off the roof.

As he fell, Victor wondered whether after failing once again in the bed he would now die of a broken neck in the matted winter grass. A final insult. But not to worry: The skip off the roof had oriented his body so that he landed flat on his back. He bounced a bit and came to rest looking up at the cottony black sky.

The vampire still screamed, doing herself harm in

the bedroom above. No one in the surrounding houses came out to check on the big naked man on the Blankenship lawn.

After expecting to be dead now, after saying goodbye to every aspect of his life, Victor had nothing going on in his head and nowhere to go. Spring was coming, the temperature neutral in a rare way for Houston. A couple hours later Buddy finally dared take a peek out the basement window and assumed Victor was dead, as still as he lay.

WEEDING

Laughter. That was an unexpected side effect of being dead. Victor Thetherson watched Tripp administer a reflex test to a 70-year-old woman while she fondled the scientist's kneecap. Victor laughed and the old gal laughed with him.

She slid a hand up Tripp's thigh, up and tickle, up and tickle, until Tripp was forced to grab it. "All we can say for sure," she told Victor, "is that my effective age is younger than Dr. Tripp's. No way it would have taken my brain that long to let my hand know I was about to get fingered."

Tripp arched an eyebrow at Victor and instructed the large lascivious lady to stand up and stand on one leg.

"It's not that Tripp is old for his years." Victor was in robe and slippers, he and his wheelie IV bag in transit from the bathroom back to his old quarters. One look and Dr. Regnald Speer had had no objection to readmitting him. There was clearly no residual vampire. Very little residual Victor of any sort. He had stared at the floor during the admittance interview— not at all like human Victor who always made eye contact as a courtesy for the other person. Now he didn't care. How long could he milk this limbo? *I might enjoy numbness.* "He's a floozy."

The woman cackled. "What a nice coincidence!" She hooked Tripp's calf with her levitating foot and rubbed him.

Tripp made a note on his e-pad. "Balance, A-plus."

The gently wrinkled, vibrant woman looked at Victor. "Are you in the longevity study, too?"

Victor had to laugh again. He knew this woman—she was maybe 25 when he had joined the study as its only child. They had been in this very exam room together a handful of times over the intervening years. Vancine was her name. Victor always thought they had a bond; the *V* if nothing else. Yet he was a stranger to her.

"Not anymore."

Vancine wasn't the least bit intrigued. She cocked an eyebrow at Tripp. "Is it time for my suppleness test?"

"Honey." Tripp flipped the cover on his e-pad and pushed away her hand, and then her other hand. "You already CLEP'ed out of Suppleness 101." He whistled in admiration as Vancine did a back bend into a bridge. "That's extra credit, for what it's worth."

"You tell me what this is worth," said Vancine as her body started to quiver.

Tripp awkwardly helped lower her to the floor. "You scan skip today's blood draw."

"A month ago I would have been disappointed not to have you sucking my blood like a vampire." Vancine retrieved her coat. "But now it's hot that you don't want to."

"Not getting your blood drawn is hot?" Tripp confirmed.

"Slayers, sweetie," said Vancine. "Today's sex symbols. Just say no to dirty vamps. I'm an honorary member of S.T.A.K.E. We're meeting later at Eugene's hunger strike slumber party, if you want to join us."

Victor chortled. "I could have saved a lot of money if we had hosted the hunger strike instead of the hospital vigil."

Vancine ignored him and tweaked Tripp's nipple. "Just as soon as they find Eugene, you need to give that young man the treatment. We need to keep him strong and supple. He's a national treasure."

"Vannie, you are in the presence of a national treasure." Tripp winked at Victor, the source of the Longer Labs' longevity breakthrough, the genesis of the injections Vancine had been receiving the past four months. "Thank you for coming in, as always. Can I get one of the aides to escort you to your car?"

"My coupe, you mean?"

"So you bought the Kia?"

"The Camaro, you mean."

"Dammit, Vannie, I don't think I can outrun you anymore."

"So stop trying, Dr. Tripp." Vancine ran her hand over his cheek and left the exam room, brushing past Victor without a glance.

Tripp typed in a final e-note. "At some point you're going to be famous. We're not ready to formally go to the FDA with a proposed trial but in the meantime they gave informal permission for the limited treatments we're doing on Vancine and a few other long-timers in our study. Once we go national and the press gets hold of it, they're going to dub you St. Augustine."

"Mm."

"That's where the fountain of youth was."

"Uh-huh."

Tripp pretended to see excitement. "Don't get stars in your eyes yet. We don't know if it works."

"Judging by Vancine, you have a winner."

"She's naturally frisky and flexible." Tripp swapped out Victor's nearly-spent saline bag. "We got you making regular trips to the potty now?"

"That's all I do."

"That's what I hear. I'd like you to take more walks. Longer than to the WC. The movement would do you good."

"What's 'good'?"

Tripp wrinkled his forehead as he checked the flow from the new IV bag. "Okay, Aristotle, I'll bite. Something is 'good' if it produces a net gain for all concerned."

"Then it's impossible to make an argument for me continuing to take up space."

"Ouch. That was about the meanest thing my pop could say to me. 'Trippanzee, you're just taking up space.'"

"Your real name is Trippanzee?"

"No. Good to see there's some curiosity in there, though." Tripp studied him with a faint grin. "Must have been some sight. The undead and the oh-to-be-dead making sweet whoopee." Victor had told him about his attempted suicide. "I don't see how it could have ended any other way than with you naked and alive on the front lawn." He pulled Victor's chest hair through the bathrobe's décolletage. Victor slapped away his hand and Tripp grabbed his hair with the other hand. "With a new lease on life."

Victor stood and took it. "I'd call it a short-term rental."

Tripp let go. "Don't dress so provocatively if you don't want your chest hair pulled." He shut the low-cut robe like drapes. "I figure you're here. That means something."

"I had nowhere else to go. And no idea how to end it."

"My friend, that was an attempt for the record books."

"Mm." Victor's muscles sagged around his bones, allowing his fat to hang heavy, dragging him lower to the floor.

"It's my fault you're in this depression. I have you trapped in transition between vampirism and humanity. You're awash in conflicting hormones and neurochemicals and that's not going to change until we fully eradicate the vamp genes that are right now in every one of your cells, dormant but still causing trouble. You need to trust me and hang in there until we have you cured."

Victor shook his head. "Whatever's happening inside me doesn't change reality. I know what I am."

"I disagree. What's happening inside *is* who you are. Or at least it's coloring who you *think* you are."

"Honestly, Tripp. I do know what I *want* to be. And it's not possible. So why should I go on?"

Tripp sighed. "Normally I would say let's go get ten beers and talk it over. But I've heard alcohol can be a depressant for some. So the coffee shop it is. We'll dump a few shots of espresso in your bag. Put some pep in your step."

"I'll pass."

"Fine, you big dick. Then I'll go back to work. Because you know what? If things go well, tomorrow's the day. We have the cure, Mister Victor. Assuming the vampire monkey doesn't die overnight I'm going to give it to you tomorrow morning."

There was the laugh again, deeper and throatier than his norm and bursting unexpectedly from his slumped belly. "So those slayer nuts were right. You do have vampire monkeys."

"Of course. We also have two chimps and three pigs that seem to be getting younger. The FDA doesn't know about those subjects." Tripp waited for Victor to shuffle into the hall with him. "If things continue the way they're going with our more or less hairy subjects, then we have something. Something huge. And it's all thanks to our national treasure."

"It's nothing I did intentionally."

"So maybe you're meant to be here for all kinds of unintentional acts of goodness. Not a bad reason to be alive."

Victor gave him a muted scowl. "That sounds stupid."

Tripp nodded at the cart of cleaning supplies

blocking the door to Victor's room. "Housekeeping will be in there for a bit. Why don't you get some air?"

"I'm not going outside like this."

"Really? What do you care?"

The scowl felt good so Victor left it there as he shuffled into the reception area and out the front door.

A beautiful day, the campus busy with walkers, dawdlers, nappers and the studious. Victor was slower than most, more animated than some. He slid along the sidewalk unnoticed, faintly registering how these rare spring days were his favorites, the air unburdened by anything baked or steamed.

"Please tell me I'm not too late."

Leaning against a thick mimosa tree, ignoring the bees buzzing the bud nubs just overhead, was a man in a sunhat nearly as broad as the canopy. He removed his sunglasses and approached Victor. He didn't seem to like what he was seeing.

It was Dr. Linciome. His sideburns had grown down his jaw, approaching a new goatee. "I can't believe you're back," said Victor.

"Not officially. Not even unofficially." Linciome glanced toward the Labs building and put his shades back on. "Speer would have me incarcerated. And from what I hear, the D.A.'s a vamp, so that would likely be the end of me."

"Why?"

He motioned for Victor to show his top teeth and received a humorless, revealing smile. Linciome groaned. "I failed you." He retreated to the shade tree to slump and sit against it. He surveyed the Rice students spread across the greensward. "I failed us all."

Victor was surprised to feel anger slicing through the numbness. In his reduced state he was able to watch it, even enjoy it as it prepared to lash out at Linciome, to make the disgraced scientist feel just as hopeless and worthless. "Yes. Let's start with Nikki. If

I had known my vampirism was still full bore I could have been prepared."

"I apologize but there was nothing—"

"Your lie started everything." Victor picked up his IV pole and marched across the grass to loom over Linciome. "Everything that brought me to this point. You ruined me. All for your research."

"For what it's worth now, it was for something bigger."

"What? Why was it so important that I remain a vampire?"

"Please." Linciome entreated Victor to keep his voice down as heads turned. "To stop the vampires."

"Keep me a vamp to stop the vamps? That doesn't make any sense."

"You are not—*were* not—like the others." He got to his feet. "They are rising. I've been in Old Europe with the men and women who have dedicated their lives to keeping them in check. Turns out we were fooling ourselves."

"We?"

"They're evolving and moving into key positions. Like the D.A. Like at the NIH. We're in trouble. And you were the key to stopping them."

Victor gaped at him. "You're crazy, aren't you? Not just unethical. You're nuts. I can't believe it."

It took a moment for the fire in Linciome's eyes to burn out. "The world went there first. A guy's gotta fit in." He nodded at the Longer Labs. "If you're cured already, why are you here?"

"It's still in my genes. But Tripp is taking care of that tomorrow."

"It's not too late!"

"Believe me, it is."

"As long as it's in your genes—"

"I tried to kill myself!" Victor felt all eyes upon him and didn't care. "*That's* why I'm here." He grabbed the IV pole and made for the sidewalk. "Actually, I don't know why I'm here."

"I'm so sorry. What you've been through I can't imagine." Linciome hustled to stay alongside Victor's hard march back to the Labs. "But I can give you a reason to care. Get out of there right now. Don't tell Tripp, just leave. Meet me—" He became suddenly suspicious of their spectators and donned glasses and hat and lowered his voice. "I'll text you."

"Don't bother."

"Big V, superstar, there is so much you need to understand. About your true inheritance." Linciome grabbed his arm. "And your Heel. I was given something in Romania. Something you need to see." From an inside pocket of his safari jacket Linciome pulled out a sealskin pouch and began to extract from it a small and apparently ancient leather-bound book. "I told you about Morbius's diary—"

Victor batted the book from Linciome's hand. Pages burst from the binding, making the scientist yelp and scramble to carefully retrieve them. He watched Linciome attempt to reassemble the diary with the lightest of touches. "You don't get it. I don't trust you. You tricked me; you tricked Tripp and Dr. Speer. For your research, for whatever. You don't care about me— don't you think I see that?"

"I care about you more than you know."

"Stop it. You care about yourself. I'm guessing you're only back here because your Romanian friends figured it out, too." Replaying Linciome's words, Victor became increasingly certain the scientist was a madman. "I won't let you do it to me again."

"I understand your anger—"

"I'm beyond mad." Victor continued walking. "I'm done. Leave me alone."

"Vic, please." Linciome stuffed the diary back in the pouch and his pocket and hustled in pursuit. He grabbed Victor's robe. "You cannot go back in there."

A campus policeman approached them. "Everything

okay here, gentlemen?"

"Of course, officer," said Linciome, reluctantly letting Victor go.

Victor pointed at him. "You might want to ask for this gentleman's ID and run a background check."

The campus cop was considering this as Victor entered the Labs.

"You want to hold him? He won't bite."

Tripp stood in the middle of Victor's room with a chimp in his arms. He prepared to transfer the big-eyed ape as it stretched out his arms to Victor.

"Good grief." Staying numb around Tripp was hard. The scientist was constantly popping into his room or sending nurses, the receptionist and even Dr. Speer to check on him. Last night Tripp had hired two young thespians from a local acting troupe to perform a scene from his favorite book, "The Picture of Dorian Gray" in Victor's room. This morning a barista from his favorite coffee shop had special-delivered a caramel macchiato.

And then there were the phone calls, which were not Tripp's fault.

"This is Victor." He hadn't recognized the number, the first of four such calls in the past 24 hours from a consulting company, a national bank, Facebook.

"Hi, Victor. I'm having trouble loading the XFP on my iPad."

"Uh ... who is this?"

"Peggy from the Department of Public Safety. Here in Texas. You're in Houston, right?"

"Yeah? How did you get this number?"

"It's on the sticker," said Peggy from the Texas DPS. "The one labeled 'Metafist helpdesk.'"

Metafist. X's consulting company. "Are you, uh, are you working with EnerGreen?"

"Who?" said Peggy.

"Or Playco?"

"I told you. I have XFP on my desktop, but I can't

figure out how to get it on my iPad."

"You have the Xtensive Feedback Predictor software on your desktop?" Victor played back her words but they didn't make any more sense coming from his mouth. "And you want it on your iPad, too?"

"I'm the head of IT here at DPS," said Peggy, tersely, irked. "I was told by your salesman that each license was tied to the person not the machine. We bought it with the understanding that we would be able to load it on multiple devices. Including my iPad."

"I don't know," Victor stumbled ahead blindly. "I didn't program it for this type of—"

"We paid you two-hundred grand." Peggy escalated to livid. "And now we don't have the ability to load this to other devices? Are you shitting me? Is it a licensing issue?"

"Well, I really couldn't say."

"My God, you are killing me. Do you want me to share my desktop?"

"I'm not at a computer."

"Are you *serious?*"

"Ma'am, I understand your frustration ..." Victor was a layer of sticky befuddlement atop a dense base of numb.

"Stop being polite. You can call me the Lone Star Bitch for all I care. I want resolution, Vic."

"Uh, can I ask what you're using the XFP for?"

"Big data, Victor. Isn't that the buzzword? Isn't that what your company promised? Isn't ... what?" Peggy's rant was interrupted by a nearby coworker. "You do? Hang on ... yep, I see it. I'm downloading it right now. Okay Victor, I see the Apple compatibility patch out on your website. Thanks for nothing, asshole."

Even through his dull confusion the words *two-hundred grand* made an impression. I should sue Metafist, Victor mused. *If only it weren't run by a ruthless vampire who would bite my wife and daughter and turn them into emaciated sisters of the undead.*

The safest world for Barbara and Amberly, Victor was constantly reminded, did not contain him.

Soon after Peggy hung up, Tripp had conducted back-to-back fire drills. Victor's private showing of "Dorian Gray" had started shortly thereafter. Then more "helpdesk" calls. Other than a five-hour sleep, Victor hadn't been alone more than 20 minutes at a stretch since returning from his walk the previous afternoon. He had not told Tripp about Linciome's surprise appearance.

The chimp settled comfortably in Victor's embrace, sitting high on his chest and interested in his wispy hair. Victor pushed up its lip. "He still has fangs."

"I would hope so," said Tripp. "The other chimps would laugh at him. You should have seen them before the cure. Couldn't get his mouth closed."

"I know a vamp like that."

"We'll cure him, too."

"I don't think he would go for that."

Tripp tried to gauge Victor's state of mind. "How about you? Ready to go full human?"

Victor shrugged. He was fine just standing there and holding the chimp, feeling the prickle of its fur through his lightweight pajama top.

"Close enough to a yes. Come on, Chuckles. Let's go give you Ebola and see if we can't cure that, too. While we're on a hot streak." He winked at Victor's concern as he took Chuckles the chimp. "Kidding. Marcella will get you prepped for the treatment. We'll do it our animal surgery center." He led Victor down the hall. "I know you're a priss about germs so we had a service come in and sterilize the joint. It's our only full-fledged operating room." Tripp stopped at the door to the animal pens and pointed Victor to continue on to the last door on the left. "Gene therapy has a spotty history. It's remote but possible you'll have a reaction. We need to be prepared. But we're sure you'll be fine."

At the end of the hall, Nurse Marcella beckoned to Victor.

"So sure," said Tripp, "that we opened up the room to spectators."

Nurse Marcella didn't make much eye contact with him these days and didn't now as he and his IV pole squeezed past her to find Barbara waiting in the operating room. Arms crossed, Barbara took a couple steps toward him. "How are you?"

Victor started to tell the truth and had to stop as he choked up.

Nurse Marcella guided him to an exam table in the corner and pulled out the step. "There's nothing for you to do. When Dr. Tripp gives the word we'll swap your saline for the solution. Then we wait an hour for the bag to empty. That's about it. You'll be awake the whole time." She glanced at Barbara, arms still crossed and staring at the floor. "So you two can just chat away." Marcella touched Barbara lightly on the arm as she left the room. "It's nice you're here."

Barbara looked uncomfortable to be alone with him. She did a constricted tour of the room, walking a circle roughly ten feet in diameter. She finished facing the door.

"You don't have to be here."

She faced him. "Are you excited?"

"Excited." That was a hard word to process. "For what?"

"To put everything behind you."

Victor had never been a laugher despite a good sense of humor. Now laughs wanted to burst from his belly, although without accompanying smiles. Each big laugh released another taut cord strung through his gut, leaving him closer to emotionless.

"Did you get my voicemail?"

"Of course." Barbara took turns glancing at the door and Victor. "So you're moving out? If you'd rather I did, that's fine."

Victor chuckled dryly. He couldn't even leave an effective suicide message. "The house is yours, Barb."

"Uh-huh, well, Amberly won't be there long either. I'm sure I'll get stuck with the dog."

"You love Porkie."

"Why is it always ..." Barbara's retort trailed off. Her shoulders relaxed as the defensiveness left. "You're right, I love that dog." It was her greatest confession to date. "And I know you don't. I appreciate you tolerating him."

Victor held out his hand. Barbara reluctantly came closer but would not uncross her arms. He let his hand rest in his lap. "I'm sorry for not holding up my end of the bargain."

She put a knuckle to her lips and shook her head.

"I hope you can start painting again after I'm gone."

This sent tears streaming down her cheeks. The way she looked at him could have been passion or hatred. "I promised to be with you forever. I know you need me."

"No." Victor reassured her and repelled a remnant of self-pity wanting to grab hold of her guilt. "That's not how I want you. I won't have that. Not for either of us."

Tripp entered the room and took in the tears. "Glad to see you two are talking. That's a start." On his heels was Nurse Marcella, wheeling a medical cart. "Marcie, let's not waste any time putting an end to Vic's curse." He pulled on gloves as he approached. "Before Dr. Speer has second thoughts. Barbie, I know I promised you a dazzling medical light show, but this is going to be the epitome of anticlimactic."

"Don't bother apologizing," said Marcella. "I already stole your fake thunder."

"The thunder was bogus but there was really a storm behind all that noise." Tripp disconnected the saline drip and hung up an IV bag from the med cart. "Right here, storm in a bag. Bringing a hard rain to wash you clean, my friend."

Marcella snorted. "Our metaphors are awful. But our procedures are topnotch." She connected Victor's IV tube and opened the flow regulator. "How fast, Doc?"

Sounds of commotion came from the lobby. "Wide open," said Tripp. There seemed to be a footrace in process with the animal surgery center at the finish line.

First in the room was Edna Campbell, pescetarian, former member of PETA, devoted slayer, out of breath. "Found him!" She was followed by the Labs' receptionist, Jordie, walking backward and protesting the arrival of the third racer, Slayer Sven, carrying Eugene Foreman, still in his hospital gown.

Barbara rushed to greet the slayer. "We've been so worried. Amberly told me she saw you."

Eugene reddened like he'd been slapped. "Over there." He directed his ride to Victor's operating bed, mush-mouthed as if shot-up with Novocain.

"You can't be in here." Jordie tried to impede Sven's progress. Edna dove at her. When she hit Jordie's hip something audibly cracked and Edna dropped to the floor, arms and legs splayed out.

"Here we go again." Tripp squared off with Sven and his passenger. "No bloodsuckers here, boys. Vic's cured. If your blood's too far up I'll let you slay a couple of our vampire rats and monkeys." With a tip of his head, Tripp directed Jordie to go lock the door to the animal pens.

"I'm gonna knock you out and let those poor critters drink you dry," Edna said from the floor, motionless but for her mouth. "And then when you turn into a monkey-man vampire, I'm going to lock you in my basement and feed you nothing but GMO bananas with a gene for Ex-Lax."

"I hope your basement isn't finished," said Tripp.

Eugene forced Sven to put him down. "Didn't you

cure Vic once already?" the famous slayer mumbled while Sven tightened the tie on the backside of his gown. "I'll believe a vamp is cured when I stake it and it doesn't turn to ashes."

Tripp shed his surgical cap and peeled off his gloves. Victor wasn't getting any imminent slaying vibes from the trio and Tripp seemed to conclude the same even as he struck an aggressive stance. "You need to head back to the hospital. From the look in your eye you're carrying a corker of a concussion." He frowned at Sven and Edna. "And why aren't you two in prison?"

Edna struggled to her feet. Her head was stuck looking hard left. "There must have been a mix-up in the coppers' evidence room. They claimed our vial of deadly toxin was just methane."

"And luckily," said Sven, "zit is no crime to try to keel zee vampire."

Lethargic, not far removed from catatonic, Eugene rummaged in Sven's slide-slung satchel. Finally he extracted an e-pad and handed it to Victor. "I have something you need to see."

On screen was a picture of an uncrumpled handwritten note:

We have the Thetherson girl. She will be released unharmed

"Amberly?" Victor jumped off the operating table. Marcella grabbed the tipping IV pole. "Who has her?"

Barbara became frantic as she read the message. "Are you saying she's been kidnapped?"

"Oh honey," Marcella commiserated.

Edna turned sideways to glare at Victor. "It comes with the territory."

Marcella glared at Edna. "Would you like me to fix that neck?"

"Scroll down," Eugene instructed. "The note has a backside."

Victor slapped and rubbed the screen. "I can't get it..." Now the note disappeared, replaced by a draft blog post on Eugene's *Sage Slayer* website titled "Awakening From Your Marketing Coma." He stuck it in Eugene's face. "I see you still have time to work on your revenue stream."

"That was before they took her." Eugene's glassy eyes relived a painful memory. "Before Amberly told me she's leaving me."

"You can't leave what you were never with." Victor shook the e-pad like an Etch A Sketch.

Barbara took the device, tapped and swished and brought the backside of the note onscreen.

as soon as you slay the vampire Victor Thetherson.

Sven held up a pale blue swatch of cotton.

Barbara gasped. "That's from the dress Amberly wore to your hunger strike."

"I don't know why she bothered," said Eugene, monotone. "She must have decided she needed to lose a few pounds."

Victor lunged at him but Barbara and Marcella slowed him down and Tripp beat him there, grabbing handfuls of Eugene's gown and popping his rear snaps. "You need to get your mind right."

"If my mind were right I'd be slaying Victor like I'm supposed to."

Tripp shook him like Victor shook the e-pad. "That's not happening."

Eugene grit his teeth at the rough handling. "Only because I don't know his soft spot."

"*When* and *where* did you get this note?"

"I woke up this morning in my apartment." Eugene shook free and then had to be steadied (and re-snapped) by Sven. "The last thing I remembered was getting stomped by the vamp X. I called Amberly and she came over and filled me in. And then she announced the end of our love affair."

"What about the note?" Victor growled.

"It came through my window rubber-banded to a five-pound kettlebell. Hit me on the bounce while I was weeping on the floor." He parted the gown to reveal his bare ass and a burgeoning bruise on ribs that cried out in malnourishment.

"One of your ribs is cracked," Marcella diagnosed, although they could all see it, third rib from the bottom.

"Who sent the note?" Tripp demanded.

Tremors wracked Eugene's body. "I failed her! I lost my way! I sold out!" Fists clenched and back bowed, the slayer howled, throaty with a high tremolo overtone. "And now I've lost my soul! My Amberly!"

Eugene's bad leg failed him. Victor made as if to catch him with alligator arms. His shoulder struck the slayer and accelerated his descent. Eugene's face ricocheted off the exam table pull-out step on the way down.

"Whoops," said Victor.

A goose egg grew on Eugene's temple and his head lolled side to side. "So blind, so blind ..." Sven and Edna rushed to his aide. "I was so blind ..."

Tripp checked Victor's IV insert while waiting out Eugene's lamentations. "Barbie and I will give you a ride back to the hospital. I'm sure they'll do a better job keeping tabs on you this time. On the way we'll stop at the police station and report Amberly's abduction."

Edna cradled Eugene's head in her lap. "Can't trust the cops. Vamp infiltration."

A spark of life flared in Eugene's eyes. "We can find her."

Victor towered over him. "Who has Amberly?"

"X," said Barbara. "It has to be him. It's his leverage over you."

"X already has me where he wants me," said Victor. "And this would turn the team against him."

Barbara knelt at Eugene's side. "Honey, who took Amberly?"

He coughed once, kitten weak. "The Civil War

Soldier."

"Who?" came simultaneous voices.

Eugene squeezed his eyes shut and rubbed his forehead. "My sensei."

"Of course you have a sensei." Victor rubbed his forehead, too. "Who was a Civil War soldier."

Tripp was confused. "Why would your sensei kidnap Amberly?"

"Because her papa is Morbius reincarnate!" said Sven.

"So what," said Victor. "I'm ..."

He looked down at the tube ferrying agents that were presumably making for his chromosomes, programmed to delete the genes inserted by the vampire crone Agnes in her final earthly act.

"Almost cured." He peeled off the adhesive dressing securing the IV catheter. Mesmerized by the sight of the tube leaving the hole in his forearm, he pulled it out.

"Whoa, no," said Tripp. While Marcella scrambled to swab the blood and tape a cotton ball over the site, Tripp yanked open drawers in her medical cart until he found another pair of gloves and IV kit. "Vic, we have time to finish the treatment. I'll call the cops and get them over here. Buddy, come on," he appealed as Victor wandered away. "You know that's the only way to do this."

Victor despaired at how tired he was. How his thoughts slogged through molasses. How his muscles ached from the fall from Florence's window. He imagined himself "bursting" into some slayer hideaway command center and doing hand-to-hand combat with this Civil War Soldier whom he pictured as William Tecumseh Sherman astride a horse, holding a stake in one hand and a torch in the other. Since he had no idea what Sherman looked like, he imagined Russell Crowe looking more like a gladiator and dismounting to beat him to death.

And where would that leave Amberly? As bait and blackmail for the next vampire that Eugene's "sensei" wanted slain.

He went to Eugene. "How much time do we have?"

Eugene gave him a steely slayer stare. "The clock is ticking."

"We need to rescue her *now*," said Barbara.

"I'm sure this Russell guy didn't leave it open-ended," said Victor.

"Who's Russell?" said Sven, confused like everyone else.

Victor ignored them. He could rescue his daughter, but he needed a little time. "What deadline did he give you?"

Eugene indicated that Barbara should swish down another page on his e-pad. "That one came through my window inside an empty bottle of sloe gin. Missed me."

They passed around the scanned message: *She dies Sunday at 11:59 p.m.*

Barbara pressed her forehead against clasped hands and began to pray. "Does he mean it?"

"Oh for sure," said Eugene.

"We must begin with what we know." Sven assumed the role of detective. Edna closed her eyes for enhanced focus and nodded for him to continue. "I do not comprehend zee significance of eleven feefty-nine. Why not simply say 'midnight'?"

"Because otherwise," said Edna, "you wouldn't know whether that's the midnight between Saturday and Sunday or the one between Sunday and Monday."

"*Bon, bon,*" Sven congratulated her. "So we are dealing with someone who appreciates precision."

"That gives us two or three days," said Victor.

"That doesn't give us *anything*," said Barbara. "Victor, we can't waste any time."

"I won't be wasting it. Where is she being held?"

"I have some ideas," said Eugene.

After a deep breath, a moment to confirm what he

intended to do, Victor took Barbara by the hand. "I need your assistance." Shuffling even without the IV pole, muscles protesting, he led Barbara out of the surgery room, picking up speed until they reached the bathroom.

"I'm not going in there with you—"

Victor pulled her in and locked the door. He placed in her hand a scalpel purloined from the medical cart. "I have a job for the steady hand of a painter." He removed the pajama top and probed under his clavicle, on the faint scar from the outpatient surgery nearly three months ago.

His finger dug as if for the root of a noxious weed deep in soft earth. He felt the implant, the inhibitor. "Right here."

Eyes wider all the time Barbara put her fingertips to Victor's chest, steadying herself, the scalpel upright and inches away. "You want me to stick this knife in your skin."

"It's more than skin deep." Victor put his hands on Barbara's hips. "I've been anesthetized for a while. I won't feel a thing."

Barbara searched his eyes. "You're going to ..." She swallowed, and again. "You're going to save Amberly."

"It's the right way to die."

Eyes moist and voice husky she stood on tiptoes and put a soft kiss on his lips. "I'd rather you didn't die."

Victor tried not to think about her words or the way they warmed his brain like rays of sunshine. For the moment he preferred the fog to remain. "The clock's ticking."

Barbara took a settling breath. "Okay. Let's cut the fucker out."

"Whoop, hold on." Victor reached in his pajama pants pocket and produced an alcohol swab packet. "Wet wipe me. Why don't you wash your hands, too?"

Barbara grimaced at the toilet, which wasn't spotless. "For what it's worth ..." After scrubbing herself to the elbows she swabbed the scarred patch under his clavicle.

A knock at the door. "You two behaving yourselves in there?" Tripp. Did he suspect what they were about to do?

The scalpel blade pressed against his flesh. Wide-eyed, Barbara's looked at her ex. "You trust me?"

"Like Dr. Linciome said, you know me. You know what's good in me and you know what's not." Victor looked down. "And you've already started."

The sharp blade was halfway in him. "Hey, look," said Barbara. "I'm a surgeon."

"Do it." Victor's breath became shallow. The gleam in Barbara's eye was a laser beam focused on the inch-long gash on his chest so that the scalpel need only follow its lead. Victor closed his eyes and leaned against the wall, knees shaking.

He remained conscious until the bloody scalpel clattered to the sink, until Barbara knuckled his pec to push her pointer and middle fingers deeper with her thumb dug in over the topside of his collarbone to keep the implant from shifting away. Numbness left Victor before the implant; bellowing like a birthing water buffalo, he felt everything and then nothing.

Chimps and rats screamed as Barbara tried to slow Victor's descent to the bathroom floor, one hand under his back and the other with an inside-outside grip on his collarbone. Terrible sounds for Tripp, Marcella and the slayers standing dumbly in the hall. Barbara didn't register the cacophony, lost in the moment, humming as she relieved Victor of his inhibition.

A STORY FOR ANOTHER DAY

No matter how many times Tripp sighs and shakes his head in disapproval, you can't get enough of pushing up your ex-husband's lip and pressing your fingertip against his burgeoning fang. If you were home with Victor, you'd draw blood and suck it in front of him. See where that gets you.

Winnie Linciome chuckles every time.

"There's not a single good thing about it," says Tripp.

You pull the straw out of Victor's sippy cup and drop a drip of water on your fingertip, lubricant for Victor's upper lip to safely lower it over the small but pointed fangs. "Rescuing Amberly doesn't make your list?"

Tripp wastes no time putting his arm around you. He can piss you off all he wants; a hug from the tall lanky buck is always welcome. "You're worried and so am I. But this is a job for the police. Not Viccy."

"Very soon," says Winnie, "you'll see that Victor is so much more than you could have imagined."

Tripp bristles against you. "Vic is so much more than any of us give him credit for. Without the vampirism."

"Tripp, honey, you've seen it."

"I sure have."

Your first impulse is, *Being a good buddy isn't the same as being a great husband.* "He's a different man this way."

"Different *than* a man. A vampire, Barbie. That's

nothing to fool with." Tripp looks down on Victor lying in the hospital bed, sutured where you pierced his body and on the inside where you ruptured a major artery and almost killed him. For a good cause. "I've seen him at his worst. So have you. That's not Victor."

"I know there are risks—"

"I've seen the genetics." Tripp's passion is something you can admire. His voice rises because he loves you both, and Victor most of all. "With the curse he's a different *creature.*"

"I know it, Tripp." You take Victor's (slightly cooler?) hand. "And I love it. Do you think *maybe* it's possible we love different things about him?" You gently tweak Tripp. "The part of him you love is still there. Please don't judge him too quickly."

"I'll judge his actions. And they'll be scary, Barbie. The *Xtreme Makeover* show wasn't an anomaly. The direction Victor is headed is dangerous for him, for you—and for Amberly."

Victor has been basically comatose since passing out in the Longevity Labs bathroom yesterday. In the meantime Eugene has been working to find Amberly's abductor on no sleep. He has checked in regularly— most recently as he crawled through the old Maxwell House factory ductwork at 2 a.m. with the sound of large agitated dogs in the background, because it had occurred to him that his sensei's assistant always reeked of coffee

You believe in Eugene. Maybe it's the romantic in you, as his efforts are for a love that will be unrequited. Eugene has not asked whether you believe Amberly was resolute when she told him goodbye. The truth would be, yes. You've never seen Amberly alter a course she decides is true. You saw resolution in her eyes.

This would be hard for Victor to hear but the young man has probably seen Amberly's resolve, too. They have spent more time together than Victor realizes and more intimately, you have reason to believe, than Victor could bear.

But even without Eugene's commitment, you would be focused right now on Victor. You hate yourself for this; your daughter *has* to come first.

You justify the flawed prioritization by telling yourself repeatedly that you are here by Victor's bedside because he is Amberly's best hope.

"Tripp, I know he tried to commit suicide."

You would have bet the house Victor wouldn't have the fortitude to go through with it. Now, listening to Winnie, you wonder if there isn't a higher power at work. "I'm sure you knew that. You probably know how. I don't and I don't care. I'm just so very thankful for the man who is going to wake up in this bed."

Winnie delicately slips into the conversation. "I'd like to tell you about that man, if I could."

"Dr. Speer should be here any moment," says Tripp. "I don't think you have time to tell us any more stories."

Victor sighs. That's the way he wakes up. This one, though, this sigh is more resolution than resignation.

"Ow. Barb, did you get it?"

Is his voice deeper? Cleaner, as if a solvent has been taken to his throat, scouring the accumulated crud, allowing you to hear his pure voice. You're sure his hair is thicker, his widow's peak a little bolder.

You lean in and whisper. "It's out of you. You're changing again, my love." Your tone and your term of endearment tell Victor exactly where you stand. There is no transition period in your mind, no wait-and-see. This is the man you married, the man you love. There must be no nagging doubt in his mind (or yours) with what lies ahead. He needs to know you are behind him.

Through drooping eyelids he scowls at his ample stomach. "Where's Amberly?"

"Eugene is looking for her."

He sits bolt upright. "What time is it?"

"Almost noon," says Tripp. "Thursday."

"You're relying on *Eugene*?"

"I'm ashamed to say we haven't called the police," says Tripp.

Victor's tongue assesses his incipient fangs. "No police. On that I actually agree with him." He again surveys his body with disgust. "Maybe I should have let him kill me."

"I don't think he could," says Linciome. "You're evolved, Victor. With a very unique Heel. One we need to talk about."

"That's it," says Tripp. "I'm an idiot. As soon as Dr. Speer gets here I'm calling the cops."

"You can't." You force Tripp to look away from Linciome. "You said they'll bring charges against Victor if he chooses to be a vampire."

"Our only priority is Amberly."

"Do you think I disagree?"

"Vic's screwed either way." Tripp nods to the monitor above the bed. "Look at his temperature. And his heartbeat." Ninety-two degrees and 41 beats per minute. "The hospital has to file a report on any vampire they treat."

"Then it's time to go." Victor yanks the monitor off his finger and brandishes the IV tube in his arm. "Get this out of me."

Your phone sings. "That's Eugene."

"Put him on speaker."

"Eugene," you connect the call, "did you find her?"

"I did."

Tripp pauses removing Victor's IV.

"I'm headed there now," says Eugene.

"Where?" says Victor.

"You survived." Eugene fumes audibly through his nose. "What's your status?"

"You'll see for yourself," says Victor. "Where is Amberly?"

"Get yourself a ticket to Tucson on the United 11:25 flight out of Bush."

"She's in Tucson?"

"No. She's in the desert."

You exchange looks. "We'll meet you at the airport."

"I don't fly commercial," says Eugene. "We're already in Tucson."

Victor reaches over to end the call. "I can't believe we're relying on that punk. Book us tickets."

"This has snafu smeared all over it." Tripp sighs. "I'll pay you back, Barbie."

Linciome is crestfallen. "I can't go. My efforts in eastern Europe landed me on the no-fly list."

"Good," says Tripp.

"To get back to the States I had to take a job as a deckhand on a tramp steamer out of Riga," says Linciome while you search for the designated flight to Tucson. "Someone with connections got me on that list. They're trying to restrict the movements of the few people who understand what's happening."

"Which is what?" Tripp challenges as he patches Victor's IV hole.

"A vampire takeover."

Victor cinches his belt a hole beyond where he was 24 hours ago. The transformation is happening just shy of Hollywood-speed. He surreptitiously flexes as he strips off the gown, disappointed in his muscles' response.

"I'll call bullshit," says Tripp. "And how the hell would you know?"

"I belong to an organization that tracks them." Linciome's German accent suddenly sounds less buttery, less playful. He looks a little more ... focused. "The longevity research was real and very important. But it's not my primary occupation." He stares at your ex-husband. "It's not why I interfered with your cure."

Victor ignores him as he puts on his shoes.

"What do you mean?" you ask.

"Knock-knock." A nurse is entering.

"One second." Linciome shuts the door in the nurse's face and stoppers it with his foot. "Your ancestor and now you have a special power: the ability to *see* other vampires' Achilles heels. It's all in the diary. The slayers, including the one who has Amberly, they have it all wrong about you. You are their ally, not their enemy."

Victor is scornful. "Oh, so it turns out Morbius isn't *king* of the vampires, he's their worst nightmare?"

"Victor, you're not Morbius."

You're embarrassed to admit this is a little disappointing.

"Never thought I was," says Victor. "So if I have this great *sight*, then why is it news to me?"

"Tell me how you knew how to kill Sennett McGumphrey."

"I didn't. I got lucky."

"A lucky punch to the armpit?" Linciome shakes his head. "No way."

You are the only one intrigued. Victor shoves Linciome out of the way and opens the door to an aggravated nurse. "I am checking myself out."

"You're fine to leave." The nurse makes notation in her chart while her eyes dart to Victor's mouth. "We've had enough bad publicity lately. Although thank goodness Eugene is okay." She beams. "I just saw his tweet."

Victor strides down the hall with only a hint of yesterday's limp. "He's tweeting instead of searching for Amberly."

You redirect his intensity. "I just bought three tickets to Tucson."

"I'll drive you to the airport," says Linciome. "We can talk about your history ... and your future."

The elevator door slides open. Tripp puts a hand in Linciome's chest and nods to Dr. Speer, standing perplexed in front of Victor's empty room. "Why don't you tell him instead?"

"Victor," Linciome protests. "It is essential you understand your power. And your Heel."

"Some other time," says Victor as the door closes in Linciome's face.

HANSEN

A little more emphatically this time Jay turned down the offer from the woman with the appetizers. From the look on her face as she moved on to the next cluster of guests, that would be the last time he was offered.

"Did I just see what I think I saw?" Mitchell Harms the Playco CFO stirred the ice in his gin and tonic, wadded up his appetizer napkin and threw it cleanly into the wastebasket under the "Fire Ice" demonstration project display.

"I'm working out later." Jay sipped sparingly on Riesling, not much more than a dip of his lips. "I'll eat after."

Mitchell shook his head, in awe. "She wasn't offering you food. The waitress just propositioned you."

Jay smiled, a tight recoil of his cheeks. "Barrie owns this catering service. I suggested her to the EnerGreen event planner."

Harms took a drink. "And?"

There would be no answer until Jay had glanced around the vicinity. With the two CFOs talking, the walls had ears, including a well-heeled few browsing the paintings on display and the well-oiled crowd gathered around the methane hydrate display, watching their spent breath travel down a tube to be injected into the "fire ice" and marveling at how their exhalations were then blown back upon them, after a few black-box processes, as refreshing, oxygen-rich air conditioning.

"She catered an event for the chamber of commerce a month ago. What can I say? I was on that night."

"Yeah?" Harms was titillated. "She was smitten ... and?"

"And I said no."

Harms watched Barrie the caterer smiling at an observation from Carl Yorbo the EnerGreen board president as he enjoyed a painting. Harms whistled softly. "Because you're gay?"

"Knock it off." Jay had lost the taste for ass-grabbery as he ascended the Finance ladder. Everyone assumed that since he was a well-paid executive, in a construction firm no less—in Texas to boot—he must be deeply conservative, Republican, close-minded. But every rung he climbed gave Jay a broader viewpoint. He had a deep sense of obligation to the downtrodden. He preferred they didn't work for him but he was always ready to give, at benefits like this and by squelching encoded hate speech from people like Harms.

"Then it must be because your wife fulfills your every need. I hadn't considered that."

"Pretty much true," said Jay. "Madeline is an incredible woman."

Harms chuckled as he realized Jay was serious. "Well, now we don't get any more fucking appetizers." He took another drink. "Everything seems to be going all right with our fanged friend, am I right?"

"Thetherson?"

"Who? I'm talking Mr. Metafist."

Jay had to unwind the knot that had instantaneously formed in his gut at the thought of Thetherson. He was seeing a therapist, a "mindfulness" trainer as he styled himself, to convince his deepest psyche that everything he felt about Victor as a vampire was now an anachronism.

In fact his goal was to go deeper, or rather to step

outside that depth and observe his fear of vampires in general, thereby reducing *fear* to mere thoughts, which could be controlled. (That last phrase was Jay's; his trainer didn't seem to understand the need for control in this chaotic world.) Jay focused on his breath, in and out, levitating inside his lungs and watching the diaphragm floor expand and deflate.

The gut knot loosened. "Of course you love him. He got you in the door." *In* and soon to be *out.* "No complaints. He's getting the job done."

"I've been impressed with his new forecasting system."

"Might be revolutionary," Jay acknowledged. "The way it autonomously captures data and uses it to predict the future."

Harms raised his eyebrows. "I've also heard he's selling that system to other companies. We might be able to argue that it was internally developed and proprietary to our joint venture."

Jay didn't want to go there. "Let him."

"Don't I remember *your* vampire at the board meeting, describing a system that sounded a lot like this XFP software?"

The gut knot tightened again. Jay was sick of thinking of himself as that little lung-and-diaphragm man. "Mitch, I don't give a shit."

Harms winked and took a drink and turned his attention to the Fire Ice demo. "So what do you make of our client's grand plans?"

"Downright incredible. Hello Carl," Jay greeted Yorbo the EnerGreen board president. "We were just marveling at your future."

Yorbo stared at Jay. When he was about to converse on a topic he loved, his eyebrows rose, his eyes flared and his head tilted back, like a silent-film vampire. "The *planet's* future. There's more methane hydrate energy to be had along the continental shelves as there is in all the other fossil fuels combined. Just takes a little commitment to get to it." He leaned in for the punch line. "And this group should definitely be committed."

"Takes some crazy," Harms agreed.

Yorbo savored his pun and then his eyes flared again. "I love this visitor center idea. If this demo doesn't get people excited about what we're doing ..." He gazed at the big snowball held aloft by ice hooks, a stainless steel tube going in to inject the attendees' CO_2, and a stainless steel tube going out carrying liberated methane—natural gas—piped to a mini-power station and converted to electricity which fed the air conditioning system which blew cool air that could not budge the wiry fringe around Yorbo's bald pate.

Harms said, "Jay is incapable of getting excited," and walked away.

They moved away from the demo and Jay was captivated by a painting: An alley with precipitous sides and darkened windows, midnight blue, purple and magenta. It evoked exactly the emotions Jay didn't want to feel, claustrophobia and fear, the ground out of focus but the walls so textured that he felt the litter underfoot, heard sour whispers hanging in the air. At the far end of the alley was a light—no, just a glow that disappeared when he looked directly at it. That shy glow allowed Jay to walk through the alley's menacing darkness comforted by the salvation ahead. "I really, really like that work."

Yorbo sidled up to the painting and read the card. "Barbara Thetherson."

Jay gritted his teeth. "You have got to be kidding me."

"Yep," said Yorbo. "It's a Thetherson." He paused for effect. "What's a Thetherson?"

"Such a boon to our community, isn't it?" A newcomer joined them, smooth skin with shifting hues the color of the Thetherson painting.

Yorbo's eyes flared and his eyebrows rose. "Art is essential to the spiritual health of a city."

"I meant the construction project," said D.A. Goodnight. "The jobs. All without tax breaks and public giveaways."

"Oil companies and banks." Yorbo was equally warm to this topic. "The only industries that giveaway to the public for the right to do business. We serve at your pleasure."

"Reduces the bribes and cronyism. Makes my job easier." Goodnight telegraphed his desire to have a private word with Jay.

Yorbo cleared his throat, attempting to cool down gracefully. "Just let us know what else we can do to make your job easier, Mr. District Attorney."

Goodnight waited until Yorbo moved on. When the D.A. turned his eyes to Jay, the Bizco CFO could have sworn the visitor center had cleared out and left him alone with the vampire.

"Follow me," said Goodnight.

Outside they skirted the perimeter fence for 50 yards and then through a gate that maybe should have been locked. Inside the construction zone the ribs of various massive buildings were visible in the night safety lights. Goodnight pointed to a trailer. Jay preceded him inside—reluctantly, he observed, in the dispassionate way his mindfulness trainer had taught him.

Goodnight locked the door. They stood together in the limited space between an old desk and the sink, in the smell of construction sites past, rain and humidity gone musty, solvents, foot odor, overripe banana peels, Old Spice. "I am sad to report your neighborhood has gone to hell."

Jay fought the urge to remove his glasses. They were no good for up-close viewing but right now that was okay, as his eyes kept darting to Goodnight's teeth. "What do you mean?"

"You're telling me that in a neighborhood you own twice over," Goodnight spoke as if to a child, "you don't have anyone walking the streets?"

Jay's mindful breath whistled through his nose. "You must be talking about Thetherson. There's nothing to report, right? He's cured. We did the job at the Labs. It was final a few days ago. And we've got him buried at Bizco under X Anthony from Metafist. I'm sure you probably know him." He told himself what he told his direct reports when they rambled attempting to anticipate everything he might possibly ask: *Stop talking.*

For a moment Jay thought Goodnight was smiling. "You're curious about my teeth," said the D.A. His lips peeled far too far up his gums and his tongue traced the edge of his pearly, fangless whites. "These are real. No falsies. I'm not like the other vamps. My weapons are back here."

He tipped his head back and dropped his jaw, unhinged except for the striated tension lining his cheeks.

There they were. Fangs top and bottom, converted molars, thick at the root and tapering to gracefully curved points. Jay saw how the system worked: The victim pierced on both sides of his throat, the hook set by the angle of the fangs, the seal vacuum-tight, blood siphoned as fast as the vampire could swallow.

Goodnight's breath smelled like CEO Fasset's when he hadn't eaten for a few hours. "I hear this is one of the next steps in our evolution."

"What do you want from me?"

"Your vampire. Thetherson. He's back."

Jay shook his head.

"He abandoned the cure." Goodnight's tone suggested that Jay should have known it was inevitable.

Cold swept up Jay's neck and soaked through his scalp. His first thought was an image of his wife

Madeline screaming as Victor advanced on her. One knot after another tangled his insides. "So?" His hands shook removing, folding and pocketing his glasses. He jutted out his jaw. "You're a goddamn vampire, too. What do you care?"

"Because I hate *this* vampire!"

Jay was backed into the desk, at an angle and sliding along the front edge, hand behind him looking for an anchor, finding only papers and folders. He stumbled and grabbed at a folding chair and managed to sit without crashing to the floor.

In a flash the D.A. was behind him, pinning him in place and breathing in his ear. "I'm going to bring Thetherson in on a murder charge against your employee Nikki."

"I thought—iiiy!"

Goodnight ran a razor blade across Jay's throat, dull and yanking at his skin, drawing blood in three places. His jaw twitched side to side, molar fangs clicking like a cicada. "Hold very still." The vampire put his mouth to the cut and lapped up the blood.

"Please," Jay whimpered. *Be brave for Madeline.* "I thought you couldn't get a conviction."

"We were fortunate that the county recently had to replace its judge."

"Rodriguez ... that wasn't an accident," Jay realized. The Houston judge had reportedly had a heart attack and drowned in his swimming pool. "Marlboro," he named Judge Rodriguez's replacement. "He's a vampire? But why would he set precedent by convicting another vampire?"

"Because he's not like the rest of us. He is much, much worse."

"Then put him away already." Jay struggled not to whine. "Why do you need me?"

Goodnight grabbed his hair and wrenched his head to the side. One vertebra popped, audible for both. Then another. To engage a single muscle in resistance

Jay was sure his spinal cord must unravel. "We don't have the appeals court yet. You have one more chance. One more opportunity to clean up your neighborhood. Before I take it over." Goodnight dragged his tongue across Jay's neck. "And charge you for it."

On the brink of madness and ready to accept paralysis, Jay tore away with everything he had. "Get away from me. I *get* it," he barked to keep the D.A. at bay. "I want Victor dead as badly as you do."

The vampire's jaw clicked like a Geiger counter. He pointed at the door. "Go do it."

Thirty minutes after Jay peeled out of the construction site in his Audi, the EnerGreen benefit had wrapped up. Barrie left the visitor center and walked along the security fence to the gate. Heart pounding with a reckless attraction she didn't want to end, she slipped through and hurried forward beyond the reach of the visitor center's lights. In her hand was a note.

Meet me in the construction trailer. J

At the steel mesh steps she stopped and took a deep breath, revealing the smile swelling her heart ever since one of her staff handed her the note. She knocked.

"Come in."

The lights were out in the trailer so there elapsed some five seconds after Barrie closed the door behind her for her brief scream to taint the night.

Project Well Done text chat

Jay 9:15 p.m.

I hope your heirs enjoy their high-performing Detroit REIT.

Larry 9:16 p.m.

??

Jay 9:16 p.m.

Vic is a vampire again. I doubt he'll let any of you live.

David 9:17 p.m.

Dude o no

Larry 9:18 p.m.

This is not good. He knows we hired Eugene.

David 9:19 p.m.

Im moving take me off this distribution

Jay 9:21 p.m.

Too late for that. We're all in this together.

Teddy 9:21 p.m.

Panic much douche bag?

Jay 9:22 p.m.

Who are you calling douche bag?

David 9:23 p.m.

Who do you think, db. Now take me off

Jay 9:24 p.m.

Okay db.

Larry 9:25 p.m.

Gentlemen, allow me to be the db. Jay, what are we supposed to do?

Jay 9:27 p.m.

I gave you one job. So do it. Do your job.

Teddy 9:28 p.m.

You're not the boss of us! Except for Larry.

Larry 9:32 p.m.

OK let's tell Eugene that either he does the job or we get our money back.

David 9:33 p.m.

How does that stop vv from sucking me dry?!?

Teddy 9:34 p.m.

Man up, dude.

David 9:34 p.m.

Then y dont you do it?!?

Teddy 9:36 p.m.

Didn't you hear Eugene? He's evolved! Do u no his sweet spot? Do u?!

Teddy 9:38 p.m.

Bsides I thot Eugene killed some other vamp for our $$.

Larry 9:40 p.m.

He failed, that's how he wound up in the hospital.

Teddy 9:41 p.m.

Watta pussy, y don't we hire a real slayer m I rite?

Larry 9:43 p.m.

Jay that's a good question. How about X? He wants Vic gone too.

Larry 9:47 p.m.

Jay?

Jay 9:48 p.m.

I'm actually in front of X's house now.

David 10:05 p.m.

So ... what did he say?

Jay 10:08 p.m.

I haven't gone in yet.

Teddy 10:09 p.m.

Man up bro.

Jay 10:10 p.m.

Big shot why don't you come over here and ask him?

Teddy 10:13 p.m.

I swear I should just get some homies together and do it mself.

David 10:15 p.m.

Do u no anybody who does remote control bombs?

Larry 10:18 p.m.

Jay you're X's boss right?

Jay 10:28 p.m.

Ok. I'm going in.

Teddy 10:29 p.m.

God ur a putz, db.

David 10:30 p.m.

F-u!!

Teddy 10:31 p.m.

The other db, dude.

David 10:32 p.m.

db should pay him with a little suck m I rite?

Teddy 10:32 p.m.

Ha ha ha from his tiny little tube

David 10:33 p.m.

Hey this doesn't taste like blood … ?

Larry 10:33 p.m.

Ok you two.

Jay 10:59 p.m.

It's a done deal.

Teddy 11:00 p.m.

Congrats you limp rag.

Larry 11:01 p.m.

Hey did you hear Raj is working for Metafist?

EVICTION

They looked down on a little cabin in the middle of the Sonora Desert. The full moon painted the smoke curling from the chimney in lustrous silver. A lit window glowed warm golden yellow. Perfectly picturesque, from the outside.

On the inside, the insane leader of the vampire slayers held Amberly Thetherson. Inside, Victor couldn't stave off blood-red rage, blooming in successively larger toxic plumes. The next one was going to pollute his surroundings.

How did I let myself degenerate to this pathetic state? Victor swore at his inept mind as it foundered through accumulated layers of worry and distraction. He cursed his body, fat, sluggish and weak. This Civil War Soldier and his assistant were waiting for him down in that cabin. He could assume they were the real deal, not braggart fakes like Eugene. And Victor wasn't ready. With his daughter counting on him, he would be no match for her abductors.

This was playing out just like last time, when Amberly was attacked by a vampire. In her own home, the one place where Victor should have been able to keep his daughter safe. He had failed then; he had been too weak. Thanks to the rapid decline he had permitted himself over the past few weeks, he was in no better shape now.

Fury polluted Victor's mind, fallout from the toxic fumes released by his self-loathing. But his fury also had external sources. There were others just as responsible for Amberly's situation.

Certainly that list included the punk in the wheelchair.

Eugene pushed a lever and a pair of night-vision binoculars rose on a spring-loaded arm. He peered through them, his breath chilled to vapor. "A little closer, please."

Slayer Sven muscled Eugene's wheelchair to the edge of the bluff above a dry creek and the cabin. He blew into his hands and rubbed his arms, bare past the shoulder. "The desert, it is not hot, no? I am surprised, yes?"

At the Tucson airport, in the passenger pickup zone, Eugene had taken one look at Victor and attempted to slay him on the spot. Tripp saw it coming and tipped Eugene backward so that his armed wheelchair shot its silver-tipped stake into the overhanging sun shade. Sven and Edna had assumed action poses, ready to provide backup, as Barbara chewed out Eugene.

Victor had simply stared. His mind didn't have room for anything other than worrying how he was going to perform when matched up with real slayers, and Amberly's fate if he failed. And after surviving so many unsuccessful slaying attempts maybe he had bought into Linciome's depiction of him as an evolved species.

The slayers had rented a handicap-accessible van but Eugene refused to ride with Victor. After the slayers spent 20 minutes trying to fulfill Eugene's demand that he and his wheelchair be strapped on the roof, Victor rented a car and with Barbara and Tripp followed the slayer van west on State Highway 86. They arrived at the disembarkation point with the sun sinking past a ragged range of barren mountains.

While Sven and Edna unloaded the wheelchair Eugene had tried to run over Victor.

That had been one attempt too many. Victor dove to

safety, rolled through the gravel and scrub, and then dragged Eugene him from the driver's seat and wrestled him to the ground.

"Do you want to know how to kill me?" he had roared in Eugene's face. "Do you?"

"Sure."

"*Screw* me, punk! Have sex with me!"

"What?!?"

"You heard me. That's how I die."

"That's the stupidest soft spot yet."

"So how bad do you want me dead? Are you ready to put your money where your mouth is?"

"Why not. It wouldn't be the first Thetherson I screwed."

Victor slugged him in the mouth, bouncing the slayer's head off the ground. He slugged him again and would have kept it up if not for Sven and Tripp hauling him off. Eugene had lay on the ground for a moment before bursting into tears.

Victor would have left him lying and bawling by the highway but only the stringy fool knew where to find the cabin. They had taken turns pushing his wheelchair over inhospitable terrain. That the desert was hardpan rather than sand dunes was nice, but they were forced into repeated detours around ridges and washouts, fields of spiny yucca and cactus clusters, so that the mile and a half took three hours.

Victor took his turn behind the chair, slapping Eugene across his concussed head every time he yelled, "Unhand me, vamp!" He had treated it like a workout, looking to replicate the way P90X had accelerated his physical development as a vampire.

And it worked; Victor swore he could feel his body responding, repairing, regenerating dormant muscle and rewiring fast-twitch nerves. He just needed more *time*.

Now they looked down on the cabin from their washout bluff. The sun had set two hours ago, carrying off every bit of the desert's heat.

"What do you see?" Edna hissed in Eugene's ear.

Eugene shuddered and brushed her away. "They appear to be forcing Amberly to eat boiled Gila monster."

"My baby," Barbara moaned.

"Time to take them out," Victor growled.

"Possibly," Eugene qualified. "It could be a corn-based porridge, and it might not be Amberly. Really hard to tell."

"I really hate this kid," Tripp whispered as Eugene swatted at Edna trying to cover his legs with her shawl.

Victor yanked Eugene out of his slayer-mobile, threw the slayer over his shoulder and started down the hill.

"Unhand me, vamp!"

Eugene's pulse hammered against Victor's shoulder, the young man's heart urgently pumping blood through his veins. A squirming blood sac, that's what he carried down the hill. A big CamelBak. Victor could hike for miles well-provisioned like this.

Bloodthirst had been upon him for hours now. It aggravated his anger. There had been no time to stop at the blood bank on the way to the airport. He hoped his appetite would be a weapon in the battle to come.

He skirted the picked-over woodpile beside the cabin and unslung Eugene from his shoulder.

"Gently," Eugene requested right before he hit the hardpan. To his credit he was on his feet in an instant. He found a sturdy pine limb and used it as a crutch to hobble after Victor.

A bloodcurdling scream froze Victor.

This time I will not be paralyzed by my fear.

He kicked the door in.

They had killed the kitchen light but the fireplace provided plenty illumination. Someone to his left and someone to his right. A third person scurried into the next room. Amberly must be in there. At the fireplace a man grabbed an iron poker. In the kitchen a woman armed herself with a knife for each hand.

Victor bared his fangs and roared, freezing them enough to reach the bedroom door. There came the scream again. He threw open the door, ready for an attack. Inside was a young boy and a baby crying on a thin mattress too big for the underlying metal cot.

Eugene entered the cabin. "Vamps!" On one leg he hopped once, twice, planted the pine bough like a vaulting pole, cleared a ratty couch and began clubbing the short Hispanic man-vamp like a baby fur seal. The Hispanic woman vamp ululated in the kitchen and charged. Through the door came Tripp; shoulder lowered, he leveled her.

Sven and Edna were right behind him to pin and disarm the smallish she-vamp. Eugene called for one of the knives, caught Sven's toss and began whittling his crutch-cum-club into a stake.

In the bedroom the boy bared his fangs and hissed horribly. The cherub-faced curly-haired baby did the same. Victor closed the door.

Barbara was on top of the woman. "Where's my daughter? Where's Amberly?"

The she-vamp hissed and then answered in decent English. "I don't know who you say."

Barbara slapped her. "You know exactly who!"

Eugene hauled the man-vamp over by the hair. The lightweight club hadn't done too much damage; the vampire was conscious, struggling and complaining. "Illegal immigrant vamps," Eugene explained. "They don't know anything. The CWS isn't here. Looks like I was wrong."

Victor looked around the cabin. This was it. There was no hiding place. "Are you kidding me?" He pictured the shanty as from Google Maps, at a sufficient altitude to see all the distance and time separating them from Houston, where they had been

14 hours ago, where Amberly surely awaited his rescue. "You weren't *sure*? You dragged us here on a plane, made us drive a hundred miles, through a Border Patrol checkpoint ..."

He worked himself into his own version of a frenzy. No one needed to see and he was ashamed to admit that he was more relieved than furious that Amberly wasn't here. It granted him extra time.

" ... and across this *desert*, in your *wheelchair* ..."

With his lame foot on the man-vamp's throat Eugene tested the point of his fresh-cut stake. He moved it slowly in front of Victor's face as if administering an eye test. "Keep it under control, Victor."

The illegal immigrant vampires on the floor brightened. The man-vamp spoke as best he could with Eugene's boot under his chin. "Are you Veector Tetterson?"

Barbara stole a proud look at Victor. "You've heard of him?"

"You are famous in Honduras," gushed the she-vamp. "Veector *es el santo patrono de los vampiros*! Our patron saint."

"Just what we need," said Tripp.

"King of the vamps," Sven spat the accusation at Victor. "Morbius reborn." He eyeballed the cabin for a weapon. Edna likewise checked kitchen drawers, cupboard and pantry, tapping her foot and muttering a limerick:

"There once was a vamp from Valentine,
who enjoyed drinking people like wine;
*   but along came a stake, that his stomach coul'nt take,*
*   and now his flesh feeds the grapevines."*

"We heard you were dead," the man-vamp explained.

"Nearly." Victor scowled at Tripp. "Thanks to my 'buddy.' Best slayer I know."

"Ha!" Edna disagreed from the kitchen. She hefted a frying pan and gave it a test swing.

Sven eyed Tripp skeptically. "I have heard of you?"

"I've been so blind!" Eugene's outburst startled everyone. "Of *course*—they took her to Chateau d'Ussé. We need to get there ASAP. Hiiiyah!" In the slayer version of the Karate Kid's crane kick, Eugene came off the floor by driving his bad knee to the ceiling, and then dropped into the splits, bad leg out front and across the man-vamp's throat, stake plunged in his heart.

The vampire sucked a dry rattling gulp of the cabin's smoky air and turned his head for one last apologetic look at his wailing wife.

"Sweet Jesus." Tripp joined Barbara and Sven tracing the cross.

"You know where Amberly is?" said Victor

"Were you listening? Chateau d'Ussé!" Eugene gave the vampire some space in his death throes. "French castle. The Civil War Soldier's Euro base." He pulled out his smartphone and got someone on the other end. "Fuel up the Gulfstream, 6 a.m. departure." He evaluated the freshness of his wheelchair bearers. "Make that 8:30."

The bedroom door creaked open. There stood the 5-year-old boy vampire, holding his crying baby sister vampire. The boy looked from his sobbing mother to what remained of his father, now in accelerated dry-rot, face disintegrating, desert camo shirt sagging over his ribcage which caved like a late-November carved pumpkin. The young vampire's tears began to flow.

Eugene snapped his fingers. "Sven and Edna. Do 'em." With little trouble he extracted the knotty pine stake from brittle ribs and limped for the she-vamp.

Sven stared at the vamp-children. "I, uh ... I didn't bring a stake."

"No more mercy!" Eugene pointed at a splinter hanging from the rough pine-plank wall. "Improvise." He turned to Barbara and nodded at the she-vamp. "Hold her still, Mom."

"Don't ever call her that again," said Victor.

"Veector!" the illegal immigrant vampire beseeched her santo patrono. "*Mis hijos*! My children!"

With Barbara frozen in wild-eyed horror Eugene left the ground, not so much a dive as an all-star wrestling freefall, legs spread and stake extended in a two-handed grip.

Tripp's cowboy boot made solid contact with his knuckles and deflected the slay-strike. Eugene grunted as he bounced on the wood-shavings floor. Using the stake as a crutch he labored to his feet. "Grave mistake, cowpoke."

Tripp put himself between the slayers and the she-vamp. "You're not killing this woman." He gave Barbara an appreciative nod as she took the vampire baby in her arms. "And you're not killing those kids."

"Showing a vamp mercy?" Eugene pointed at Victor while gaping at Tripp. "Haven't you learned anything?"

Edna hopped up behind Tripp, brandishing the frying pan. Victor easily intercepted her and twisted her hand up behind her back until she dropped the pan. Then he twisted a little further. "We need to go," he told Barbara. He had training to do.

"Not until these little ones are safe." Barbara soothed the whimpering infant. "I won't sacrifice this woman's children to save ours." The baby-vamp tried to bite her wrist. "No-no," she admonished.

"You'd rather have them sucking human kids' blood at the detention center?" said Eugene.

Sven flung the splinter into the kitchen. "She is correct. I will not slay children."

"We'll send them back across the border," said Barbara.

Eugene took a stand at the door. "I'm not letting

vamps walk in either direction."

"So we're agreed," said Victor. "We kill Eugene."

Tripp dug in his vest pocket and pulled out a business card. "Science to the rescue again." He helped the she-vamp to her feet. She hurried to take her baby-vamp from Barbara. "Do you want to cure your children? Make them human again?"

Suspecting a trap, the woman finally nodded. She drew the 5-year-old to her hip. "A man in our neighborhood did this to them. To all of us." She sobbed, kissing her baby-vamp's forehead. "Our neighbors drove us from our home."

"A wise choice by your village elders," said Eugene.

Tripp gave the woman his card. "I can cure you. I'm in Houston. If you can find some way to contact me ..."

"Perhaps via cell phone?" said the she-vamp.

Tripp nodded, embarrassed. "Then I'll find a way to come to you."

They left the single-parent illegal immigrant vampire family in the cabin. Sven and Tripp took turns carrying Eugene up the hill, slow progress, slipping and stumbling, dumping the slayer more than once. Victor waited for them at the top, arm around Barbara to ward off the increasing chill.

He accosted Eugene as they dumped him in his wheelchair. "What made you think Amberly would be here?"

"Partly because the CWS told me not to look here." At their blank looks Eugene pulled out his smartphone and brought up a picture of the backside of the second message.

Don't bother looking for us in the old familiar places.

Victor was torn between his extreme disgust at the very sight of Eugene and the desire to drink him dry. "Then why are we here?"

Eugene smirked. "Have you ever heard of a reverse decoy? It must be the Chateau." He snapped his fingers. "Driver!"

Sven's sweat was freeze-drying. He shivered violently as he took a grip on the wheelchair handles and put his back into it. "*Allons*! To the Chateau!"

"She's in Houston," said Tripp. "Bet on it."

The three of them reached their rental and its heater a little after 6 a.m. as the desert's ultimate heater was clearing the saguaro-stubbled horizon. They had literally carried Edna with them after the little old slayer lady tripped and fell face-first on a cactus, blinding her. She elected to wait for her fellows at the van, and received no argument.

Two miles down the road they hit the Border Patrol roadblock again.

Tripp rolled down his window as an agent approached the car. "Good morning, officer. Remember us?"

The agent waved his compatriot back to their running SUV and leaned into Tripp's window. "Anything to declare, citizens?" He looked at Victor in the passenger seat and grinned. "I know what you were doing in the desert." His eyes darted to Barbara in the back seat. "And I know you're coming back empty-handed."

"Right you are," said Tripp. "You can check the trunk. Nothing but legals here."

The agent stared at Victor. "I'm talking about your daughter." With some effort and slobbering, he removed his falsie-mouthpiece to reveal himself a vampire. Tripp stiffened; Barbara could see gooseflesh on the back of his neck.

Victor flung open his door and charged around the front of the car. As the other border agent left her SUV, chambering a shell, the vampire met Victor halfway, slugged him in the solar plexus and threw him on the hood.

"You need to shut up and listen." The vampire pushed up Victor's lip. "Ah, yes. I see you are undergoing a resurrection."

"Where is my daughter?" Barbara flew at the vampire and gouged at his eyes.

He knocked Barbara to the road with a backhand. Tripp had a mind to punish him but he found the female agent's shotgun barrel under his chin and then his arm behind his back, and cuffed, in short order face-down and halfway under the rental's front end, anchored to the axle.

Victor vibrated with adrenaline but there was no breaking the vampire's grip. "Do you know the Civil War Soldier?"

The vampire's teeth were stained brown and his breath putrid. "I work for X Anthony."

"Does he have Amberly?" Barbara was back on her feet.

The vampire border agent chortled in Victor's face. "X knows how Amberly can be freed. X says you owe him. Perhaps you should come through on the outstanding coding you promised. Or ... maybe there's something else he wants?"

The vampire was baiting him. Victor struggled to find the mental calm that vampirism promised. But he was preoccupied with a tortured singing of sorts emanating from the agent's throat. As if the vampire border agent's tonsils were crying out to him.

"I'll give him whatever he wants."

"You're a terrible negotiator," said the vampire. "Which means you should be able to make a deal." He set Victor back on his feet and nodded for his compatriot to un-cuff Tripp. "Noon Saturday. X will see you at the office."

As they pulled away the agent put his falsies back in and leered. "Come ready to deal, Victor."

12 May 1588

Today I chanced across this record, my history. I had forgotten it existed. Truly I had nearly forgotten my prior life, that of N., along with that human desire to recount the day's events. I cannot count the heads that have rolled since I last picked up this quill.

In these last two years what have I had to document? Would posterity find interest in the screams? The blood? Or how my power has grown by the day and with it the legend of Morbius? How I stride through the streets of Bucharest and Tirgu Mures and Constantinople wearing a Greek hero's armor of invincibility?

Ah but my suit of armor <u>is</u> interesting. Like Achilles, I too have a chink, the smallest of slits for the assassin's blade to penetrate.

That chink, that Heel; yes, it is worthy of recording, worthy of the song of Homer himself. Sacrifice! that Holy rite of purification and submission. Sacrifice! you who will lay me to rest, must be prepared to make. Sacrifice! a fitting dispatch for a vampire.

I harbor no fear of that dispatch, as I cannot imagine any of these poor wretches willing to give their own pathetic lives to end my reign. Poor, pathetic wretches! They are my kin, these men and women, and yes, the children. Yet I stalk them and destroy them. I see the world through their eyes while I lust for their slaughter.

But now as their numbers dwindle and the streets flow as rivers of their blood, I am compelled to

[entry stops mid-sentence; translated from Romanian]

12 May 1588, continued...

It is some hours since I set down my quill unexpectedly. I had to step away to slay Dragomir's family. Dragoș himself was out but the opportunity was too good to pass up. I'll catch up with him later.

Where was I? Ah yes, compulsion. Now that the vampires' ranks are thinned, I am compelled to reach out to the past and reflect on what brought me here. And to look to the future and dream of better things.

Love—that is the compulsion. I believed my life complete, and yet love has played no part. Murder, you have fulfilled me! Such a thrill to <u>see</u> the chinks in the vampires' armor and deal them final death.

I forgot what real, human love is. Dare I claim to love as a human? I will leave that judgment to the one who has crossed what many believe to be an un-Holy divide. Trubadur Maistru, my first and only true love, to you I give my heart.

What of M., the vampire Mortimer Canterpark? I believed I was in love, but I might better have been called in thrall. M., to this day my only regret was driving you from my bed that fateful night, ashamed for what I had done and afraid for what I would become. Trubadur finally confessed to slaying you that very night. I only pray you did not die with a broken heart.

With my uncanny vision and your steady hand, Trubadur my love, we will soon put to dusty rest the remaining vampires. We will bequeath to your precious Ugenosz and Stela a world free of this menace. Now Stela can someday start a family of her own. And Ugie can focus, as you so longed to do, on the pan flute. I only pray he can find a way to grow to love me as his father has. For I do grow weary of his little slayer attacks.

Trubadur Maistru, to you I give my heart. And on this blessed night I finally give you my body. I cannot wait to wake tomorrow in your arms, finally fully yours, with the rest of our lives to be lived and made as we choose.

I am Morbius, and the woman who was once, and will soon again be, Nadia Mihai Rákóczi

[translated from Romanian]   .

13 May 1588

Yesterday did not go as planned. Nadia, as soon as we finished our beautiful love-making, before the welts began to rise on my flesh, you died. I know there is no need to describe it to you, as even good vampires surely do not go to Heaven, but you went out with a production worthy of the greatest stage-performer and most creative story-teller. I am heartbroken.

And, it appears, a vampire. You promised not to bite me.

The other slayers are going to hate me.

T. Maistru

[translated from Romanian]

X Anthony the exceptional businessman vampire finished reading Trubadur Maistru's entry in the diary of Nadia Mihai Rákóczi, aka Morbius. He gently thumbed through subsequent entries on the dried-out, near-to-crumbling pages. Reading for another day.

"Where did you locate this?"

The question came to Dr. Linciome as if he might be sitting across from X having tea. In fact Linciome hung upside down, strung up by his ankles over the rafter in X's attic.

He was not presentable for tea. His normally natty clothes were disheveled and here and there torn. His face was battered, the worst of it a gash over his eye steadily dripping blood caught in a cake pan. That eye was swollen shut and he kept the other one closed.

"The diary, Doctor. You located it while in eastern Euro—the old country. Who had it?"

Linciome shook his head.

"You don't need to worry. Soon you are with us. Although not quite like X, sorry." He took Linciome by his thick plume of hair and lifted his head so they were face to inverted face. "With this diary the war is done.

Thetherson is done."

Linciome looked into X's glowing yellow orbs. "Even if you can fool everyone into believing he is Morbius, what the original Morbius wrote long ago is still true. No vampire will be willing to give his life for the cause."

X had what he wanted—Linciome's visual attention. "*B*ut," he said, fangs drawing his own blood, "there is a *slayer* willing to die for the cause."

The scientist closed his eye to the blood running down X's chin. There was no blocking the sound of the vampire's rapid breathing or the predator's pheromones permeating the air. "We will never stop hunting you. With or without Victor."

"We?" X demanded. "In a *m*inute you will no longer *b*elong to the set of 'we.' And so now you have a choice, a *f*inal choice as a hu*m*an. Tell X who ga*v*e you the diary and I will drink you dry and *m*erci*f*ully *p*ut an end to your accursed existence."

Linciome's mouth curled into what would have been an impish smile before his face was messed up. "So you admit the life of a vampire is for the damned."

X breathed faster and flexed his taloned hands, fixated on the blood dammed up under Linciome's eyebrow. "Doctor, you're going to tell X, now or a*f*ter. You'll *b*e sur*p*rised how di*ff*erently you a*pp*roach the world as a *v*am*p*ire."

He knelt before Linciome, something close to compassion on his face. "*F*or *m*e and *m*y *m*aster, the new world we're *b*uilding is going to be hea*v*enly. *B*ut not *f*or the une*v*ol*v*ed. Not *f*or you." X pushed Linciome's collar back from his throat. "I reco*mm*end you take the easy way out."

MURDER

"Ten more seconds," said Tony Horton, to Victor and Barbara. "Hang in there. Time to dig deep. Time to bring your swagger!"

This is for Amberly, Victor reminded himself when he wanted to quit at five seconds, at three, and again right before Tony said, "Time!"

The workout hurt, left him ready to throw up, reopened his sutures and made him dizzy, delirious and weak. His shoulder was nowhere near healed from the last time he had worked out with Tony, his back still ached from the one-story fall from Florence's bedroom, and instead of growing stronger with exercise he had only grown agitated, and then ashamed that he wasn't looking for his daughter.

He made it to the end of the routine, completed his last burpee even after Tony and his P90X crew had wrapped up.

Barbara was in better shape. She was able to work out at high intensity from the moment Tony started the clock until he called time, again and again. Exhausted, she walked it off, hands on hips, moving beautifully if wearily on 15 square yards of cushioned interlocking exercise mats.

It was coming up on 10 o'clock Saturday morning. X's instructions were to meet him in the office at noon. Barb hated the delay; every few hours she had insisted he call X and demand to meet immediately. But she understood Victor's mindset, and she put her faith in his approach, in her words and her deeds, with him every mile he ran and every pushup he cranked out.

Extremely lightheaded and finally breaking a cold, greasy sweat, Victor fell to his knees and threw up just off the mat.

Barbara toweled off below her throat and glanced at the mess, on top of a patch of oily dirt left behind by her sedan. "I was going to clean that spot, anyway." As she scattered a liberal amount of floor-sweep compound over the red-hued vomit, Barbara studied him, his physique, his posture, his expression. "How do you feel?"

Victor was constantly appraising himself in the same way for the same reason. Over the 20 hours since returning from Tucson, other than during a tortured attempt to sleep, they had been exercising. He felt awful.

He nodded. "Let's go get her."

Relief swept over Barbara. "I need five minutes to change." She shut off the television and hurried for the house. "I'll call Eugene."

On her heels, peeling his shirt off clammy skin, Victor envisioned Eugene and his slayer pals on the Bizco floor running amok, seeking revenge on X and hoping to score a twofer on him. Being their normal bungling selves. "We don't need him."

Barbara worked to hide her concern as she shed her clothes, giving Victor a small thrill in spite of the circumstances. "Wouldn't it help? You're just coming back." She was naked now, sleek and flushed, beautiful. "He wants Amberly back as much as we do."

Victor darkened. "X isn't looking for a fight. He's doing this at Bizco for a reason." He hurried to towel off his fleshy body and clothe it. "You heard the border agent. This is a blackmail move. He wants me to continue contributing to the software program."

Now Victor was the one to study his ex as she stood before the mirror brushing her hair. He wondered how much she could bear to hear. "X made it clear from the start he would use the two of you to get to me. Eugene is wrong, as usual. I don't think this Civil War Soldier has Amberly. I think it's X."

Barbara turned away but Victor saw the tears. "Does it matter?" she said. "You'll do whatever it takes to get her back."

Traffic was a bear. They didn't walk into the Bizco lobby until 11:30. As Victor signed in at the security desk in front of the well-built and expressionless weekend guard, he scanned the ledger and saw signatures from Darla, Florence, Larry, Kirby, Tessa, Quinten— nearly a full house. X was there, too.

And a couple surprises. Raj Dajiv was signed in as a Metafist employee. And David Copperfield, magically appearing at all kinds of interesting moments.

Victor tilted his head at Barbara. "She can't come up."

"What?" Barbara took his arm. "What are you doing?"

He kept his eyes on the guard, hoping he was committed to doing his job. "She's not an employee."

The weekend guard lived for these moments. He came around the desk to come between them. "Sorry ma'am. You'll have to stay here."

He went quickly to the elevator bank. "Victor!" Barbara's voice was raw with anguish. "I want to be up there with you!"

The doors slid open. "Meet me at the car."

"Find her. Please."

Victor wished he could say everything began to move in slow motion as the doors opened on the 14th floor, as he walked into the accounting department, as he scented a full palette of different warm foodstuffs. But no, life sped up, and he was a step behind.

Exclamations and murmurs rippled across the floor. On cue X emerged from the break room followed by

Raj and a man Victor didn't know, like Raj a soft and stylish Indian who bared his fangs at the sight of Victor. Raj smiled and he too sported fangs.

David Copperfield jumped to his feet at Larry's workstation. He had been playing with one of Larry's micro-taxidermy mounts, a tusked boar. In his eagerness to leave the line of fire and perhaps handicapped by the hunchback's constriction of the tendons in his right arm, David missed on his attempt to replace the pig on Larry's shelf and then sought to leave it on the next desk. He recoiled at Florence's snarl and hurried on, desperate for hands-free operation, finally flipping the micro mount into Quinten's inbox.

Quinten had his headphones in, didn't notice the little arrival, kept working. Florence grabbed him by the scruff of the neck and hauled him in the direction David Copperfield had fled.

Monique picked up a handheld video camera and began recording.

Larry kept one eye each on X and Victor as he wheeled backward in his chair. He tucked his pant leg behind a calf-sheathed Bowie knife and whistled a warning to Kirby.

Casey strapped on her bike helmet.

Reading the sign-in sheet in the lobby, Victor knew something was wrong. X hadn't invited him here to bargain for Amberly, not at all.

It wasn't long ago that Victor had decided to end his life. Restarting his conversion to vampirism wasn't a change of heart; it was solely to save Amberly. And so while he recognized it was Death that approached, there was no thought of running.

Neither was there confidence he would survive. In mind and body, Victor simply wasn't ready yet.

Kirby hopped from his chair and met Victor a few steps out of the elevator. "You're probably wondering why we're here, since we don't normally work weekends. I hope you don't think we do. He's really been a good boss." Kirby pointed at a buffet table in front of Darla's empty desk. "X brought in brunch. And at noon the bar opens. Four microbrews on tap in the break room. I hope there's a milk stout."

"I don't care, Kirby."

"And we'll all get a ten-thousand-dollar bonus if the XFP goes standalone for EnerGreen by the 15th." Words didn't fly out of Kirby's mouth, they were squeezed out, extruded, no open spaces between them, one elongated syllable linked to the next by his sustained earnestness. He took a breath. "Sorry X doesn't like you."

"None of us like you now!" Tessa yelled at Victor as she approached, with Monique trailing in a crouch, shooting low-angle. "X said you reversed your cure. Is that true? Show us your goddamned teeth!"

Her vitriol stunned him. As did the rest of the team's reaction when he bared his fangs. They booed him. Quinten's hands megaphoned his mouth, putting his voice closer to Victor's ear. "You suck, VV!"

"How could you?" Tessa looked with righteous awe at the three vampires fanning out, Raj to Victor's left and his fellow Indian Metafist-er to his right. X came head-on, a ribbed steel briefcase under his arm. "You broke your vow."

"I had no choice. X has my daughter."

"Oooh," X protested, playing to his little crowd. "You know that's a lie. I have it on good authority you've been told exactly who has your daughter." His tongue flicked at the rubber fang tips. "A slayer. A slayer who understandably wants to eliminate the modern-day legacy of the most evil vampire in history."

"And I have it on good authority that my ancestor was a good vampire."

"There's no such thing!" said Tessa. Victor tried to focus on X while Tessa and the accountants leaned into their booing. They might as well have been holding pitchforks. All except for Casey, who burst into tears. "If you had stayed human," said Tessa over Casey's sobbing, "your daughter would be all right."

"Amberly was abducted before I stopped the cure."

"Because you're wishy-washy," said Larry. "I'm sure this slayer recognized it. You had finally made a good decision, Vic. But you just couldn't leave it there, could you?"

"Ah, Larry." Raj strolled to his old workmate. He enjoyed Larry's subtle recoil and Monique's camera. "You can't understand what our poor old boss was missing." He flexed his hands and showed his fangs. "Welcome back to the club, Victor. I mean that. For a few minutes."

Florence marched up to Victor. "You're changing again." Her irises turned a deeper red as she drank in his enhanced state. She slapped him. "That should have been mine." Hatred glistened in her tears. "You selfish fucker." She slapped him again, vampire-strength, driving Victor to a knee. "Now your daughter is suffering. All because of your gutless, selfish failure."

X seized her raised arm and forced her out of the way. "Don't beat him senseless. Give me at least a glimpse of what all the fuss was about."

"I'd like to see that too, actually," said Raj. "Vic was fussy. But that was about it."

"I am just so surprised Raj became a vampire," Casey spoke to the camera and blew her nose. "You never think it will happen to someone you know."

"He just grew fangs," said Tessa, disgusted. "He's always been a vampire."

"I'll take that as a compliment. It's how business gets done, Tessa." Raj held court for the accountants and a future YouTube audience. "The public, you think you're holding Big Business accountable to a moral standard. When you get an occasional glimpse of what you deem immoral through some tell-all book, we have

always had to *bite* our tongues and endure your
outrage and pretend those actions were outliers. But
we know that progress only occurs through the
exercise of power. Finally, the time has come that we
can *waggle* our tongues." He closed his eyes, to make a
passionate point. "Everyone is going to label this the
rise of the vampires, but it's really just Business—"

"Enough," said X. After ensuring Raj's eyes were
open and receiving the message, he manufactured a
disappointed look for Victor. "You didn't write the XFP
code I requested, did you? At the very least, you
deserve to be fired. But given that you are heir to
Morbius, firing is insufficient."

The elevator dinged and disgorged Darla, satchel
over her shoulder, wearing a headache. She was a few
steps onto the floor before registering the unusual
circumstances: past and present accountants in a
ragged semi-circle, Monique recording the scene,
Victor the center of attention.

Darla looked at Raj and David. "What are you two
doing here?" She noticed the blood on Victor's swollen
lip and unslung her satchel, let it fall to the floor.
"What's happening?"

"I told you I didn't need you this weekend," said X.

"Then why is my team here?"

"As witnesses."

Victor worked to divert his mind from going down
paths leading to panic. "Tell me where Amberly is. Let
me pass along that information. Then do whatever you
want to me."

"I didn't say I knew where she is," said X. "I told you
I could help you free her."

"What happened to Amberly?" Darla pushed past
Tessa and Quinten to get to Victor. "Is she all right?"

With a nod from X, Raj intercepted her. "You
shouldn't be here, Darla." His voice was syrupy calm
over her protests.

Victor bristled as Raj enjoyed the opportunity to

wrap up Darla and hold her tight. "X, please ..."

"Thetherson," X said, "don't beg. I want to remember you at your best. I'm sure everyone here feels likewise."

"Come *on*." Eugene the vampire slayer wheeled out of X's black tubular teepee, followed closely by slayers Sven and Edna. "I'm sure your introduction was going to be dramatic but I can't wait another second in that stinking vamp sweat lodge."

"I was that close to going on a vision quest," said Edna. "Now I'll probably never meet my totem animal."

"Ze goose, zat is mine," said Sven. "Fed by force, with a beeg liver."

Edna cackled. "After we're done here I'm going to pickle your liver with some grade-A gin and have my way with you. Edna gets randy after some good slaying."

"You do not need to tell Sven," said Sven, goosing Edna's ass through her culottes, getting only trousers, going deeper until he found a pinch of meat. "My hot, desert-dry amour! *Mon Dieu*, zee friction! Zat is why we can only slay every other day, *ma chère*."

"Let's get this over with," said Eugene.

"Monsieur Eugene," said Sven, "allow me ze honor." He winked at Edna as he unsheathed a long slender steel-tipped stake from the utility belt around his skintight capris. He assumed a fencing stance and pointed the weapon at Victor with a lean, muscled arm. "En *garde*! But only if you wish to prolong your agony."

"I'd love to get your May-December night of passion off to a rousing start," said X. "But this kill must go to the slayer bearing the famous name. Maistru, in its original form." X turned to Eugene like a minister performing a wedding. "You've read the diary, Eugene. Do you accept the special sacrifice required?"

"I do." Eugene was solemn like Victor had never

seen him. "I finally understand what the CWS tried to tell me." The slayer rolled forward, came to a halt and reared back, spun his wheelchair 360 degrees to again face Victor. He rocked back and forth, little front wheels hovering off the ground. "But first I thought we'd try it the traditional way." A skinny stake shot out from his chair-mounted launcher and plunged into Victor's chest.

Accountants screamed. Darla broke free from Raj to support Victor as he sank to his knees, clutching the polished mahogany stake protruding between button and shirt pocket.

He slipped into shock. His chest was so tight no breath could fill his lungs. Victor gasped for it, he needed air to think ... to remember Barbara, his family, his life. His daughter.

Monique zoomed in.

"Victor Thetherson," Darla whispered. "You will not go ..."

Florence dragged Larry forward for a closer look. David peered from behind them. Larry turned away and knelt before his wastebasket, being sick.

"Amberly," Victor managed to say. "Amberly."

Eugene pointed his chair at David.

"I'm not a vamp!"

"Obviously." Eugene nodded to Larry. "You two tell Berry I refunded your deposit. This one isn't for the money." He wheeled to within a few feet of Victor, leery of getting too close to a high-speed decomposition. "You have my word: Amberly will be safe. The CWS will fulfill his promise."

Victor sat back on his heels, and marveled at how loose his knees were, how this pose didn't hurt in the least.

"I'm sure he will," said X. "But you still haven't made good on *your* obligation." He slapped Victor across the face and received a full-fanged snarl. He was off his heels and would have stood but for X's foot on his shoulder. He didn't appear to be on the verge of decomposition. X looked at Eugene. "You see?"

"Crap," said Eugene. Now he appeared to lose his oxygen, too.

With an unseemly grunt X leaned forward and yanked the stake from Victor's chest.

Victor wheezed. There was room again in his chest to breathe. Blood oozed from the hole, but not a frightening amount.

X tossed the stake at the accountants, who yelped and jostled to avoid the bloody thing.

"Oh my God." Tessa crossed herself watching Victor recover from the staking. "It's true. You are a monster."

X placed his briefcase on the nearest desk, popped the clasps and carefully cradled a loose few pages, some of them just fragments, all of them amber from age and covered with faded blood-brown writing. He displayed them for Victor as Monique gave her viewers a close-up. "Does this stir something deep in your black soul, monster?"

With Darla's assistance Victor struggled to his feet. "Morbius's diary, I suppose." He felt like Frankenstein forming his first words. "How did you get it?"

"It was a fortunate find." X clutched the diary excerpt to his chest, playing to the camera. "If we left you to your wicked ways, Victor Thetherson, the world would have soon revolted against us. We would have been slaughtered." He acknowledged his accounting team with a cinematic flourish. "These hardworking Bizco team members have seen how wonderful life can be with a vampire at the helm. They know I will lead them to a higher status within the organization. And higher compensation." He received a muted but still enthusiastic cheer.

Darla appealed to her team. "You know Victor. He's not what X is saying—how can you believe that?"

"You love Victor, Darla," said Casey. "That's why you can't see how evil he is. I can't see it, either, but I lost that part of my brain in the accident. I think everyone is good."

At Tessa's urging, Quinten and Kirby hustled forward and tore Darla away from Victor.

"Stop it!" Her team manhandled her. They forced her into a roller chair and strapped her down with power cords pilfered from various workstations.

X prevented Victor's feeble intervention and mugged for the camera. "I wish we could deal with you through normal law enforcement channels. But the legal system hasn't yet adapted to vampires." He nodded to his other Metafist employee.

The vamp plucked a can of SpaghettiOs from the lunchroom donation bin and hurled it with perfect cricket form. The can ricocheted off Victor's head and whacked David Copperfield in the throat. Both went down.

"Took your wicket," the vamp said with crazy eyes and a thick Indian accent. Victor wanted to vomit from the concussive pain.

X applauded his employee's prowess and set his briefcase in Eugene's lap. "For the uninitiated," he addressed his audience, "there is a vampire concept known as the Achilles' heel. Victor, as Morbius's heir, has an exceedingly rare Heel."

He kicked Victor in the stomach, sissy-style, packing a wallop nonetheless. "To obtain rare things one must pay a high price." X removed one rubber tip. The action seemed to give him relief, like removing shoes after a long day's labor. He knelt before Eugene. "What would you *pay* to sa*ve* your *pre*cious A*mb*erly?"

Eugene hesitated only long enough for his eyes to dart to the blood trickling down X's chin. "Everything, vamp. You know that."

X's smile was of the wolf, the devil, the viper. "Then do I ha*ve* just the stake *fo*r you."

He opened the briefcase as if an otherworldly light might spill forth and bathe his chinless face in supernatural incandescence. Reverently he revealed a double-tipped stake and held it in ready position, the wicked ends pointing at slayer and vampire.

"No!" Sven leaped to stand over Victor, who was struggling to clear his head. "The sacrifice will be mine! It is a far, far better thing that I do, than I have ever done; it is a far, far better rest that I go to than I have ever known." He pointed to Edna, rheumy eyes drinking in her paramour's bravery, her withered chest heaving. "Or she can do it. Either way."

X cuffed Sven with a stake-reinforced fist, sending the slayer sprawling into Quinten's desk, knocking over his 64-ounce vat of Mt. Dew, soaking everything. Larry growled and rescued his soggy little boar.

"The choice was *m*ade centuries ago." X removed the other rubber nipple. "When Eugene's ancestor, Tru*b*adur *M*aistru, killed *M*or*b*ius." The pheromones of his frenzy filled the air faster than the building's green, LEED-certified recirculation system could freshen it.

Eugene breathed it in, looking for intoxication.

X fixed him with wolfish eyes. "I didn't show you the whole diary. You think your ancestor was so *bra*ve to slay *M*or*b*ius." He grabbed the handicapped slayer by the front of his shirt and hauled him from the wheelchair. "In *f*act Tru*b*adur was a coward."

"I'll slay *you* for that," said Eugene. He ripped the double-tipped stake from X's grasp and cocked it double-handed over his head.

Lightning quick, X forced Eugene's arms down and behind him, making him goggle-eyed with pain. Shoulders would have dislocated on a less flexible slayer. "You'll slay *V*ictor for that." X released him, turned his back on him and played to the assembled. "Eugene's ancestor had the chance to end *M*or*b*ius's legacy *f*orever. He was too gutless to *m*ake the sacri*f*ice."

Eugene rotated life back into his shoulders. "I don't

believe you."

X pointed at Victor. "That is all the proof you need." The vampire was having a hard time maintaining his lawyerly presentation style, blood pulsing from his bottom lip and the frenzy threatening to possess him. Raj and his fellow Metafist Indian stalked back and forth like rappers onstage, feeding off their leader's energy.

"Your ancestor did kill Morbius. But he refused to make the sacrifice! He would not give his life to save humanity. And so the bloodline continued and Victor stands here today." He was close to screaming. "That is why 'Maistru,' the name Foreman, is reviled to this day!"

Eugene's face was berserk with tortured confusion. He strangled the stake and pressed one pointed tip into his chest.

X side-kicked Victor's chest, putting him on his back. "The choice is yours, Eugene. We are all audience to your decision." He nodded to the assembled, for the camera. "Will you finally redeem your name?"

Eugene screamed as the stake pierced his tight black t-shirt.

"Eugene Foreman," X bayed as if at the moon, "will you fulfill your legacy? Will you save the woman you love?"

"For Maistru!" Eugene thrust the stake in the air. "For Foreman! And for you, Amberly. I am yours forever!" He turned the true believer's sightless gaze on Victor. "Die, Vamp!" Slayer Sven and Edna began to ululate.

Raj and his fellow Metafister pinned Victor's arms to the floor. Eugene went airborne and anchored the stake in the starter hole in his chest.

Victor met him with his feet but Eugene's momentum was too great and the stake reached its target.

The slayer was suspended at a steep angle of attack,

on three points of contact: Victor's feet in his gut,
Eugene's hands gripping his shoulders, and the
double-tipped stake in each man's chest. They stared
at each other, faces inches apart.

"You're completely insane," said Victor. He sweated
furiously. His body temperature plummeted. This
stake, this time, was different. "You're going to kill
yourself, to kill me?"

Blood pumped into Eugene's flame-red face. He
ground his teeth in pain and effort as he strained to
pull them together. "Of course."

From her little prison Darla screamed. Larry sat
beside the wastebasket, taking in the scene with a
glazed expression. Slayers Sven and Edna offered
intense words of encouragement to Eugene while doing
double-duty as crowd control. Everyone else watched
fascinated, horrified, and reconciled to the ending.

The stake sank deeper. "Someone," Eugene grunted,
"make sure Amberly sees the diary. She needs to
understand why."

Victor pushed with his legs, but the slayer would
not be budged. "Eugene," Victor used his name for the
first time he could remember. "You haven't seen the
whole diary. Maybe I am Morbius, but my ancestor
killed *vampires*. Not humans." Victor grunted in fear
as his body began to shake. "He could see vampires'
Heels. He had the sight. I think I have it."

"You're lying." Eugene redoubled his efforts. A vein
burst on his forehead. Blood from his chest painted the
wood and mixed with the blood spreading across
Victor's shirt.

"No, no ..." Victor was exhausted. He couldn't feel
his legs, couldn't tell how hard he was pushing.
"Remember I told you in the desert that sex is my
Heel—Eugene, listen to me! Do you remember? That's
also the only way my curse is passed on. Sex kills me
and turns my partner into a vampire."

"Shut up and die already, Morbius."

"If Trubadur Maistru killed Morbius, then how can I be Morbius's descendant? Think, Eugene! There's only one way that could happen!"

Eugene's eyes bulged and his face vibrated with the attempt to end them both. "Are you saying—" He loosed a tortured groan. "Are you saying my ancestor had gay sex with a vampire?"

Amidst a system-wide shutdown Victor could only say *yes* with his eyes.

"Why?" Eugene gasped.

"He's lying," X hissed.

Victor couldn't look at him; but he pictured the oily quivering skin atop the vampire's balding skull.

Just like the armpit of Sennett McGumphrey.

X screamed at Eugene. "Why would a slayer love a vampire?!"

"Indeed," Victor rasped.

Eugene stuttered through the pain and confusion. "Then Trubadur became a vampire? Which means— which means!—he's your ancestor, too?"

Victor's reply was a contorted wince. His eyes darted to X and back. "He's deceiving you and your sensei, too."

"*Victor Thetherson*," X raged, "is a ra*b*id dog that *m*ust *b*e *p*ut down!"

Victor's eyes remained locked on Eugene's while all he saw was the top of X's head. "And he's got a squishy fontanel."

Eugene's face transformed into a different type of hate. Victor saw his opportunity and gave him a mighty push. Eugene shot up into the air, stake in hand, and landed behind X.

The vampire spun but Eugene was gone—with one nimble step he used Casey's desk to launch himself. X was slow to understand the slayer was above him. As he came down Eugene drove the stake into X's brain through a soft entry at the tip-top of his skull—the stellar businessman vampire's Heel.

All the air in the room was sucked into X's lungs. His final taste of Life.

"Slayers," Eugene commanded as X fell dead on his face. "Do your thing."

Sven and Edna each pulled a stake from their utility belts and charged the Metafist employees. Sven jabbed Raj's compatriot in the throat and rammed the stake into his chest. Raj punched Edna in the face and drove the little old lady hard to the floor.

"This will be like drinking powdered milk," Raj quipped as he bit her.

Edna's stake lay in her open hand. Victor picked it up, raised it high, howled at the white-hot fire coming from his much-abused chest and plunged the stake into Raj's back.

The former Bizco accountant vampire arched his back, gave a rattling squeak and rolled off Edna. He looked up sideways at Victor. "It figures that you would be a 'good' vampire." Raj feebly added the rabbit-ear quotes. "Because you were a terrible manager." He died, the stake propping him on his side.

"Great fucking video," said Monique, ending her recording.

On shaky legs Victor went to Darla, knelt before her and untied the power cords. She took Victor's face and kissed it and then looked at Florence and Larry, he sitting slumped like a lost puppy in a dark alley, she inching toward the elevator bank. "You're both fired." Darla took into account the rest of her befuddled, traumatized team. "I'll have to seriously consider the rest of you." She began worrying about Victor's chest wounds. "Kirby, call 9-1-1."

Sven hauled Edna's limp frame into the wheelchair. Her eyes rolled around in their sockets. "Some *juice d'orange, s'il vous plaît?*" he appealed to the Bizco accountants. "Ze lady has just given blood."

"And another wheelchair," Eugene requested, slumped against Casey's desk, giving his chest wound a lackluster daubing with napkins Quinten had fetched from the brunch buffet. He stared vacantly at the floor, lost in recently-introduced thoughts.

Victor threw the power cords at him, receiving most of the slayer's attention. "We need to find Amberly. Now."

"I don't know—I don't know where she is."

Edna patted the wheelchair arm, head lolling and semi-conscious. "I had this very same model. First time I went vegan. I lost 156 pounds. My kids had me involuntarily committed to the nursing home. Ranching community. The staff force-fed me beef to get my strength back."

Eugene stiffened as if he had been electro-shocked. He limped to Edna. "Get her out of there."

Sven tenderly lifted the little lady out of the wheelchair.

"My lover smuggled in humane sushi," Edna continued the reminiscence. "Sweet Jesus he was a cool drink of water." Her eyes fluttered open. "I could use a drink of water." Her head fell back against Sven's hardbody chest. "That's the day I lost my virginity and became a pescetarian."

The elevator opened and policemen poured onto the floor. "Everybody stay put!" said a grim-faced officer. Victor raised his hands and kept his mouth closed.

The officer saw the three staked vampires. "Good Lord." X was in early-stage decomposition, skin going gray, the underlying tissues liquefying.

One of the officers spotted Monique's video camera. "Oh goodie, we got a movie." He had her place the camera in an evidence bag.

Eugene knocked the wheelchair over. A stake discharged and cracked a window.

"You!" One of the officers rushed him. "Down!"

Just before the officer drove a knee into his chest wound, Eugene read the underside of the wheelchair. "Cool Breezes nursing home. The CWS gave me this.

That's where—ungh!"

The slayer struggled as the officer pinned him on his stomach and handcuffed him behind his back. Victor didn't need Eugene to fill in the blank. "That's where Amberly is. Officers, we need to get to the Cool Breezes nursing home." His voice rose as one of the officers approached him with something other than urgency. "My daughter is there! She was kidnapped!"

The officer saw his fangs. "Are you Victor Thetherson?"

"I am."

"We're here to bring you in." He produced handcuffs and indicated Victor should turn around while two officers positioned themselves as backup.

Victor held up his hands and backed away. "For what?"

The policemen were in no mood, a moment away from an involuntary cuffing. "You're being charged with the murder of Nikki Haley."

"Hey," an officer called from Raj's body. "Who staked this one?"

Many eyes went to Victor. He nodded. "Guilty."

The officer put his fingers in Raj's mouth and pulled out falsie fangs. "Looks like the D.A. can add another murder charge."

IN AND OUT

Hilda called Cornelius W. Sanders, aka the Civil War Soldier amongst other names, into the hall on the east wing of the Cool Breezes retirement village. She relayed to her master the gist of the call she had received. Cornelius uttered a Civil War-era curse and walked back into the room. He told Hilda to revive Amberly Thetherson.

Hilda excelled at putting people out and bringing them back. She had done it to Eugene Foreman more than once, to give him some solid shut-eye while his body healed from various extreme insults. Amberly had been fed intravenously the past few days. Now she came to.

She had seen Hilda briefly when the henchwoman lured her into an alley beside police headquarters, as Amberly had been arriving to tell the hunger strikers Eugene was safe. This was her first time laying eyes on Cornelius as he sat next to her on the bed.

"The CWS." Amberly was groggy, understandable under the circumstances. Her skin was paler than might have been expected. "Eugene has told me so much about you."

Cornelius smiled the way a southern gentleman does. He did not have a drink in his hand. "Then you also know my assistant, Hilda."

Amberly looked at her. "Nope. Never mentioned you."

Hilda shrugged but couldn't stop the color from

moving up her neck.

"Not even during pillow talk?" said Cornelius.

"None of your business." Amberly blinked to straighten out her vision while assessing the tightness of the tape binding her hands and feet to the bed frame.

Hilda's lip curled in disgust. "How old are you, girl?"

"Old enough."

"That's another spanking for Eugene," Hilda decided.

"I'll be the only one spanking Eugene," said Amberly.

Cornelius admired her spunk and her legs. "You are obviously a smart girl. Maybe you can tell us why we have you here."

"Where's here?"

"The Cool Breezes retirement home. You're surprised I told you. Worried, maybe. The police will be here within the hour. But we'll be long gone by then."

Hilda believed Amberly was contemplating screaming. She slapped the leather strap she kept handy, making it *pop*.

"No," said Amberly. "I don't know why I'm here."

"You have been kidnapped. Your ransom is Eugene slaying your father."

"Not happening. I broke up with Eugene. It's over and he knows it. So there goes his incentive. And my dad is cured so it would be a murder charge even if Eugene did kill him. Sorry." She sighed. "You'll have to kill him yourself."

Cornelius's wrist twitched, an aborted reflex that would have normally brought a mint julep to his lips. "I doubt your Dear John was enough to snuff out Eugene's commitment. However, the end result is it appears you are correct. Eugene did not slay your father." He removed his white hat and talked into it. "Chances are he's going to miss the deadline."

Amberly waited until she could produce enough saliva to answer coolly. "What's the deadline?"

"Tomorrow night. Midnight."

"And?"

"And I promised to kill you."

Amberly couldn't stop her eyes from filling with tears. "Why? Why do you want me dead?"

"I want your father dead."

"Okay, why? What did he do to you?"

Cornelius gazed into his hat. "It's what he is *going* to do that I'm worried about."

"For God's sake, my dad is an accountant."

"And Jesus was just a carpenter." Cornelius took a last glance in the hat before donning it. He groaned pushing his old, old body to its feet. "Damn good one, too."

Panic crept into Amberly's voice. "You have him all wrong."

Cornelius chuckled. "I'm the only one who knows who your father really is. Publicola gets some credit for that." He refreshed a laptop sitting on the corner desk. "For instance, he's about to feed the slayer community a load of horse hockey about Victor being Morbius and rallying all the evolved vampires to his evil cause." After a final scan of the Publicola blog post, he hit *Send*.

"You're saying he's not Morbius?" This was enough to keep Amberly's breathing a notch below rapid. "Then why would you want him dead?"

"To *protect* Morbius, of course. Which brings us to the other reason why I kidnapped you. Yep."

Amberly waited until her patience and saliva ran out. "Yep what?"

"Yep I'm not going to kill you."

Amberly sobbed loudly in relief. Hilda slapped her. Amberly spit on her and was slapped again.

Cornelius watched the stripes from Hilda's fingers go white and then fill with blood. He tossed his hat aside. "I'm not going to kill you. But neither am I giving you up."

Amberly wiped her tears against her shoulders and looked up at the IV bag. "You're going to drug me again, aren't you?"

"I need you unconscious," said Cornelius. "But I'm not going to drug you." He knelt beside the bed on a level with Amberly's face. "This is for you, Stela."

Amberly frowned. "Stela?"

"You don't know how long I've been waiting for this."

Hilda moaned. "Master, you didn't need to wait."

"Quiet," said Cornelius.

Hilda sobbed, eyes filled with hatred for Amberly.

Cornelius reached into his mouth and after considerable effort removed his falsies. His natural teeth weren't as white, straight, or dull.

Amberly thrashed and dug her chin into her chest to cover her throat. "Please don't. Please don't. I've already been bitten."

"So I've heard."

"I'm already changing! You're wasting your time!"

"I'm sure that's not true." Cornelius breathed raggedly. "You'll find *my* bite has a very different effect." He pinned Amberly's head to the bed and dropped his mouth on her throat.

Amberly screamed until she couldn't. Her body bucked until it came to rest. She whimpered in her last moments of consciousness. "You're so fucking gross."

George and Boris had finagled the best room at the Cool Breezes retirement village. They had a great view of the duck pond and tiny copse of trees that blocked the hot winds off the nearest refinery.

That was reason enough to upset Samuel Grivens across the hall. After all, Samuel had his name on that room's waiting list for six months prior to George and Boris showing up. But it was the fact that the two men were vampires that really teed Samuel off.

The confrontation in the lobby between X and Eugene had cinched it for Samuel. Even though George and Boris never bit anyone in the retirement village, most of the residents had already been sure. Of course, some folks also thought well-heeled Maria Santos in Room 1501 was actually Imelda Marcos.

Besides the view and the wind-block, George and Boris also had easy access to the parking lot. The exit door was right outside their room. Perfect for coming and going late at night, and for visitors who appreciated a low profile.

George and Boris now helped their visitors to the parking lot, carrying a big rolled-up Persian rug. They stuffed the rolled rug in the trunk of a Cadillac de Ville. A minute after the de Ville pulled out of the parking lot, a stream of squad cars pulled in.

JAILHOUSE

On a cot in the middle of the Houston police department vampire pit, Victor stared at the ceiling. Directly above him the plaster was dry, while a broad crown molding of beaded condensation ringed the cell. This humid border corresponded to the 50 or so vampires maximizing their distance from Victor.

A woman ventured forth. The curve of her hair, now dull and thin, and the gentle grace of what was left of her makeup marked her as a one-time Southern belle. She knelt like a creaky geisha at Victor's cot.

"Are you him?" She had a lilting drawl and sour-blood breath. "Is it true what they're saying?"

The bruises on Victor's face were already turning pretty colors in the final healing stage. "What are they saying?"

The Southern belle vamp carefully backhanded hair that wasn't out of place to begin with. "I heard it from a policeman. He said you know how to kill vampires." She leaned in to whisper confidentially, although it didn't appear to be a secret in the vamp pit.

Victor repositioned on the cot to alleviate the poke from a sprung spring. The puncture wound in his chest was no longer unbearable—it was starting to itch. "Sounds far-fetched."

"Please. Please help me."

Victor saw an eternity of sadness in her eyes. "How?"

She started to answer, bit her lip, drew blood and

dropped her head. Tears plunked on his cot. "I liked what I had. I liked who I was. Do you understand?"

Victor looked at the ceiling. "Can't say I do."

Her hand was on his arm. "If you could—"

"Make room." A deputy at the cell door ran his nightstick across the bars, prompting reluctant vampires to move. They jostled each other to maintain a buffer with the room's central occupant. "Thetherson," the deputy barked. "Visitor."

Victor sat up and vampire dug her nails in his skin. She pulled close to him. "Denise Masters. Come find me. Please."

Victor took a moment and looked at her. A yellow glow emanated from the hollow of her throat. He nodded and left the pit.

The deputy led him to an interrogation room. Barbara and Tripp waited inside. The cop stabbed his fingers into Victor's abdomen and took hold of his bottom rib.

"We're watching you, you fucking weasel. And I don't mean the cops."

He shoved Victor into the room and shut the door behind him. Barbara ran into his arms.

"Amberly?" Victor prayed for good news despite their expressions.

When Barbara couldn't speak, Tripp stepped forward. "Police didn't find anything at the retirement home. Eugene was wrong."

Victor screamed, desperate to tear out this Civil War Soldier's throat. He searched the bare room for something to break and finally settled for jamming his forehead against the raised frame of the door's little window. "They're in on it."

Tripp was dubious. "The police?"

Victor had had his fill of Tripp's refusal to believe anything that existed outside the paradigm he chose to live in. He slammed his palm on the table—it felt so good, and not nearly good enough, that he did it again and again and again until they received a warning knock. He pointed at the door. "The one who let me in here, for starters. The D.A., Tripp. One of the top dogs at the NIH—you told me that yourself! How hard does it have to hit you over your thick head?"

Tripp gave Barbara a pointed look.

"Yes! I'm more aggressive as a vampire. That's why I stopped the treatment! It's the only way we're getting Amberly back."

"But don't you see that doesn't make any sense?" said Tripp. "That's why she was *taken*. To convince you to take the cure."

Barbara put her hand on Victor's forearm and spoke to Tripp. "That's not exactly what the message said."

"This Civil War Soldier wouldn't care if you were dead if he knew we have the cure."

"He seems to know everything else," said Victor. "Or at least everything X was telling him. I think X was playing him, feeding him a bullshit line that I'm legacy to the most evil vampire the world has ever known. When in fact ..." He had a hard time voicing something so incredible. "It appears I'm the one who can bring them down."

"You know this how?"

"The diary. From Dr. Linciome. Is he ..."

"We visited him at the hospital on the way here," said Barbara. "They found him dumped by the river."

Tripp paced, battling his emotions. "He was bitten and nearly drained."

"X must have found out Dr. Linciome had the diary. According to Winnie, it proves I'm not Morbius. And it describes my ability to see a vampire's Achilles' heel." He reacted to Tripp's disbelief. "I *used* it, Tripp. On Sennett McGumphrey and on X. I told Eugene how to kill him."

Tripp started to respond, then thought better and continued to listen.

"I thought it was bullshit, too. But I felt it. The

diary also describes how to kill me." Victor pointed to his chest where the wound had seeped through the bandage onto his jailhouse-issue shirt. "I felt that, too."

Tripp nodded at the wound. "Eugene?"

"Who else?" He faced Barbara. "We have to get me out of here."

"I know. But I don't know how."

"When you decided to be a vampire again," said Tripp, "you opened yourself up to being prosecuted for Nikki. Now this second murder didn't help."

"Raj was a *vampire*. He looked like one, he acted like one. He was biting the old slayer woman. Why does it matter whether he had real fangs?"

"Fair question. For the court."

"There's no time." Victor worked to manage his rage. "What about Eugene? Is the punk going to make it?"

"He'll be okay," said Barbara. "He's a few rooms down from Winnie. Under 24-hour guard this time. He's facing charges, too."

"In Eugene's words," said Tripp, "he hired a 'high-powered slayer defense attorney.' He's confident his lawyer will get him out. Along with the other two slayers, for what it's worth."

Victor grimaced. "Not much."

"The diary," said Barbara, eyes widening with nervous excitement. "We just need this Civil War Soldier to read it. Then he'll see the truth and realize he was wrong about you. Right?"

Victor caught Barbara's spark. He thought back to the showdown with X. "The cops have an excerpt. The part X wanted Eugene to see. I'm sure X had the rest of it, somewhere."

Tripp was all in. "I'm on it. I'll try to beat the cops to the rest of the diary."

Barbara was at the door. "I'll work with Eugene's lawyer to get a copy of whatever the police have."

Victor pounded for the deputy. Barbara stepped into his arms and kissed him. "I love you," she told him.

That was all Victor needed to hear. "I will never let you down again." Inches apart without his readers and she was still in pretty good focus. The curse, his wonderful curse, was working its magic.

Be on the lookout for the final chapter in the
Vampire Vic trilogy,
coming soon ...

ABOUT THE AUTHORS

High in the mountains of Colorado, up where the air is clear and one's thoughts soar, you can look down and see Castle Rock, a little south of Denver. That's where Harris Gray lives and writes. Crowfoot Coffee is where each day begins, and then continues, as evening comes and the coffee shop lets its hair down and slips into something a little more comfortable, called the Crowbar. Caffeine and craft beer, they go together like Gray and Harris. They are each married, but people still consider them a couple.

The website: harrisgray.com
The marketplace: amazon.com/Harris-Gray
The tweets: twitter.com/harrisandgray
The posts: facebook.com/HarrisGrayAuthor
The sharing:
plus.google.com/u/3/102066651638902173967
The community: www.goodreads.com/harrisgray